KU-207-251

The
SECRET
KEEPERS

Tilly Bagshawe is an internationally bestselling author of more than twenty novels. A mother of four, Tilly and her family recently returned to England after many years based in Los Angeles. They now divide their time between London and Gloucestershire.

Also by Tilly Bagshawe

The Secrets of Sainte Madeleine
Adored
Showdown
Do Not Disturb
Flawless
Scandalous
Fame
Friends & Rivals

The Swell Valley Series
One Summer's Afternoon (Short story)
One Christmas Morning (Short story)
The Inheritance
The Show
The Bachelor

Sidney Sheldon's Mistress of the Game
Sidney Sheldon's After the Darkness
Sidney Sheldon's Angel of the Dark
Sidney Sheldon's The Tides of Memory
Sidney Sheldon's Chasing Tomorrow
Sidney Sheldon's Reckless
Sidney Sheldon's The Silent Widow
Sidney Sheldon's The Phoenix

The
SECRET
KEEPERS

Tilly
Bagshawe

HarperCollins*Publishers*

HarperCollins*Publishers* Ltd
1 London Bridge Street,
London SE1 9GF
www.harpercollins.co.uk

HarperCollins*Publishers*
Macken House, 39/40 Mayor Street Upper
Dublin 1, D01 C9W8
Ireland

First published by HarperCollins*Publishers* Ltd 2024
1

A catalogue record for this book is available from the British Library

ISBN: 978-0-00-852191-2

Set in Sabon LT Std by HarperCollins*Publishers* India

Printed and bound in the UK using 100% Renewable Electricity by
CPI Group (UK) Ltd

For England.
My heart never left.

"His heart is filled with longing to return home.
In the heat of the sun, to return home."

PROLOGUE

Paris, France, 1952

'Tell me about the dream.'

Dr Auguste Clemenceau leaned back in his leather Eisler & Hauner chair with an audible creak, carefully crossing one leg over the other. The eminent Freudian's office, just off the Champs-Élysées, was a study in minimalist chic. One chair, one desk, one pristine white Jean Prouvé couch. And, today, one beautiful but tortured patient.

'I've already told you, doctor. So many times. Nothing has changed,' Ines Challant sighed. She tried to believe that the famous psychoanalyst could help her. That he could make these awful nightmares stop. Or at least explain them, so she could be at peace. But after so many years, it was hard to keep the faith.

'I understand it's frustrating,' said Clemenceau. 'But please tell me again. Close your eyes.'

Ines did as he asked.

'It's dark,' she began.

'Good. Where are you?'

'I'm in my bed at Beaulieu. I'm nine years old.'

'Mm hm.'

'It's the summer of 1928. August twenty-fourth.'

'Stay with your sensations,' Dr Clemenceau instructed. 'How do you feel?'

'Hot.' A bead of sweat formed in the tiny groove above Ines's upper lip. 'Unbearably hot.'

'And?'

'Frightened.' Her breath quickened. 'My heart's racing. There's a storm outside. I can hear the dogs barking and the boy's screams. Awful screams.'

Unconsciously, she gripped the sides of the couch with her slender, manicured fingers.

'They're chasing him. Hunting him. He's terrified.'

'Go on.'

Ines shook her head. She didn't want to go on. She didn't want to go back there, to remember.

'What happens next? What do you see? Hear?'

'Nothing,' she lied. 'That's it. That's all there is. I hear the barks and the screaming and then . . . *Bang*. I wake up.'

Auguste Clemenceau leaned forward, looking at her intently. 'Bang?'

Ines looked down, but said nothing further.

At thirty-three, Ines Challant had the world, or at least Paris, at her feet. A successful interior designer, accomplished, wealthy, strikingly beautiful. But for all her outer luminescence, there was a darkness inside her. Some secret shame that she had spent her life trying to suppress, but that her subconscious returned to her every night in the form of this same recurring nightmare, like a cat dropping an unwanted gift of a dead bird at its mistress's feet.

They'd talked about her childhood countless times. About her complex relationship with her late father, a classic Electra complex in Clemenceau's opinion. They'd talked about guilt and transference, and how as a little girl Ines had felt responsible for the terrible, tragic accident that occurred at her family's bastide in the summer of 1928. But still the dreams kept coming.

'Ms Challant. Forgive me,' he said. 'But I know there's something more. Please, try again. Keep your eyes closed. You hear your father's guard dogs, and the boy's screams. But what else?'

'*Oiseaux*.'

The word tumbled out of her mouth before Ines even knew she had thought it.

'Birds. I hear birds.'

2

Clemenceau inhaled sharply, unable to hide his excitement. This was new. Not what he'd expected, exactly. But still new. Progress.

'Maman's birds. They're in the aviary squawking and panicking,' Ines continued, wringing her hands together, visibly distressed. 'They're beating their wings frantically against the bars of the cage, trying to escape. They need . . . Oh God. Someone needs to let them out!'

She sat up suddenly, her eyes wide.

'*You* need to let them out, Ines,' said the doctor. 'Is that it? Is that what you're feeling? That you should have released your mother's birds?'

Ines nodded, sobbing. Things – terrible, long-buried things that she couldn't name – were rising up inside her. Things for which there were no words.

Her dream wasn't about the boy. It was about the birds.

It had always been about the birds.

I should have set them free.

PART ONE

SUMMER

CHAPTER ONE

Beaulieu-sur-Mer, France, June 1928

'So.' Clotilde Challant carefully folded her napkin and surveyed her children's happy faces around the breakfast table. 'What are everybody's plans for the day?'

It was the Challants' first morning at Beaulieu, the luxurious seaside home that they decamped to en masse every summer, leaving the hubbub of Paris behind. The bastide, originally a fortified medieval dwelling built of thick stone, had been added to and softened over the years. Fairytale turrets now punctuated the house's four corners, and pale blue wooden shutters framed its pretty windows, with bougainvillea running riot over much of the façade. The house perched atop a high hill, with sloping formal gardens cascading down around it, like water from a spring. Lavender, rose and kitchen gardens all had their own exquisitely delineated spaces, and there were lawns and fountains and intricately laid gravel paths weaving among the grounds, always raked to perfection. True to its fortress roots however, the whole property was encircled by forbiddingly high walls of brick and stone, protecting those lucky enough to live within from whatever dangers might lurk without.

Years ago, a family friend had likened the Challants to a flock of migrating birds; glamorous and exotic but constantly on the move between their Paris mansion on Place Dauphine, their bastide at Beaulieu in the summers, and their vast chalet in Megève every Christmas. The trope had stuck, not least because Clotilde Challant herself happened to be an avid collector of exotic birds, with an aviary at Beaulieu to rival that at any of the local zoos.

'I'm going down to the farm first thing.' Renée, fifteen years old and the Challants' second daughter, practically bubbled with excitement. Pretty in a tomboyish sort of way, with short dark hair and a smattering of freckles across her nose and cheeks, Renée was Clotilde's 'uncomplicated' child. Independent, cheerful and perfectly satisfied as long as she could spend most of her time outdoors, ideally around animals.

'Sandrine told me last night that the Martins' spaniel bitch has had puppies, *and* they've bought a whole flock of new geese that Monsieur Martin needs help with.'

'Puppies?' Nine-year-old Ines, the baby of the family and a blonde, fat-cheeked cherub whose angelic look wholly belied her mischievous personality, sprang up in her chair like a jack-in-the-box. 'I *love* puppies! Can I come with you, Renée? Pleeeeaaase?'

'Of course you can, darling,' Renée assured her. 'What about you, Charles? You could come and help me with the geese if you like. Monsieur Martin might let us have some eggs if we do a good job.'

Twelve-year-old Charles Challant, known as Charles Fils, rolled his eyes grumpily.

'No thanks.'

The only boy of the family, Charles had been nicknamed *Niverolle* (snow finch) by his sisters because of his love of all things alpine and ski related. He lived for winters in Megève and always sulked when the family arrived at 'Boring Beaulieu' for the summer, complaining that there was nothing to do.

'Well what are you going to do today, Charles?' his mother pressed. 'I don't want you moping around the house all day, getting under the servants' feet.'

'He could go down to the yacht club? See if any other obnoxious boys he knows have arrived for the season yet.' At seventeen, Genevieve was the eldest and most sophisticated of the Challant children. She peered at her little brother disdainfully over the top of her romance novel. Gen was also in a 'difficult' mood. Under normal circumstances, she looked forward to family summers at Beaulieu. But having been forced to spend most of the last year bored out of her mind at finishing school in Switzerland, it had been a real wrench to leave Paris and all of her friends again. One friend in particular.

'That's a good idea,' Clotilde said, ignoring the barb and smiling at Gen warmly. 'Would you mind taking him?'

'*Me?*' Genevieve looked horrified.

'I'd do it myself, but I have two new grey parrots being delivered this morning for my aviary, so I'm rather stuck till they arrive.'

'Sorry, Maman. I can't.'

'Whyever not?' Clotilde frowned. Just once it would be nice if her eldest daughter would make things easy.

'Because.' Genevieve pouted. 'I'm busy.'

'Doing what?' Renée teased her older sister good-naturedly. 'Mooning over that dog-eared photograph of Aurelian again? It's a wonder it hasn't disintegrated completely by now.'

Aurelian de la Tour was the son of family friends in Paris. A would-be playwright, he was also Genevieve's latest *interet amoureux*, despite being at least five years older and mixing in a much more sophisticated, cosmopolitan crowd. Nonetheless, Aurelian seemed to enjoy Genevieve's unconcealed adoration, and as a result the two of them had spent a good deal of time together last year, before Gen's banishment to finishing school in Switzerland.

'I'm sure I haven't the faintest idea what you're talking about, Renée,' Gen responded breezily. 'All the sea air must have gone to your head.'

'For your information, I don't need to be "taken" anywhere,' Charles Fils piped up angrily, bringing the subject neatly back to himself. 'I'm perfectly capable of cycling down to the club by myself.'

'You see?' Genevieve smiled sweetly at her mother. 'I'm superfluous. He doesn't need a chaperone.'

Clotilde glanced questioningly over at her husband. 'What do you say, cheri? Are you happy for Charles to go into town by himself?'

Seated at the head of the table, in the grand, oak-backed

chair that Ines always thought made him look like a king on his throne, Charles Challant had declined thus far to join in the general breakfast conversation. Not a man given to small talk, especially not of the domestic variety, with his full grey beard and striking, light blue eyes, Charles Père radiated benign patriarchal authority, rather in the manner of an Old Testament prophet. Generally he preferred to rise above the fray, leaving most of the day-to-day decisions about family life to Clotilde. But occasionally, he did take an interest in Charles Fils that ran deeper than his concern for his three girls, whom he seemed to regard almost as charming pets, rushing about and occasionally presenting him with demands for this or that.

In this case, however, a single, brief nod indicated his assent. Charles Fils could bicycle into town if he wanted.

'Right then,' Clotilde exhaled. 'In that case everybody knows what they're doing. I've asked Eloise to lay out a picnic lunch on the *terrasse* for anyone who wants it at one o'clock. Otherwise I'll expect you all back here at six for . . .'

She was interrupted by four slavering dobermans, barrelling into the room in a sudden flurry of sound and fury, knocking into sideboards and table legs as they went. Instinctively, Clotilde shrank back in her chair.

'There's no need to cower, darling,' Charles Père assured her. 'They won't hurt you.'

But Clotilde wasn't so sure. She was a strong woman, but her husband's dogs terrified her. She couldn't understand what had possessed him to bring such savage creatures into their home. None of their neighbours in Beaulieu had guard dogs. But this summer, Charles had insisted they acquire some.

'You're good boys, aren't you, hm?' Bending his bearded face low, Charles grabbed one of the dogs by the collar, nuzzling against its powerful jaw like a child with a teddy bear. Little Ines looked on in astonishment. She adored her father, but knew him as a distant, almost God-like figure, not a man given to physical displays of affection, to either humans or animals. But he seemed as smitten by his new pets as much as Maman was distressed by them. For her own part, Ines was also scared of the dobermans. But it did make her smile to see her beloved papa so happy.

'*Pardonnez-moi, madame.*' Sandrine, one of the maids, ran into the room with a volley of apologies to Clotilde as she attempted to round up the dogs. 'I opened the kennel door to feed them and they took off into the house before I could stop them.'

'It's all right, Sandrine,' Clotilde said kindly, watching with relief as the pack followed the maid out of the door, tempted by a handful of treats. From the girl's harassed expression, it was clear that Charles's dogs were as unpopular with the bastide's staff as they were with its mistress. Somehow, Clotilde supposed, they would all have to get used to them.

Retreating upstairs to her bedroom the moment breakfast was finished, Genevieve locked the door behind her. Her room was at the front of the house, with spectacular views across the rooftops of the town to the sparkling, azure expanse of the Mediterranean beyond. There was a pretty, antique bed, dressed with crisp white linens, an armoire and a kidney-shaped dressing table complete with drawers and an inlaid mahogany mirror, placed directly beneath the blue-shuttered window.

Sitting down at the table, Gen let out a sigh of relief. Thank God she hadn't been roped into chaperoning Charles for the morning. It was good to be alone with her thoughts. With herself.

The face staring back at her in the mirror wasn't classically pretty. Not like her little sister Ines, who was clearly destined to become a raving beauty, or even Renée, with her wholesome, tomboyish charm. But there was a playfulness and intelligence to Gen's features that made them attractive anyway, and she liked what she saw. With her long, vole-like nose and dark, sardonic eyes, she bore little physical resemblance to any of the other members of her family, an odd-one-outness she had always been rather proud of. Artists were supposed to be different.

11

Opening her dresser drawer, Gen pulled out a well-thumbed manuscript. Her latest play, a comedy, was set in a Lausanne finishing school, and if she did say so herself it was coming along nicely. She'd been secretly posting segments of it to Aurelian for advice all last term, and had followed his editing tips to the letter.

Thank God for Aurelian. Sometimes Gen felt like he was the only person on earth who understood her. Even though she hadn't seen him in the flesh for well over a year now, he remained the only member of her immediate circle who took her writing seriously.

Perhaps it was because he was such an old father, but Papa had very rigid, absurdly old-fashioned views about women's education – about women in general, come to that. And though Genevieve tried to remain a loving and loyal daughter, it was hard not to be resentful at all the opportunities that had been denied her. She'd *begged* both her parents to allow her to attend the lycee in Paris and to spare her the grimly vacuous litany of flower arranging and deportment that constituted an 'education' at finishing school. Especially after her baccalaureate results were so outstandingly high.

'I don't need to be finished,' she pleaded. 'I need to be allowed to start! How am I ever going to succeed as a writer if I'm not exposed to other writers? If I'm not allowed to hone my craft?'

'"*Hone your craft*",' Charles Challant had chuckled, with affectionate disdain. 'You're a lady, Genevieve, not some sort of artisan.'

'I'm talking about writing plays, Papa. Not becoming a shoemaker,' Gen snapped back, frustrated. 'You know how highly I scored on my language papers. At the lycee . . .'

'Examination results are all very well,' Charles cut in. 'But what a young woman in your position actually needs is to learn how to manage a household and succeed as a hostess. They won't teach you that at the lycee.'

Helplessly, Genevieve had turned to her mother for support. But Clotilde had fallen in line behind her husband, unwilling to precipitate a marital battle on the matter. What made it worse was that Genevieve knew that her mother felt stifled at times, both creatively and intellectually. That she had so much more to offer than her traditional roles as wife and mother allowed. And yet she seemed willing to stand by and watch while her daughters were frog-marched blindly down the same constricted path in life.

Anyway, it doesn't matter, she told herself now, arranging her manuscript carefully out on the dressing table along with the silver pen that Aurelian had given her as a going-away present the last time they saw one another. *I will rise above parental narrow-mindedness. I will publish my play, and one day they'll come to see it in Paris, and then Papa will have to admit he was wrong.*

'There's a gentleman for you at the tradesman's door, madame.'

Sandrine poked her head around the door of Clotilde's *boudoir*, the small but elaborately decorated sitting-room-cum-study where she spent most of her mornings whilst at Beaulieu. A spectacular mural of jungle flora covered one entire wall, while bright, hand-knotted rugs and eclectic lamps in rainbow-hued glass completed the overall feeling of wonder and magic. Clotilde's unique creativity had been allowed to flow unfettered here; but only here. The little jewel of a room was her sanctuary.

'I believe he has your new birds?'

'Wonderful!' Clotilde clasped her hands together excitedly, her face lighting up like a child's. 'Would you have Louis walk him down to the aviary? I'll meet him there in around fifteen minutes, once I've dug out my cheques.'

Clotilde Challant's hobby was an expensive one. But her birds brought her such joy, such blessed release from the frustrations and disappointments of her life, they were worth every penny. Today's acquisition, a breeding pair of grey parrots shipped over especially from the Côte d'Ivoire, was relatively modest compared to some of her other purchases. Last year's addition of five goliath cockatoos to the Beaulieu aviary had cost almost as much as Charles's new Rolls-Royce Silver Ghost, a gleaming extravagance that sat for the most part outside their Paris mansion, undriven.

There were aspects of her marriage that caused Clotilde Challant both pain and regret. However, her solution was to make a conscious effort to think about them as little as possible. To focus only on the good, or at least the tolerable parts of married life, and ignore the parts of herself that had died when she slipped on Charles's ring and promised to love, honour and obey. Parts like her ambition, and her own artistic and creative talents, that would never now bear real fruit.

But . . . the children were lovely. The homes were lovely. Charles himself, when in a good mood, could be engaging company. And no one could deny that he was a generous, even an indulgent, husband when it came to his wife's spending. All the more so given how much he disliked Clotilde's 'squawking bloody birds'.

Those who knew Charles Challant well – his business partner, Baron Maurice de Rothschild and his handful of old friends from Paris – had been astonished when he announced his intention to marry the then twenty-year-old Clotilde Jamet, the shy, artistic, unassuming younger daughter of a venerable old family from Nice. Already in his mid-forties at that time, and a confirmed bachelor whose only known interests in life were work and religion, it seemed miraculous that Charles would even have *met* Clotilde, let alone that he would want to marry her. But something about her artistic, whimsical nature captivated him and after a whirlwind romance, if it could be called that, involving a summer of Charles paying court to Clotilde's parents and inviting her on a series of heavily chaperoned excursions, he proposed and was accepted.

The marriage was loving and harmonious at first, notwithstanding their huge differences in character. By Christmas, Clotilde was pregnant with their first child, but a miscarriage ended that pregnancy, and a second, before she finally gave birth to Genevieve in the spring of 1911. Over the course of the next eight years, she was to suffer further failed pregnancies in between the births of her healthy children. The effects of these losses on Clotilde's health, both physical and psychological, were tremendous. But Charles never fully understood this, just as he never really appreciated how badly Clotilde needed an outlet for her creativity beyond her roles as wife and mother. His response to the miscarriages (*prayer, penance, try again*) never wavered. It was the first, and perhaps most fundamental, brick in the wall of distance and misunderstanding that began to build up within the Challant marriage. Even when, as a family, they ostensibly sailed on to greater successes and higher heights.

As for Clotilde, it had never occurred to her to question *why* she had married Charles in the first place. Like most young women of her generation and class, she had stumbled into matrimony passively, having been brought up to see it as both her destiny and her duty. Her parents, whom she loved and trusted, believed Charles Challant was a good match. He was hard-working, a pious and devoted Catholic, of good moral character and already respectably well off – although nothing like as eye-wateringly rich as he was later to become. He was also tolerably attractive, not that that factored into the Jamet parents' judgement of him as a suitor, but it made it easier for Clotilde not to think of him as such a *terribly* old man. In any event, the way Clotilde saw it, she would have needed a reason *not* to marry Charles. Not being in possession of such a reason, she married him.

Scrabbling around on the shelves behind her desk, she eventually found the gilt box in which she kept her unused cheques. Only two left. She would have to see Charles about that, especially with both the older girls needing new summer dresses for the season. Taking one cheque out of the box, Clotilde grabbed her shawl and hurried eagerly out into the garden towards the aviary.

It was four o'clock by the time Ines and Renée got back from the home farm, laden with a groaning basket of fresh goose eggs.

15

The high summer sun was still punishingly hot, and the air as thickly humid as soup. Both girls' cheeks were flushed pink, and tendrils of hair stuck, limpet-like, to their foreheads with sweat.

· 'Well now, that's quite a haul!'

Marie, the cook at Beaulieu, peered into the basket approvingly. With her rounded cheeks, gap-toothed smile and arms that seemed to be made entirely of rolled fat, like two string-tied joints of pork, Marie was beloved by all the Challant children. But especially by Ines, who would sneak down to the bastide kitchen regularly in hopes of sweets or treats.

'You must have been mightily helpful for Monsieur Martin to give you so many.'

'We were,' boasted Ines. 'We fixed the coop and put all of the new wire fencing in. It had to go six feet deep because of the *renards*, although I think the new geese could see off a fox. They're almost as big as me, aren't they Renée?'

'Some of them.' Renée ruffled Ines's damp blonde mop of hair indulgently. Naturally maternal, Renée had always had a soft spot for her baby sister. Ines had been no help whatsoever today, rolling around with the adorable puppies and collecting stray goose feathers to try to fashion a makeshift fan, while Renée had done all the hard work, helping the bastide's tenant farmer hammer in stakes and unwind endless rolls of chicken wire beneath a blazing sun. Not that she minded. It was a joy to be out of the city, with animals all around her and the faint summer breeze carrying the scent of the ocean to cool her as she worked.

'Can you make a cake with them, Marie?' Ines turned one of the still-warm, white eggs over in her palm, feeling the weight of it.

'I could make twenty cakes with that little lot,' the cook grinned back at her.

'Chocolate ones?' Ines asked hopefully.

'I don't see why not. But perhaps we should save some for tomorrow's breakfast, *non*?' said Marie, relieving Ines of her egg.

'Papa's always hungry after mass,' observed Renée. 'He loves a nice goose egg.'

'I daresay he does,' Marie sniffed, frowning. 'But it's not him I'm thinking of.'

It hadn't escaped the children's notice that Marie was often somewhat disdainful of their father, making no secret of her preference for her mistress over her master. No one really knew where her dislike or disapproval of Charles Père came from, but at moments like these it could be quite pointed.

'Could we quickly make just one cake now, Marie?' pleaded Ines, who didn't want to think about Papa, or tomorrow, or boring old mass. 'I'm *starving*.'

'You're always starving,' laughed Renée.

'I could help?' Ines offered eagerly.

'Help me eat all the batter you mean?' Marie rolled her eyes. 'I think I'll be faster on my own.'

'We need to go and get cleaned up anyway, Ines,' said Renée firmly. 'You've more straw on your head than hair, and if Papa sees either of our fingernails he'll send us both back to Paris before you could say knife.'

'I'll tell you what, *Chipie*,' said Marie with a laugh, watching little Ines's face fall. 'Take some of these madeleines to tide you over while you make yourselves nice again.' Reaching over to the enormous range cooker, she scooped up four or five miniature sponge-cakes from the cooling rack and divided them up between the two girls. 'And I'll get started on that chocolate cake for tonight's dessert.'

Ines looked doubtful, even as she stuffed the first of the delicious madeleines into her mouth.

'If we hurry up, you might have time to see Maman's new birds before supper,' Renée cajoled, ushering her little sister towards the stairs.

'Oh, yes!' Ines brightened. She'd forgotten about the parrots. She would run down to the aviary as soon as she was clean to take a look at them. 'Thank you Marie. *Â bientôt!*'

Ines loved Marie, and she loved summers at Beaulieu, more than anything. Puppies, geese, boiling sun, chocolate cake, new parrots, and tomorrow maybe the beach, or sailing with Papa and Charles. It was all going to be just wonderful. And to think that this was only day one.

'Do you think they'll be happy in there?'

Ines looked up at her mother doubtfully. The two grey parrots were perched by themselves in the far corner of the aviary, on the branch of one of Clotilde's newly planted fig trees.

'They look a bit lonely. What if the other birds don't make friends with them?'

Clotilde rested a loving hand on her youngest child's shoulder.

'I'm not sure birds do "make friends" exactly,' she explained. 'But they will have a wonderful life here. I'll make sure of it.'

It was rare for the two of them to be alone together like this, especially at Beaulieu, and Clotilde was delighted that Ines had asked to come with her to see the new birds before dinner. Always a daddy's girl, Ines hero-worshipped her father, despite Charles's often distant manner towards her and her sisters. (Or perhaps because of it.) The family's long summer and winter migrations represented Ines's best chance to spend time with him, and with her adored older brother, so Clotilde was often ignored once Paris had been left behind. But the aviary remained a draw, another thing that mother and daughter had in common, along with their love of art and design and colour, their natural flair for all things feminine and beautiful.

A couple of weeks ago, Clotilde had begun work on a new silk screen, painted with an array of exotic birds, and had brought it with her to Beaulieu in the hope Ines might want to help her with the project. When it came to her live birds, however, Clotilde's feelings were of straightforward love. Whereas Ines's were more complex, falling somewhere between fascination, admiration and unease. The little girl definitely felt an affinity to these inscrutable, magical creatures, some sort of instinctive connection that made her happy. But at the same time, Ines felt it was wrong to keep them captive, even in a prison as vast and abundantly lovely as the Beaulieu aviary.

'Tell me about that one again.' Ines pointed to a twilight-blue bird with a line of black feathers across its eyes, like a highwayman's mask.

'I call him Luis. He's a jay,' said Clotilde. 'From the Andean cloud forest.'

'*Andean cloud forest*,' Ines echoed wistfully. 'That sounds so lovely.'

'Doesn't it?' Clotilde lit up, delighted by her daughter's interest. Ines had the same romantic nature that she had felt as a child, the same yearning for adventure and magic. '*He's* not so terribly lovely though, I'm afraid. They really are the noisiest birds. That's one of the reasons I don't have many jays. But this one was such a beauty, I couldn't resist. Do you see how bright turquoise that plumage is on his throat?'

Ines nodded, entranced. 'Like a jewel. And what about that one, at the feeder?'

'Ah.' Clotilde cocked her head affectionately to one side. A completely white bird with a spectacular, crested fan of feathers on the top of its head clung precariously to one of the hanging seedballs towards the back of the enclosure. 'That's Elena, my umbrella cockatoo. She's an old lady now. But so intelligent. They're the closest to humans, I think, cockatoos.'

'How old is Elena?'

'I'm not sure exactly. Older than me, though.'

'Older than Papa?'

Clotilde's smile faded slightly.

'No. Not older than Papa,' she replied. 'Cockatoos don't live past sixty. Now, do you remember what that one's called?'

Changing the subject, she pointed up to a tiny yellow and black bird, swooping down from the very top of the cage to the edge of the ornamental pond.

'Ooo, yes!' Ines hopped up and down, screwing up her eyes in an effort to dredge up the name. 'Oreo!' she said finally. 'It's a finch. Like Charles.'

'*Oriole*,' Clotilde corrected. 'But very good. It's an oriole finch. And Charles is our *Niverolle*.'

'What am I?' Ines asked shyly, gazing deep into the recesses of the huge wrought-iron cage. 'Do any of your birds remind you of me?'

Bending down so that their eyes were level, Clotilde cupped her daughter's face in her hands. Maman looked so sad and serious all of a sudden, Ines felt a stab of panic. She loved her mother deeply and hated to see her upset. Had she done something wrong? Perhaps she shouldn't have asked the question.

'You're very beautiful, Ines,' Clotilde told her, her voice cracking. 'Like Carlotta.'

Ines knew about Carlotta. She was Maman's prized hyacinth macaw, the most valuable bird of her entire collection.

'Really?' Ines wanted to smile. This sounded like a compliment. And yet the tears welling in Clotilde's eyes suggested that it wasn't. Or at least not entirely.

'Is that . . . bad?' Ines asked, confused. 'To be beautiful?'

'Not bad.' Leaning in, Clotilde planted a kiss on her forehead. 'But beauty can be a dangerous thing, sometimes. The whole world will want to possess it. Beautiful birds get trapped.'

The sun had already started to sink low in the sky, and the long, dark shadows of the trees felt colder all of a sudden, the heat of the day snuffed out like a pinched candle. Ines shivered. She wished she were back inside with Renée and Charles playing cards in the salon. Even Genevieve should have come downstairs by now, and Papa would probably join them all shortly. Things back at the house would be fun and light and safe like they used to be, Ines felt sure of it. Something was changing this summer, a subtle, negative shift between her parents that Ines felt but could never quite name or describe. Here in the garden her mother's sadness hung like a weight around her neck, and she wanted to run from it, and from the birds, whose screeching was starting to grate on her ears like fingernails on *un tableau*.

'I don't think I'm a macaw,' she said, unpeeling Clotilde's

hands from her cheeks and clasping them bravely in her own.

'No?'

'No. I think I'm a cockatoo, like Elena.'

'Is that so?' Standing up, Clotilde forced a smile. 'And why's that?'

'Because they're intelligent,' Ines replied firmly. 'Come on. Let's go in.'

Clotilde allowed herself to be led back up the path to the house, past the walled kitchen gardens and through the lavender beds that still buzzed lazily with bees, even at this late hour. She knew she had unnerved Ines before, and she was sorry for it. Summers at Beaulieu were the family's happy time. Ines deserved that happiness, and all the pure childhood innocence that went with it, no matter what she and Charles might be going through.

'You mustn't worry, you know, Maman,' Ines announced, sounding much happier now as they approached the warm orange glow of the house. 'Charles may be our Niverolle. But I think Genevieve, Renée and I are all cockatoos. We're *much* too clever to get trapped.'

Please, let that be true, Clotilde prayed silently. *Let my daughters have the freedom that I was denied. Let them all soar.*

CHAPTER TWO

Nestled between Saint-Jean-Cap-Ferrat and Villefranche-sur-Mer on the French Riviera, Beaulieu-sur-Mer, or 'Beaulieu' as the locals knew it, was fast becoming the resort of choice for France's wealthy elites. Famously described by Queen Victoria as 'a paradise of nature', with its spectacular beaches and harbour, its magnificent clifftop villas, and its charming cobbled medieval streets, giving way onto leafy, open squares, Beaulieu now boasted no fewer that eighty-two hotels and had everything that the discerning Parisian family could hope for, both as a summer resort and, increasingly, as a warm sanctuary during the winter months.

Charles Challant had realized early on that prime land in Beaulieu was available at a significant discount to what was being offered in neighbouring resorts such as Villefranche and Eze. Since 1920, he'd been investing heavily in the town's building boom, with part shares in two new grand hotels as well as multiple villas and the expansion of the marina. Having successfully earned a small fortune from these endeavours in Beaulieu, over the past eighteen months Charles had turned it into a big one by repeating the same trick in Megève, the once sleepy town in the French Alps that had been the Challants' winter home for almost two decades. Alongside Maurice de Rothschild and his wife Noémie, Charles had helped transform Megève from an obscure mountain village into a booming ski-Mecca to rival the famous Swiss resort of St Moritz.

Not everybody in either Megève or Beaulieu appreciated the changes that men like Charles Challant were effecting in their towns, or the unprecedented influx of money and tourism that those changes triggered. But this was 1928, a thrilling new era, full of innovations that would have seemed unimaginable a generation ago, and the clock could not be turned back. Across France and across the world, motorcars were beginning to replace horses, the luxury of electricity was becoming commonplace in even the sleepiest towns, respectable women were cutting their hair short and demanding the vote of all things, and the advent of moving pictures from Hollywood was transforming the way that ordinary people thought about the world.

Perhaps ironically, Charles Challant himself shared many of his Berlugan neighbours' concerns. Raised a devout Catholic, Charles revered all the laws of the church, and took his positions as both the head of his family and a prominent civic leader seriously. Money and success were all very well, but only if dedicated piously to the glory of God. With his taciturn manner, full white beard and penchant for heavy, three-piece suits even in June, Charles was in many ways a Victorian moralist, trapped in a twentieth-century developer's body. A man out of his time.

As a result, today's family trip to the new cinema that had just opened next to Beaulieu's grand Hotel des Anglais had become an unnecessarily fraught affair. The children's excitement troubled Charles, who worried about the moral suitability of the film (Buster Keaton and Charlie Chaplin's *The Circus*, a wildly popular slapstick comedy featuring a tightrope-walking Chaplin and sev-eral hilariously misbehaved monkeys).

'We can't be seen to endorse lewdness,' Charles had grumbled pompously to Clotilde, pointing to the publicity poster of Merna Kennedy in a moderately low-cut dress posted on the cinema walls.

'Come on, darling,' Clotilde replied reasonably. 'It's hardly the Folies Bergère.'

'Even so,' Charles muttered. 'It isn't suitable for Ines. Perhaps she should go home with you? You could work on that silk screen together. You know, the bird-thing you've been tinkering with?'

Clotilde stiffened. Even after all these years, his dismissiveness of her art still rankled. They'd both been born into a world where men worked and women 'tinkered', but familiarity with her position had not made it any easier for Clotilde to accept it. She said nothing, however.

By the time they all took their seats and the *ouvreuse* came by with her tray of ice creams and patisseries, the party's happy mood had already been soured. Only Charles Fils seemed unaware of the tension between his father and everyone else, laughing loudly throughout the show and repeatedly whispering comments to his sisters.

'That was *so good*!' he announced breathlessly afterwards, as the family emerged into the foyer. 'Wasn't it? I love Chaplin.'

'Everybody loves Chaplin. The man's a genius,' said Genevieve, languorously lighting a cigarette. In a fringed silk Lanvin sundress and jauntily tilted cloche hat, Ines thought her eldest sister looked especially glamorous and sophisticated this afternoon.

'Wasn't it brilliant when he got stuck in the lion cage?' Charles enthused. 'I'd be scared stiff.'

'So would I,' said Ines. Then, looking up, 'Maman? I think that boy's waving at you.'

Across the red-carpeted foyer, close to the doors, a boy a little younger than Charles Fils was hopping up and down, signalling animatedly at Clotilde. Ines had seen him before. They all had. He was well known around Beaulieu as *simplet*. No one knew exactly what was wrong with him, but he'd been born slow and was clearly never going to be like other children.

'Poor thing,' replied Clotilde, waving back kindly. 'He was peeking through the back gates at the bastide last week. I think he's fascinated by my birds.'

She began to walk over to the child, but Charles Père put a restraining hand on her shoulder. 'Don't,' he said gruffly. 'You'll only encourage him.'

Clotilde laughed. 'But Charles, I can hardly just ignore him.'

Before Charles could respond, the boy rushed over and flung his arms around Clotilde in a sincere, if unexpected, show of affection.

'I'm Bernard,' he announced blithely, gazing beatifically up at Clotilde.

24

'Hello Bernard.' Clotilde smiled back, ignoring Charles's ever deepening frown.

'You're Madame Challant,' said Bernard.

'I am.'

'Madame Challant who did the jungle paintings in the school hall?'

'That's right.' Delighted, Clotilde reached down and touched his face tenderly. 'Do you like them?'

Bernard nodded. 'They're lovely. Especially the birds.'

Last summer, Clotilde had volunteered to paint some murals at the dilapidated local school, St Hélène's, to give the children something more inspiring to look at than peeling plaster. It was a modest act of charity, but one that had given her more pleasure than she liked to admit. Of course, it was a far cry from the grand commissions she'd dreamed of working on as a teenager, back when she still fantasized about becoming an artist in her own right. Before her marriage to Charles. Before reality. But it still warmed her heart to hear that her work was being appreciated and enjoyed. That it meant something, if only to the sweet, simple boy from the village.

Watching her mother engage with the boy, Ines felt a warm glow of pride at her kindness. Maman showed compassion to everyone, and all of Beaulieu loved her for it.

'You like birds, don't you Bernard? I think I've seen you sometimes, looking at the ones in my aviary.'

The boy blushed, worried for a moment that he'd done something wrong.

'Clotilde, for pity's sake,' Charles protested, sotto voce. 'People are *staring*. Do let's leave.'

It was true that a growing crowd of onlookers had gathered to watch Bernard monopolizing one of Beaulieu's grandest ladies like a love-sick puppy. But Clotilde couldn't understand why Charles seemed so flustered by it.

'I'm afraid I have to go now, Bernard,' Clotilde told the boy, still smiling warmly to try to put him at ease. 'But perhaps one day I could introduce you to my birds? If you'd like to take a closer look at them.'

'Oh, yes! Yes please, Madame Challant! I would like that very much.'

He was still waving and smiling as the Challants walked away, Clotilde and the children following a displeased Charles into the horse-drawn *caleche* waiting to take them home.

Back at the house, Charles pulled Clotilde aside.

'I won't have that boy coming here,' he told her sternly, as soon as they were alone. 'Do you understand? I won't have it.'

'All right Charles.' She looked at him perplexed. 'Although I can't for the life of me see why you care about it so much.'

'Be that as it may!' he bellowed, so loudly it made Clotilde jump. 'If he turns up here, you're to send him away.'

'I said all right!'

What sounded like defiance in her voice was actually shock. Shock and a creeping, more insidious feeling. It took Clotilde a few moments to recognize it as fear. Charles had always had a temper. But in the last few months, his anger had begun to spill over. The small tremors that had always punctuated their marriage were becoming more frequent and more intense. Try as she might, Clotilde couldn't help but worry that a big earthquake was coming. And that when it did, it would devastate all of them.

A few days after the cinema 'incident', another unfortunate event occurred to disturb the fragile peace up at the bastide.

Sandrine, Clotilde's maid, was bitten by one of the dogs.

'Stupid girl. She should have been more careful,' Charles observed tetchily, fiddling with his silver cufflinks as he and Clotilde walked down to dinner. 'She knows not to approach them when they're feeding. I'm sorry if it sounds unsympathetic, but really, she has been told.'

Clotilde said nothing. It did sound unsympathetic, especially as poor Sandrine had had to see Dr Lefevre for several stitches in her hand and arm. Besides, according to Sandrine, the dogs hadn't been feeding at the time, she was merely clearing away their empty bowls. But Clotilde had no appetite for getting drawn into another argument with Charles. Especially one she knew she couldn't win.

'I just hope we don't lose her,' was as far as she would go, linking her arm with her husband's as they reached the bottom of the stairs. 'Sandrine's been with me since Gen was a baby.'

'Lose her? Why on earth would we lose her?' Charles replied dismissively. 'She won't find another position as good as this one in Beaulieu, that's for sure.'

The children were already sitting at their places when their parents entered the *salle à manger*, formally dressed for dinner as their father insisted. Charles took his usual place at the head of the table.

'*Au nom du père, du fils et du saint esprit,*' he intoned.

'Amen.'

Ines sat quietly, uncomfortable in her starched white muslin dress, watching the two new maids serve the coq au vin. Perhaps it was her imagination, but, as they spooned the tender chicken onto her father's plate, Ines sensed an unhappiness in their faces that hadn't been there yesterday. She knew that all the servants were talking about what had happened to poor Sandrine. It was a conversation to which the little girl was acutely attuned, since privately she, too, was quite terrified of the dobermans.

'I had news from Megève today,' Charles Challant told his son cheerfully, apparently oblivious to the tension in the room. 'Maurice expects the new ice skating rink to be finished in time for next year's season.'

'Really?' Charles Fils's eyes lit up. 'Two ice rinks! Imagine that. Will it be as grand as the one in the Palace des Neiges, Papa?'

'Grander, I daresay.' Charles Père sipped at his wine contentedly. 'It will certainly be bigger.'

'I can't see what you're so excited about,' Genevieve drawled, with a pitying look at her younger brother. 'You can only skate on one rink at a time. Besides, I thought all you wanted to do was ski?'

'It is,' Charles puffed out his chest. 'But you can't ski at night. The new town rink will be all lit up at, won't it Papa?'

Gen stabbed at her food savagely with a silver fork, not sure exactly what it was about this father–son exchange that so annoyed her. Certainly the attention that Charles Challant focused on his only son and denied his daughters – or at least denied Genevieve and Renée – had long been a source of resentment. Not that Papa was ever particularly *loving* to Charles Fils. But what rankled was that, as a male, Charles Père considered his son's life to be worthy of his interest in a way that female lives intrinsically were not. This extended to everything from her little brother's hobbies, to his education, to Papa's willingness to include him in adult conversations about things like business or finances, even at twelve.

Meanwhile, Renée was more concerned with Ines, who'd barely touched her food and looked pained.

'Are you not hungry, dearest?' she asked kindly. 'Is anything the matter?'

Ines shook her head, shoving a large forkful of *haricots verts* into her mouth to avoid being asked to say anything. What she really wanted was to know how Sandrine was, and whether the dogs were safely locked away for the night. But something told her it wasn't a safe line of enquiry.

Conversation turned to other things. Genevieve's latest letter from a girlfriend in Paris, the contents of which she was keeping mysteriously close to her chest; Renée's recent escapades down at the home farm; Charles's camp in the woods above the town that he'd spent the last three weeks building with two of his local Beaulieu friends, and of which he was inordinately proud. Ines had been making friends too during her trips to the beach with Maman. But she didn't want to talk about that in front of everybody, nor about the fact that she had twice seen Bernard Angier, the simple boy from the cinema, and that the last time she'd chatted with him happily for nearly forty minutes about Clotilde's birds, and their different eggs, and all the marvellous, romantic, far-flung places they'd come from.

'Perhaps we could go on one of our twilight walks after dinner, Ines?'

Her father's low, resonant voice jolted Ines out of her reverie.

'I'd love to, Papa.' She smiled back at him.

Charles and Ines's 'twilight walks' were a tradition at Beaulieu. Because the sun set so late here, and often so spectacularly, father and daughter could stroll into the grounds after supper, right before Ines's bedtime, and watch the deep red orb bleed into the horizon. Sometimes they would see bats flitting dramatically through the dusk, sweeping down from the bastide's eaves and turrets in search of moths, which they would devour mid-flight. On other clear nights, they'd spotted shooting stars. But even without these excitements, the walks were a magical experience for Ines, one of the few occasions that she had her father completely to herself.

'Don't keep her out too late, Charles,' pleaded Clotilde. Privately, she was feeling increasingly anxious about the dobermans. Charles hadn't beaten them, or shouted, or anything when they'd gone for poor Sandrine – Clotilde was terrified that she, or God forbid one of the children, might be next.

'I won't,' said Charles without looking up. He found his wife's fussing irritating. As if he didn't already have enough on his mind. His hands shook slightly as he thought back to the unwelcome 'visitor' at the bastide a few nights ago. On that occasion he'd been able to slip out of the gates without anybody seeing and meet the man in private. Thank God he'd managed to convince him that whatever issues remained between them could be dealt with in Paris. His secret was safe for now. But Genevieve had still been up when he returned to the house, and Charles suspected she had witnessed his agitation.

Clotilde's present anxiety only added to his burdens. Couldn't a man enjoy a relaxing evening stroll with his daughter without being berated for it?

Half an hour later, her small hand ensconced in her father's gnarled, age-spotted, warm one, Ines felt profoundly happy. All the worries that had made her lose her appetite at dinner evaporated the moment they stepped outside into the cool night air. Behind them, the house's blue shutters glowed almost purple in the evening light, and Genevieve's turret bedroom looked for all the world like Rapunzel's tower, softly lit from within. The dogs were barking intermittently, but Ines could tell that the sound was coming from far away and the safety of their locked kennels. There was nothing to fear after all.

'Did you have a nice time at the beach today, little one?' Charles asked her.

'Oh yes,' she replied happily, inhaling the scent of the lavender beds on the still-warm air. 'I always do. The water's cool, and there are *sooo* many crabs this year. Maman and I always meet interesting people there.'

Unconsciously, Charles's grip on his daughter's hand tightened.

'Really? What sort of people is your mother meeting?'

'Oh, well, it's not really Maman,' Ines corrected herself hastily, sensing she'd made a mis-step. 'I'm the one who meets people. Maman mostly just reads her book.'

Charles's fingers loosened slightly. 'I see. So who do *you* meet?'

'Just . . . other children.' Ines thought about Bernard, and hoped her father couldn't see her blush in the gathering darkness.

'Tourists?' Charles asked.

'Sometimes. Or summer people like us. A few of them live here all the time,' said Ines.

'And what is it that you like about these children?'

Ines hesitated. She had the feeling she was being tested, but she wasn't sure what it was her father was hoping to hear. In the end, she opted for the truth.

'I just . . . I like trying to imagine their lives,' she told him, tugging him through the clipped yew hedges and onto the gravel path that led down to the aviary.

Charles frowned. 'Imagine their lives?'

'Yes. You know, what their houses are like inside. How they're decorated, and where they go to school, and what they eat for breakfast. Things like that,' Ines explained. 'On the beach, we're all sort of the same, with our nets and buckets and bathing costumes. But when we migrate back to Paris . . . where do *they* go? What do *they* do? Don't you ever think about things like that, Papa?'

She looked up at him, wide-eyed and hopeful. But Charles's face was a blank.

Releasing her hand, he turned away. 'No,' he replied gravely. 'I never do.' After a pause he said, 'Remember Ines, you might look the same as those children. But you are not the same inside. You're a Challant. That makes you different.'

'Of course, Papa,' Ines answered seriously. 'We're special. Like Maman's birds.'

They'd reached the aviary now. Unusually, barring a few soft chirrups from the cockatiels, all was quiet.

'I wonder about their lives too,' Ines said idly, pressing her forehead against the cool metal of the cage and coiling both hands around the white bars. 'Whether they ever think about flying free, back to the Amazon jungle. Maman says they don't . . .'

'Your mother is right,' Charles said firmly.

'But how do you know?' Ines pressed him. 'Maman told me that one of her jays, the really dark blue, squawky one, comes from the Andean cloud forest. If *I* came from a cloud forest, I wouldn't swap it for a cage in Beaulieu. Would you?'

For a flicker, Charles Challant looked uncomfortable, unsure what to say. But when he spoke again it was with his usual certainty.

'None of these birds would survive a day in the jungle, Ines,' he told her. 'Beaulieu is their home. It's where they belong.'

Ines tried to feel reassured. Her mother had said the same thing after all; her mother who knew the birds better than anyone, and loved them more than anyone. But still, the slow-burn of anxiety lingered in Ines's chest. Because sometimes, especially when she spent time with her mother or even with Genevieve, it struck her that a place could *be* someone's home, and where they belonged, but still a prison.

That was not a comforting thought.

CHAPTER THREE

'I mean it. I'll do it.' Fourteen-year-old Laura Gunn lifted up the heavy chain and padlock with which she intended to shackle herself to the garden railings, and shook them threateningly at her mother. 'You can't make me leave, Mummy. You *can't!*'

With her pale skin, mane of fiery-red hair and passionate green eyes alight with anger, Laura looked more like an Irish revolutionary than an English gentleman's daughter.

Gingerly setting down the rare hyacinth macaw egg she was holding into a specially prepared, straw-lined box, Edie Gunn pressed her hands to her temples wearily.

'You're right darling. I can't,' she replied, sealing the box's lid. 'But the new owners can. And I suspect, chain or no chain, they will.'

Laura let out an ear-piercing, animal wail.

Whatever happens, thought Edie, *I mustn't lose my temper.*

As hard as today was for her, for all of them, she suspected Laura was hurting the most. In the space of two short months, the poor girl had lost the father she adored, every scrap of her financial security, and now she was about to lose Maltings, the pretty Cornish manor house that had been in the Gunn family for over eight generations. It was the only home she'd ever known and where she and her brother had never been anything less than blissfully happy.

An Elizabethan stone manor house in the classic Cornish style, with a large Victorian wing added somewhat incongruously on its western wall and acres of gloriously unkempt gardens, Maltings exuded a sense of romance and charm that few grand houses could match. In the old part of the house, small higgledy-piggledy rooms with flagstone floors and stone-mullion windows made it feel almost castle-like, while the high-ceilinged Victorian drawing room with its elaborate cornicing and vast bay windows had always felt to Edie like the old house's brasher, richer cousin. A bit vulgar, but infinitely more comfortable, and pretty in its own confident, un-apologetic way.

It was an odd, lovely, utterly magical house. And if Edie felt the injustice of its loss so keenly at forty, how on earth could she expect her daughter to control her emotions at fourteen?

'Come on, Laur.' Hector Gunn, Laura's nineteen-year-old brother, emerged from the house staggering under the weight of another enormous packing crate. 'The chaps from the British Museum will be here any minute for Pa's collection. I can't sort it all out on my own.'

'Well you'll have to.' Tossing her hair back defiantly, Laura fastened the padlock before dramatically flinging the key deep into the long grass on the other side of the drive. 'Because I'm. Not. Moving.'

'Suit yourself,' Hector shrugged.

Known to everyone outside his immediate family only as 'Gunn', Hector was Edie's eldest child and only son. At nineteen, he was already strikingly handsome with his thick blond hair, strong, masculine features and tall, muscular physique, none of which he had inherited from his late father.

William Gunn had been red-headed with a round, freckled face and was no more than five foot eight with his boots on. But what Edie's husband had lacked in stature, he had more than made up for in charm, intelligence and naked courage. An explorer, adventurer and passionate collector of artefacts of all kinds, from rare birds' eggs to Aztec gold drinking vessels to stone tablets from ancient Babylon, William Gunn had lived life on his own terms, stuffing his ancestral home at Maltings with a collection of treasures to rival that of many great museums. Unfortunately, it was this same, untamable spirit that had led to his untimely death in early May, swept away and drowned in the treacherous currents of Borneo's Kinabatangan river. Which in turn had led to Edie's discovery that the family were, in fact, in quite an appalling state of debt. Having bequeathed his entire collection to the British Museum in the event of his death, William had effectively left his widow with nothing to sell, and no means of repaying their (many) creditors, short of emptying what little was left in the family bank accounts and selling Maltings.

'Help me, will you?' Edie asked Gunn, striding frantically into the long grass in search of the jettisoned padlock key. She really couldn't face the prospect of having to cut her daughter free with a metal saw in front of the people from the museum. Not to mention the time it would waste. The moving van needed to be packed, loaded and on its way by six o'clock.

'Not a chance.' Gunn shot his sister a stern look. 'If Laura wants to play silly buggers and make a spectacle of herself, that's her lookout. I've got more than enough work to do, and so have you, Ma. Just leave her.'

By three o'clock, miraculously, the party from the British Museum had already been and gone, Edie had retrieved the key and Laura had grudgingly allowed herself to be unchained from the garden railings. Emotionally exhausted, Gunn had announced he was taking the family dog, Friday, for a walk and set off in the direction of the cliffs.

It was a glorious summer's afternoon, ironically uplifting weather for such a distressing day. The sun blazed down from a brilliant blue Cornish sky, flecked with only occasional small white clouds, like stray sheep in a vast, azure pasture. Bending down to let Friday off the lead, Gunn looked on with envy as the springer spaniel took off across the bluffs, tail wagging, utterly oblivious that today was different to any other. That she would never sleep another night beside the cast-iron range in Maltings' kitchen, listening to the heavy *tick, tick* of the grandfather clock and the constant creaks and wheezing of the house's ancient pipes.

For the time being, the family were only moving about half

a mile up the road into a vacant farm cottage that a neighbour had kindly offered after William's death. But eventually, Edie would need to find a permanent new home. With the very modest amount of money still left to her, it was likely she would have to move further inland. Perhaps even to St Austell or Truro if, God forbid, she ended up needing to find some sort of work to make ends meet.

It won't come to that, Gunn told himself firmly. *It's up to me not to let that happen.*

Sometimes it disturbed him, how angry he felt towards his father. Gunn had loved William, very much, and was utterly devastated by his sudden, unexpected death. Growing up, he'd felt a huge sense of pride at how much more exciting and interesting and fun William was compared to any of his friends' boring, run-of-the-mill fathers. True, Pa was away a lot. And Gunn had sometimes felt that he left a bit too much of the work of running Maltings and raising a family to Ma, while he gallivanted around the world on exciting adventures. But whenever he returned to Cornwall, it was always in such a happy whirlwind of hugs and kisses and presents, regaling them all with gripping stories about ancient cities or dangerous animals or caves full of stalactites or hidden treasure, that everybody immediately forgave him.

But now there would be no more stories, no more love and joy. Only loss, grief and the devastating betrayal of what had been concealed.

It wasn't just the *fact* of his father's financial mis-management, of his reckless and frankly unforgivable dereliction of duty as the breadwinner and head of the family, that hurt Gunn so much. It was the magnitude. Sifting through the scores of unopened letters from the bank that William had stuffed to the back of one of the drawers in his bureau, Gunn and his mother had discovered truly *huge* debts, many of them going back years or even decades. Gunn had always struggled with reading at school, and to his embarrassment it still took him a lot longer than other people to plough through a letter or a bill. But even he could see at once that the interest payments on his father's debts alone were more than double what it cost to run Maltings for a year. And Edie had already been doing that on a shoestring, cutting back in order to help fund her husband's 'passion', or so she'd believed.

The worst part for Gunn, the part he simply couldn't comprehend, was that *knowing* how serious a situation they were in, *knowing* that they would almost certainly lose the house unless something changed, William had continued to borrow more money to fund even more expeditions.

Gunn could see now that the brave, adventurous father he had so idolized had actually been a desperate addict. That while his friends' 'boring' fathers had toiled away at their 'boring' jobs, what they were actually doing was sacrificing their own happiness in order to support their families. Meanwhile William Gunn's relentless, compulsive pursuit of the next thrill, the next treasure, had not only cost him his life, but had left his widow and children borderline destitute.

How did one forgive that? And how was Gunn supposed to grieve, if he couldn't forgive?

Whistling for Friday, and turning his face up towards the sun, he tried to push these unhappy thoughts out of his mind. It was good to be outside, away from the crushing atmosphere of the house and the packing crates. Good too to be in his beloved Cornwall. Pa had always said that, no matter how far he roamed, he had yet to see anywhere as beautiful as the countryside around Port Isaac, and on this point at least Gunn agreed.

Taking the steep, winding path that led down to the shore, he picked up a stick and threw it for the dog, who was just beginning to tire after her explosion of energy up on the bluffs. Despite the warm day, the beach wasn't particularly crowded. While Friday sniffed about on the sand, randomly digging, Gunn searched for a smooth, round pebble suitable for skimming. Tossing stones out over the water, seeing how far they could bounce, was another game that he and his father used to play together, often for hours at a time. But despite that association, Gunn still found it calming and satisfying to watch his missile leap gracefully from wave to wave.

I must move forward, he told himself, gathering another stone.

Looking back won't change anything.

He was the man of the house now. It was his responsibility to take care of his mother and sister. Not just to learn from his father's mistakes but one day, God willing, to rectify them.

Gunn had passions of his own. The new sport of downhill skiing, in particular, held a deep fascination for him. He was good at it too, regularly beating the local Swiss hopefuls in the few amateur races he'd entered. For the last two winters he'd spent every penny of his own savings funding trips to the Alps to indulge his hobby. But that would all have to take a backseat now. He needed to make money. A lot of money.

From now on, Gunn vowed, he would dedicate his life to accumulating wealth. He would achieve the financial security that had eluded his father and one day, as soon as he could, he would buy back Maltings. Gazing out to the horizon, he imagined himself leading his mother back into their ancestral home, and proudly pressing the keys into her hand. In his fantasy, the Maltings he restored to Edie wouldn't be the run-down, dilapidated version that they were leaving today, the result of years of his father's neglect. Instead, Gunn would return to his mother a restored, majestic version of the manor, with gleaming paintwork and a new roof and pipes that didn't creak like the boards of an old, sinking ship.

Gunn wasn't academic, like his sister Laura. And just at this precise moment he didn't know how he was going to do it. But he was determined to put right the wrongs done by his father. He would mend his mother's broken heart, and restore honour and glory to the Gunn family name.

CHAPTER FOUR

Beaulieu-sur-Mer, France, July 1928

'Let's see now.'

The four Challant children were gathered expectantly in the hallway, huddled around Sandrine as she sorted through a thick stack of post. The scar on her hand from last week's dog bite was still lividly visible, but they all tried not to stare.

'What do we have today? One for you, Miss Renée.'

Renée stepped forward eagerly. 'It's from cousine Louise,' she announced. 'I can tell from the handwriting on the envelope.'

'Nothing for Master Charles today,' Sandrine went on. 'Or for you, I'm afraid Miss Ines.'

Disappointed, Charles and Ines both wandered off, leaving only Genevieve hovering anxiously at Sandrine's shoulder.

'That one's mine!' Reaching into the pile, she picked out a stiff cream envelope, with her name printed on the front in elaborate gold lettering.

'As is this,' Sandrine smiled, handing over a second, more ordinary-looking letter before heading into the salon to deliver the rest of the post to Clotilde.

Sinking into the deep, maroon velvet sofa near the bottom of the stairs, Renée tucked her stockinged feet beneath her and began skimming through her letter.

'I love Louise, but honestly and truly, she can be such a dreary correspondent,' she complained to Genevieve. 'I mean, no offence, but what do I care about Uncle Albert's gout? Who's yours from?'

Genevieve didn't reply.

'Gen?'

Looking up, Renée saw that her sister stood frozen in her dressing gown, rooted to the spot. She had what looked like a formal invitation card gripped tightly in her left hand and a second, unopened envelope dangling limply from her right. Her jaw and neck had gone strangely rigid, and she was breathing in the fast, shallow way that dogs did when they were frightened, or about to whelp.

'Genevieve, what is it? What's wrong?'

Wordlessly, Gen handed over the card. Judging by the format and the elaborate, cursive script, it was clear that it was a wedding invitation.

'*Monsieur et Madame Gustave Allenceau request the pleasure of the company of Mlle Genevieve Challant at the wedding of their daughter Sylvie Celeste,*' Renée read, '*to Monsieur Aurelian de la Tour . . .*

'Oh darling.' Wrapping a comforting arm around Genevieve's frozen shoulders, she read on. '*The wedding will take place at L'Eglise Saint Etienne-du-Mont, on Saturday September eighth. Répondez s'il vous plaît a . . .*'

Gen took the card back.

'He didn't tell me.' Her voice was monotone, numb with misery. 'He wrote to me ten days ago, didn't say a word. He let me find out like *this*.'

'I'm so sorry, Gen,' said Renée with feeling. 'I know you liked him.'

'I *loved* him,' Genevieve whispered hoarsely, allowing herself to be pulled down onto the couch. 'I just . . . don't understand. He loved me too, Renée. I know he did.'

'Do you, my love?' Renée asked gently. 'Did he ever actually tell you that?'

'Yes!' Gen sobbed. 'I mean, perhaps not in actual *words*. But in his actions. His intentions. All last year he wrote to me.'

'About your play,' Renée reminded her.

'Yes, but . . . you don't understand. We were so close before I had to go to stupid old Lausanne. Oh Renée! Why did Papa have to send me away?'

39

It was the complaint Genevieve came back to again and again, like a dog digging up an old bone.

'He forced me to go to finishing school, and now Aurelian's marrying Sylvie Allenceau. *Sylvie Allenceau*, of all people!' She ran a hand through her short hair in despair. 'I mean, you tell me what those two have in common?'

Sylvie Allenceau was a casual acquaintance from Paris, the daughter of a vastly wealthy family of shipbrokers, originally from Marseille. Pretty, well-connected and with an inheritance and income that was easily triple Genevieve's, it wasn't hard at all for Renée to imagine the appeal Sylvie might hold for an ambitious young man about town like Aurelian de la Tour. Truth be told, it had been obvious to Renée from the beginning that Aurelian had never shared her older sister's feelings, or at least not in any serious way. The 'big romance' had always been in Genevieve's head. But even Renée hadn't expected things to end like this, in such a dramatic and painful way.

Opening the second letter listlessly, Gen read the first few lines before folding it away. The tears that she'd been trying so hard to stop from coming streamed down her cheeks now in a silent torrent.

'It's from Juliette,' she told Renée miserably. Juliette was Aurelian's younger sister. 'She's trying to be kind but I . . . I just can't!'

Getting up suddenly, she ran, sobbing, up the stairs to her room. Renée thought about going after her, but decided in the end to leave it, at least for the rest of the morning. Having never been in love herself, and not possessing the romantic disposition of either of her sisters, Renée had never experienced heartbreak. But she understood instinctively that there were some griefs that could only truly be faced alone.

Poor Gen.

The morning after Genevieve received the devastating news about Aurelian, Ines was sitting on the kitchen stairs with her back pressed against the wall, listening.

'Spying' was one of her favourite games. She used to play it with Charles, where the two of them would try to sneak into a room as quietly as possible and then hide, in order to eavesdrop on adults' private conversations without being discovered. But at twelve, her brother now deemed the game 'babyish'. He'd also pointed out, with some justification, that they never heard anything interesting anyway, the lives of both their parents and older sisters being 'so damned dull, you almost wish they *would* catch you and liven things up a bit'. Occasionally one of the servants or tenant farmers might drop a juicy nugget of information. Some gossip about who was courting whom, or who could no longer fit into their pinafore and might even be *enceinte*. But none of it was enough to tempt Charles, and so today Ines was on her own.

'You have to admit it's a bit odd, Marie. The way he keeps coming back up here, like a lost cat trying to find its way home.'

Hercule, one of the manservants, was talking to Ines's friend, Marie the cook.

'I don't think he knows where he is half the time, poor mite,' Marie replied. 'He just likes looking at Madame's birds.'

Ines's ears pricked up. Who *were* they talking about? If only Charles were here.

'Hmm.' Hercule sniffed sceptically. Through the crack in the kitchen door, Ines could see him rubbing his big, ugly nose with the back of his hand. She didn't much like Hercule, who never smiled or joked around with her the way that Marie and Sandrine did.

'If it's all so innocent, why is Monsieur so hellbent on chasing him away? That's what I'd like to know. I mean, what harm could a simple boy from the village be doing, if all he wants is to look at some parrots?'

Ah, thought Ines. *He means Bernard.* She hadn't seen him at the beach recently and wasn't aware that he'd been to the bastide again. *I wonder why Maman never mentioned it?*

'Mark my words. There's more to it.' Hercule wagged his finger sagely in Marie's general direction. 'That lad knows something. Something about Monsieur.'

'Don't be so silly!' Marie replied, more defensively than she'd intended. 'The boy barely knows his own name.'

Hercule's eyes narrowed. '*You* know something too, don't you Marie?' he said slowly. 'You're keeping secrets. Go on, admit it.'

'I'll admit no such thing!' Marie laughed, trying to lighten the mood. But Hercule was having none of it.

'What *does* that lad know?' he pressed her. 'Something Monsieur doesn't want him blabbing about to Madame, I'll bet.'

Ines leaned slightly forward, alarmed by Hercule's increasingly angry, ominous tone. The horrid man was clearly implying that Papa had done something wrong or shameful. But everyone knew what a good man he was. To her dismay, however, she heard Marie hesitate before replying, 'Hmmm. Maybe.'

'I mean, let's face it,' Hercule went on, 'we all know what a hypocrite Challant is. With his preaching and praying and all his holier-than-thou . . .'

At that moment, mortifyingly, Ines somehow lost her footing and slipped, noisily and with an embarrassing clatter, to the bottom of the kitchen stairs.

Marie came rushing out, her capacious aprons rustling like a ship in full sail.

'Miss Ines! What on earth happened? Are you all right? What are you doing down here?'

'I'm fine,' Ines blushed, picking herself up and taking care to avoid eye contact with horrid Hercule. 'I came down to see if you had any treats I could take up to Genevieve.' The lie was quick and, Ines thought, convincing. Certainly it seemed to satisfy Marie, who immediately began retrieving some macarons from the larder and asking after 'poor Miss Gen' as she handed them over.

Muttering *merci*, Ines took the paper bag full of treats and fled back up the stairs, her heart pounding. She decided that perhaps she wouldn't tell Charles what she'd heard after all. Suddenly being a spy didn't feel like quite as much fun as it did before.

*

Much later that night, Clotilde sat at her bedroom dressing table, brushing out her fine gold hair and watching in the mirror as her husband pulled on his flannel dressing gown and sank to his knees in prayer.

Praying before bed was a regular part of Charles Challant's nightly ritual, like brushing his teeth or putting on his pyjamas. Often, when they were at Sunday mass in Paris, or here at Beaulieu, Clotilde had the uncomfortable feeling that there was an element of theatre to Charles's piety. To the deep, resonant voice with which he intoned the familiar Latin prayers, and the look of saintliness on his face – as if he were secretly hoping that the other members of the congregation were watching and admiring, perhaps aspiring to be as virtuous as he. But in Charles's defence, this definitely wasn't the case with his bedtime prayers. These were sincere; a habit, learned in early childhood and never outgrown. Watching him drop to his knees beside their bed each night, closing his eyes tight, Clotilde could see the little boy in her often overbearing husband in a way that wasn't usually visible. It was a rare glimpse of vulnerability, one that she had often clung to in order to keep affection alive during difficult times in their marriage.

Getting slowly back to his feet after a perfunctory sign of the cross, Charles Challant approached his wife's dressing table in an unusually ebullient mood. 'What a week, eh? First the bank in Megève came through with the financing we wanted, just when I'd begun to think it was hopeless. And then the incredible gains we made at the *bourse*.'

Reaching down, he placed both hands on Clotilde's shoulders and began to make amorous circles with his thumbs.

'Things do seem to be going well.' She smiled back up at him, trying to mirror his sudden burst of optimism. But it wasn't easy. All summer, Charles had seemed anxious and secretive. It had started with him buying those awful dogs, for 'protection'. But protection from what? Now, all at once, he seemed at ease and happy again. Clotilde couldn't keep up with his turbulent mood swings.

'Better than well!' Charles insisted, puffing out his chest

43

like a cockatiel trying to impress its mate. 'I'll be giving old Rothschild a run for his money if I can keep up this winning streak.'

Sensing some hesitation, despite Clotilde's best efforts, he released her shoulders. 'Is something the matter, my love? You seem a bit subdued.'

'Not really,' Clotilde replied hastily, pinning her brushed hair back up into its loose, nightly bun. 'I'm a little concerned about Genevieve, that's all. She only came out of her room today for meals, and you could see she'd been crying.'

'Oh, she'll get over it,' Charles announced breezily. 'She's too young to marry now anyway, but when the time is right I'll expect her to make a far better match than that dilettante De la Tour.'

'She's only a year younger than I was when we married,' Clotilde reminded him. 'And she was very fond of Aurelian, you know.'

'God knows why,' muttered Charles. 'The boy always struck me as a frightful popinjay. And he was for-ever encouraging Genevieve's nonsensical ideas about becoming a playwright. As far as I'm concerned, Mademoiselle Allenceau is welcome to him.'

His hands were back on his wife's shoulders. Soon his fingers began to edge downwards, beneath the thin muslin collar of her nightgown.

Clotilde steeled herself for what was to come. In the early years of their union his libido had been prodigious. But as he'd aged it had become more of a sleeping bear, roused only very occasionally and almost always as a result of some kind of business success.

Clotilde didn't begrudge this wifely duty. But neither did she enjoy it. Perhaps if he could have been just a little bit kinder and more sensitive about Genevieve's disappointment, she might have felt more amenable to his advances? Or if he hadn't been so prone to anger, so volatile, so *different* these past few weeks, especially since they'd arrived at Beaulieu? As it was, she felt nothing as Charles lifted her nightgown over her head, shielding herself in the cloak of numbness that she found herself wearing more and more often recently.

Bernard, the simple boy, had come to the house again today, to look at her birds. The servants had sent him away, and Clotilde had instructed them not to mention the incident in front of Monsieur, or any of the children. But as Charles led her to the bed and climbed on top of her, thrusting away mechanically, her thoughts drifted back to the child.

She felt sorry for him. Sorry and sad. Watching him gazing, rapt, at her aviary, Clotilde could tell that the child felt the same transcendent joy around these magnificent, rainbow-plumed creatures as she did. She longed to invite him in and share that joy, as a kindred spirit. But Charles had made it clear that there was to be no interaction between them. His growing obsession with the boy was troubling.

The sooner Bernard accepted the situation and found himself a new passion, the better it would be for everyone. Until then, Clotilde reflected, they were all trapped in their different ways – her, Bernard, Charles, the birds. *We just have different cages.*

'Do you think Gen will start to feel better soon?' Ines asked as Renée switched off her bedside lamp.

'I'm sure she will,' Renée replied. 'I'm just not sure how soon.' She pulled the thin summer blanket right up to Ines's chin, tucking her in tightly the way that she liked.

'I don't think Aurelian behaved kindly,' said Ines.

'No,' agreed Renée. 'Nor do I.'

'He should have told her that he liked someone else.'

'Yes.' Renée kissed the top of her sister's blonde angel-head. 'He should have. But sometimes people are scared to say things that they think might upset somebody else.'

Ines bit her lower lip awkwardly and looked away. Try as she might to forget it, the conversation she'd overheard between Hercule and Marie in the kitchens earlier kept coming back to her. Marie had been scared to say something about Papa. Horrid Hercule clearly didn't care who he upset.

But Marie had been holding something back, Ines was sure of it. If only she hadn't fallen down the stupid stairs before she could find out what it was!

'Renée, what's a "hypocrite"?' she asked guilelessly.

'A hypocrite is someone who says one thing but does another,' answered Renée. 'Someone who isn't honest or honourable, they just pretend to be. Why?'

'Oh, no reason,' blustered Ines. 'I read it in a book.'

'You and your books!' Renée smiled, tickling her again. 'You should come down to the farm with me again tomorrow. Get your nose out of Hans Christian Andersen and play with the puppies while you still have time. They'll be weaned soon and off to their new homes.'

'How could they be weaned so soon?' Ines wailed. 'I feel as if they were only just born.'

It would be good to get out of the house tomorrow, away from Gen's sadness and all the other tensions whispering in the walls of the bastide, Ines thought. Things that she felt and fretted about, but didn't begin to understand. What she *did* know was that her precious summer at Beaulieu was being tainted somehow, spoiling like a ripe peach left too long out in the sun.

CHAPTER FIVE

London, England, July 1928

Gunn looked listlessly out of the train window, watching the West Country scenery fly by. The dry summer had left everything parched, with fields more yellow than green and leaves already starting to fall from the trees as if it were autumn. It was still beautiful though. Gunn watched as flint Cornish cottages gave way to mellow Devon thatch, and then on into Hampshire with its grand Georgian rectories and manicured parks and estates. More money the closer one got to London, or so it seemed to Gunn.

Everything came down to money in the end.

On the rare occasions that he'd travelled by train as a child, Gunn had always gone first class. Pa had paid for their tickets, and it would simply never have occurred to an upper-class, landed gentleman like William Gunn to proceed in any other fashion. Not that Gunn's father had been flashy or vulgar with his money. Quite the opposite. But the Gunns travelling first class was the same as the sun rising in the east. It wasn't a choice or a decision. It was simply the natural order of things.

Not any more, though. After a gruelling week helping move his mother and sister into Briar Cottage, a romantic name for an entirely charmless, farm-worker's house on a neighbour's estate, Gunn was now headed to London to meet with his father's lawyer.

'He's asked me to travel up to town, but I truly can't face it,' Edie had told Gunn, handing him the letter from a Mr Merriweather on smart Lincoln's Inn paper. 'Apparently Pa had some sort of life insurance policy that needs to be untangled, but I honestly haven't the energy to deal with solicitors. And besides, I'm useless with figures. Would you go, darling?'

Gunn still struggled with reading, and anything remotely legalese was completely beyond him. But he did understand numbers, and was also good with people, both a natural salesman and a confident negotiator.

'Of course, Ma,' he'd told her reassuringly. 'You just concentrate on settling in. From now on you must leave this sort of thing to me.'

It had felt good to be able to help, to *do* something practical in a set of circumstances that were almost completely out of his control. But as soon as Edie dropped him off at Newquay railway station, Gunn had felt the positivity start to drain out of him like dirty water through a dishcloth. He was poor. The whole family was poor. Even if tomorrow's meeting with James Merriweather went well, it was unlikely to change that fundamental, dispiriting fact.

Despite the lateness of the hour when he arrived in London, Gunn decided to walk from Paddington to his guesthouse in Bayswater, a modest but clean and comfortable affair run by a bossy, overweight woman named Mrs Fisher and her small, hen-pecked husband. By the time he'd agreed on the rates, unpacked his small case and washed his face after the long journey, he felt too tired even to eat. Crawling under the covers he fell asleep immediately.

He woke late the next morning to Mrs Fisher's loud banging on his door to inform him that his breakfast was ready. An hour later, fortified by a large plate of kippers, mushrooms and fried bread, washed down with very strong, sugary tea, Gunn was on his way to Lincoln's Inn to meet his father's lawyer.

'Ah, yes, Hector, isn't it?' James Merriweather was not at all what Gunn had been expecting. In his mid-sixties, with a shock of wispy white hair, and a suit that looked as if it had been made for somebody else at least forty years ago, and possibly not cleaned since, he came across as more of a confused, elderly uncle pottering about his flat than an expensive London solicitor.

'Jolly good, jolly good, yes, your mother did say it would be you coming.' Smiling, he picked up a pile of papers from the seat of a rickety-looking chair, which he proceeded to offer to Gunn. 'Sit down, dear boy, please. Sit, sit, sit. Now, would you care for a cup of tea?'

The pleasantries over, Merriweather got down to business, outlining the situation regarding William's various life insurance policies without pulling any punches.

'Your father didn't keep up his payments,' he told Gunn bluntly. 'I'm afraid that's the long and the short of it. So while there is *some* money available to your mother, it certainly doesn't amount to a livable income.'

He showed Gunn the figures.

'Christ.' Gunn ran a hand through his thick blond hair. 'Is that really all there is?'

'I'm afraid so. Has your mother . . .' The solicitor hesitated. 'I don't mean to offend by asking this. But has your mother considered some sort of employment? She's still a relatively young woman, I understand.'

Gunn shook his head vehemently. He wasn't offended. And Edie had considered it. In fact the two of them had discussed the matter endlessly since Pa's funeral. But the reality was, his mother had few if any marketable skills. And, as Gunn saw things, it was his job to provide. He was the man of the family now.

'Ma still has Laura to think of. I'll be the one earning.'

'Right.' Merriweather nodded sagely. 'And what sort of employment had you been thinking about, Hector? If you don't mind my asking.'

'I'm not sure yet,' Gunn mumbled awkwardly. 'I'm a pretty good skier.'

'Skier?' Merriweather looked confused.

'Yes, you know, downhill skiing. It's all the rage in St Moritz,' Gunn explained. 'I had thought about perhaps downhill racing competitively. For prize money?'

The old man's eyes widened, but he said nothing.

Gunn frowned. 'What? You don't think it's a good idea?'

'I couldn't possibly say, my boy.' The lawyer spread his hands in a gesture of innocence. 'I'm afraid I know very little about the world of ski racing.' He pronounced the last two words with visible distaste. 'However, I would imagine one would have to win quite a large number of prizes simply to cover one's costs. Don't you agree? Travelling back and forth to Switzerland and what have you?'

'Maybe,' Gunn admitted grudgingly. Stupidly, he hadn't factored the cost part of it in at all.

'Perhaps something a touch closer to home might be . . . more practical?' offered Merriweather kindly. 'Give it some thought, anyway. I'm sure you have plenty of skills that an employer would value.'

Walking down the Strand half an hour later, with his hands thrust deep in his pockets, Gunn tried in vain to think of what those skills might be. He was fit, strong and willing to work hard. But manual labour wasn't going to pay enough to provide a decent life for his mother and sister, never mind himself. What else? He could make things. One summer he and his father had built a canoe, a marvellous vessel that they'd forged from the wood of a fallen elm tree at Maltings, and triumphantly paddled down the Polperro river together. But Gunn couldn't imagine there was much money in canoe-building, especially given it had taken him almost three months to make just one.

Feeling defeated, he found himself standing in front of the Savoy Hotel and, on a whim, decided to go inside for a drink. He couldn't afford it, but he needed it, and who knew, perhaps it would help him think.

'Good afternoon, sir. Welcome to the Savoy.'

Stepping through the heavy brass doors into the grand, red-carpeted lobby was like stepping into another world. All around him, well-dressed, obviously wealthy men and women lounged around in brocade armchairs, talking and laughing and exuding a practised ease that Gunn at once admired and envied. A glittering crystal chandelier shimmered overhead, casting a warm, flattering light over everything. Soft piano music wafted through the air, and a pleasant smell of wax furniture polish, scented lilies and some other aroma that Gunn couldn't immediately pinpoint, but might simply have been money. *This is the life I want to live,* Gunn found himself thinking. *But how to get here?*

The bar was an intimate, oak-panelled room, tucked away at the end of a corridor a few steps down from the lobby. Even at this early hour it was relatively busy, with couples tending to opt for the tables, while singles perched on stools. Gunn ordered a scotch and soda, and took a seat at one end of the bar. He quickly became aware of a middle-aged woman sipping a martini at the other end. Partly because she was notably attractive with elaborately curled auburn hair and a full bosom, displayed to some advantage in a low-cut, wildly expensive-looking silk dress. But mostly because she was openly staring at Gunn, in a manner not unlike that of a lioness eyeing up a tasty-looking gazelle.

Before Gunn knew what was happening, the woman had sashayed over, drink in hand, and introduced herself.

'Joan Keating,' she announced, taking a seat on the empty stool next to his. She was American, with the sort of low, husky voice he associated with a heavy smoker. 'And who might you be?'

'My name is Gunn.' He raised his glass to hers. Reaching into his jacket for his silver cigarette case, a sixteenth birthday present from his father, he pulled out two Chesterfields. Lighting one for himself, he offered her the second.

'Just Gunn?' she smiled, slipping the cigarette between her lips and leaning forward for him to light it, revealing even more of her really quite exceptional chest.

'Just Gunn,' he confirmed. He noticed that 'Joan' wore a wedding band, along with a diamond engagement ring the size of a small grape. But it was crystal clear from her manner towards him that conjugal loyalty was not a big priority for Mrs Keating.

51

'Are you and your husband here on holiday?' Gunn asked her, sipping his scotch and thinking how much he would enjoy uncovering the rest of that phenomenal bosom.

'Holiday?' She laughed bitterly. 'My husband never takes holidays. Doesn't believe in 'em.'

'That doesn't sound like much fun,' Gunn smiled.

'It isn't.' Joan's diamond-encrusted hand closed over his. Looking up at the barman, she said, 'Another round for me and my friend please, Henry. You can put it on my tab.'

At that moment, a number of thoughts flitted through Gunn's mind simultaneously.

The first was, *this day just got a lot better.*

The second was, *I must step into hotel bars in the afternoons more often.*

And the third was, *what if this is it? What if my most marketable 'skill' is getting rich, bored women to like me?*

'Joan Keating', whoever she was, had already paid for his drinks. Or rather, Mr Keating had. Gunn couldn't help but wonder what more she might be willing to pay for, if he were to keep her entertained? And not just Joan specifically, but the countless other bored, rich, beautiful women he'd encountered over the years in places like . . . St Moritz, for example.

All of a sudden his conversation with his father's solicitor came rushing back to him. '*I would imagine one would have to win quite a large number of prizes to cover one's costs. Travelling back and forth to Switzerland.*'

But what if one's costs were already covered? What then?

Returning the pressure of Joan's fingers, Gunn drained the rest of his first drink while the barman mixed his second.

'You're too kind,' he told her. 'Thank you.'

'Oh, don't worry, sweetheart,' she replied, knocking back her own martini with disconcerting aplomb. 'You can thank me later.'

CHAPTER SIX

Beaulieu-sur-Mer, France, August 1928

Friday 28 August dawned grey and ominous at Beaulieu, the sky swollen and heavy with gathering storm clouds.

Ines awoke to the dull whine of the wind, which was already starting to pick up, although the actual rains weren't expected till the evening. Pulling back her bedroom curtains, she stared numbly out at the shivering plane trees, and the spindly palms as they swayed side to side. She wondered whether Maman's birds were frightened by the change in weather, or felt any of the foreboding that she did. She would go and check on them later.

At breakfast, Charles Père was in a foul mood, brooding about potential damage to the property if the coming storm turned out to be as bad as expected.

'Well there's really not much we can do about it,' Clotilde pointed out reasonably, earning herself an irritated glare from Charles, who was in no mood to be sanguine.

'Where the hell is Genevieve?' he snapped, nodding towards his eldest daughter's empty chair. He was clearly looking for a fight.

'She's sleeping in, Papa,' Renée answered on Clotilde's behalf. Papa had been a particularly terrible bully these last few weeks at Beaulieu and it pained Renée to watch her mother shrink in the face of his bad temper, like a withering flower. 'I don't think she had a very good night.'

'Well go and bloody wake her,' commanded Charles. 'I've had about as much as I can stand of this wallowing. All over some ridiculous boy.'

Renée pushed back her chair to do as he asked, but Clotilde raised a hand for her to stop.

'Leave your sister be, please Renée.' Her mother's voice was quiet but unusually firm. Turning to Charles, she added, 'There's no need to drag the poor girl down to breakfast if she's not hungry.'

Charles Père's eyes widened, then narrowed. 'Fine,' he grumbled, dropping his napkin on the table and stalking away. 'Have it your own way. I have work to do.'

'Well done, Maman,' Renée said, glancing admiringly at her mother once he'd gone. She couldn't remember the last time that Clotilde had openly opposed her husband. Or that Papa had so easily allowed himself to be overruled, albeit with a bad grace. She wondered whether there was something more going on between her parents, something that had shifted the power dynamic between them in some unspoken way?

Brushing away her daughter's compliment, Clotilde reached for her *tasse de café*. But she quickly set it down again when she realized that her hand was shaking violently enough to make the cup rattle in its saucer.

'Are you all right, Maman?' Ines asked, worried.

'I'm fine, cherie,' Clotilde replied, although her voice carried less of its usual warmth.

Ines's anxiety lingered. It was only nine o'clock in the morning, but already a feeling of foreboding had descended over the day, as thick and cloying as the humid air. Something had *happened* overnight. Something that had put Papa in such a terrible mood and made Maman so different. Something that had changed the natural order of things.

Bernard Angier wasn't frightened at all by the prospect of a storm. In fact he found the whole thing quite thrilling.

Standing in the doorway of his family's modest fisherman's cottage above Beaulieu harbour, he gazed up excitedly at the darkening sky, wondering when it would all begin.

'Will there be thunder, Tante Eloise?' he asked breathlessly. 'And lightning?'

'I hope not,' his aunt yawned. She'd raised Bernard since his mother died when he was a toddler, and loved him like a son. But taking care of a child with his needs could be hard work.

'I love lightning!' The little boy clapped his hands.

'I daresay. But you mustn't go out once the rain starts,' she told her nephew sternly. 'Do you understand?'

During the last big storm in Beaulieu, trees and timbers had fallen everywhere, and neighbours had seen seven-foot waves wreak utter havoc down at the quayside. Bernard couldn't swim. If his curiosity were to get the better of him, he could be in real danger.

'But I'll put my coat on,' the boy pleaded. 'Also my boots.'

'No, darling.' Tante Eloise was firm. 'I'm sorry, but it just isn't safe. You can go out and play now if you like. But if the storm hits before nightfall, you must promise to come straight home.'

Wolfing down his bread and *lait chaud*, Bernard decided to head out and explore while he could.

Outside, the change in the air made everything feel hot and wet, like a jungle. Bernard liked jungles. He'd read lots of picture books about them at the library. The streets of his beloved town looked different today beneath the dark blanket of clouds. Bernard wondered whether the potholes he skipped over today would become puddles tomorrow, after the rains? He loved puddles, and splashing, and wearing his special rubber boots that his uncle had given him.

Bernard waved and smiled at everyone as he weaved his way through the streets, and most people smiled back. He knew that he was different. But he'd been raised to view his disability as a fact, not a problem, and it was not something that had ever made him unhappy. On the contrary, growing up in Beaulieu, among his aunt and uncle's friends and neighbours, Bernard had always felt lucky and safe. The town was his playground and its residents his playmates, and although from time to time his curiosity had landed him in trouble, in general he moved through life with a buoyant confidence that made folks warm to him even more.

The one confusing exception to this rule was the Challant family. Tante Eloise said that it was because the Challants were rich, and rich people were different. That they said one thing and did another. But this made no sense to Bernard.

Madame Challant had told him at the cinema that he could come up to the bastide and visit her birds. He remembered it clearly. But when he went up to the bastide and asked for Madame Challant as instructed, she never came. Servants greeted him instead and chased him away. Sometimes they even shouted at him. He mustn't come back. He wasn't welcome. Monsieur said *non*.

At first, Bernard had ignored them. They had made a mistake. Madame Challant wanted him to come and see her birds. But as the weeks went by, and the same thing kept happening, his confusion deepened. In the end, his aunt and uncle made him promise not to go back to the Challants' bastide.

It was hard, though. So hard. The birds were so lovely. So pretty and enticing with all their coloured feathers and the cawing, jungle-y sounds they made. He just wanted to be *near* them. Just to look, with his eyes. Surely it couldn't do any harm for him to look with his eyes?

Perhaps he would sneak out tonight, after his aunt and uncle went to bed? They always went to bed really early. When it was dark, and no one could see him, he could take the electric torch he'd been given for Christmas and go and look by himself. Then he could see the birds *and* the lightning!

I won't ask for Madame Challant this time, he thought. *Or pull the bell at the back gate. I'll just go in and look. Tante Eloise won't even have to know.*

*

56

Leaning over the bathroom basin, steadying herself with one hand, Genevieve steeled herself to drink the fizzing glass of Enoz that Sandrine had kindly brought up to her.

'This isn't the answer, you know,' the maid had told her, retrieving two empty brandy bottles from beneath her bed. Yanking open the curtains, Sandrine had clearly been shocked by the state of Gen's room, with clothes lying everywhere, overflowing ashtrays on every surface and the torn, half-burned remnants of her play manuscript shoved roughly into the wastepaper basket. But it was the overpowering smell of stale alcohol that worried her the most, prompting the search for the bottles.

'Isn't it?' Gen had replied desolately, shielding her eyes against the daylight. 'What is the answer then, Sandrine?'

'I don't know, Miss Gen,' said the maid. 'But if I were you I'd start with a nice bath and a big glass of Enoz salts. They're revolting but they get the job done, and you can't stay in bed the rest of your life.'

The Enoz was, indeed, revolting. Gagging violently after the first sip, it took all of Genevieve's willpower to finish the glass. But after a few minutes, she did start to feel marginally better, her throbbing headache and raging nausea both lifting as she stepped gingerly into the bath.

That was nice too. Although it was a struggle to feel even a moment's pleasure without the pain of Aurelian's betrayal sneaking back in and overwhelming her, dragging her back down into the dark well of depression that had become her world ever since she heard the news. Yes, she could force herself to wash and dress and come downstairs. Perhaps she could even eat a little, as her mother had been begging her to do for days.

But why? What was the point of it all? That was the question. And to Genevieve it felt very much as if brandy *was* the answer. Given that she would never now marry the man she loved, never publish a play, never do anything or be anything that *meant* something or mattered to anyone. Papa had already ruined her life and crushed her dreams so that she could conform to his idea of the perfect Challant daughter. So what did any of it matter any more? Why not stay in bed, and drink, and escape it all?

After a few minutes soaking the heat became too much. Gently easing herself out of the bath, Genevieve wrapped one of the soft, Beaulieu towels around her skinny body, and walked over to open the bathroom window. Strangely, the air outside was almost as damp as it was in the steamy bathroom, thick and muggy.

Pulling on the first dress she saw, and roughly brushing her hair back from her face, Genevieve headed downstairs. The house felt quiet, but that wasn't unusual for early afternoon. Gen assumed her siblings were out and about. Papa would be holed away in his study working. And Maman . . .

Before she could finish the thought, she heard raised voices coming from the library. Her father's familiar, resonant bass, mingled with another unfamiliar, high-pitched voice: her mother's, but in a state of either anger or distress that made her sound quite altered from her usual calm, compassionate self.

Concerned, Genevieve crept downstairs, drawing as close as she dared to the half-open salon door.

'Because you're my wife, that's why!' she heard her father insisting. 'It's your duty to support me.'

'My duty? And what of your duties, Charles? To protect me and the children?'

'I *am* protecting you.'

'From a danger of your own making!' Clotilde shot back. 'What if they come here, to the house?'

Genevieve's heart pounded. What 'danger'? What was her mother talking about? And who were 'they'?

'They won't,' insisted Charles.

'I'm frightened, Charles. All these secrets! What else don't I know?'

'I won't discuss it any more, Clotilde. I mean it. You will honour me as your husband . . .'

'*Honour*,' Clotilde scoffed. 'Please.'

'God damn you, woman!' Charles Père's voice shook with rage, and Gen heard his heavy footsteps pound heavily across the floor. She had heard her father angry before, but not like this. The air of menace in his voice was unmistakable. Instinctively, without even thinking, she moved to protect her mother, pushing the door open wide and bursting into the room.

'Papa!'

Both parents turned to look at her, Clotilde ashen-faced, Charles Père ruddy and dishevelled. If Genevieve didn't know him better, she would have thought her father was drunk. As it was he had his right arm raised – *had he been going to strike Maman?* But the moment he saw his daughter standing there he let it drop, limp to his side.

'What is it, Genevieve?' His voice steadied again. Controlled. As if everything Gen had just heard and seen had been a dream. But it hadn't. Had it?

'Nothing. I just . . .' she hesitated. 'I slept late, that's all. I was just wondering where everybody was. And whether Maman wanted to, er, come on a walk. With me. It looks like it's going to rain later.'

'I'd love to, darling,' Clotilde answered, composing herself. 'I'll be out in just a minute.'

Genevieve withdrew, her heart pounding and her mind racing.

Did Papa beat Maman? Even now, after the tableau she'd just witnessed, she found that hard to imagine. She would have known, surely? They all would have known. Maman would have had bruises or . . . something. And Papa, for all his old-fashioned, occasionally selfish ways, had never been a violent person. If anything he was the opposite: ordered and virtuous, the living embodiment of self-control.

What had her mother said, though? About being afraid?

All these secrets.

Papa had secrets.

Genevieve's clever mind was already calculating. What if she were to discover the things her father was concealing? Would that knowledge give her the power over her own life that she so desperately craved? Might Papa's secrets, whatever they were,

59

be her key to freedom? To a life outside the stifling future that he had planned for her?

Yes, Genevieve had slept in late. Too late. But she was awake now.

Wide awake.

The rains started just as the sun went down, and within less than an hour the storm had begun in earnest. After an early supper, Bernard announced he was tired and going straight to bed, knowing that his aunt and uncle would take this as their own cue to turn in. For half an hour he lay quiet, listening to the deep boom of the thunder, and watching excitedly through his rain-lashed window for flashes of lightning. Then, once he felt sure Tante Eloise was asleep, he slipped on his rubber boots and raincoat, grabbed his special torch, and crept out into the night.

Everything outside was changed. The streets were slick and wet and beautiful, cobblestones glinting in the pale moonlight. But there was detritus everywhere, tree branches and shutters from buildings torn off by the wind, and gutters and drains overflowing. The rain when it hit Bernard's face was surprisingly warm. But the gusting wind made his wet skin feel cold, and he shivered as he made his way up the hill, towards the bastide.

He was happy, though. Happy and excited, and perhaps just a little bit guilty, because he'd broken a promise to Tante Eloise. Two promises really, about the storm *and* about not going to the Challant house again. But he'd had to do it, because Tante Eloise didn't understand about the birds. And anyway, he would be safe in the storm, because he had his rain boots and his flashlight. So everything would be all right.

As he got to the high wall surrounding the bastide, a flash of lightning lit up the sky above him making him squeal with excitement. Now he would finally get to see Madame Challant's birds up close – no servants to stop him, everyone asleep or sheltering inside. Bernard felt clever and proud for having thought of this plan. Soon he'd be there with the parakeets and the parrots, the finches and the jays, the macaws and the cockatoos. He wondered whether Madame kept any mynah birds? The man at the library had told him that mynah birds could talk. If you said *Bonsoir*, the bird would say it right back to you! Bernard couldn't think of anything more wonderful than saying *Bonsoir* to a bird and having it reply. Apart from maybe growing wings and being able to fly himself. But things like that never happened except in stories.

Climbing the bastide's wall was harder than it looked, especially in the dark and with the rain lashing down. Everything was slippery, and twice he scraped his knuckles scrambling for a handhold between the bricks. But at last he reached the top, edging along it on his hands and knees, moving slowly towards the aviary. The white-painted metal was clearly visible in the moonlight. It was quiet. Most of the birds were probably sleeping, or trying to shelter from the storm. But he could hear one or two of them letting out little whirring chirps.

Looking over into the bastide gardens for a suitable spot to jump down, he felt a sudden, unexpected wave of dizziness. The steep bank rising up from the lane meant that you didn't need a ladder to scale the wall from the outside, and although high, it was clearly climbable. But on the other side, the drop was vertical and much bigger than Bernard had realized. He wanted to pull out his flashlight to take a better look at the ground he'd be landing on, but that would mean lifting one hand up from the top of the wet wall, and that didn't feel safe. His aunt had told him he must always stay safe.

Oh no! Panicking, he gripped the top of the wall more tightly. What should he do? He had to stay safe, but he needed to see the birds and the wall was so high.

Closing his eyes tightly to shut out the danger, he dug his fingertips as hard as he could into sodden bricks and swung both legs over onto the garden side, his skinny legs flailing wildly in the wind like twigs. Then, with a whimper of pure fear, he let go.

*

'Do you hear that?'

Renée laid her cards down on the green baize table and cocked her head to one side. She and Genevieve were playing after-dinner cribbage, to try to keep Gen's mind off Aurelian, while Maman busied herself with needlepoint by the fire. But Gen had been distracted all evening, and there was a palpable frisson of tension in the air that Renée felt but couldn't fully understand.

'What?' Genevieve also stopped to listen. Apart from the relentless hiss of the rain and occasional clap of thunder, she couldn't hear anything except the dober-mans' distant barking. 'Do you mean the dogs?'

'Yes,' said Renée. 'They were quiet before, but now suddenly something's spooked them.'

Gen shrugged, turning back to her cards. 'Animals often behave strangely during a storm.'

'Even so. They sound very agitated,' Renée frowned. 'Don't you agree, Maman?'

Standing up, Clotilde walked over to the window and peered out into the rain-lashed darkness.

'I'm sure it's nothing, darling.' She tried to sound reassuring but inside her heart was hammering away at her ribs. What if the dogs had seen something – or someone – who'd caused them to panic, or raise the alarm? Charles had promised her the family were safe. But how could she rely on Charles's promises, when he'd already kept so much hidden from her?

Tugging anxiously at the material of her gilet, she made some excuse to the girls and slipped out of the room. Perhaps it *was* nothing. But if not, Clotilde intended to be prepared.

Charles Challant carefully made the last entry in his daily ledger, blotting the ink with the old-fashioned wooden roller he kept on his desk for the purpose. Most men in his position would pay a secretary or an accountant to manage such things for them. But Charles preferred to keep track of his burgeoning empire himself. Like his neatly ordered study, and immaculate copperplate handwriting, it gave him a feeling of control.

Recent events may have proved the feeling illusory, but he clung to it nonetheless.

Outside, the dogs were barking. To Charles's ears, it was a comforting sound. He was well aware of how much Clotilde feared and disliked his dobermans. But the simple fact was that they were there for her protection. For the whole family's protection.

Closing his ledger, he smoothed his beard with his hands, brooding on the events of the day. It troubled him that Genevieve had walked in on him and Clotilde arguing earlier. He couldn't help but wonder how much she had heard, or how she might have misinterpreted things. If only Clotilde understood! She was so quick to judge. But what did she know about the pressures a man like him faced? An important man, with growing business interests and a reputation to maintain?

I am a good man, Charles assured himself. *I'm devout. I provide for my family. What more does she want?*

It was one thing for strangers or even servants to spread malicious gossip. Great wealth and success engendered great envy after all. That was only to be expected. But to be questioned and berated by one's own *wife*, and perhaps thought less of by one's daughter? That was quite wrong.

At least the damned dogs know who their master is, Charles reflected bitterly, getting to his feet and turning out the office lamp. He would walk down to the kennels later and check on them.

A spectacular blue macaw let out a squawk of alarm, dazzled by the beam of Bernard's electric torch.

'N'aie pas peur,' the boy whispered, gasping in awe at the bird's lapis-blue plumage. 'Don't be afraid of me, Mr Bird. I'm Bernard. I'm your friend.'

His ankle throbbed from where he'd twisted it, jumping down from the wall. He also had a gash on his knee, which he would have to cover up with long trousers tomorrow, so Tante Eloise didn't see it and start asking questions. And he was soaked to the bone. But it had all been worth it to be here at last, up close to the beautiful birds and with Madame Challant's magnificent aviary all to himself.

'I wish I could live in there with you,' he sighed. Lying down on the saturated ground he stuck one spindly arm through the bars as far as it could go, and grasped around, trying to find a feather to keep as a souvenir.

It was the birds that first alerted him to the danger. Suddenly it wasn't just the macaw squawking, but a whole chorus of anxious, awakened birds, flapping and chirruping in various stages of distress.

Initially Bernard thought it was his light that was bothering them. Or the fact he was reaching into their enclosure. But when he pulled out his arm and stood back up, a treasured parrot feather clutched between his fingers, he heard it.

The loud snapping of a twig.

Quelqu'un est là?

Dogs barking. Getting louder. Coming closer.

The birds' panic triggered his own. An awful churning feeling began in the pit of his stomach. Scrambling to his feet in the mud, Bernard began to run.

BANG!

Ines sat bolt upright in bed, her heart pounding.

Was it thunder? It sounded terribly loud for thunder.

Sweat poured down her back and chest, soaking her nightgown. The room was stiflingly humid. But that wasn't the only reason.

She'd been having a lovely dream about cloud forests. There were waterfalls and mangrove trees and brightly coloured parakeets swooping back and forth against a crisp blue sky, delighting in their freedom. But then all at once, everything changed. The sky went dark, all the sweet jungle flowers began to smell putrid, and the most awful, frightening cacophony of squawking birds filled the sweltering air.

And then the bang awakened her.

It must have been thunder, Ines told herself. Whatever it was, it wasn't only Ines who'd been frightened by it. Outside, the dogs were once again barking furiously, but this time their snarls and yaps were mingled with an appalling shrieking coming from Clotilde's aviary.

And in the midst of it all the unmistakable, blood-curdling sound of a human scream.

In the salon, the older Challant children all heard it at once.

'What the hell was that?' Charles Fils jumped to his feet.

'Maybe a tree fell,' said Genevieve. 'Let's go out and see.'

'No!' Charles Père appeared in the doorway looking ashen. 'I'll go. All of you are to stay here till I return. All of you.'

'But Papa . . .' Charles Fils began.

'STAY!' his father bellowed, as if the boy were a dog. Shaken, Charles sat back down.

'Where's your mother?' Charles Père demanded.

Charles, Renée and Genevieve exchanged shrugs and glances.

'Upstairs?' offered Genevieve vaguely.

'Has something happened, Papa?' Renée asked boldly. 'Perhaps we should call the police?'

'You're not to call anyone,' Charles snapped, turning towards the front door. 'Do you understand? Just . . . stay inside.'

And with a heavy slam of the door he was gone.

The older children did as they were told. But, unbeknownst to anyone, Ines had already escaped.

Creeping downstairs in her nightgown, she'd slipped outside barefoot through the kitchen door and out into the rain, heading straight to the aviary.

Another bang. The rain lashing down.

The tight knot of fear in her chest swelled until she could hardly breathe. And yet somehow her feet kept propelling her forward, across the slippery lawn into the moonlight gloom, towards the dreadful sound of the shrieking birds. The dogs' barking had died down now, and there were no more screams, or claps of thunder. But the awful, desperate cries from Maman's birds grew louder and louder, an unbearable symphony of anguish that Ines simply had to put a stop to, no matter how frightened she was.

I must open their cages. The thought was like a drumbeat in the little girl's head, hypnotic and utterly compelling. *I must set them free.*

But as she approached the aviary, the drumbeat stopped abruptly. The birds were still crying. But Ines's attention was seized by something else.

Her parents, standing with their backs to her, both frozen like statues.

Behind them, three dobermans cowering submissively in the grass.

A few feet away, a fourth dog, sprawled out dead, its legs jutting at a grotesque angle in the faint glow of the moonlight.

And beyond that, a dark shape slumped on the ground.

'Papa?'

Ines called out, her voice a frightened rasp. She wanted her father to hold her. To reassure her. To press her against his solid, warm chest and tell her that she had nothing to fear. That whatever the danger had been, it had passed.

But instead Charles Père spun around wildly as if he'd been shot.

'Get back!' he snapped at Ines, his eyes wild. 'Don't come any closer.'

'But why?' Ines started to cry. 'What's happened? Maman?'

If Clotilde heard her daughter, she showed no sign of it, but remained still and silent, rooted eerily in place.

'GET BACK IN THE HOUSE!' Charles Père roared, almost lunging at Ines.

Petrified, she turned and fled.

As soon as Ines was out of sight, Charles sank to his knees.

While Clotilde watched mutely, he began to pray.

CHAPTER SEVEN

London, England, August 1928

'Dear Lord. What an awful story.'

Lady Antigone Hanborough, known to everyone as Tig, carefully folded her copy of the *Sunday Telegraph* at the appropriate page and handed it to Gunn.

Frowning, he began slowly to read the article. It was about a French family named Challant, who he vaguely thought he'd heard of, and a dreadful accident involving a mentally disabled child wandering onto their estate and being killed by a pack of dogs.

All reading was a challenge for Gunn, but he found newsprint particularly tiresome. The small size of the letters and the way the words were crammed together in columns made everything even harder to untangle. But he wasn't about to admit the weakness to his lover, so instead ploughed diligently through the gruesome account.

It was mid-morning on a dull, late summer weekend and Gunn and Tig were in the Hanboroughs' four-poster marital bed in Chelsea, reading the papers over what was left of breakfast. The fact that Lord Hanborough knew all about his wife's affair, and apparently wasn't the least bit troubled by it, eased Gunn's conscience somewhat.

'Johnny's with his own mistress up in Scotland, darling,' Tig assured him, the first time he'd spent the night at the house on Old Church Street. 'Lovely girl. Does all the ghastly shooting and bridge parties for me while I'm in town. Honestly, I'd be lost without her.'

But it still felt strange, having another man's footman wander in in the morning with the newspapers and a tray of toast and eggs for two. As if it were the most normal thing in the world for the mistress of the house to be waking up with a strange nineteen-year-old boy in her bed.

'Horrific,' said Gunn, finally getting to the end of the piece. 'What an appalling way to die.'

'Isn't it?' Tig shuddered. 'I feel sorry for the French family too, though. To have something so dreadful happen on one's estate, knowing that your own dogs were responsible? You'd never get over it, would you?'

'No,' said Gunn. 'You wouldn't. Although reading this, there seems to be quite a lot of bad feeling towards them in this town. Beau-whatever-it's-called.'

'Beau*lieu*, darling!' Tig laughed, extracting the paper from Gunn's hands and straddling him, swinging one soft, warm thigh across his waist. 'It's *the* place on the Côte d'Azur these days. But I do love that you haven't heard of it.'

At thirty-eight, Tig Hanborough was still an ex-ceptionally beautiful woman. Her glossy dark hair was cut in a short, boyish bob, but everything else about her was all woman, from her full, pink lips, to the long lashes framing her hazel eyes, to her jaw-dropping figure, with its sensuous curves in all the right places. Gunn had never met Lord Hanborough, but understood 'Johnny' to be in his late fifties, somewhat dour, and considerably more interested in both shooting and salmon fishing on the Tay than he was in his wife, or even his mistress.

Despite this, or perhaps because of it, the Hanboroughs' marriage was considered an extremely happy one. Tig had produced not one, but two male heirs, and was consequently free to live her life exactly as she pleased.

Gunn, although every bit as upper class as his older lover, had never been exposed to the sort of uber-wealthy, permissive circles that the Hanboroughs and their friends moved in. The closest he'd come was in Switzerland, skiing with a schoolfriend's family in the impossibly ritzy St Moritz, where adultery was no more frowned upon than borrowing another man's skis. Gunn had made a mental note of this at the time. But it had never occurred to him that, less than two years later, he'd be a part of this same racy, aristocratic crowd, or at least hovering on its periphery.

'That's it!' he said suddenly, reaching under Tig's negligee to cup her heavy, magnificent breasts with his hands and feeling himself harden instantly. 'That's where I heard the name. In St Moritz.'

'What are you talking about, darling?' Tig breathed huskily.

'*Challant*,' said Gunn. 'I knew I recognized it. From the paper? Charles Challant's a great friend of Maurice de Rothschild. I think they might be business partners.'

'Really?' Reaching down, Tig wrapped her fingers tightly around Gunn's rock-hard erection, arching her back as she guided him inside her for the second time that morning. Evidently she had lost interest in the Sunday papers, and the sad story of the boy and the dogs. For the time being, at least, so had Gunn.

Later that same day, after ordering himself a new sports jacket courtesy of the Hanboroughs' tailor on Savile Row, Gunn had lunch with Basil Tooley, an old friend of his father's at Brooks's.

'Have you seen William's collection yet? At the British Museum?' Basil asked Gunn.

'You mean they're showing it?' Gunn looked surprised. He'd just assumed that his father's treasures would be stuffed away in a basement somewhere, safe but, in large part, unseen.

'Oh yes,' said Basil. 'They've put on a whole exhibition. You really must go. It's marvellous.'

Usually, anything to do with his father was a non-subject as far as Gunn was concerned. The pain of William's death, combined with the scale of his betrayal and the ongoing crisis in the family's finances, meant everything was still too raw. But having just been treated to a stodgy but delicious meal of steak and kidney pudding and treacle tart, all washed down with a decent bottle of house claret, Gunn was feeling in a more convivial mood than usual.

'I haven't,' he admitted. 'But perhaps I'll pop in this afternoon. I've got a few hours to kill before dinner.'

Basil Tooley was right. William Gunn's collection of 'miscellaneous exotica' looked quite fabulous, even packed as it was into two relatively small rooms towards the back of the museum. It was popular too, with a surprising number of patrons willing to brave the five flights of stairs in order to look at William's shrunken pygmy heads, or the stuffed Carolina parakeet, now extinct, staring back at them glassy-eyed from beneath its bell jar.

Weaving his way through the birds' eggs and headdresses and earthenware pots that he remembered so vividly from Maltings, Gunn felt a heady mix of emotions. Pride, in his father's undeniable achievement as a collector: his vivid, some might say genius, eye for the compelling or absurd. Grief, for all that had been lost, and the fact that William Gunn himself would never see this triumph. But there was something else there too. Some deep affinity for these remarkable, fascinating objects, from far away or long ago. Running his finger lovingly over a display case of ancient Indian tribal coins, and then another of rare butterflies, lovingly pinned and labelled, Gunn felt something akin to yearning. A sort of longing to immerse himself in a world that was bigger and more varied and more magical than the one he lived in.

Was this what Pa felt? he wondered. *Or some hundred times more powerful version of it? Was this what took him away from us?*

In the end Gunn spent two full hours at his father's exhibition, and when he finally emerged onto Great Russell Street, it was already dark. Glancing at his watch, he realized he'd have to get a move on if he was going to make it to tonight's dinner party.

Normally he'd have been excited by the prospect of an evening with Tig's high society friends. Not only for the wealthy connections he might make over dinner – Gunn took his responsibility as family breadwinner seriously, and was already turning 'gifts' from Tig into cash that he could send home to his mother – but also because he was an innately sociable and curious person. Tonight, however, as he hurried home to his modest rented flat through a Bloomsbury bathed in moonlight, Gunn's thoughts lay elsewhere.

They were with his father, claimed by a treacherous stretch of river in the Borneo jungle. And in two rooms at the back of a museum, full of dead things that had touched Gunn's heart, and brought him back to life.

CHAPTER EIGHT

Beaulieu-sur-Mer, France, September 1928

'It's disgusting, Marie. Truly. I don't understand how you can sit there and defend them.'

Marie's husband, Géraud, stared moodily into the dregs of his glass of Bourgogne rouge. It was unlike him to pick a fight. But feelings were running high in the Lancon household after the verdict of misadventure in Bernard Angier's tragic death, as they were among many families in Beaulieu.

'For the last time, Géraud, I'm not defending anyone,' Marie replied, clearing away their plates with a genuinely pained look on her face. 'I'm as sad about what happened to that poor boy as you are.'

'Are you?'

'Of course I am,' Marie shot back, hurt. 'I'm simply saying that I don't know what purpose would have been served by sending Monsieur Challant to prison. Whatever happened that night was an accident.'

'Accident!' Géraud Lancon scoffed. 'Those dogs were a menace and Challant knew it. You told me yourself they'd already attacked poor Sandrine.'

'Well, yes . . .' Marie admitted guiltily. God knew she did not relish playing the role of Charles Challant's defender. But there were certain things she knew that her husband didn't. Things she'd confided only in her closest friend, Marianne, but that she knew she could never tell Géraud.

'He may as well have kept lions,' Géraud ranted on. 'And what did he need them for, eh? In a peaceful community like ours?'

Marie bit her lip and began pumping water into a basin for cleaning the dishes. There was no point discussing it. Géraud's mind was already made up.

'I mean, you tell me. How is it that a little boy is killed, and *that man* walks out of court with barely a rap on the knuckles, hm? It's obvious he has the magistrate in his pocket.'

Marie scrubbed silently.

'He got away with murder, that's what I reckon. And I'm not the only one who thinks so, Marie.'

It was certainly true that many in Beaulieu believed that Charles Challant should have been imprisoned for failing to control his dogs on the night of the storm. But Marie suspected that while sympathy for poor Bernard and his family might have had something to do with people's anger, there were also less noble motives at play. Most notably a spiteful sense of delight, watching a member of the town's self-proclaimed 'elite' suffer such an ignominious fall from grace. Charles Challant was perceived by many as holier-than-thou, lording it over his neighbours at church as if he were not just richer than they, but morally superior as well. Charles's only 'punishment' over Bernard's death was an order demanding that his dogs be destroyed – and that stuck in many people's craw. The fact that he had been foolish enough to try to appeal that ruling only made things worse.

'Any normal person would have wanted rid of those dogs,' Géraud had pointed out, outraged.

On this point at least, Marie fully agreed with her husband. What she didn't agree with was the lynch-mob attitude. In particular, the pernicious way that blame was now being extended beyond Charles towards the entire Challant family. That wasn't right. Poor Madame had wanted nothing to do with those dogs. And she'd been devastated by Bernard's death, suffering a serious nervous collapse that had seen her take to her bed, so debilitating was her guilt. The doctors were really quite concerned for her.

As for the children, just the other day at the pier, poor Charles Fils and Ines had been set upon by a mob of village kids who called their father a murderer and spat at their feet, telling them they weren't welcome in Beaulieu. That broke Marie's heart.

Drying the last of the plates with a tea towel, she returned to the table, placing her rough hand over her husband's.

'I do understand how you feel, Géraud. More than you know,' she told him.

Softening, he entwined his fingers with hers.

'I'm sorry for taking it out on you,' he replied. 'I just wish you didn't work there, that's all.'

'Don't say that,' Marie chided him gently. 'I'm grateful for my position there, and you should be too. To be kept on all year, and only have to cook for three months of it? There aren't too many jobs like that in Beaulieu, or anywhere, I daresay. And the pay's very generous.'

She was right, of course. Géraud hated taking Charles Challant's money. But with his work at the docks so piecemeal and unreliable, they needed Marie's regular salary.

'Besides,' Marie reminded him. 'The family will be back in Paris soon. Then we can start to put all this heartache behind us.'

We can, maybe, thought Géraud. But try telling that to Eloise Angier, Bernard's aunt and surrogate mother. Since the tragedy of the storm that changed everything, the poor woman had aged twenty years overnight.

Neatly folding her 'church dress' with the help of a large square of tissue paper, Renée watched amused as Genevieve flung her own trunk down on the bed and began stuffing clothes into it willy-nilly.

'You'll ruin them if you do it like that,' she said. 'Everything will come out creased and spoiled.'

'What do I care?' Genevieve pouted, crossly. 'They're only clothes. And who's going to see them anyway? Nobody, that's who.'

Renée frowned. Typically, she was the one who didn't give a fig about jewels and dresses. It was Gen who always overpacked and ummed and ahhed over every outfit choice, like Cinderella before the prince's ball. Something was definitely wrong. Renée just wasn't sure whether it was Aurelian, or the prospect of her return to Switzerland, or the ghastly tragedy with the boy from the village that was putting her sister in such a sour, miserable mood.

Walking over to the window, Gen pressed her forehead to the glass. She looked tired and thin, but also harder somehow, different to the carefree girl she'd been at the start of the summer. It seemed to Renée as if anger and disappointment were poisoning her from within, but she didn't know what to do about it.

'Look at him.' Genevieve nodded bitterly towards the bastide lawn, where their father was pacing slowly back and forth, hands clasped solemnly behind his back. 'Poor Maman's been in bed all morning, ill with stress, and he couldn't care less.'

'You don't know that,' Renée countered. 'I'm sure he's worried about her. And, well, everything that happened.'

'What on earth makes you sure of that?' Gen let out a mirthless laugh. 'All that man ever worries about is himself. He was more upset when the vet came to put his precious dogs to sleep than he was the night that boy died.'

'Genevieve!' Renée gasped, genuinely shocked. 'You mustn't say things like that.'

'Why not?' Genevieve shrugged sulkily. 'It's true. All Papa cares about is how "this business" as he calls it might damage his precious reputation. Be honest, Ren. Have you once seen him show a shred of remorse?'

Renée looked away uncomfortably. It was true that Papa hadn't cried or officially said that he felt terrible about what had happened. But then he wasn't a de-monstrative man at the best of times, so she'd tried not to read too much into it.

'Meanwhile, poor Maman's thin as a rail and either bed-ridden or staggering around the house like a ghost, feeling too guilty and broken to do anything,' an impassioned Genevieve continued. 'As if *she* could have prevented what happened!

As if any of us could. But Papa seems to view her unhappiness as some sort of personal affront. They were arguing again last night, you know.'

'I know.' Renée returned to her packing, praying that Gen would drop the subject. The whole house had heard Charles's raised voice and Clotilde's sobs up in the marital bedroom.

'Doesn't it upset you?' Genevieve pressed. 'Doesn't it make you hate him?'

'I don't hate him.' Renée chose her words carefully. 'And for what it's worth, I don't think you do either. You're just angry. Which I understand.'

'But aren't *you* angry, Renée?' Gen couldn't hide her exasperation. She wanted an ally, someone willing to bitch along with her. But Renée wasn't playing ball. 'I think he hits her, you know,' Genevieve announced bluntly, trying another tack.

'Rubbish,' said Renée, refusing to take the bait.

'It's not rubbish,' insisted Gen. She lowered her voice. 'Something had been building for weeks, you must have felt it. And earlier that morning, on the day of the storm, I walked in on the two of them rowing in the salon. Papa had his arm raised like this.' Balling her fist, she pulled back her elbow menacingly in imitation of Charles. 'If I hadn't walked in . . .'

'If you hadn't walked in you don't know what would have happened,' said Renée.

'I do know,' Gen shot back. 'You weren't there. I'll tell you something else as well,' she added ominously. 'Papa has secrets.'

'What do you mean?' Renée's eyes narrowed. 'What sort of secrets?'

'I don't know exactly,' Genevieve admitted. 'Not yet. But it's clearly something bad. So bad he was too ashamed to share it, even with Maman.'

'This is nonsense,' Renée bit down on her lip unhappily. 'I won't listen to this.'

'Don't then,' Gen shrugged. 'But it's not nonsense. I heard Maman confront him about it, and the next thing I knew . . .' She drew back her arm again and put on her best impression of their father's maddened face. 'He's scared of something, Renée.

Or someone. That's why he bought those awful dogs in the first place.'

Angrily, Renée snapped her own case closed.

'I'm going to the farm,' she told Genevieve. 'I love you, Gen. We all do. And I know you're angry with Papa. But all this blame and hatred and suspicion. It's just making things worse. It won't help you and it certainly won't help Maman.'

'Really?' Gen called angrily after her sister's retreating back as she disappeared down the hallway. 'So what *will* help Maman, Renée? Doing nothing? Is that the answer? Putting our heads in the sand and just pretending none of this ever happened?'

But it was too late. Renée was gone.

Ines collected the last of the goose eggs – eighteen in all today – and set the heavy basket down on a straw bale at the back of Monsieur Martin's barn.

These last days of summer felt even hotter than the weeks before, and everything seemed to move more slowly as a result. From the beads of sweat coursing down Ines's forehead and between her shoulder blades, to the fluffy white clouds drifting across the sky, to the leisurely pace of the carthorses as they ambled in from the fields, life at Beaulieu felt stretched out, like a reel of film played in slow motion.

In one way, Ines was glad of the slowness. Despite everything that had happened, she didn't want to leave. Paris, with its strict formality and routine, felt like worlds away. Going back didn't just mean a different house, a different season. The Challants' migration was far more than that. It meant that Ines would be a different person, a version of herself that bore no resemblance to the wild, carefree girl she got to be here during the summers.

Or at least, she had been. Until this summer.

This summer had been different. And not just because of *it*. The tragedy. The 'accident'. The thing she couldn't bring herself to speak out loud, and did her level best not to think about. Even before the night of the storm, something at Beaulieu and within her family had fractured. An unwelcome, jarring note had begun to sound through the carefree idyll of Ines's childhood. Something intangible, but important, had already changed. Bernard's death had simply set those changes in stone.

Scuffing her way across the dusty barn, she headed for the pig-pen, pushing these uncomfortable thoughts from her mind. Elodie, the old sow, had recently produced a fine litter of seven piglets and Ines never tired of watching them play, snuffling around in the straw, falling over each other to secure the prime spots at one of their mother's swollen teats.

Coming to the farm with Renée had been the best thing about this summer. Monsieur Martin's animals weren't as exciting or as mesmeric as her mother's birds. But neither did they worry and consume Ines, the way that the birds did. Since Bernard's death, she'd been unable to bring herself to go down to the aviary at all. At night, she still heard the parakeets calling. In less of a frenzy than they had that awful night, but calling nonetheless, a sound that Ines couldn't help but interpret as agitation and distress. Perhaps they missed Maman, who'd taken to her bed and no longer visited them? Or perhaps they sensed in some instinctive way the same darkness and threat in the air that Ines did.

Sometimes she was tempted to go to them. To throw back her covers as she had on the night of the storm, and pad her way barefoot across the lawn, and do what she'd intended to do back then: set them free. But she was too afraid. What if some other terrible thing were to happen, just as she approached? What if Maman became so upset by their loss that she never got better?

You mustn't think like that, Ines scolded herself. Maman *would* be well again. And people in Beaulieu would realize their mistake and stop spitting at her and Charles Fils when they passed them on the pier, and calling Papa a murderer.

'I thought I'd find you here.'

Renée, sweating and dirty after a long afternoon helping Monsieur Martin unload hay bales, sneaked up behind Ines, wrapping her arms around her.

'You'll miss them, won't you?'

Both girls gazed down at the piglets, rooting happily around their exhausted mother.

Ines nodded sadly. 'I'll miss everything. I hate going back to Paris.'

'Me too,' admitted Renée.

Ines hesitated. 'Maybe it's good we're leaving, though.'

'You do know it was an accident, don't you my darling?' Renée whispered kindly into her ear. 'What happened to Bernard wasn't your fault. It wasn't anybody's fault.'

Tears welled in Ines's eyes. She wished she believed what Renée had just said wholeheartedly. But a small part of her couldn't help but feel that it *was* her fault, even though she couldn't say why. She could no longer remember exactly what she'd seen that night, out in the dark and the rain with Maman and Papa and the dogs. All that was left was a heavy, lingering guilt. As though she were complicit in something, even if she'd buried the memory deep inside her somewhere.

'I just want Maman to get better,' she said aloud.

'She will get better,' Renée insisted fiercely, turning Ines around so they were face to face and then hugging her tightly. 'She's already much stronger than she was. She made it down to lunch today, didn't she?'

Ines nodded. That was true. Maman had come downstairs to eat, for the first time in several days. She just missed her *so* much. Working on their silk screen together, and talking about all the different birds. Ines had barely cared about those things at the time. But now each moment, each shared confidence with her mother felt wildly precious.

'And I heard her tell Genevieve that she planned to take a turn in the gardens this afternoon,' Renée added brightly.

Just then Charles Fils, red-faced and panting, came racing into the barn.

'Come quick!' he wheezed, bending double to try to catch his breath.

'What is it?' Renée asked, alarmed.

'It's Maman's birds,' Charles gasped.

Ines gripped Renée's hand so tightly her nails left marks.

'Someone unlocked the cages and they flew away. They're gone. They're all gone.'

Renée, Charles Fils and Ines were all waiting outside in the hallway when Genevieve emerged from their mother's room.

'Will she be all right?' Ines asked, her voice wire-taut with fear.

The news about the birds had shocked Clotilde profoundly. She'd once again taken to her bed, and the doctor had been called.

'Is she going to die?'

'Of course not,' Gen squeezed her little sister's hand. 'Dr André's with her now. She's going to be absolutely fine.'

'It wasn't me,' Ines blurted defensively.

Her siblings gave her a curious look.

'I didn't set the birds free.'

'Of course you didn't, dearest!' Renée laughed. 'Nobody thinks that.'

Maybe not. But I've thought about it countless times, Ines reflected guiltily. *I've* wanted *to do it. And I never imagined how much it might upset poor Maman.*

'Someone from the town probably sneaked in and opened the cages out of spite,' Charles Fils piped up. 'They all hate us, after all.'

'Charles!' Renée scolded him.

'What?' Charles shrugged. 'They do.'

'Can I see her?' Ines stood on tiptoes, straining her neck to peer around Genevieve and into their mother's room. She didn't want to talk about the birds any more, or how much everyone in Beaulieu disliked their family. She just wanted her mother.

'Tomorrow,' Gen said firmly. 'The doctor says she needs complete rest now.'

Charles Challant was at the desk in his study when Genevieve walked in.

An hour earlier, he'd been in a brooding, self-pitying mood. Dr André had briefed him on Clotilde's condition, which was stable but serious. A weak heart that had caused her problems as a child was now once again putting her at risk, triggered by the 'trauma' of witnessing Bernard's death. Charles had come away with the distinct impression that the young medic seemed to blame *him* in some way for what had happened. But after the doctor left he'd poured himself a large scotch, followed by another, and then a third. So by the time Genevieve appeared, unannounced, a warm, welcome fug of inebriation had enveloped him, successfully smothering any uncomfortable thoughts or feelings.

'Darling.' A relaxed, tipsy smile spread across Charles's face.

'Was it you?' Gen demanded.

'I beg your pardon?'

Her blunt tone jolted him momentarily out of his stupor. Even with his hazy vision, he could see that his daughter's face was set like flint.

'Did you release those birds?'

The smile died on Charles's lips. He met Genevieve's gaze, but tellingly said nothing.

'It *was* you!' she gasped, glaring at him accusingly. 'How could you? You did it out of spite, didn't you? To hurt her.'

'You don't know what you're talking about,' Charles responded, gruffly. 'Why would I want to hurt your mother?'

'I don't know,' hissed Genevieve. 'And I don't know what else you're hiding. And I don't know why you want to hurt me either, but you keep doing it.'

His eyes narrowed angrily. 'For pity's sake, Genevieve. This isn't about *you*.'

'No. It's about Maman's birds,' she shot back, shaking her head in disgust. 'You're not even sorry, are you? You're *never* sorry for *anything*.'

A tiny muscle twitched at the top of Charles's jaw, and he tightened his grip on his whisky glass. But he managed to keep his temper.

'One day, Genevieve,' he replied steadily, 'you'll understand how wrong you are about that. I'm sorry for many things.'

'Admit it!' Gen hissed at him. She was growing hysterical. 'Admit it was you who opened those cages!'

Again, he returned her gaze calmly and in silence.

'I hate you,' Genevieve whispered. Turning on her heel, she left, slamming the door behind her.

CHAPTER NINE

London, England, September 1928

'So, Hector. I gather you're a skier?' Lavinia Scott flashed a horse-toothed smile at Gunn. 'How thrilling.'

Gunn returned the smile politely, not quite sure how he was expected to respond. He understood that it was an honour to have been seated next to the hostess at tonight's dinner party – a grand affair thrown by one of Tig's friends, Lavinia, at her mansion on Eaton Square. Particularly as he'd never set foot in the Scotts' palatial townhouse before, knew nobody present apart from Tig, was the youngest person by at least a decade and decidedly the least accomplished. But it wasn't an honour he'd asked for or expected, and the attention was beginning to make him uncomfortable. As if he were the star attraction at some sort of freak show. Or worse, Lady Hanborough's new, exotic pet.

'Do you compete?' Lavinia asked him. 'I've heard that downhill ski racing can be *frightfully* dangerous.'

'I raced last season, in St Moritz,' Gunn admitted.

'Not *professionally*?' Alasdair Scott, Lavinia's husband, adopted a horrified expression to match his tone. Clearly the very idea of competing in a sport for money repulsed him. The son of a millionaire Scottish steel magnate, Alasdair Scott hadn't needed to stoop to anything as grubbily middle class as earning his own keep.

'Not so far,' Gunn replied, bridling at his host's tone. 'But I might this winter.'

'Good God!' Scott shuddered.

'The sport's only really in its infancy,' Gunn explained to Lavinia. 'But investment's already pouring in.'

'He's right, you know,' Tig piped up supportively. 'Half of our friends are buying chalets in St Moritz. Johnny and I looked ourselves, but the prices are *eye-watering*.'

'Are they really? And to think, the place is full of Swiss,' another of the male guests observed, apparently without irony.

Gunn smiled gratefully at Tig, determined to make the most of the evening and enjoy himself, despite the small-mindedness and rampant snobbery of his fellow guests. Clearly, learning to tolerate bigotry and allowing older, richer men to patronize him without losing his temper was going to be an important skill in the world Gunn hoped to conquer. Seducing bored, rich women was the easy part. But he was canny enough to know that he would need to find a way to appeal to their husbands and brothers and fathers as well, if he were ever going to become a rich man himself.

Which I am, he promised himself, sipping Alasdair Scott's expensive port and letting his eyes rove around the impressive dining room. Everything reeked of money, from the gleaming silverware to the fussy, embroidered silk curtains, to the gilt-framed portraits that hung from the panelled walls. Gunn didn't yet know much about things like art and antiques, but he was already starting to educate himself, and Tig had assured him he had a good eye. *I want this*, Gunn admitted to himself. *I want all of it. The big house, the servants, the silver, the world-class wine cellar.*

At the beginning he'd told himself that he only wanted money to provide for Edie and Laura. To buy back Maltings and to make right all that his father had done wrong. But the more time he spent in London, in Tig's rarified world, the more Gunn came to appreciate that riches were worth having for their own sake. Those who, like him, were neither going to inherit, nor had the sort of brain or connections that were going to catapult them into an Oxford degree and a high-flying career, would have to find an alternative path to achieving the wealth they craved. They would have to hustle.

Happily for Gunn, hustling – like skiing – turned out to be something for which he had a natural, God-given gift.

Not until after pudding, a rich lemon syllabub sprinkled with deliciously crisp shards of meringue, did the conversation turn back to the craze for downhill skiing in the Alps, and the vast sums of money being invested there.

A rather jovial banker at the other end of the table, Toby something-or-other, became quite animated on the subject.

'I wish to God I'd invested in St Moritz ten years ago, when I had the chance,' he complained. 'There's precious little profit to be made in any of the Swiss resorts now. They say France is the future.'

'Megève,' said Gunn. It was the first time he'd spoken in several minutes and everybody turned to look.

'Right!' Toby pointed a finger at him, impressed. 'That's exactly right. Megève.'

'Where on earth is that?' asked Lavinia.

'France,' said Toby. 'It's Baron de Rothschild's latest pet project. He reckons it'll be the new St Moritz. I daresay he's right.'

'And I daresay he isn't,' Alasdair Scott grumbled, bitterly. 'I heard Noemi got fed up in Switzerland because no one there invites Jews to parties.'

'Ali!' Lavinia chided. 'Really, darling. What a thing to say.'

'It's true,' her husband shrugged.

'Well if it is, I highly doubt France will be any better,' observed Toby. 'I've never known a more antisemitic country. Jew-baiting's their *pain et beurre*.'

Gunn noticed that everyone seemed amused by this, even Tig, and struggled to hide his distaste. It seemed to him to be taking class snobbery one step further when a racial element was added, a step from which he instinctively recoiled.

'I admire Maurice Rothschild,' he heard himself saying, once the laughter had subsided. 'I'm sure he'll make a success of Megève.'

'Maybe you could ski there this winter?' Tig said cheerfully, sensing a tension in the air and hoping to defuse it. 'See it for yourself?'

'Maybe,' said Gunn. He found his mind wandering back to the newspaper article they'd read recently about Charles Challant, Rothschild's French friend and partner. Perhaps he was involved in this grand new project? Idly Gunn wondered whether there was money still to be made there. Usually, by the time one heard about these things, the opportunity had already passed.

Not that he *had* any money to invest. At this point, he barely had enough to pay for his own supper. But that would change. In fact it was already changing. Dinner parties like tonight's brought it home to Gunn how very small and incestuous the world of the rich and connected actually was. The most important thing was to step inside the circle. Then, once admitted, the trick was to stay inside.

If I *can manage that*, he told himself, *I'll make it eventually*. It was just a matter of time.

CHAPTER TEN

Paris, France, December 1928

Charles Challant pulled sharply on his reins, bringing his excited bay gelding to a shivering, wide-eyed halt.

It was cold in the Fôret de Chantilly. Cold enough for the horse's exhausted breath to plume in front of it like a puff of dragon's smoke as Charles waited and watched, peering through the trees for the roe deer he was certain was there. In fact he'd glimpsed two; small does, but where there were two females there were bound to be more camouflaged among the birch, the faithful harem to a solitary, elusive stag.

Charles badly wanted to see the stag. He wanted to be the one to sound his horn and have the rest of the hunt come hurtling towards him. To hear the hounds giving cry and his fellow *chasseurs* thanking and congratulating him as they closed in on the magnificent beast, hungry for the kill. Although it wasn't the kill Charles wanted so much as the *win*.

He knew that he wasn't well liked among his fellow huntsmen, but it didn't bother him particularly. He assumed it was due to the fact that he preferred to ride alone, rarely engaging in the chit-chat and socializing that the other fellows seemed so keen on. Not being liked was one thing. But not being respected, envied or admired? That rankled.

Feeling the young horse twitch beneath him like a live electrical wire, its nostrils flaring and ears twitching wildly, Charles nudged the animal gently forward. *You want to win too, don't you lad?* he thought to himself, willing the deer to break cover.

The men Charles hunted with used to respect him. They used to envy him too, for his wealth and success; his beautiful houses; his young, well-born wife and the glamorous, migratory life they led together with their children, between Paris, Megève and Beaulieu. But something had shifted. Not openly. Not in any way that he could put his finger on. But of course, that only made it worse. The whispers. The sly, pitying looks.

'You're being paranoid, Charles,' his old friend Lucien Archambault had told him bluntly over lunch at their club last week, when he'd complained about the situation. 'Clotilde's not well. It's only natural for people to express concern.'

'Clotilde's fine,' Charles had insisted, ignoring Lucien's raised eyebrow. The truth was that Clotilde hadn't set foot outside the house at Place Dauphine since she arrived months ago, and spent most of her time in bed. 'She just needs rest, that's all. People should mind their own business.'

'In Paris?' Lucien chuckled. 'Don't be ridiculous, man. The entire city runs on gossip, as you well know.'

'Hmn.' Charles had stabbed at his gristly steak morosely.

It was the gossip that upset him the most, mainly because he had no control over it. He'd heard the world 'Beaulieu' mentioned more than once, and guessed that a link had formed in people's ignorant, ill-informed minds between the tragic accident at the bastide – the unfortunate death of the *enfant simplet* – and Clotilde's declining health. But of course, no one would admit as much.

'They're blaming me,' he complained to Lucien. 'For Clotilde. For the boy.'

'No one's blaming you, Charles,' replied Lucien loyally. But of course, certain people were, and they both knew it.

Charles was grateful for Lucien's steadfast friendship. But he remained unhappy and uncertain about how to behave. He worried dreadfully about Clotilde, of course. But months into her illness, the house at Place Dauphine had started to feel like a mausoleum. And he resented the reproachful looks on the servants' faces when he chose to go out hunting, rather than sit around uselessly at his wife's bedside, conflabbing with ineffectual doctors.

It wasn't rational, he knew. But some days it almost felt as if Clotilde herself were turning people against him. As if she were ill on purpose.

A crack and a rustle a few yards deeper into the forest jolted him out of his unhappy reverie. Seconds later, a large family of roe deer leaped up from their respective hiding places and began bolting due south towards the forest edge and the open meadows beyond.

'There you are, you beauties!'

Reaching triumphantly for his horn, Charles blew it with expert skill. *Pah pah pah pah, pah pah pah pah!* The familiar staccato rhythm of the 'sighting' call echoed through the crisp winter air. Already Charles could hear the hounds returning it, their distant barks growing louder as the master and huntsmen realized their mistake, and turned to head in Charles's direction.

A win. His first in quite a while.

Perhaps today would be a good day after all.

Crossing the Pont Neuf with her nanny on the walk home from school, Ines gazed down at the beautiful Seine as she skipped along, wondering about the lives of the people on the rickety old tug boats, and how wildly different they must be to her own.

Immediately on the other side of the bridge, they turned right into Place Dauphine, the leafy garden square of imposing brick mansions where the Challant children had all been raised. With its gleaming wrought-iron gates and railings enclosing an immaculate front garden, and its imposing, double-fronted brick façade, studded with six-foot sash windows, and topped with an elaborately tiled roof, Place Dauphine was easily the grandest of the family's homes. As big as an embassy, with marble floors and massively proportioned 'state rooms', it was a house to be admired rather than loved.

Once inside, Ines headed into the morning room while her

nanny dashed off to talk to cook in the kitchens. As it was a more modestly sized and furnished room than the mansion's other *salons*, Ines often chose to do her homework in the morning room at the little desk under the window; it provided a good vantage point over the various comings and goings in the square. Unpacking her satchel, she scribbled some lines half-heartedly in her *cahier*, while keeping an eye on the door to the hall. A new doctor was visiting her mother upstairs, and Ines wanted to see when he left, and if possible to get a good look at his face. She'd come up with a theory: that grown-ups often lied to children with their words, but their facial expressions usually told the truth. Especially if they didn't know you were watching them.

The last few months had been hard for Ines. Not only because of Maman's illness, although naturally that was her biggest worry. But ever since the family had returned to Paris, pretty much every aspect of the little girl's life had taken a turn for the worse.

Place Dauphine had always been a grand cavern of a house, big enough to roll a hoop down the corridors or to hear your own voice echo from the ballroom ceilings. But in years gone by it had also been a busy, happy home, full of noise and laughter. Maman's relentless charity work and Papa's business dealings had conspired to create an endless round of parties, luncheons and social events, from small intimate dinners, to larger political soirees, to spectacular cocktail parties for two, three, four hundred people out in the gardens and *grande terrasse*. Between all this and the army of servants that Ines had grown up with as an integral part of her childhood, the one thing she never remembered feeling at Place Dauphine was lonely.

But that had changed overnight. It didn't used to matter that Papa would retreat from family life significantly once they returned to the city from Beaulieu. Because Maman had more than filled that gap, with her laughter and her warm, constant love. When Papa was darkness and silence, Maman was beauty and colour. But now, not only were both Ines's parents effectively 'gone', but Genevieve and Charles Fils as well; the former banished to Switzerland, and the latter to some awful boarding school north of the city. Of her older siblings, only Renée remained at home. And she spent every waking hour not earmarked for school either out riding in the Jardin du Luxembourg or in the gardens with her pesky bees and stupid old hives. (Ines could get behind piglets and puppies. But really and truly, bees hardly even counted as animals. *And* they stung you, which hurt a lot, whatever Renée said to the contrary.)

The point was that without Maman, or Gen, there were no parties to be thrown, no guests to be invited. Nanny had been kind and told Ines that she was welcome to ask her own schoolfriends over to play whenever she liked. But it wasn't the same. Besides, deep down, Ines felt embarrassed to bring people home to the heavy, sad atmosphere of Place Dauphine, with Maman's poor health and Papa's bad temper hanging over its empty rooms like a great storm cloud.

The ringing of the dinner bell made Ines jump. Could it really be that late already? Pushing her unfinished homework to one side, she stood up and was about to head to the dining room when she suddenly stopped. There came the doctor, at last.

One of the maids, Evangeline, was helping him into his overcoat. Which meant he was leaving. Which in turn meant that things couldn't be *too* bad with Maman, at least for this evening. Despite craning her neck this way and that, Ines was able to catch only the briefest glimpses of his face, and only in profile. But from what she could tell he seemed calm enough.

Relieved, she headed off for another lonely supper with just Nanny and Renée. Later, when no one was looking, she would sneak into Maman's room and check on her in person. It was a ritual the little girl performed as often as she could, especially on nights when Papa was out late. She tried not to think of it as a penance, but in truth that was exactly what it was.

Though she'd never admitted as much to her siblings, secretly Ines still blamed herself for her mother's nervous collapse. In the beginning, she'd convinced herself that her crime had been *not* releasing Maman's birds. Because if she'd only done that when she'd first thought of it, at the start of the summer, Bernard wouldn't have come to try and see them, and he wouldn't have trespassed into the garden and been attacked by Papa's dogs, and none of those dreadful things would ever have happened.

But later, when someone else *did* release the birds, and Maman's heart condition worsened, Ines blamed herself for having wished that the creatures would be set free. As if her thoughts alone had somehow manifested both her mother's illness and her father's unhappiness.

She understood that such magical thinking made no sense rationally. But in her heart, her soul, Ines simply knew it was true. *She* was to blame. *She* was the one who had brought this curse to Maman and to all of them.

It was a heavy burden to bear.

Clotilde's eyelids fluttered briefly open. She was aware of Ines lying beside her. The sweet, clean scent of her baby's hair and skin, the trusting yet tentative touch of Ines's fingers on her neck and shoulder.

She sighed, her own fingers reaching back. She felt overwhelmed with love, but simply too exhausted to keep her eyes open, let alone begin a conversation. Still, she sensed that it was enough for Ines simply to be here with her, physically close, the heat of their twin bodies affirming a love that did not need words. Did not need anything.

This was how things were now for Clotilde. Her world had shrunk to this room, this bed, and to her own five senses. The smell of her daughter's skin. The softness of clean sheets beneath her own. The comforting taste of sweet rose tea on the rare mornings she felt able to drink it, soothing her rasping throat.

Not that she deserved such comfort. Like her daughter, there was a part of Clotilde that viewed her reduced existence as a penance. A justified act of atonement, for a guilt that would otherwise be too heavy to bear. If only she could explain that to her husband . . . if she could just make Charles understand?

But things were too far gone between them for that. Clotilde couldn't reach Charles, any more than he could reach her. The physical pain of her symptoms could be quite appalling at times. But it was nothing compared to the emotional pain that preceded it.

I've made so many mistakes, she thought wearily.

Before she'd married Charles, things had been different. *She'd* been different. Confident. Creative. Not ambitious, perhaps, in the common sense of that word. But a person in her own right, someone with talents, hopes and dreams.

Wild and free. Just like my beautiful birds, before I caged them. Locked them in, just like Charles locked me in. And called it love . . .

Fumbling blindly behind her, Clotilde entwined her thin, cold fingers with Ines's. Feeling her youngest child squeeze back, she felt a rush of true happiness. Fleeting, but real. Amid the darkness of her world, her little daughter was light. Because light *could* come from darkness, as Clotilde knew better than anyone. Good could come from bad, just as beautiful roses could grow from dirt and shit and filth. So, she prayed, it would be for Ines.

She squeezed again, just once, before sleep snatched her away.

Charles Challant stood in the upstairs hallway, peering into the darkness of his wife's room. For all his outward bluster, he was desperately worried about Clotilde's health, and the weak heart that kept threatening to take her from him. It was late, after one a.m., and he was still in his hunting clothes. He'd expected to find Clotilde sleeping alone but startled when he caught sight of little Ines, curled up with her. Lying behind her mother, with one delicate arm draped protectively across Clotilde's frail ribs, she too was asleep in that open-mouthed, heavy breathing way that the very young had in common with the very old. In that instant, Charles felt a stab of love for his youngest child so sharp and unexpected it made him reach for his chest.

None of the others loved him quite like Ines did. Charles Fils looked up to him, the way that boys generally did to their fathers, but his heart had always been Clotilde's. As for Renée and Genevieve, they were older now, and so had naturally begun to view both their parents through a more nuanced lens, tempering their affection accordingly. But Ines's love remained utterly pure. A wild, instinctive, unbreakable adoration that meant more to Charles than he chose to admit. On nights like tonight, it sustained him, comforting him in a way that nothing else could.

Creeping over to the bed, he scooped Ines up in his arms, carrying her silently back along the corridor to her own room. Peeling back the covers on her inlaid mahogany bed, he laid her down, carefully tucking the sheets and blankets back in around her. Then, stooping low, he planted a single tender kiss on the top of her head, brushing her sleeping face with his beard, before tiptoeing out, softly closing the door behind him.

Only once the door was closed and the sound of his footsteps had completely died away, did Ines open her eyes.

What had just happened?

Papa never put her to bed. *Never*.

But tonight, he *had carried her there*. Not only that, he had tucked her in and kissed her. Actually kissed her!

Wrapping her arms tightly around her own chest, she clutched the magical memory to herself, trying to hold on to the wonder of it for as long as she could. Tomorrow, no doubt, he would revert to his usual distant self, the way he always did in Paris. Locked away in his study or at his club. Or perhaps at mass, where he'd taken to going more and more recently, not just on Sundays *en famille* but for the weekday services as well by himself. Stations of the cross and vespers and all that extra, boring stuff that only widows or nuns usually went to.

But tonight had been real. Tonight, Papa had picked Ines up and put her to bed. He hadn't been angry that she was in Maman's room. He'd been kind and gentle. He had kissed her.

It was a sign. A turning point.

It had to be.

Things would start to get better now.

Feeling happier than she had in many months, Ines fell back asleep.

CHAPTER ELEVEN

Charles Fils and Genevieve both returned to Paris the week before Christmas. Due to Clotilde's illness, this was the first winter in a decade when the Challants had not made their annual migration to Megève. A catastrophe for poor Charles Fils, who'd had a rotten term at school and lived for skiing and the mountains, but a blessed relief for Genevieve, who'd seen enough mountains in Switzerland to last her a lifetime and who was pining dreadfully for city life.

'I want to see everybody once I'm home, and I mean *everybody*,' she'd written excitedly to Renée the week before she left Lausanne and her dreaded finishing school. 'Even the new Monsieur and Madame de la Tour.'

Renée had expressed her doubts on this last point, but Genevieve was giddily insistent when she got back to Paris. 'There's no need to worry, dearest, I assure you. I am *completement* over Aurelian.'

'Really?' Renée frowned.

'Really. But I do miss talking to him about plays and writing, and I do *so* miss all our mutual friends and Paris gossip. Besides, if you had even an inkling of how deathly dull the girls at Lausanne are, you'd understand. One more conversation about flower arranging or whose dreary brother is engaged to who else's dreary cousin, and I *will* shoot myself.'

Gen and Charles Fils's homecoming provided a much needed boost to everyone at Place Dauphine. Overnight, it seemed, the gloom and loneliness that had hung over the house since September dissipated, and the mansion was once again filled with life, noise and laughter.

At Genevieve's prompting, and to everyone's surprise, Charles Père had agreed to host a large, impromptu drinks party at Place Dauphine on the night before Christmas Eve.

'We'd be entertaining if we were at the chalet,' he'd explained over breakfast, as if he needed to justify the decision. 'Maman's condition confines us to town, but it shouldn't make us any less magnanimous as hosts.'

'Hear hear!' grinned Genevieve.

'Can my friends come?' Charles Fils asked. He still wasn't fully over his grump about missing out on skiing, but even he was cheered by the idea of a party.

'Of course,' said Charles.

'Even Jean-Yves?'

A general groan rose from around the table. Jean-Yves Peppan had been Charles's close friend since they were babies, and was without doubt one of the most badly behaved and obnoxious thirteen-year-old boys in the whole of Paris. Last year he'd famously been banned from attending mass in the cathedral after gluing the pigtails of a girl sitting in front of him to the back of her pew. So thorough was the job that the poor child had needed her head shaved afterwards. As Charles Fils had pointed out, when Jean-Yves committed to a prank 'he makes a good fist of it'.

'The Peppans *are* invited, as it happens, *en famille*,' Charles Père replied, to his son's delight. 'But if that little tyke brings glue or any other destructive element into this house it'll be the last thing he does, I guarantee you. So you'd better warn him in advance, Charles.'

Clotilde's health seemed to have stabilized, at least according to the doctors monitoring her heart, although she remained very weak. Certainly in no fit state to attend a party, never mind host one.

'Are you sure it won't disturb you too much?' Renée asked up in their mother's bedroom. 'Hearing all the commotion downstairs?'

Clotilde shook her head, smiling weakly. 'I like to think of you all being happy.'

There was something knowing about her mother's smile that made Renée feel anxious, but she tried to push it out of her mind.

'I just hope Genevieve doesn't drink too much on the night,' Clotilde added, her expression clouding. 'You know how she gets. And how your father hates a scene.'

'I'm sure it'll be fine, Maman.' Renée had tried to sound reassuring. But privately, she shared her mother's worry.

After a few frenzied days of preparations, the night of the party rolled around. Everything began well. Genevieve looked stunning in her new Jean Patou cocktail dress, a riotous affair of drop-waisted silk and feathers in vivid emerald green.

'She's like a cockatiel!' Ines exclaimed admiringly, watching her eldest sister greet the guests as they arrived, acting as hostess in Clotilde's place. 'Doesn't she look exotic?'

Renée agreed that she did. More conservatively attired herself in a simple black evening skirt and sweater with grey Tahitian pearls sewn into the neckline, Renée was perfectly happy to remain in Gen's shadow. She'd never been much of a social butterfly, and secretly loathed having to put on a dress and make small talk with half of Paris. But tonight was about making everybody else happy, especially Gen and Ines, who'd been awfully down recently. And concern about their mother's health was still at the backs of everyone's minds.

It would have surprised Renée to know how nervous Gen felt as she flitted from group to group, kissing cheeks and *Joyeux Noel*-ing everyone. The house looked and smelled wonderful, with the enormous Christmas tree in the grand foyer decked out in silver bells and clove-studded oranges tied with red ribbon. A pianist played carols softly on Clotilde's grand piano while guests continued to flood in – everyone who'd been invited seemed to have accepted – and Genevieve knew she looked good, and that all Papa's friends were admiring her as she assured them that Clotilde was on the mend, and that finishing school in Lausanne was 'fabulous'. Even so, beneath the confident exterior, her heart was racing.

Where was he?

Minutes passed, then an hour, and there was still no sign of Aurelian. He and *Sylvie* . . . Genevieve still couldn't bring herself to think of that vile, unworthy girl as his wife, had both RSVP'ed yes, and the Allenceau parents were both already here, yukking it up with Papa in the ballroom. But Aurelian himself was nowhere to be seen.

Reaching for a glass of champagne from a passing footman, Genevieve drained it instantly, then helped herself to another. All of this was for Aurelian. The decorations in the house, the dress, the confident smiles. Despite what she'd told Renée, Gen thought about him all the time. At the very least she wanted him to see what he was missing. But secretly she hoped that if she could convince him she'd moved on and wasn't interested, he would suddenly long for her again the way she was *sure* he used to, and would ask her to become his mistress.

Genevieve had long believed she'd make a better mistress than she would a wife. It was the role she was born to play in fact, one that would allow her time to write and live life on her own terms. Sex without the burdens of domesticity! What could be more perfect? Plus it would madden and appall Papa, who she still hadn't forgiven for his dreadful treatment of Maman over the summer.

When he'd agreed to host tonight's party, and Aurelian had said yes, Gen had been sure she'd have a chance to put the first part of her plan into action. But Aurelian hadn't even bothered to come. *Sylvie* had probably talked him out of it. And all of her hard work and hopes had come to nothing.

'Be careful, darling.' Renée walked up behind a visibly swaying Genevieve, attempting to steady her as she made her way back into the ballroom to refresh her empty glass. 'You've had a lot to drink already.'

'So?' Turning around, Gen scowled at her sister. 'It's a party, Ren,' she slurred. 'I'm enjoying myself.'

'Are you?' A worried Renée drew her to one side. 'I don't know why you always do this,' she said, more in sadness than in anger and dropping her voice to a whisper. 'If Papa sees you in this state, he'll have your guts for garters.'

'Papa.' Genevieve waved an arm dismissively. 'What do I care about Papa? Hmm? Who is *he* to judge me?'

'Care about yourself, then,' pleaded Renée. 'Or Maman. You know how much it upsets her when there's tension between the two of you. Don't you want her to get better?'

It was a low blow, but there was no getting through to Genevieve when she drank. Renée had to try something.

'Of course I do.' Gen took a step back, stung.

'Genevieve!'

At the mention of her name, both girls turned around. There, standing in the doorway looking dapper in a velvet smoking jacket and brushed cotton evening trousers, was Aurelian de la Tour. Alone and, in Renée's opinion, looking mightily pleased with himself.

In an instant, all Gen's anger and sour mood vanished. Renée watched, embarrassed, as her sister rushed for-ward, flinging herself into Aurelian's arms like a lost puppy greeting its master.

'You came!'

The aloof, alluring siren of two hours ago – or perhaps more pertinently, six glasses of Laurent-Perrier ago – was long gone, replaced by this uncontrolled, adoring lush.

'Well of course I came,' said Aurelian, looking both flattered and amused as he wrapped an arm around Gen's shoulders. 'You seem a trifle flustered, my dear. Perhaps we should go outside and get some air?'

'Where's Sylvie?' Renée asked pointedly, looking past him to the guests milling around in the hall. 'Is she not with you?'

'Alas, no,' he smirked. 'She had a ghastly headache, poor lamb. That's why I'm so late. I wanted to make sure she was all right before I . . .'

'Went out to enjoy yourself at a drinks party?' Renée

finished for him, in a distinctly withering tone. It wasn't that she minded him coming out without his wife. It was more his general character. His vanity, and the shameless way he led poor Genevieve on. She might be only fifteen years old, but Renée Challant knew a charlatan when she saw one.

'Renée!' Genevieve scowled at her little sister.

'I didn't want to let you all down, that's all,' Aurelian pouted. 'Especially Genevieve. As we haven't seen each other for so long.'

'Of course you didn't, dearest,' slurred Genevieve.

'So how's your writing going?' he asked, leading Gen out onto the *terrasse*, away from the prying eyes of her irritating little sister.

Renée watched them go, Genevieve leaning into Aurelian like a sapling in the wind, vulnerable and trusting.

Why wasn't she angry with him? Why didn't she protect herself?

She's like a baby turtle, thought Renée, *running across the beach towards the open ocean. She sees the danger. But she can't help herself.*

'So how are you?' Aurelian asked, casually stroking Genevieve's hair as she laid her head on his lap, gazing up at the stars. 'Enjoying the young ladies of Lausanne?'

'Ugh.' Fumbling for a cigarette from the silver case in her bag, Gen stuck it between her lips and arched suggestively upwards for Aurelian to light it. 'It's such a relief to be back in Paris. You've no idea.'

'Back in the bosom of your family?' he asked knowingly, obliging with his Dunhill lighter and a casual flick of the wrist. 'How *is* your poor mother?'

'Improving,' Gen's voice hardened. She didn't want to talk about Clotilde's illness. Not with Aurelian, who, much as she loved him, saw everything as an opportunity for gossip.

'Is it true she had a nervous breakdown at Beaulieu?'

he asked, true to form, dropping his voice to a stage whisper. 'After, you know . . . *the accident?* With the boy?'

'You mean the night when my father's guard dogs mauled an innocent child to death?' she answered loudly.

'Shhhh dearest!' Aurelian blushed. People had turned to look at them.

'I'm not sure I'd call that an *accident*,' Gen went on, oblivious. 'Although the coroner did, so what do I know?'

She dissolved into giggles, quite clearly three sheets to the wind. Already regretting bringing it up, Aurelian looked for ways to change the subject.

'I imagine your father must be missing Megève? Your brother too.'

But Genevieve was on a roll. She didn't want to talk about Megève. She wanted to talk about her father, and the unfair way he treated her, and the secrets she was sure he kept, although she didn't yet know what they were. The champagne had loosened her tongue, and inhibitions. But it had also reopened a door to memories from the summer. Unpleasant memories that leaped out at her now in a mad, chaotic jumble.

'Papa caused that boy's death, you know.' She jabbed a drunken finger into Aurelian's chest. 'And Maman's illness.'

'You mustn't say things like that, Genevieve,' he looked at her seriously.

'Why not, if they're true?' she demanded. 'He let her birds go. On purpose! He opened the cages and she just . . .' She made a fluttering motion with her hands, as if a house of cards were being knocked to the ground.

'Perhaps we should go inside? Get some coffee . . .'

'He beats her, too. D'you know tha'?' Genevieve slurred. 'I bet you didn't know. No one knows! Charles saintly Challant, pillar of the church, hitting his wife. Can you imagine?'

She laughed but there was no joy in the sound. Then, sitting up suddenly, she lunged towards Aurelian, pressing her lips aggressively to his, kissing him with tortured abandon.

For a split second he responded. But then he pushed her

away, scrambling to his feet. It had been a mistake to come here. He'd wanted to see Genevieve, wanted the ego boost that he knew she could be relied on to give him. But not at the expense of his reputation. Not like this.

'For heaven's sake. What are you doing?'

'Kissing you,' Gen answered defiantly.

'Sylvie's father is here!' Aurelian hissed. 'As is yours.'

'And?' Genevieve looked up at him, wide-eyed. '*And?*'

'You love me, Aurelian. You've always loved me.'

He shook his head. 'Genevieve . . .'

'You came here by yourself,' she slurred. 'Without *her.*'

'I already told you, Sylvie wasn't feeling well.'

'You called me "dearest"!' Genevieve wailed.

'Because you are dear to me. As an old friend,' insisted Aurelian. 'Come on, Gen. Be reasonable. I'm married. You know I'm married.'

'I'll be your mistress, then.'

She said it so matter-of-factly, and in a voice loud enough to have Aurelian glancing around in panic, certain that someone must have overheard them. *Merde.* How the hell had he got himself into this?

'You've had too much to drink, and you're saying things you don't mean,' he told her bluntly, deciding that honesty was the only way to get himself out. 'I'm going home.'

'No!' she called after him desperately as he started to walk back inside. 'Aurelian wait, please. I'm sorry!'

When he didn't stop, she followed him, shouting wildly as she stepped through the French doors into the salon.

'You're lying!' she sobbed. 'You love me! You do!'

Every one of the remaining guests turned to stare at the dramatic scene unfolding. Genevieve Challant, make-up smudged and black tears of mascara streaming down her cheeks, pursuing Aurelian de la Tour as he bolted from the house like a hunted deer.

She would have followed him onto the street had Renée not grabbed hold of her.

'No, my darling. No,' she said firmly, giving a signal to the pianist to resume playing. Genevieve gave her sister one last despairing, heartbroken look and fled to her room.

The party was over.

In the general melee of departing guests, endless 'Good nights' and '*Joyeux Noels*', nobody noticed the late arrival of Clotilde's doctor. Nobody except Ines, that is, who was busy stuffing the last of the pink sugared almonds greedily into her mouth before the footmen cleared them all away, when she saw the ashen-faced young medic bolting up the stairs, two at a time.

'What's happened?' she asked Charles Fils, her stomach starting to churn. 'Has something happened to Maman?'

Charles had just said goodbye to his friend Jean-Yves, arriving at the foot of the stairs just in time to witness the doctor's rapid ascent.

'I don't know.' Instinctively he slipped his hand into hers. Ines knew at once that he was frightened too.

Doctors didn't make house calls after midnight unless it was something serious. Did they?

'Do you think we should go up?' she asked.

Charles nodded.

Later, Ines would remember the way that the stairs creaked as she and her brother climbed them, hand in hand. She would remember the smell of pine needles from the Christmas tree in the hall, and of woodsmoke and cinnamon and cigars, still lingering from the party. Just minutes before it had been too loud to hear one's own thoughts at Place Dauphine. The whole house had been alive with conversation and laughter and love. But, once again, an eerie silence had descended like a blanket, heavy enough that Ines could hear nothing beyond the beating of her own heart.

When they reached Clotilde's room, the door was open.

Papa stood on one side of the bed. He looked tall and oddly frozen, like a statue, doomed to look on helplessly, doing nothing. On the other side were Father Guillaume, the priest, who'd attended tonight's party, clutching a rosary; and the

103

young doctor, Carpentier. The latter was leaning over Maman, so low that the children couldn't see her face. He was pressing the palms of his hands hard and rhythmically against Clotilde's chest – *push, push, push* – the muscles in his arms locked tight in a desperate battle. But the expression on his face told Ines and Charles Fils that the battle was lost, even before Dr Carpentier looked up at their father and shook his head.

It was over.

Maman was dead.

PART TWO

WINTER

Ten years later . . .

CHAPTER TWELVE

Megève, France, December 1938

'Well done, darling. Third place!'

Julia Valaperti opened the door of her horse-drawn carriage, patting the fur-lined seat beside her. In a pristine mink coat and hat, and with diamonds the size of barnacles flashing at her fingers and wrists, Julia was still an attractive woman at fifty. But what she really radiated was not beauty but wealth, glittering like a Snow Queen at the foot of the Mont d'Arbois.

Hector Gunn, officially Julia's 'ski instructor' and one of the competitors in today's downhill, handed his skis to Julia's driver and climbed in sullenly beside her.

'I should have got silver at least,' he grumbled, fingering his bronze medal with dissatisfaction. 'My own stupid fault, though. I took that last turn far too wide. Came in at the wrong angle.'

Julia rested a comforting hand on his knee as they drove away. It was typical of Gunn to be hard on himself when it came to his racing. Despite being twenty years Julia's junior, and more handsome than any man had a right to be, he had always been a complicated person, and much more than just eye candy. From the beginning of their unofficial relationship, Gunn had challenged her intellectually and on every level. He had also always been respectful, treating her as a friend and an equal and not merely as a cheque book. That meant a lot.

'You can't beat everyone all the time,' she reminded him.

'Can't I?' he shot back. And although he did then have the good grace and self-awareness to laugh, Julia suspected that he meant it.

A heady combination of youth, ambition and innate arrogance all fuelled Gunn's ferocious will to win. He had the talent to do it too, and make it to the very top as a downhill skier, if he continued to apply himself and train as hard as he had been. But he also had to accept that he was coming from behind. As Julia had repeatedly pointed out, most of his competitors were French, Swiss or Austrians, born in the Alps and skiing since before they could walk. Gunn hadn't touched a ski until he turned seventeen. Since then, like most Englishmen, his experience had been hit and miss at best, based on the relatively short time he'd been able to spend in the mountains each winter. It was only in the last two years, since he'd been with Julia, that he'd had the luxury of spending months at a time in Megève, travelling as her 'private instructor'. With her support, he had been able to train with the best in the world, not to mention kit himself out with state-of-the-art skis and equipment.

Today's race had been the last of the pre-Christmas 'trials' in Megève; friendly, warm-up events with no prize money at stake. But after the holiday the professional season would begin in earnest. Gunn had not spent all winter training like a galley slave to be satisfied with a bronze medal, or bronze medal money. Julia had been incredibly generous. But eventually he needed to earn something of his own, beyond the beer money he brought in as a part-time ski guide for his lover's rich friends.

'I thought the Challant boy was good,' said Julia, as they approached the Palace des Neiges, Noémie Rothschild's grand hotel and her home-from-home for the season. She and Gunn had separate suites, for good form's sake, although a hidden door in Gunn's dressing room connected the two of them, and they'd effectively lived as a couple since November.

'He was,' Gunn agreed, albeit slightly grudgingly. 'Damn good for an amateur. Nice fellow, too. If he hadn't fallen on that nightmare left through the trees, I reckon he could have won it.'

'Really?' asked Julia.

Gunn nodded. 'He's reckless, though,' he added, his tone making it clear that he meant this as a compliment.

'Isn't that what people said about you?' Julia nudged him affectionately.

'When I was Challant's age, maybe,' Gunn replied ruefully. 'Not now. Now I'm a cautious old man of twenty-nine and it bloody shows. It did today, anyway.'

Julia rolled her eyes. 'What nonsense you talk, my love. If you're an old man, what on earth does that make me?'

Gunn could smell her Chanel scent, and feel the growing pressure of her hand as it inched further up his thigh. She was bound to expect sex tonight, and probably before dinner, while he was still sweaty from the race. She always wanted him more after a competition for some reason. Not that he was complaining. He was genuinely fond of Julia, and enjoyed making love to her. Besides, he could use the distraction after his stupid mistakes on the piste.

She was right about Charles Challant. *Charles Fils*, the other fellows called him, as opposed to his father, the illustrious *Charles Père*, one of Megève's founding fathers. The boy had real talent. Gunn remembered reading about the family years ago in London, back when he was with Tig Hanborough.

Christ, what a marvellous woman she was, Gunn reminisced affectionately. *I wonder where she is now?*

He'd approached Charles Challant after the race to congratulate him and had to fight his way through a swarm of pretty girls to get near. Gunn had admirers of his own of course, but there was no doubt that Charles Challant was considered Megève's most eligible bachelor.

When they finally spoke, Gunn had found Charles to be quite charming, and disarmingly modest. Thankfully, he confirmed he had no plans to compete on the professional circuit which meant Gunn was unlikely to race against him again this season. But he still found himself hoping their paths might cross socially – although between Julia's nocturnal demands and his gruelling training schedule, he had little time for making friends.

It might be worth making an exception for the Challant boy, though, he reflected now. It certainly wouldn't hurt to make an ally of such a rich and influential fellow. One day, after all, Charles Fils would become Charles Père.

Filing the thought in the back of his mind, Gunn returned the pressure of Julia's hand.

'You go up first,' he whispered to her. 'I'll be five minutes behind you.'

'Is he here yet?'

Nineteen-year-old Ines Challant cast a worried glance up at her brother Charles from beneath snow-encrusted lashes. She'd watched him race earlier, and been alarmed by his spectacular, high-speed fall. But as soon as she realized her brother wasn't injured beyond a few bruises, her anxieties had returned to the imminent arrival of a certain houseguest.

'No idea,' Charles replied, gallantly relieving his little sister of her skis and exchanging them for his much lighter poles as they walked together towards the main square. 'I haven't been home since breakfast.'

'Nor have I,' Ines groaned. 'I made sure to have lunch in the village with Gen, just in case the train got in early.'

It wasn't that she disliked David Walton, the enormously rich American hotelier whom her father had invited to join the family for the holidays. Indeed, based on her few interactions with him at Beaulieu last summer, she already considered David *far* preferable to the decrepit and downright physically repellent Duc d'Annecy, the other 'suitor' that Papa had decided might make a suitable match for her. This despite his nose hair, veiny old man's hands and inability to talk about anything except hunting and his stupid horses, as if Ines gave a fig about either! It was just that she'd prefer not to have to make small talk with *any* potential husbands. Especially not at Christmas.

Until this year it had always been tacitly understood that the Challants' winter migration to their chalet in Megève, in the shadow of Mont d'Arbois, was family time. For Ines, it was a precious, festive coming together of all their scattered flock. They still gathered at Beaulieu and Paris too. But those places held painful memories for Ines, of her mother's death and the awful summer that preceded it, both of which had become taboo subjects within the family, never to be spoken of out loud. Only Megève remained free of those associations, a safe, happy place where everybody's memories were pure and intact, untouched by tragedy. A place just for them.

This year, though, things were different, and not just because David Walton had been invited to stay. The shadow of a possible war that had been hanging over Europe ever since Herr Hitler became Germany's chancellor appeared to grow heavier and darker with each passing day. Charles Fils and Genevieve didn't seem to notice particularly, or care. But Ines was worried, and she could sense that Renée and Papa both were too. While life for the rich and leisured denizens of Megève chugged along as normal, Ines found it increasingly hard to shake the feeling that they were all fiddling while Rome burned.

'It looks beautiful, doesn't it?' Charles Fils pointed up at the Challants' spectacular family chalet, its lights twinkling invitingly even from this distance.

'It does,' Ines agreed, sighing wistfully. *If only David weren't coming.*

The irony was that there was certainly no need for Ines to marry money. In the ten years since her mother's tragic, untimely death, her father had managed to amass an even greater fortune, most of it through his wildly profitable property portfolio right here in Megève. And yet Charles Père had become almost obsessed with Ines making the 'right' match.

He'd changed since Clotilde died. Hardened, some might say. With no desire to remarry, instead he'd thrown himself ever more deeply into his work, using it to distract from his grief and any other unwanted emotions. Perhaps inevitably he'd grown further apart from his older children, rarely interacting with them even when they were all under one roof. But he still doted on Ines, clinging to her unchanged adoration like a drowning man clutching at a buoy. Many people respected Charles Challant these days, and still more envied or feared him. But nobody else loved him like she did, with a blind, uncritical eye.

Trying to keep her mind off Walton, Ines turned back to her brother. 'You skied very well today,' she told him.

'Do you think so?' Charles Fils's face lit up. 'A lot of people congratulated me, even though I made an ass of myself with that fall.'

Ines enjoyed skiing, and was naturally quite good at it, but nowhere near in her brother's league. 'Niverolle' had always been the snow bird of the family, born for the mountains and naturally gifted at any sport or activity that involved snow, ice and terrifyingly steep drops. At twenty-two, he'd become a respected amateur, although Charles Père was still adamant that his son would never race professionally.

'It's simply not what people like us do,' had been his firm and final word on the matter.

If his adult children wanted access to the family fortune, Charles Père was happy to grant it – to be generous, even – but only on his own terms. His need to control was as strong as ever, and with no Clotilde to rein him in, his word at home became absolute law. For the Challant girls that meant finishing school followed by a suitable marriage. And for Charles Fils it meant following his father into the business. His offspring's individual tastes, talents or preferences didn't factor into Charles Challant's thinking at all. He knew what was best.

A light snow was falling, as it had been all day, and Megève looked like a Christmas card in the fading afternoon light. The town was built on a hill with the large square at the bottom, overshadowed on three sides by mountains – Rochebrune, Mont d'Arbois and Le Jaillet. The lower slopes of these three giants were all heavily wooded, giving the town a cosy, hemmed-in feel, while the snow-capped peaks glistened and sparkled majestically above it all like white sugar icing. Ines and Charles watched children ice skating and throwing snowballs around the rink in the square, shadowed by the vast Norwegian fir that served as this year's town Christmas tree.

'If David has arrived, do you promise to talk to him at

dinner, and afterwards?' pleaded Ines, her anxiety mounting the closer they got to home.

'Can't Genevieve?' Charles complained. 'He won't want to talk to me.'

'Genevieve's useless,' grumbled Ines. 'You saw how she was with him at Beaulieu. She either ignores him or makes fun, and I can't keep the whole conversation going on my own.'

'Better not marry him, then.' Charles Fils nudged a playful elbow into her ribs as they walked. 'There won't be anyone to save you from Dreary Dave when it's just the two of you at dinner every night, *á deux*. Not to mention afterwards,' he winked.

'Don't be disgusting,' replied Ines, appalled. 'Besides, I'm not marrying anyone. Not soon anyway. I've only just left school. I'm actually thinking of trying to get a job.'

'What sort of job?' Charles laughed, not unkindly. 'Flower arranging?'

'Not far off actually,' Ines retorted cheerfully, ignoring the barb. 'I thought I might go to work for one of the big interior design houses. Lots of people say I've inherited Maman's flair for colour and making places beautiful.'

'You have.' Charles looked at her with affectionate admiration. 'But I wouldn't set your heart on life as a working girl if I were you. I think Papa might have given up on Genevieve or Renée ever finding a husband. But one more hopeless, unmarried spinster daughter would finish him off completely. You know he wants his "dynasty".'

Ines frowned but said nothing, largely because she feared her brother might be right. At twenty-nine, Genevieve was already considered past her prime marrying years. As for Renée, she had about as much interest in men as Ines had in mathematics, which was to say none whatsoever.

Renée was in England over the holidays, staying with her friend Charlotte, whose family owned farms in Yorkshire and whom Renée had met at a fine arts course at Christie's, another one of their father's failed attempts to throw his second daughter into the path of eligible young men.

All of which left Ines as the family's matrimonial great white hope. Other than Charles, of course.

'If it's a dynasty he wants, that's your department,' Ines told her brother matter-of-factly, jogging past him to take the lead as they neared the top of the cobbled hill.

'Me?'

'Of course, you,' said Ines. 'You're the keeper of the family name. Which means you're the one who has to go forth and multiply. Not me.'

'I'm perfectly happy to do both.' Charles grinned at his sister. 'But you won't catch me anywhere near an altar for at least ten years.'

'Nor me,' said Ines with feeling.

Or at least, not with David nice-but-dull Walton.

When she met her future husband, Ines felt sure, she would know him instinctively. She'd never completely lost her childhood romanticism. The little girl who'd dreamed of joining the circus, or travelling to the cloud forests of the Amazon to see her mother's beautiful birds flying free, was still inside her.

Unfortunately, so was the little girl who lived for her father's approval. When she was younger, she had longed for her father to fill the void left by her mother's death. But of course, that was impossible. Clotilde's warmth, her laughter, her easy physical affection and unceasing flow of maternal love were not things that Charles Père had the capacity to give his children, even had he wanted to. His reluctance even to talk about Clotilde meant that the children were thrown back on themselves when it came to keeping Maman's memory alive. But keep it alive they did. For Ines, in particular, it burned deep and brightly.

She didn't yet know what her future might hold. But she did know that she wanted more than life as an American hotelier's wife, however rich and successful he might be.

She would simply have to find some other way to make Papa happy.

*

'Tell us about New York, David.'

Charles Fils leaned across the table, passing the decanter of delicious Swiss Chasselas to their American guest. It was fondue tonight, and the rich, nutty-sweet smell of the bubbling raclette mingled perfectly with the crisp notes of the wine as the family took their seats in the enormous, vaulted dining room.

'Is there much talk of war there?'

'Not as much as there should be.'

David Walton refilled his glass gratefully, trying not to look too obviously in Ines's direction as he answered her brother. David had yet to figure out Charles Challant's youngest daughter. It was clear that the older girl, Genevieve, disliked him. But Ines gave him mixed signals. When they'd last met at Beaulieu over the summer, she'd given him hope on a few different occasions that she liked him; or at least that she wasn't actively averse to his attentions. But at other times he'd sensed he was boring her, or that the age and cultural differences between them were too wide to bridge. Tonight she seemed reticent in his presence, even shy. Which could be a bad sign or a good one.

'I think Roosevelt underestimates Herr Hitler,' he went on. 'To most Americans, Europe and her problems feel pretty far away.'

'Or perhaps people are just bored with politics,' Genevieve drawled, draining her own wine glass at frightening speed before extracting a dripping hunk of cheese-soaked bread from the pot. 'I know I am. Bored to tears.'

'That's because you don't understand what's hap-pening,' Charles Père observed pithily.

'Being a mere woman, you mean, Papa?' Gen countered, her lips curling in something between amusement and disdain.

Oh God, thought Ines. *Please don't let them have a row. Not on David's first night.*

Walton was already at the chalet when she and Charles got home, bathed and changed for dinner into a business suit that was *exactly* wrong for the occasion: not formal enough for proper dinner dress, but far too formal for a casual post-skiing supper *en famille*, with no servants besides the chalet maid in attendance. He did look handsome though, in an American, older man sort of way. At thirty-eight, he was almost twenty years Ines's senior, but he was still a vigorous man in his prime, with a full head of thick dark hair and the sort of strong jaw that Hollywood studios favoured. Not quite Clark Gable, perhaps, but equally not as nondescript as Ines had remembered him. The fact that he was somewhat socially awkward also helped make him less of a terrifying prospect than he'd seemed in anticipation this afternoon. For the first time it struck her that David, too, might be feeling apprehensive, invited for Christmas as the family's sole guest, and with all eyes on him as a potential future husband.

'The Munich Conference was a disgrace.'

Ignoring Genevieve, Charles Père addressed himself directly to David, stabbing his fondue fork forcefully into a hapless cube of bread.

'Both we and the British have a lot to answer for, pressuring the Czechs to roll over like that.'

'You don't feel that sacrificing Sudeten preserved the peace?' asked David.

'For now,' Charles muttered ominously. 'But in the long run? I'm not sure it can be preserved.'

Although a staunch Catholic himself, Charles Challant had made the bulk of his fortune in partnership with Jewish businessmen, some of them from far wealthier and more influential families than his own, like the Rothschilds. Ask a Jew about 'preserving the peace' and you were likely to have your head torn from your shoulders. Charles tried not to show his children how worried he was about the geopolitics unfolding around them. But he did find it irksome sometimes, that both Genevieve and Charles Fils seemed utterly oblivious to the dangers and so wholly caught up in their own shallow lives. Both were too old for such wilful blindness, in their father's opinion.

'Let's not dwell on it tonight though, Papa,' Ines pleaded as Genevieve opened her mouth to shoot back some sassy, inflammatory riposte. 'Poor David must be exhausted after his journey.'

Charles smiled, delighted that Ines appeared so amenable to Walton all of a sudden. Nothing could shake him of the opinion that his daughters' happiness – all women's happiness – ultimately depended on them making happy, ideally economically advantageous, marriages. In a perfect world he'd have preferred to see Ines married to a Frenchman. Her distaste for the Duc d'Annecy, who was clearly wildly enamoured with her, was a blow. But the ambitious and successful American hotelier would do very well as a consolation prize son-in-law.

'I am tired,' David admitted, shooting Ines a grateful glance. 'But I'd sure like to see some of the town tonight before I go to bed. If you'd be willing to show me around, that is?'

'Ines would be delighted to give you a tour,' Charles Père answered for his youngest daughter. 'I'll have Louis ready the horse and trap now. It's the best way to see Megève, you know.' He smiled approvingly at David. 'Wrapped in furs, in a horse-drawn carriage, under the stars.'

Genevieve raised an eyebrow. 'Who knew you were such a romantic, Papa?' she observed drily. But a sharp kick from Charles Fils under the table convinced her to leave it at that.

'I won't keep you out too long, I promise,' said David, sensing Ines's discomfort and not wanting to push his luck. 'But I'd love to drive by the Rothschilds' hotel. I've heard so much about it.'

'Of course,' said Ines, suddenly eager to escape the dinner table and brewing family tension. 'It would be my pleasure.'

As it turned out, it was a pleasure. Not because David Walton proved particularly scintillating company, but because Megève did indeed look quite magical tonight beneath its blanket of stars, the thirteenth-century cobbled streets lined with simple wooden dwellings lending it a rustic, fairytale air.

There was nothing rustic about the Rothschilds' newly finished Palace des Neiges, however, the undisputed jewel in Megève's crown. Set above the town and built in the Austrian style, with castle-like turrets and arched windows, its façade as

117

smoothly white as an iced wedding cake, the hotel positively radiated luxury and glamour.

'Boy. It's quite something, isn't it?' David sighed admiringly. 'What I wouldn't give to own a hotel like that.'

'Papa said you've built a wonderful resort in Idaho,' said Ines.

'We're getting there,' David acknowledged humbly. 'But I'll be honest with you, it's not in the same league.'

Just then, an elegantly dressed older woman in a spectacular full-length mink emerged from the lobby into the snowy evening to wave goodbye to some friends. She was joined moments later by a handsome blond man; Ines was sure she recognized him.

'I think he was one of the skiers from this afternoon's race,' she told David. 'I saw him talking to Charles afterwards. He's English, I believe.'

'Do you want to say hello?' David asked, reluctantly. Even from this distance he could see that the fellow was devilishly good-looking. 'We could pop in for a drink if you'd like to?'

'Oh, that's all right,' Ines yawned. 'If it's all right with you I think I'd rather go home to bed. Besides, he's with his mother. I wouldn't want to intrude.'

'Of course.' Relieved, David instructed the driver to head back to the chalet. 'Perhaps you might show me some more of the town tomorrow?'

Ines smiled politely and assured him that she would. She was glad that David had turned out to be less boring and ordinary-looking than she'd remembered. Glad also that he seemed a kind, considerate man. But at the same time, she felt no spark with him. No passion. No soul-to-soul connection of the sort she'd read about in the romantic novels Genevieve gave her, or seen in the Pierre Alcover films she so adored.

On a dreamy night like tonight, surrounded by snow-capped mountains as ancient and mystical as the earth itself, Ines couldn't help but believe that she was destined for something more special, more magical than life as Mrs David Walton. That one day some glorious, intoxicating prince was going to show up on her doorstep, sweep her up into his arms, and gallop away with her to his fantasy kingdom.

Maman had been a dreamer. That was one of Ines's strongest memories of her. How, in her imagination, Clotilde had always been more than plain old Madame Charles Challant. She'd been a wild, beautiful, exotic bird, torn from her home in her cloud forest to live out her days among lesser mortals, brightening their lives with her brilliance.

She must have been lonely, sometimes, Ines reflected sadly as the carriage bumped and jolted its way back up the hill. *Being so different.*

It was a thought that stayed with her as she got into bed that night, keeping her awake for several hours, despite her exhaustion.

CHAPTER THIRTEEN

Genevieve Challant scanned the room, feeling more ex-cited than she had in weeks.

For one thing, it was New Year's Eve. Gen had always loved this night, with its promise of new beginnings and happier times to come. Not that it had been an *un*happy year. For Genevieve at least, 1938 had been much the same as the five years that preceded it, a practically endless litany of parties and plays and social engagements among her fun but flighty Paris 'set'. Summers at Beaulieu, sailing and sleeping late up at the bastide. And winters at Megève, her least favourite time of year, although things had been somewhat ameliorated this year by the absence of Renée, who'd decided at the last minute to stay on in England at some godforsaken farm in 'the Dales', wherever that was.

In the years since their mother died, Renée had tire-somely appointed herself as Genevieve's conscience and was forever nagging her about her drinking and not doing anything 'meaningful' with her life.

'Such as what?' Genevieve would respond, exasperated. 'I'm not going to get married to someone I don't love. But anything other than marriage, or activities that might lead to marriage, Papa won't pay for.'

'And?' Renée shot back. 'I'm not married, Gen. And I get next to no allowance from Papa. But I go to work at the Foreign Office, and I volunteer and I have my animals. I do things that mean something to me.'

'Yes, dearest,' Genevieve pointed out. 'But you do them wearing the most ghastly, cheap clothes and living in a poky little flat with that friend of yours, hanging your nylons up to dry out of the kitchen window! No offence Ren, but I want a little bit more from life than that.'

'More? You mean going to the same old parties in Paris with the same old vacuous crowd, year after year after year? Yes, Papa buys you lovely dresses and an expensive apartment, but aren't you *bored*? You have so many gifts, Genevieve. So many talents. It's painful to watch you waste them.'

Gen knew that her sister chastised her only out of love. But really, it could be very trying sometimes. Not least because she *was* bored, and frustrated, and often lonely. Unfortunately she was also too frightened of a life without money to break away from her father's control. No, until she married, as she saw it, she was trapped. But having witnessed her own mother's unhappiness with her father, she was damned if she was going to marry for anything less than true, lasting love. And that, as it turned out, was proving difficult to find.

Still, one lived in hope, and perhaps tonight would be the night? Certainly everyone who was anyone in Megève had come to Maurice and Noémie Rothschild's New Year's Eve event at the Palace des Neiges. First there were the skiers. The champion Swiss racers Walter Prager and David Zogg were both there, as was France's famous Émile Allais, who'd won the men's downhill at Chamonix last season. Evie Pinching, the dark-haired British girl who'd won the downhill and combined women's events at Innsbruck, was being fussed over by everybody, despite the fact that, in Genevieve's view, her dress was ugly and shapeless, with short sleeves that made her look like a shot-putter.

Then there were the socialites. The Rothschilds and their friends, several well-known American families including at least one Mellon from Pittsburgh, and the usual smattering of French nobility. Amelie Maupeou looked particularly ravishing tonight in a daring, pink tulle ballgown with feathers sewn into the hem. Thank-fully she was joined at the hip to her fiancé, a balding, chinless Italian count who was apparently even richer than the Rothschilds.

'She looks like a flamingo, doesn't she?'

Genevieve startled. A tall, sandy-haired young man had suddenly appeared at her elbow and was whispering conspiratorially in her ear.

'I mean, what would possess a pretty girl like her to wear a dress like that?'

He spoke French with a slight accent, which might have been German or Swiss, and had an endearing, lop-sided smile that made his eyes crinkle at the corners.

'Have we met?' Genevieve returned the smile. Any man prepared *not* to be enchanted by Amelie Maupeou was a man she was happy to talk to.

'We have now. Wilhelm Noiret.' He offered his hand.

'Genevieve . . .'

'Challant,' he interrupted, bringing Gen's hand up to his lips and kissing the back of it gallantly. 'I know who you are, mademoiselle. My friends tell me that your family are practically royalty in this town.'

Genevieve frowned. 'Your friends are misinformed, I assure you.'

Wilhelm Noiret. She wondered whether he was German or French. With a name like that he could be either, but she fervently hoped it was the latter. Now was not a good time for a French woman to become romantically entangled with a German man. But she was getting ahead of herself.

'Would you care to dance, Genevieve?' Wilhelm asked.

'Absolutely not,' replied Gen with feeling. 'I'd rather stick pins in my eyes. But I'd love a drink, if you're offering.'

'A girl after my own heart,' Wilhelm grinned, linking his arm with hers. 'Follow me.'

Charles Fils was leaning against the fireplace, chatting to Gunn and some of the other skiers on the men's circuit, when he noticed Genevieve and her admirer heading to the bar.

'Do you know that fellow?'

Gunn looked languidly over his shoulder.

122

'Not really. He's a friend of Marcel Lefevre's, I believe. I've seen the two of them in town together.'

'He's a Kraut,' someone else piped up, disapprovingly.

'Are you sure?' Charles asked, worried.

'Quite sure. A soldier, in fact. You'd think they'd know they aren't welcome.'

'Now, now,' Gunn observed mildly, puffing on his pipe. 'We're not at war yet, old chum. Besides, every German's a soldier these days, now that Hitler's brought in conscription. It doesn't make him a Nazi.'

Maybe not, thought Charles nervously. *But Papa's not going to like it. Not one bit.*

On the dancefloor, Ines did her best to look enthusiastic as David Walton waltzed her around the room. His dancing was like everything else about him. Proficient, perfectly adequate, but devoid of passion.

Maybe I'm being unfair, she thought, as they weaved their way through the other couples. *After all, it's not as if I'm putting my heart and soul into it.*

Christmas had passed off better than Ines had expected, and she couldn't fault David for his good manners or his kindness. In fact, in some ways it had been a welcome distraction having him there, defusing the inevitable moments of tension between Genevieve and Papa and forcing all of them to be on their best behaviour. But try as she might, she could not conjure up any sort of spark between them. *He's attractive*, she admitted. *He just doesn't attract me.*

'I hope you'll write to me,' David said, drawing Ines's attention back to the present moment. 'With luck it won't be too long till I see you again, but until we know what Germany's going to do next it's hard to make any sort of plan.'

'Of course,' said Ines. No doubt it was a terrible sin to wish for war, or at least for the continued threat of it. But it did provide one with a cast-iron excuse not to make any plans for the future. Such as an engagement, for example.

Glancing across at her brother, she saw him deep in conversation with the good-looking Englishman she'd seen outside the hotel with David, the night he'd arrived. She'd learned since then that the man's name was Gunn and that he worked as a ski instructor when he wasn't racing. Rumours were rife that he was also being bank-rolled by a wealthy widow from Rome, but Charles Fils insisted that was just gossip.

Both he and Charles were surrounded by half the pretty women at the party, but neither of them seemed particularly interested.

Ines surreptitiously sneaked a glance at the cuckoo clock on the wall, a rare touch of alpine kitsch in the otherwise elegant room. It was eleven fifteen. Forty-five minutes until they would all ring in the new year with champagne and toasts, and no more than an hour until Papa bundled the Challant party into their coach and home to bed.

Parties were all very well, in Charles Père's book, but like all other pleasures were to be partaken of in strict moderation. Or as Genevieve put it in one of her many, hilarious impressions of him, 'Of course you can go, darling. Just make sure you have no fun at all, and remember to go to confession the next morning to offer penance, for *wishing* that you had.'

Julia Valaperti had also noticed the crowd of young women around Gunn. She despised herself for feeling jealous. It really was too feeble, at her age. But there it was: a fact.

Julia had loved her husband, Roberto, and been a faithful wife until his sudden, unexpected death from a stroke five years ago. Now a wealthy widow who pleased herself, she had no desire to remarry. But she'd been taken aback by the loneliness she felt after Roberto's death, rattling round their apartment in Rome on her own.

Her initial intention had simply been to travel, and meet new people. She had not been looking for a lover when she met Gunn at a party on Elizabeth Street on one of her regular shopping trips to London. But he'd been so attentive and funny, and had brought such a strong, youthful energy into her life, that in the end she had run out of reasons to resist.

Julia wasn't stupid. She knew that, were it not for the money and the lifestyle she could afford him, Gunn wouldn't be with her. She also knew that all her friends and acquaintances saw straight through the whole 'ski instructor' conceit. And yet she carried on, growing closer to her young lover by the day despite her best intentions. It was all very vexing.

Gunn himself had said nothing and seemed happy enough to continue with things as they were. But since they'd come to Megève, Julia had found herself idly wondering whether perhaps she *did* want to marry again. She tried desperately to picture in her mind a world where this man-boy half her age would be accepted as her husband by her high society friends. And though she knew it was a fantasy – she'd be laughed out of Rome, out of everywhere – watching Gunn laughing and flirting by the fire now, surrounded by girls, it was a hard one to relinquish.

Catching her watching him, Gunn made his excuses and walked over to join her.

'Everything all right?' Relieving her of her empty glass, he replaced it with a new one.

'Everything's fine.' Julia smiled at him gratefully. Notwithstanding their 'arrangement', there was genuine affection there. 'You?'

'Oh, you know,' he shrugged.

'You're missing your family?'

It was an unexpected guess from Julia, but an astute one. Gunn rarely went home to Cornwall any more, and when he did it was only to visit his mother. Edie now lived in a pretty extended cottage in Wadebridge, close to Port Isaac and about twelve miles from Maltings, which was fortunately too far for her to pass by her old family home and be reminded of the life that had been lost.

Gunn had paid the deposit on the cottage, and Edie seemed happy enough there, with her large, rambling garden and her beehives and fruit trees. But, as his sister Laura had pointed out waspishly the last time they spoke, almost two years ago now, that was 'only because Ma doesn't know where the money came from. She'd be horrified if she did, and you know it.'

Laura Gunn disapproved vehemently of her brother's lifestyle, 'exploiting' rich, lonely women for money rather than finding himself a real job. Gunn told himself she was wrong. Julia wasn't being exploited. She knew exactly what she was doing and was perfectly happy with the set-up, thank you very much. Besides, it was impossible to compete as a downhill skier without some sort of private funding behind you. And it was hardly Gunn's fault that his inheritance had evaporated.

But deep down, Laura's criticisms stung because he knew they were true. After too many rows to count, brother and sister were now more or less estranged, a situation that pained Gunn more than he cared to admit.

'New Year's Eves used to be a riot back home, back when my father was alive,' he told Julia, his face lighting up at the memory. 'We'd have fireworks in the gardens at Maltings and a big bonfire if it wasn't raining. Pa taught us these terrific tribal dances from the Amazon, and the four of us would clap and stomp around the fire with drums. We must have looked like utter lunatics.'

'It sounds fun,' Julia said kindly, briefly brushing her hand against his.

'It was.' Gunn smiled, grateful for the kindness, but wary of appearing too intimate with Julia in such a public setting, and of slipping into syrupy nostalgia. If there was one thing he abhorred it was self-pity. 'But tonight's been fun too. Just in a different way.'

He told her about his conversation with the other skiers earlier, about the young German soldier who was still monopolizing Genevieve Challant. 'They've been stuck together like glue all night. It seems a shame that people make such a fuss about him being German. Almost as if we're already at war. As if it can't be avoided.'

'Goodness, don't say that,' Julia shuddered. Since Mussolini's conquest of Abyssinia in 1936, Il Duce and the Führer appeared to have grown ever more closely allied on the world stage. Any war between France or England and Germany would leave Italians like her in a difficult position. If nothing else it would spell the end of cosy trips to Megève or London with Gunn. 'I expect your friends are only gossiping because one of the Challant girls is involved,' she said confidently, as if a firm tone could make it true. 'You know how obsessed people here are with that family.'

Gunn did know. After the Rothschilds, the Challants were probably the richest family in Megève, which these days was saying something.

'Marie Guerlain told me last week that the youngest daughter's soon to be engaged,' she added, nodding to-wards Ines and David Walton, who were now standing together at the bar, talking to Ines's father.

'Really?' Gunn followed her gaze. Charles Fils hadn't mentioned anything about an engagement. Tonight was the first time Gunn had seen any of the Challant sisters in the flesh. The general consensus around town was that they were all attractive girls, but that the youngest one was the prettiest. Glancing at Ines, Gunn concurred. The girl was an absolute goddess. Certainly far too beautiful, not to mention far too young, to be with the chap standing next to her, who must have been forty if he was a day.

'Who is he?' he asked Julia.

'An American hotelier,' she replied. 'I forget the name.'

'And is that the father?' Gunn asked, looking at Charles Père.

Julia nodded.

'Looks a bit Old Testament, doesn't he?' whispered Gunn. 'With that beard? Christ. Makes me want to confess my sins just looking at him.'

Julia laughed. 'I wouldn't do that if I were you, darling. We'll be here all night.'

*

The party roared on until midnight when, with a great clinking of glasses and raising of toasts, everyone moved on to the hotel's rear terrace to watch the fireworks being set off at the foot of the piste.

'To better things in 1939.' Wilhelm raised a glass to Genevieve, who raised hers unsteadily in reply.

'To better things.'

They were both quite drunk. But my goodness, what a lovely evening it had been, and what a happy, easy time Gen had had in Wilhelm's company. How strange it was to have just met someone, and yet feel as if one had known them for years.

Would the next year bring better things? Watching the fireworks beneath a peaceful alpine moon, shards of coloured light streaking against a backdrop of snowy white peaks, Genevieve could almost believe it.

For appearances' sake, Julia Valaperti went up to her room first, as soon as the fireworks were over, leaving Gunn to follow a little while later.

Settling into a fleece-lined chair on the terrace, Gunn lit a cigar and puffed on it contemplatively as the carriages drew up to take people home. There was a lingering smell of phosphorus in the air after the fireworks, mingled with the sweat of the horses below, one of his favourite smells from childhood.

It was funny, Julia bringing up his family tonight. He did miss them, and England and the old days, perhaps more than he'd realized. But what was the point in looking back? The life that he pined for had died with his father ten years ago. Wishing wasn't going to bring it back.

Watching the Challant party climbing into their two horse-drawn carriages, both of them larger and finer than all the rest, Gunn thought about families, and how different and ultimately fragile each one was. There was white-bearded Charles Challant Père, looking like a character from Dickens in his long frock coat and black top hat, being helped into the first carriage by his footman. And following his son, Charles Fils, and the

American hotelier here to woo the youngest daughter.

The two Challant girls, both now swaddled in furs, stepped up into the second carriage. The older, dark-haired one first and then the youngest. Ines.

She paused for a moment before she got in, turning and looking up at the star-filled sky with an expression that struck Gunn as both wistful and melancholy, hopeful and yet oddly sad.

Yes, he confirmed to himself. *She's very beautiful.*

But after the carriage had gone, as he stubbed out his cigar and headed in to join Julia, it was her sadness he remembered. Perhaps because, in that moment, it mirrored his own.

CHAPTER FOURTEEN

By late January, most of the casual ski tourists had returned home, and Megève was considerably emptier. The snow was fabulous though, feet-deep and as fine and soft as icing sugar. For those lucky enough to be able to stay later into the season, it was a magical time.

'Do you really have to go back to Germany?' Charles Fils asked Wilhelm after skiing one afternoon. The two boys were enjoying warm slices of tarte tatin smothered in crème anglaise at L'Alouette, a new café that had just opened close to the square. 'You realize poor Genevieve will be heartbroken.'

'So will I,' Wilhelm admitted, spooning up the last of the custard from the edges of his plate. 'Believe me, I'd love nothing more than to stay here longer. But I've already taken my full allowance of leave. If I'm not back at the barracks by six o'clock on Sunday . . .'

'You'll be shot at dawn?' Charles raised an eyebrow dramatically.

'Perhaps not *shot*,' Wilhelm smiled. 'But it wouldn't go down well. Let's put it that way.'

He'd become good friends with Genevieve's younger brother over the last few weeks. And although it was Gen he would really be sorry to part from, everything about his time in Megève had been perfect, a beautiful, unexpected dream.

That was the trouble with dreams, though. Eventually, one has to wake up.

If only his parents had settled in his father's native France after they married, rather than in his mother's hometown of Hamburg. Wilhelm had always felt just as French as he was German, and privately loathed the Nazis and their preposterous, strutting, mustachioed leader. But as a young German man of fighting age, he'd been called to military service along with everybody else he knew. Which meant that if there *were* to be a war, he would have no choice but to fight in it. And on the opposite side to Genevieve, and Charles Fils, and all his French friends and family.

'How long will you stay?' he asked Charles, signalling to the waitress for a refill of the thick, syrupy hot cocoa he'd just finished. 'Will you go to Mürren?'

The last, big race of the professional downhill season was being held in Mürren, in Switzerland's legendary Jungfrau region, in two weeks' time.

'I doubt it,' Charles replied ruefully. 'Papa wants me to start working for one of our subsidiaries in Paris, and the sooner I start the better. We'll see. I'd like to go and support Gunn. If he keeps up his current form, he could win it,' he added excitedly.

'Hm.' Wilhelm frowned.

'Oh, come on,' said Charles. 'I know you don't like him. But you have to admit the man skis like an angel.'

'If he does, that's the only angelic thing about him,' Wilhelm said gruffly.

It wasn't that he didn't like Gunn, exactly. The fellow was eminently likable: charming, funny, generous with money. More than that, he had stuck up for Wilhelm on more than one occasion when others in Megève's incestuous social circle were being unkind about his German roots. It was more that Wilhelm didn't trust him, especially when it came to his burgeoning friendship with Charles Fils. Now that he and Genevieve were an item, Wilhelm considered the Challant family's affairs to be his business. Particularly in so far as they involved an obvious chancer like Gunn, who made no secret of his desire to become rich and to achieve it through the subtle art of association.

'You know the man's a terrible gossip. Wildly indiscreet,' he told Charles. 'Just the other day I overheard him discussing your father.'

'"Discussing", how?' Charles Fils frowned.

'Musing aloud about where his fortune came from,' Wilhelm replied bluntly. 'He pretty much implied to my friend Marcel that your father had been involved in some sort of fraud.'

Charles shrugged. 'Those old rumours have been around for years. There's no truth in them.'

Wilhelm was taken aback. He'd expected a far stronger reaction. Concern at a minimum, perhaps even outrage. If someone he considered a friend had called *his* father a crook, it would have been no shrugging matter. But Charles Fils seemed utterly unfazed, forking up the last of his delicious tarte with undimmed relish.

'Look,' Charles explained, clocking Wilhelm's dismayed expression. 'I've lived with these whispers for most of my life. My mother used to let the malicious gossip get to her. I'm sure that was part of what led to her nervous breakdown and, you know . . .'

He left the sentence hanging, choking up for a moment. Then, clearing his throat, he went on.

'Anyway. I made a decision long ago to simply rise above it. I expect Gunn's just curious. It's not a crime.'

'No, it's not,' acknowledged Wilhelm. 'But I hear that he's also *curious* about your youngest sister.' He gave Charles Fils a knowing look. 'You do know the man's a fortune hunter?'

'That's a bit rich, coming from you,' Charles teased him, as their second mugs of cocoa arrived. 'Seeing as you're all over Genevieve like a rash.'

'Not for her money!' Wilhelm replied, seriously. 'I hope you don't think . . .'

'Of course I don't,' Charles interrupted, waving the idea away with his hand. 'Not for a moment. I was only joking. I just think you should give Gunn a break, that's all. If he were seriously interested in Ines, he'd have told me. And I'd have told *him* not to waste his time. My sister is going to marry David Walton, the American.'

'Really?' Wilhelm was surprised. But Charles Fils seemed quite sure.

'She doesn't want to, but she will,' he insisted. 'You watch.

It's what Papa wants. Ines always does what Papa wants in the end.'

Only a few days later, Charles Fils found himself thinking back to his conversation with Wilhelm at L'Alouette, and not in a good way.

He'd been heading back to the chalet earlier than usual one afternoon, after a problem with his ski, and happened to walk past the ice rink. Over Christmas and New Year it would have been packed at this time, but now it was virtually empty. Charles saw the two of them instantly. Ines, sprawled out on the ice laughing loudly. And Gunn, standing over her, also laughing, leaning down to offer her his hand and help her up.

On the face of it, it was an innocent enough tableau. Except that Gunn hadn't mentioned anything to Charles about going skating, or about Ines, when they'd skied together earlier. In fact, he'd made up some story about promising to play ski guide for the afternoon to Julia and one of her friends from Rome, who'd just arrived in town.

'I tell you, if I win at Mürren, I'm going to tell Julia I'm done with the ski teaching,' he'd complained to Charles. 'The money's good, but these middle-aged women are so demanding. Makes one feel like a bloody galley slave.'

Charles had said something sympathetic. But now here Gunn was. No Julia. No friend. No ski-guiding.

Just Ines, unchaperoned and alone, and looking worryingly happy to be in his company.

'I can see your brother's the only athlete in the family,' Gunn teased Ines, helping her unsteadily back onto her feet, as wobbly and useless on the ice as a newborn calf.

'Not true!' she shot back. 'I can ski *and* ride. And I'm better than Charles at tennis.'

'*Tennis.*' Gunn rolled his eyes disparagingly. 'Who on earth cares about *tennis*?'

133

Ines tried to make a cross face, but it was hard to pretend to be annoyed with Gunn. She'd seen him around Megève all winter, and even watched him race. But while she'd always considered Charles's English friend handsome, she hadn't expected him to be so clever or amusing. After six weeks of David Walton's earnest, sensible attentions, it felt fabulous to spend time with a man who only had fun on the agenda.

'Here. Let me show you.' Moving behind her, wrapping both his hands firmly around her waist while extending his arms forward, Gunn began to skate rhythmically around the rink. 'It's a bit like a waltz. Right step . . . glide. Left step . . . glide. Once you get into a rhythm it's honestly not that hard.'

Ines let him guide her, enjoying the firm, warm pressure of his hands as they made their way slowly over the ice together. She hadn't told Charles Fils or anyone about the time she'd spent with Gunn since New Year's Eve. Not because she was ashamed of it – they were just friends, after all – but because she didn't want Papa to get the wrong idea and put a stop to it.

It was truly uncanny how much the two of them had in common. Gunn's father, William, had been a collector and adventurer and had been fascinated by exotic birds, just like Maman. He knew all about umbrella cockatoos and Andean jays and hyacinth macaws; things that nobody knew about in Ines's experience, apart from herself and her siblings. Even more incredibly, Ines's mother and Gunn's father had both died in the same year, 1928, and only a few months apart.

'Everything changed after that,' Gunn had told her. 'We lost the house. My mother and sister had to move, and I was out on my own.'

He said it matter-of-factly, but Ines sensed the pain beneath.

'How awful,' she'd replied, with feeling. Much had changed for her too, after Clotilde's sudden death. But at least her homes, Place Dauphine, the bastide at Beaulieu and the chalet at Megève, had remained the same. The annual 'migration' of the Challant flock, flitting between these three nests, had been a lifeline for Ines, a vital link to her mother's memory that had sustained her through the lonely decade that had followed. Poor Gunn hadn't even had that.

'Much better,' he shouted encouragingly from behind her. 'You've got it. I'm going to let go now.'

'No, don't!' Ines shrieked.

'You'll be fine,' he reassured her, gently uncurling his fingers. 'Just keep going. Step and glide, step and glide.'

Ines did as he said, feeling a rush of cold air around her middle where moments ago Gunn's warm hands had been. But it was an exhilarating rush. She was doing it, skating properly, round and around.

'Ha!' she exclaimed in delight. 'This is easy!'

'I told you.'

'INES!'

Ines spun around. Her brother Charles was leaning on the low wall at the edge of the rink, trying to get her attention. Smiling broadly, she skated over to him, delighted to find that she could actually change direction without falling and making a fool of herself.

'Did you see me?' she panted happily, her round cheeks flushed red from both the exertion and the cold. 'Gunn's been teaching me.'

'So I see.'

'What's the matter?' Ines frowned.

'Nothing's the matter.'

'Yes, it is.' She looked at him curiously. 'Why are you so grumpy?'

Gunn sped effortlessly across the ice to join them, all smiles. 'Charles! What are you doing here? I thought you'd have been up the mountain for hours yet.'

'I might say the same,' Charles replied sullenly. 'What happened to Julia and your touring party?'

'Cancelled.' Gunn rolled his eyes. 'You know what women are like. Always changing their minds at the last minute.'

'Erm, excuse me,' Ines nudged him playfully in the ribs. 'Not all of us.'

Merde, thought Charles. Wilhelm was right. Gunn and Ines had become awfully chummy all of a sudden. He wondered how he'd managed to miss all the signs.

'Ines and I should get home,' he told Gunn curtly.

Ines looked at her watch. 'Now? But it's only half past three.'

'Papa wants us all to go to the four-thirty mass,' said Charles, thinking up a plausible lie on the spot. 'Don't ask me why,' he added, before Ines could do just that. 'All I know is, we need to go.'

While Ines went to take her skates off, Charles turned to Gunn.

'What's going on?' he asked bluntly.

'What do you mean?'

'You and Ines,' Charles spelled it out. 'What's going on between the two of you?'

Gunn's eyes widened. 'Going on? Nothing's "going on".'

'It didn't look like nothing to me,' Charles scowled. 'You were flirting up a storm when I saw you just now.'

Gunn waved a hand dismissively. 'Don't be such a prude, old man. Of course I was *flirting.* Who wouldn't flirt with Ines? She's a lovely girl. But there's nothing "going on". I'm with Julia, for my sins,' he added, lowering his voice. 'In case you'd forgotten.'

'It's not me who's forgotten.'

'Oh, come *on,*' Gunn laughed. 'You're making some-thing out of nothing. Believe me.'

Charles wanted to, badly. Gunn certainly sounded convincing. Perhaps he *was* jumping to conclusions? Reading something into an innocent situation, just be-cause Wilhelm had put the idea in his head?

'She's practically engaged,' he reminded Gunn, glancing across to the bench where Ines was sitting, patiently unlacing her skates.

'I know she is,' his friend replied. 'You told me. As has she. Although if you ask me it's a crying shame. She obviously doesn't love the chap.'

'Love can grow,' Charles replied awkwardly, looking away, and realizing how pompous and unfeeling he sounded. Privately, he agreed that David Walton was wrong for Ines, not to mention far too old. But he wasn't about to rock the boat with Papa, and he didn't want Gunn to either. 'Just . . . keep your distance. All right?'

'All right.' Gunn raised both hands in the air in a gesture of innocence. 'I'll back off. But I promise you, Charles, you're overthinking this. Ines and I are just friends.'

Ines was livid when they arrived back at the chalet later and Charles admitted there was no mass.

'What on earth were you playing at, dragging me home for no reason?'

'There was a reason,' Charles insisted. 'I didn't want people to start talking. About you and Gunn.'

'Don't be so ridiculous,' Ines snapped. 'There is no "me and Gunn".'

Charles would have been more reassured if she hadn't blushed violently when she said it.

'Are you sure about that? You looked awfully close out on the ice.'

'Of course I'm sure,' she replied, exasperated. 'Besides, I thought you liked him?'

'I do like him,' said Charles. 'He's a good friend.'

'Then why can't I like him too?' said Ines.

'Because,' Charles squirmed. 'It's different.'

'No, it's not,' insisted Ines. 'You think it is. But it isn't. We're friends, Charles. Friends. Nothing more.'

She's probably right, thought Charles. Gunn had said the same exact thing, after all. Even so, he suddenly found himself pleased that the season was about to come to an end. After the big race at Mürren, the Challants would all go back to Paris. Normal life would resume, and Megève would be forgotten for another year.

Normally this would have made him sad. But with the storm clouds of war gathering, not to mention other potentially dangerous storms brewing closer to home, it felt like the right time to go.

CHAPTER FIFTEEN

Julia Valaperti carefully folded the sleeves of her cashmere twinset around the crisp sheet of tissue paper she'd bought for the purpose, before laying it gently into her trunk.

It was a bright, beautiful afternoon in Mürren, and from the windows in her lavish suite at the Regina Palace Hotel, Julia had a clear view of the white-peaked Matterhorn, majestic beneath a dazzling, sapphire blue sky. *A day for new beginnings*, Julia thought bravely. *A day for bringing things out into the sunlight, and seeing them as they really are.*

It had been a happy trip to Switzerland, and a triumphant one. After a thrillingly close race down the famously treacherous Lauberhorn course, Gunn had beaten off the local hero Permin Halsfetter to win gold in the men's downhill; a historic first for an Englishman, but also a victory for Megève, who very much saw Gunn as one of its own.

There had been parties of course, and press events, and at all of them Julia had kept a discreet distance, making sure that she was just one of Gunn's crowd of friends and admirers. Given that others among that crowd included several Rothschilds, at least one Italian prince and the younger two Challant children, Charles and Ines, both favourites of the society columnists, it was easy enough for Julia to fade into the shadows. And later, once the parties were over, Gunn had come to her, sharing his excitement sweetly, like a puppy. Sharing her bed, too. Only there, Julia sensed, he had become more of a loyal dog than an excited one. Uncomplaining. Happy enough, or so it seemed. But in recent weeks something had changed. Julia could no longer fool herself that the physical passion she still felt for

Gunn was reciprocated. It had cooled, faded, as passion was wont to do, especially in the young. And in its place, affection. Kindness. But also a reticence, even a fear, that had convinced her it was time to act. To do what must be done, while she still had the strength to do it.

Gunn knocked and entered just as she was clicking the trunk shut, closing each of the brass buckles with a satisfying snap.

'What are you all packed for?' he asked innocently, slipping his hands around her small waist from behind and planting a kiss on the back of her neck. 'You know the train to Geneva doesn't leave till ten tomorrow. We've got ages.'

Julia turned around to look at him. In a new pair of fashionable 'Oxford baggies', the high-waisted, loose corduroy trousers that were all the rage in England, and a burgundy cashmere polo neck, he somehow managed to look even more desirable than usual. The lemony Floris aftershave didn't help either. But she held firm.

'You've got ages, darling,' she told him. 'My train to Zürich leaves in two hours.'

'Zürich?' He released her, taking a step back while the import of what she was saying began to sink in.

'From there, I'll take the overnight to Milan. I plan to spend three or four days with friends. And then home to Rome.'

'So you're not coming back to Megève?'

She shook her head.

'What about all your things? Back at the hotel?'

'I was hoping you'd be kind enough to have them sent on to me,' said Julia. 'It's only a few furs and some knick-knacks. I emptied the safe when we came here, so I have all my jewellery, my passports . . .'

She trailed off. Winded, Gunn sat down on the end of the bed.

'You don't have to go, Julia.'

Sitting down beside him, she took his hand.

'I do. We both know I do.'

Despite everything, a small, pathetic part of her held its breath, waiting, hoping against hope that he would try to change her mind. Scoop her up into his arms and insist that he did love her after all, that there was some way . . . that he would come to Rome with her. But of course, he didn't.

Instead he said gruffly, and truthfully, 'I do care about you.'

'I know that.'

'And I'm very grateful. For everything you've done for me.' Dragging his eyes up from the carpet, he forced himself to look at her. He was so earnest in that moment, and so adorably contrite, that to her own surprise, Julia found herself laughing.

'Oh for heaven's sake, darling. Nobody's died. We had a lovely time, which was always going to come to an end. And now it has. There's no need for theatrics.'

Gunn shook his head admiringly. She was a wonderful woman.

'Just, be careful,' Julia stroked his hand.

'Careful?' He looked confused. 'There's no talk of conscription yet. At least not in England, if that's what you mean. I've no intention of getting myself killed.'

'That's not it,' said Julia. 'I'm talking about the youngest Challant girl. I know you're smitten with her.'

Gunn opened his mouth to deny it, but then thought better of it. If Julia had the courage to be honest with him and call a spade a spade about their relationship, then the least he owed her was to return the favour when it came to Ines.

'I don't blame you,' Julia continued. 'She's terribly pretty. And quite the catch, financially.'

'It's not about her money,' said Gunn, primly.

Julia rolled her eyes.

'All right,' he admitted, blushing. 'It's not *just* about her money. Perhaps at the beginning it was. But now . . . I like her,' he said simply. 'And I think she likes me.'

'It won't matter, my love.' Julia looked at him pityingly. For someone who was so canny in so many ways, he could be incredibly naïve at times. 'She can't marry you.'

'Who said anything about marriage?' Gunn back-tracked hastily.

'Her father will never consent to it,' said Julia, ignoring him. 'Never.'

Gunn couldn't help but look a little offended. 'Not that I've got any intentions in that direction. But hypo-thetically, if I wanted to marry Ines . . . why do you think her father would be so against it?'

'Because you're penniless, darling.' Julia pointed out the obvious. 'Not to mention English, a Protestant . . .' she counted off his failings on her fingers one by one. 'And you have a *reputation*. When it comes to women at least.'

'What does that mean?' Gunn protested, aggrieved.

'It means he'll cut Ines off if she marries you. Believe me, my darling. He will. You won't see one franc of Challant money.'

Gunn went quiet. Julia could practically hear his mind whirring.

'You do not want Charles Challant as an enemy,' she added, a note of genuine anxiety creeping into her voice. 'I say that purely as a friend. Underneath that moral, upstanding exterior, the man is ruthless.'

Gunn was intrigued. 'Is he? I mean, I've heard some rumours of shady business practices, back in the day. Ill-gotten gains and all that. But do you know of something worse?'

Julia shook her head. 'I don't *know* anything. But I believe that, before his wife died, Charles Challant was involved with some deeply unscrupulous people. We're talking well beyond "shady". Several friends in Paris told me that the wife was living in fear the summer before she died.'

'In fear of what? Of him?'

'Perhaps,' mused Julia. 'Or perhaps it was his associates she feared. I don't know. What I do know is that by the end of the year, she was dead.'

'Well yes, but that's a coincidence, surely?' Gunn frowned. Julia was a sensible woman, not prone to conspiracy theories or hysterical speculation. 'I under-stood she'd suffered a nervous collapse after that awful accident, with the village boy being mauled to death by their dogs?'

'If it was an accident,' muttered Julia.

Now Gunn was really intrigued. 'Has anyone said otherwise?' he asked her.

He remembered reading about the case at the time, years ago. The gruesomeness of the boy's death had always stayed with him.

'Surely no one in their right mind would *deliberately* set their dogs on an innocent child?'

'I agree,' Julia exhaled. 'And I'm not saying that *is* what happened. But there were discrepancies in the coroner's report, apparently, that were never made public at the inquest. And Charles Challant did have huge financial and political influence down in Beaulieu at that time. He still does.

'Look,' she concluded, after a pregnant pause, 'all I'm saying is that that I believe there's a dark side to that man. A dangerous side. And that by all accounts he dotes on his youngest girl excessively. Be very careful, Gunn.'

'I appreciate the warning,' he said. 'But you really needn't worry. It's all a moot point. As soon as Ines gets back to Paris she's going to get engaged to that American fellow. The one she was with at New Year's Eve.'

'Really?' Julia brightened. 'Well, good. I'm pleased to hear it. You must let her go, my love. As I must let you go. Besides,' she nudged him affectionately. 'You're a famous ski racer now. A world champion, no less. You'll have all the girls back in London at your feet, just you wait and see.'

Gunn put an arm around her, pulling her to him with genuine warmth.

He would miss her. It felt so strange to think about going back to London, instead of on to Rome with Julia as they'd planned. *London.* Even the word sounded unfamiliar to him now, a half-remembered echo of a different world. A world where he used to belong.

The bubble of Megève and this year's glorious ski season was always going to end. But to have it happen so suddenly felt jarring. Julia's unexpected but heartfelt warnings about Charles Challant only served to heighten the bad taste in Gunn's mouth, a sadly sour end to such a sweet interlude.

'Thank you,' he told her, bending to kiss her hand.

'What for?' asked Julia.

'For being so kind,' said Gunn. 'For making it easy.'

Nothing about the next year will be easy, thought Julia. *For either of us, I expect.*

But Gunn would have to work out that part on his own.

Gunn waited on the platform at Lauterbrunnen until the Zürich train had pulled completely out of sight. Ignoring Julia's protests, he'd insisted on coming down with her in the cable car and seeing her onto the train, carrying her cases and giving her a 'proper' goodbye.

It had felt strange and sad watching her go. But as he rode the cable car alone back up to Mürren, he couldn't deny the sense of lightness creeping in. A growing awareness of freedom, of a burden lifted.

Twilight bathed the village's wooden rooftops in a magical, blue-grey glow, and stars filled the night sky above him as Gunn crunched his way up the snowy hill towards the main square. He was so lost in thought, he didn't notice Ines Challant emerging from the tabac, clutching a brown paper bag full of postcards and a packet of Gitanes which she proceeded to open, tapping out a single thin cigarette and lighting it, inhaling deeply. It was only when she slipped on the icy pavement and fell moments later, that he realized who it was.

'Here,' he rushed forward. 'Let me help you.'

Crouching down he reached underneath both Ines's mink-coat-clad arms and pulled her back up onto her feet.

'What happened?'

'I don't know exactly,' she answered, embarrassed and wincing in pain as she tried to put weight on her left foot. 'I must have lost my footing somehow. I'm an idiot.'

'Not at all,' said Gunn. 'These streets are a deathtrap when they haven't been properly gritted. Can you walk?'

Ines shook her head. 'I don't think so. Not without help.'

Their eyes locked, and for several moments a silence

144

descended between them that spoke a thousand words. Gunn's earlier conversation with Julia was still ringing in his ears. This was dangerous. This could never work. This would ruin him. But now that Ines was actually here, in his arms, in need of his help, he felt a pull towards her so powerful it overwhelmed all such practical considerations, like a rip-tide dragging him inexorably out to sea.

For Ines, the whole encounter was more like a dream, one of the wild, romantic fantasies of her childhood. As if she'd been meant to fall, destined to do it, so that Gunn could find her and rescue her and carry her back to his castle in the sky. Or, if not a castle per se, then at least to her hotel.

Except that of course, Charles Fils would be waiting at the hotel. And there would be people there, scores of people, watching and surmising and gossiping and reporting back to her father, ruining everything.

Except that it was too late to worry about that. Gunn had already scooped her up into his arms like a rag doll, and was striding purposefully and wordlessly up the hill towards the Hotel Beausite, where Ines and Charles Fils were staying. Closing her eyes, Ines buried her face in his chest, drinking in his warmth and his heartbeat and the faint smell of his aftershave beneath his thick sweater, knowing that these few moments might be the last she would have with him, ever.

A blast of warm air told her they'd entered the hotel lobby. Reluctantly, Ines opened her eyes as Gunn set her down gingerly in one of the armchairs opposite the reception desk.

'The young lady slipped on the ice,' he told the concierge. 'She'll need someone to take a look at her ankle.'

'Oh no, really. I'm fine,' blurted Ines. She wanted to cry. But instead she pulled herself together, calmly thanking Gunn and signalling to the bellman to summon the lift.

'I'd ask you to come up. But Charles is probably waiting in our suite and . . .'

'Of course,' Gunn cut her off. 'I understand. Best not.'

'Is it, though?' Ines heard her own pleading tone as the lift doors opened and she limped inside. '*Is* it "best"? Because it doesn't feel "best". Not for me.'

Reaching into his coat pocket, Gunn pulled out a small object wrapped in tissue paper and pressed it into Ines's hand. He opened his mouth as if to say something, presumably to explain what it was. But the lift doors began to close before he got the chance.

The last thing Ines saw was his stricken face, staring at her helplessly through the dwindling gap. And then, just like that, he was gone.

The next morning, Charles Fils sat in the first-class train carriage with Ines, watching the snowy peaks of the Eiger and the Jungfrau recede into the distance. Her ankle was bandaged and there were some light scrapes visible on her left hand and forearm. But other than that there were no visible signs of the previous night's 'incident'.

The siblings were heading to Interlaken, then Bern, and then ultimately across the border into France. They wouldn't reach Paris till late the following night. Charles Père and Genevieve had already returned to Place Dauphine, and Renée was supposed to arrive from London today. Charles and Ines were the stragglers, having begged to be allowed to come to Switzerland and watch the big race at the Lauberhorn. But now they, too, must fly home to roost.

Neither of them minded the long train journey or its multiple stops. Quite apart from the stunning scenery of pine forests, undulating lowland pastures, crystal clear rivers and spectacular, glassy lakes, it would give them both time to adjust; to leave behind the peace and beauty of the Alps and prepare for the hurly-burly of city life. For Charles, that would mean a new job. A chance, hopefully, to prove himself to Papa and to begin taking on more responsibility within the family business. For Ines, it meant a resumption of the endless round of parties and social engagements that made up the lives of most upper-class, unmarried French women. Perhaps some charitable work, through the church. And then in due course, an engagement.

It could not be avoided forever.

As a child, she'd had such dreams! Vivid, colourful, exciting dreams. Of joining the circus. Of becoming an artist, or a nomad, or both. Of travelling to the Amazon rainforest or the wilds of Africa, the exotic habitats of her mother's birds which Ines had always romantically believed to be her own, spiritual home. In some strange way she couldn't quantify, Hector Gunn had become a part of those dreams over the course of the last few weeks. But that was over now.

Wasn't that what growing up meant, after all? Re-linquishing one's childhood fantasies in favour of reality, of duty. The duty she owed Papa.

'Are you all right?' Charles asked her. With her nose pressed to the carriage window, Ines looked lost in thought.

'I'm fine,' she told him. 'A bit sad, I suppose. It feels strange to be going home. Especially leaving from here, instead of Megève. It's like we didn't say goodbye properly.'

'I know what you mean,' said Charles wistfully. 'But it's never goodbye. Only ever "*au revoir*". We'll be back next winter, just like we always are.'

'Will we?' Ines raised an eyebrow.

'Never' and 'always' felt like strange words to use in this moment, with the very real prospect of war hanging over Europe. But Charles took a more optimistic view.

'Of course we will,' he said robustly. 'And aren't you glad we came here and saw the race? Talk about a spectacular end to the season.'

Ines nodded. She was glad. The Lauberhorn had been utterly thrilling, unlike any downhill race she'd been to before. And Gunn had skied beautifully, flying down the mountain, quite literally at times as the ground fell away beneath him, like a man possessed.

'Gunn said he's headed back to London now for the rest of the year,' Charles Fils observed casually. 'I told him I thought it was the right decision. God knows what he ever thought he was going to do in Rome with Julia. He doesn't even speak the language.'

The train rattled on. Reaching into her coat pocket, Ines ran her fingers over the small, tissue-wrapped package Gunn had given her yesterday. She didn't pull it out and look at it in front of her brother. But just knowing it was there brought a warm feeling that she clung to now, like a small child to its blanket.

Inside the tissue was an enamel brooch of a cockatoo, a nod to a conversation Ines and Gunn had had back in Megève, when she'd told him about her mother's admiration for cockatoos above all other birds.

'They have brains as well as beauty, you see,' Ines explained. 'Not all birds do.'

'Beauty and brains,' Gunn had replied, with a smile Ines could see now as if he were sitting right in front of her. 'Like you.'

That fateful summer back in Beaulieu, a nine-year-old Ines had assured her mother that she and her sisters were all like cockatoos. '*You mustn't worry, you know, Maman . . . We're* much *too clever to get trapped.*'

But the older she grew, the more Ines realized that everyone was trapped to some degree. Confined by their circumstances, their beliefs, their class, their gender. Confined by war or illness, or other things outside of their control.

She wished she could remember how that long-ago conversation with her mother had started. What was it that Clotilde had been so afraid of? What 'trap' did she believe she'd fallen into, that she wanted to spare her daughters from? But the memory, like so many others, was shrouded in the thick mists of time.

Reaching into her valise, Ines pulled out a pad of letter paper and a pen.

'Who are you writing to?' Charles asked, a touch ner-vously.

'To David,' Ines replied.

'David Walton?'

'Of course. I promised to tell him all about Mürren and the race, but I haven't had a chance till now.'

Leaning back in his seat, Charles Fils exhaled. It was all going to be all right.

*

The return to the house at Place Dauphine turned out to be a much livelier and happier affair than either Charles or Ines had expected.

Renée, who hadn't been back to France or seen anyone since last summer, was full of news about England and the Foreign Office and her 'dear friend' Charlotte.

'The farm where her family lives is honestly the most idyllic place you've ever seen,' she gushed to Genevieve, as the two of them changed for dinner. Tonight would be the first Challant family meal at Place Dauphine in more than three months, and Charles Père had insisted on formality to mark the occasion. 'Rolling hills, and dry-stone walls, and the prettiest little villages dotted about everywhere.'

'My idea of hell,' observed Gen, but not without affection. Although she hadn't missed Renée's moral lectures, she had missed her sister's kind, steady presence, and was longing to talk to her properly about Wilhelm and how divine he was.

'Charlotte and I were supposed to go back to London weeks ago,' Renée went on, fiddling with the clasp on her pearl necklace. 'But her father was worried after the bombings, so we ended up staying longer. Which was fine with me, although to be honest I did feel a little bit guilty as it's all hands on deck at the Foreign Office now, what with the threat to Poland and . . .'

'Hold on,' Genevieve interrupted. 'Bombings? What bombings? I know I'm not as up on politics as you, Ren, but surely Germany hasn't started dropping bombs?'

'Not *Germany*,' Renée rolled her eyes. 'The IRA.'

'The who?'

'The Irish separatists? Come on, Gen, you must have heard of them. They bombed two tube stations in London. It was all over the papers.'

'Not in Megève it wasn't,' said Genevieve, smoothing down the skirts of her elegant black evening dress and applying a swipe of fierce red lipstick. 'I do wish you'd been with us, Ren,' she gushed, all talk of bombing forgotten in an instant. 'We had the most marvellous Christmas and New Year. Honestly I don't know where to begin, there's so much to tell you.'

'Well I'm longing to hear it all,' Renée smiled. 'Although perhaps not right this second. You know what a fuss Papa will make if we're late for dinner.'

It was a relief to see Gen looking so happy for once. Last summer, at Beaulieu, her drinking had been bad, but her sorrows had resolutely refused to drown. Renée had tried to talk to her about it, but even sober Genevieve found it hard to articulate the root of her sadness. There was the familiar soup of anger towards Papa, romantic disappointments and a general sense of being without direction in her life. And yet, to Renée's frustration, her older sister never seemed willing to take any action of her own to change any of these things.

Renée herself had long ago realized that if she wanted to lead life on her own terms, she would need to do so largely without financial help from their father. The good news was that as long as one was willing to forego certain material luxuries, this really wasn't a problem. True, Papa had shouted a bit when she informed him she had no wish to marry. That it wasn't the suitors he was proposing, but the 'entire institution' she rejected. But once that tricky conversation had been navigated, the rows had quickly ended. As Renée had tried to explain to Genevieve, you can't fight an enemy who won't engage. But the two sisters had always been very different. Since their mother's death, it sometimes seemed as if 'engaging' with Papa had become Genevieve's raison d'être. Father and daughter oscillated between bouts of outright conflict, and a brooding, uneasy 'cold war' that took a toll on the whole family. And yet while Genevieve chose to remain under her father's roof, and on his payroll, it was clear to them all that there was only ever going to be one winner.

Once the formality of grace was over and the wine was poured, dinner quickly turned into a loud and raucous affair. Ines and

Charles Fils both forgot about their exhaustion after their long journey, so thrilled was everyone to see Renée again, and even Charles Père seemed relaxed for once, pleased to be back home in Paris and with all of his children around the table. The new chef at Place Dauphine had also excelled himself and everyone agreed that tonight's food was a triumph: canard à l'orange that melted on the tongue, creamy pommes de terres dauphinoise, homemade ratatouille and a cheeseboard the likes of which none of them had seen in months.

'In Yorkshire all you get is Wensleydale,' Renée complained. 'It's the local cheese. It's white and crumbly and tastes a bit of lemons.'

'Lemons?' Charles Père looked suitably aghast.

'Yes, you know. *Tangy*,' Renée elaborated. 'You might be offered a bit of cheddar if you're lucky, but that's it. No brie. No Roquefort. No Époisses.'

They all agreed that, when it came to food, the English were savages.

'The things they do to their côtes de boeuf – it's enough to make you weep,' observed Genevieve. 'Although to be fair, I'm not sure the cheeses in Megève were much better. Unless you like chevre. Or that awful nutty goo the Swiss go in for.'

'They put beer in it,' said Charles Fils. 'In the fondue. I've seen it.'

Ines sat quietly watching her family as they exchanged banter around the table. She couldn't remember the last time she'd seen everyone so happy in one another's company. Especially Papa. He'd become irritable and tense towards the end of their time in Megève, after David left. But the return to Paris, and Renée coming home, seemed to have brought him back to life. It made a nice change to see him opening bottle after bottle of vintage Bourgogne rouge and laughing along with everyone, even Genevieve. Every now and then he would steal a glance in Ines's direction and give her one of his special smiles; the ones that had always been just that bit warmer and more loving than those he bestowed on her siblings. Even now, at nineteen, she felt a warm glow, basking in her father's approval.

As the cheese plates were cleared away and bowls brought up from the kitchen for dessert, the conversation turned to business, and to Charles Fils's new role.

'Your brother will be working closely with our bankers as we move more confidently into the hospitality sector,' Charles Père announced proudly to the table in general. 'In a year or two, I expect to be out of residential property altogether and focusing exclusively on hotels. So I'll need Charles to be up to speed.'

'I won't let you down, Papa,' said Charles, positively beaming with pride.

Genevieve pulled a sour face, but to Renée's relief said nothing to dampen the mood.

'Ines's beau, David Walton's got the right idea,' Charles Père added, nodding approvingly in Ines's direction as he refilled his wine glass. 'More accessible, mid-priced hotels, like the ones David's been building in the States. That's the future. We had some very interesting discussions about it in Megève.'

'Your beau?' Renée raised an inquisitive eyebrow at Ines. 'Why has no one told me about this?'

'Because there's nothing to tell,' Ines blushed heavily. 'David Walton's not my *beau*, Papa.'

'Well, well now, you know what I mean,' muttered Charles Père, brushing aside her objection.

'The two of them were thick as thieves over New Year,' Genevieve told Renée in a stage whisper, amused by Ines's discomfort.

'And you should have seen her writing to him on the train yesterday,' Charles Fils piled in, 'scribbling away, page after page.'

'He's a friend,' insisted Ines. 'People do write letters to friends, you know.'

But none of her siblings were having it. 'Oh, give over, Ines,' said Charles. 'He's obviously going to propose eventually, once all this talk of war dies down.'

At the mention of war, the tone around the table shifted.

'*If* it dies down,' said Renée.

'It will,' Charles Fils insisted confidently.

Renée shook her head. 'You're being naïve. You don't honestly think Hitler's going to stop at Sudeten, do you?'

For once, Ines was glad to let the conversation swing back to politics. Anything to move away from the topic of her romantic life. These moments of family togetherness and harmony were both rare and precious. Ines gathered them to her closely, like jewels sewn into the hem of a coat. Because who knew when the next precious moment would be? When they would all be together, and happy, again?

Perhaps not for a long, long time.

The rest of Renée's visit flew by. She spent most of it with Genevieve, whose life seemed to consist of nothing but leisure, affording her endless hours free to stroll along the snowy banks of the Seine or huddle over *chocolats chauds* in little cafés with her sister. Renée would listen patiently while Gen wittered on and on and *on* about Wilhelm, and how utterly perfect he was in every respect. Privately, Renée worried about how a romance with a serving German soldier, albeit a reluctant one, was ever going to progress.

'Take care of yourself, love,' said Renée, kissing Gen on both cheeks as she got into the car that would take her to Calais before her journey by boat back to England. Genevieve was the only one there to see her off. Charles and Papa were both at work and had said their goodbyes last night, and Ines had taken off right after breakfast, disappearing into the city on some mysterious errand as she seemed to do most days.

'And keep an eye on Ines for me.'

'I'll do my best,' said Gen, smiling bravely.

She was desperately sad to see Renée go. Having her here had eased the loneliness she felt without Wilhelm and filled the emptiness of her days. What on earth she was going to do with herself through the long, dull months that stretched ahead between now and Beaulieu, she had no idea.

'Don't stay away so long this time!' she shouted, waving

frantically as the Daimler pulled sedately through the mansion gates.

Renée smiled and waved back. Then she was gone.

At first the quiet in the house was awful. But it didn't last long.

Just a few days after Renée's return to London, Charles Père burst into the salon one morning, waving a piece of paper in his hand furiously.

'Where's your sister?' he bellowed at Genevieve.

'Which one?' asked Gen coolly, putting aside her novel and feigning insouciance as she met her father's angry gaze. The truth was that Papa's dark moods frightened her. But she'd rather die than let him know it.

'Don't be flippant,' he snapped back at her. 'You know very well which one. Ines. Where is she?'

'I have no idea,' said Gen, truthfully.

'So help me, Genevieve, if you don't tell me where she is . . .'

Charles Challant's face was livid red and his eyes bulged with rage as he loomed over his eldest daughter's chair. Despite herself, Genevieve flinched. Memories of that long ago afternoon in Beaulieu came flooding back to her, unbidden. Overhearing her parents arguing and walking in to find her father with his arm raised and her mother cowering, just like she was now.

'Papa,' she swallowed, holding her ground. 'I'm telling the truth. I don't know where Ines is. She'd left the house before I got up this morning.'

'Well the *second* she gets back, you send her to me,' Charles grunted, taking a step back. 'D'you understand. The *second*!'

Gen nodded mutely. It occurred to her that, beneath his anger, Papa seemed afraid too. She wanted to ask him what had happened, but he was clearly in no mood for questions. She couldn't imagine what Ines could have said or done to elicit so visceral a reaction.

Once Charles Père had stormed out, and she'd heard the door of his study slam shut behind him, Genevieve tiptoed into

154

the hallway and picked up the telephone.

'I can't talk now, Gen,' said Charles Fils, sounding utterly miserable on the other end of the line. 'Papa's apoplectic.'

'I know, I just saw him,' said Gen. 'He came home, looking for Ines.'

'Is she there?'

'No, thank God. Papa honestly looked as if he might kill her. I've never seen him so angry. What's this about, Charles? What's she done?'

A long sigh echoed down the line. 'David Walton proposed to her and she turned him down.'

Gen gasped. 'What? When?'

'More than a month ago, apparently. David proposed in Megève before he left.'

'And Ines never said anything?'

'Not a word,' said Charles. 'The first inkling any of us had was this morning, when a letter arrived for Papa from Walton. According to him, Ines said at the time that she'd think it over. But just over a week ago, she finally wrote and refused him. Said that she considered him a friend and was flattered and all that guff, but that she wasn't in love with him and she didn't want to live in America.'

'That must have been the letter she was writing to him on the train, with you?'

'So it seems.'

'My goodness, she's a dark horse,' said Gen admiringly. 'Good for her.'

Charles let out a mirthless laugh. 'I don't think that's how Papa sees it!'

'No,' admitted Genevieve. 'But *you* think she made the right choice, don't you Charles? If she really didn't love him?'

Charles paused for a moment. 'Yes,' he said eventually. 'If she really didn't love him, I suppose she did. But as far as Papa's concerned, Ines has made a fool of him, and you know how much he hates that. It was clear from Walton's letter that he assumed Papa already knew.'

155

Hanging up, Genevieve let out a slow exhale. Poor Ines. She must have been too frightened to break the news. The rest of the siblings had all clashed with their father over the years, and borne the brunt of his occasional righteous rages. But Ines had always been the good girl and his obvious favourite. She was also loyal to a fault, and had never defied him before, at least not that Gen could remember.

The reckoning when she finally got home tonight was going to be brutal. But it had to be faced. They must all brace themselves.

But Ines didn't come home.

Not that night. Not the next.

'Should we call the police, Papa?'

Charles Fils sat in the corner armchair in his father's study, wringing his hands anxiously.

'At some point we have to,' urged Gen, pacing back and forth.

Behind his desk, stony-faced, Charles Père said nothing. But beneath the neutral façade, his emotions were swinging wildly between anger, sadness and fear.

It wasn't like Ines to run off. That much was certainly true. Terrible images ran through his head: Ines hurt, or injured or under some sort of threat. Kidnapped, perhaps? These things did happen, after all, in very wealthy families. But then no one had approached him for a ransom. And surely it was far more likely that Ines was actually safe and well, hiding out at a friend's apartment, too ashamed to come home after she'd lied to him and betrayed him in such an underhand, unconscionable manner about David Walton?

Every time he thought about that, and Walton's letter, his wounded pride took over, and worry once again morphed into rage.

A knock on the door surprised all three of them.

Monsieur Cardin, the butler, approached Charles Père's desk gravely.

'A telegram for you, sir.' He bowed deferentially, offering his master a silver tray bearing a nondescript brown envelope.

'Thank you, Cardin. You may go.'

Charles Fils and Genevieve held their breath as their father cut open the envelope, removing the single folded sheet within. They watched in silence while he read it.

'Well?' Genevieve spoke first, unable to contain herself any longer. 'Is it from her, Papa? Is it from Ines?'

With trembling hands, Charles Père lowered the telegram. A single tear streaked its lonely way down his cheek, dropping onto the paper. It was the first time either Gen or Charles Fils had ever seen him cry.

'Oh God, Papa, what's happened?' Charles Fils blurted, panicked. 'Is she . . . Is she dead?'

'She is to me.'

Standing up slowly, Charles Père handed his son the telegram and left the room.

'Show me!' Genevieve demanded. Leaning over her brother's shoulder, she read the telegram for herself.

'In England. STOP,' it began.

'Married. STOP.

'Will telephone soon. STOP.

'Forgive me. STOP.'

And then Ines had signed off.

Mrs Hector Gunn.

CHAPTER SIXTEEN

London, England, September 1939

'Heavens, Ren, you look like a drowned rat.'

Charlotte Mortimer put down her newspaper and dashed to the front door of the flat she and Renée shared in Bayswater.

'Leave the umbrella in the hall,' she suggested, helping to peel her friend out of a Macintosh that was more water than fabric. 'And you'd better give those shoes to me. I'll see if I can dry them next to the heater.'

Renée allowed herself to be helped. Removing her socks, she wrung them out like dishcloths over the kitchen sink. 'Oh, disgusting!' laughed Charlotte.

Somehow Charlotte managed to make everything fun, even the dismal English weather. A week after Germany's dramatic invasion of Poland, and three days since Britain, Poland and France had all declared themselves at war, it seemed appropriate that London's usual 'scattered showers' should have taken a turn for the apocalyptic.

'Any news updates?' Renée asked, glancing at the copy of *The Times* Charlotte had left on the tiny kitchen table. She'd left for work at the Foreign Office before dawn this morning, and hadn't had a second to look at the papers.

'Not really,' said Charlotte, turning on one bar of the rickety heater they had in the living room and setting Renée's shoes down a few inches in front of it to steam-dry. 'I'm waiting for the wireless news at six.'

Tall, and what the English called 'big-boned', Charlotte

had a lovely, open, round face, the highlight of which were her dazzling, cornflower-blue eyes. She possessed a certain strong, womanly beauty, at least in Renée's eyes.

'Did *you* hear anything new, at work?' Charlotte asked. Her own job at Christie's auction house, where she and Renée had first met, was a hotbed of gossip, but wasn't exactly at the cutting edge of world affairs. Renée's job at the FO put her at the very heart of things.

'Nope,' Renée called back from their shared bedroom, changing into a dry skirt and blouse. 'No one tells me anything. I'm only a lowly translator.'

Charlotte cut them both a slice of malt loaf, spreading each thinly with margarine while the kettle boiled for tea. 'I got a long letter from Dad today,' she told Renée. 'I'll show you later. And this came for you.'

She handed Renée an envelope postmarked Cornwall, with a knowing look.

'From the runaway, I assume?'

'I assume,' said Renée. She and Ines were both 'runaways' in their father's eyes. Although thanks to her shock elopement with the rather shady-sounding Mr Gunn, Ines had definitely assumed the mantle of the family's 'black sheep', relieving both Renée and Genevieve of that burden.

'I hope she's all right.' Renée anxiously sliced open the letter with a butter knife. 'I'm not sure I could bear it if she'd got herself into any more trouble.'

Both Renée and Genevieve had corresponded spor-adically with Ines since her secret wedding and subsequent decampment to the English countryside with her unsuitable new husband. On the positive side, she did appear to be deliriously happy. Each letter overflowed with gushing praise for Gunn, and childish delight for the 'perfectly sweet' cottage they were living in down in the West Country.

'I never knew what I wanted to be before,' Ines had written to Renée over the long summer. 'I always felt sure I had a purpose, some sort of destiny that was waiting for me. I just never knew what it was. But I do now. I love being his wife, Ren!

I love it more than anything, ever. Our life here, our little garden. I long for you to see it all . . .'

Less positively, having received grudging forgiveness from Charles Fils for the sneaky way she and Gunn had gone about things, Ines seemed to be building up hope that their father would also eventually 'come around' to her new husband. But that was never going to happen.

'Papa will never forgive her,' Genevieve had told Renée. Still stuck living in the belly of the beast at Place Dauphine, Gen bore daily witness to their father's fury and wounded pride. 'Never. We're not even allowed to speak Ines's name at home. Charles mentioned her in passing the other day, quite by accident, and Papa literally got up and stormed out of the room.'

Renée could picture the scene, and it broke her heart. To think that Papa's stubbornness and need to control should clash so violently with Ines's open-hearted impetuosity that he would risk losing her forever. It was a tragedy, really. A certain degree of anger on their father's side was understandable. But the depth of bitterness that Genevieve described went far beyond that. Like a wounded lion, brooding over his injured paw, Charles Père was at his most vicious when hurt.

'They've bought geese.' Renée smiled nostalgically as she read Ines's letter. Thankfully it contained no further drama, and was full of domestic trivia.

'I love geese,' said Charlotte, pouring the tea.

'Me too,' said Renée. 'We used to have them at Beaulieu. Monsieur Martin, who ran the farm, bought a whole flock of them the summer my mother died. Ines used to help me look after them.'

Reaching across the table, Charlotte laid a comforting hand over Renée's. It was a frightening time, what with the shadow of war hanging over them. But it must be that much harder for Renée, far away from home and with her family scattered.

Entwining her fingers with Charlotte's, Renée squeezed gratefully. She didn't know where she'd be without Charlotte and the little cocoon they'd made for themselves in Bayswater. She wouldn't trade their poky rooms with the creaky boiler and

160

linoleum floors for all the grandeur of Place Dauphine, or the luxury of Megève or Beaulieu.

If home was where the heart was, then Charlotte Mortimer had become Renée's home.

Gunn watched with wry amusement as Ines attempted to herd their six geese towards their coop, really just a garden shed with a makeshift wooden ramp.

'I thought you said you'd done this before?'

'I have,' Ines puffed, red-cheeked and sweating as she attempted to steer the noisy, flapping birds in one, consistent direction. 'I'd just forgotten how stupid geese could be. And you could help instead of just sitting there!'

Hopping down from the fence, Gunn covered one side of the garden path while Ines took the other. Between them they managed to wrangle the squawking birds into the coop and close the sliding doors. Heavy thunder and lightning were expected tonight, and it wouldn't do to have the geese taking fright and disappearing off around the village. They'd only had the birds a week and already two grumpy neighbours had knocked on their door, complaining about the noise.

Ines blushed, catching him looking at her as she brushed the dried mud and feathers off the front of her yellow Liberty-print dress.

'What?'

'Nothing,' said Gunn. But desire made the word catch in the back of his throat, and he wondered if she knew how much he wanted her.

Her pretty dress was teamed with black rubber Wellington boots and a pair of old canvas gardening gloves. But even hot, flustered and dressed like a farm hand, Ines was undeniably lovely, all glowing skin and high, heaving breasts, with her pale pink lips puckered into the most exquisite pout.

'I was just thinking how badly I want to kiss you.'

'Go on, then,' said Ines, sliding into his arms.

It was strange, Gunn reflected, to feel so lucky and happy

when so much of what he'd planned and hoped for had gone so spectacularly wrong. He was supposed to be getting richer, not poorer. For all her undeniable charm and beauty, Gunn had set his sights on Ines Challant because she was a wealthy heiress, and one still young and naïve enough to be convinced into marrying purely for love. Of course, he knew that old man Challant wouldn't approve of the match and that he'd have an uphill climb proving himself as a son-in-law. Especially given the elopement. But he'd never really believed Julia Valaperti's dire warnings about Charles Père's 'ruthless' nature, and certainly hadn't expected that Ines's father would cut her off completely in such a harsh, brutal fashion.

With each passing day of their marriage, however, it became clearer to Gunn, if not to Ines, that Charles Challant had no intention of forgiving or forgetting. 'Without a penny' turned out to be the literal truth in Ines's case. Not only had she brought no Challant money to their union – not a bean – but the very fact of that union meant that Gunn was effectively cut off from what had been *his* primary source of income ever since his father died: namely, squiring wealthy, older women around the various hotspots of Europe. All of which left them in a distressing financial no man's land.

True, Gunn was now a champion downhill skier, a 'job' of sorts. But he couldn't support himself, still less a wife, on prize money from racing. Not least because the outbreak of war had put a temporary end to competitive skiing, or sport of any kind, in Europe. As of this moment, Gunn had no idea how he was going to keep supporting his mother and pay this winter's gas bill at the ramshackle cottage he and Ines were renting in a little hamlet on the banks of the Tamar, never mind support the pair of them for the rest of their lives.

And yet he felt happier than he had since he was a boy, since before his father died.

Falling hopelessly in love with his young bride had never been part of the plan. But that was what had happened. It was supposed to have been the other way round. The innocent, ingenue Ines should have become besotted with *him*, the worldly, experienced playboy. And she was. It was just that Gunn hadn't imagined himself to be capable of similar intense, uncontrollable feelings. Of adoring somebody so much that the joy of being with them almost felt like pain.

His attraction was about much more than Ines's looks. Every day she surprised him: with her sensitivity, her intelligence, her love of nature and her uncanny ability to make every space she occupied beautiful. With clever use of paint and some cheap fabric offcuts from a local haberdasher, she had immediately set about transforming their dour cottage into a cosy haven of pattern, colour and light. Gunn had never pictured himself living in such a feminine environment, full of exotic flower prints and with images of birds of paradise stencilled onto ceilings and walls. But Ines's creativity was an uncontainable part of her happiness, and for that reason alone he loved it. Most unexpected of all, though, was her cheerful willingness to accept the material privations of their present situation and to turn her hand to any sort of work, however unfamiliar or menial. Astonishingly for a young woman with her upbringing, there wasn't a spoiled or privileged bone in Ines's body. Indeed, she appeared to want nothing in life beyond her new husband's love and affection.

Apart, perhaps, for the return of her father's love and affection. Sadly, Gunn suspected that that was going to be a very tall order indeed, and one that might not be in his power to deliver.

At least they had their love for each other. That made lots of things easier, but it made other things exponentially harder. Things like the war, for example, and the prospect of Gunn going off to fight.

'Come for a walk with me.'

Grabbing her hand he tugged her in the direction of the lane that curved past the front of their rented cottage.

'Now?' Ines glanced up sceptically at the darkening sky, already pregnant with bruised, steel-grey storm clouds. 'The heavens are about to open. And I need to make supper.'

'We'll make it a short one, then,' insisted Gunn. 'Come on.'

He led her across the lane to the stile. The footpath beyond climbed up a steep scrubby hillside dotted with dandelions and thistles, that opened up at the top to a spectacular vista of rolling hills and lush pasture, all fed by the wide Tamar river as it snaked along the valley floor. There wasn't a soul out this evening. Everyone was indoors, waiting for the expected storm and glued to their radios for the latest news on the war and the Nazis' advance through Poland. Even the cattle had abandoned the open fields, lying down in huddled circles beneath the sycamore trees, some instinct warning them of the bad weather to come.

'What is it?' Ines asked, snaking her arm around Gunn's waist lovingly as they reached the top of the rise. 'What's wrong?'

They'd been married only seven months, but already she knew him so well. Gunn always broached 'difficult' conversations out on walks. The first time he'd told her about his struggles with reading, and how hard that had made it for him to find a normal job; explaining about his mother's signs of early dementia, and the pain that caused him; trying to rationalize his estrangement from his only sister Laura. All of these things had been raised while walking in the Cornish countryside, as if the walls of their little house might not be big enough to hold all the emotion he needed to express.

That was something else Ines had learned about Gunn. That he was frightened of emotion, both his own and hers. He couldn't bear it if she cried, blaming himself no matter what the cause of her tears, and viewing her sadness, or any difficult feeling, as a problem he must instantly fix.

'Nothing's wrong,' he replied awkwardly now, picking a long stem of grass out of the ground and twisting it anxiously around one of his fingers. 'But we do need to talk, my love. About this war.'

Ines took a long, steadying breath.

'You want to go, don't you?' She looked at him steadily, forcing him to meet her eye. 'You want to join up.'

He looked at her nervously. 'I think it's the right thing to do.'

164

'But why not wait until they call you? Like everybody else?' Ines asked reasonably. 'Why the rush to leave me before you have to?'

'It's not a rush to leave *you*,' he responded, anguished to hear her frame it in this way. 'I hate leaving you. You know that.'

'Why, then?' Ines refused to let him off the hook. 'Why now? Why so soon?'

It was a good question. Unfortunately, Gunn himself wasn't entirely sure how to answer it. Certainly he loathed Hitler and the Nazis as much as the next man. Over the two years he'd spent with Julia Valaperti, he'd travelled extensively in Europe and brushed up against fascist ideologies first hand and often enough to know that he found them utterly repulsive.

But he was honest enough to know that moral outrage and an innate sense of patriotism weren't the only reasons he felt compelled to put himself in harm's way. War meant adventure. It meant risk, danger, excitement, the unknown. Gunn was enough of his father's son to feel the call of those sirens, and to yearn for each one of them. More pragmatically, war also meant opportunity. The chance to reinvent himself. Stuck in England with a wife he had no means of supporting, no immediate prospects of advancement and no plan was not an appealing prospect, and was already taking a toll on Gunn's self-esteem. Proving himself in battle would certainly tick that box, and might also redeem him in the eyes of the world – perhaps even, one day, in the eyes of his father-in-law.

'I'll have to go eventually,' he told her now, circling her waist with his hands and holding on to her as she tried to walk away. 'If I did it now, it would be on my own terms. My father's old regiment have said they'll take me . . .'

'You mean you've written to them already?' Ines spun around, taken aback. 'Without even discussing it with me?'

Gunn at least had the decency to look guilty.

'Why ask me now, then, hm? If it's already done?'

'It's not done, as such,' he stammered.

'Clearly my opinion counts for nothing with you,' she hissed.

She was angry. Furious, in fact. She'd given up her life, her country, her family for him! She'd followed him here, to *his* country, without a word of complaint, jumping with both feet into this alien life willingly. And now he was just going to up and leave her here, alone? Despite herself she felt tears starting to sting her eyes.

'Ines, darling . . .'

'Don't you "darling" me!'

Before she even knew she was doing it she'd launched herself at him, fists flying, and began to pummel him anywhere she could reach, his chest, his arms. Gunn let it happen, allowing her to exhaust herself, sobbing and hitting till she had no energy left. Only when she reached up to try to claw his face did he catch hold of her hands.

'Please, Ines. I love you.'

Their frightened eyes met. And like the flip of a switch, blows turned to kisses, their lips pressing wildly and desperately together. Scooping her up into his arms like a ragdoll, Gunn laid her gently down on the grass in the lee of a clump of blackthorn bushes. Peeling her dress up over her head, he gazed down for a moment at her perfect, soft body and her heartbroken, angry face. Never in his life had he wanted someone more.

He made love to her as the heavens began to open, hot, warm summer rain pouring down on their heaving entwined bodies, like a blessing. Or maybe an absolution?

'I love you.' His breath was on her neck, warm and wonderful. Closing her eyes, Ines tried desperately to sear this moment into her heart and mind, to capture it forever. Shuddering to climax with ridiculous ease, her hands gripped tightly to his thick blond hair, while her mind began to race. How could she hold on to him for longer? What could she do to make him stay?

For a long time, Ines had believed she would never recover from her mother's death. That something inside her had been irretrievably broken. But somehow, she *had* recovered. She had survived and rebuilt her shattered heart. Not as it was before, though. The heart that emerged from that devastating grief was quite different to the carefree, innocent heart of her early childhood. It was stronger, and harder, a magnificent thing. And like a fool she had given it to Gunn, handed it over in a love-drunk stupor.

I can't do it twice, she thought, as they got back into their rain-soaked clothes and raced back down the hill together, hand in hand. *I can't rebuild myself again.*

She knew that nothing she said or did would stop Gunn from going off to fight eventually. But she was determined to make him wait until he was called up. It might only buy her a few months, or even weeks. But every minute, every second was precious, and Ines wasn't going to give up without a fight.

Please God, let him stay with me, she prayed as they reached the cottage. *At least until Christmas.*

In a hotel room in the tenth arrondissement, close to the Gare du Nord, Genevieve was also praying. Although in her case, the spiritual moment was enhanced by both a dry, warm bed and a deeply satisfying, post-coital Gitane.

'You'd better not get yourself killed,' she instructed Wilhelm, who was sprawled out beside her on his back, naked and a little shell-shocked.

The hotel, and the sex, had both been Genevieve's idea. Not that he was complaining. Far from it. It just wasn't how he'd envisaged their first time making love. Knowing that in a few short hours he must catch the first of several trains to rejoin his unit in Germany. And that from then on, presumably, he would be fighting and on the 'wrong' side, unable to be with Genevieve until the whole mess was over. It felt wrong, somehow, taking her to bed when he knew he was in no position to offer her anything, except his love.

'I'm not planning on it,' he told her. 'You will keep an eye on Grandmère for me, while I'm gone?'

'Of course,' Gen reassured him. She already adored Granny Noiret, a feisty, ancient crone of a woman with a penchant for gin rummy whose terminal lung cancer was the reason Wilhelm had been granted compassionate leave to come to Paris in the first place. The doctors had given her days at most. 'I'll visit her every day. And I promise I won't leave Paris until after the funeral.'

Wilhelm turned to face her, propping himself up on one elbow.

'Have you spoken to your father yet? About moving back down to Beaulieu?'

Gen nodded, stubbing out her cigarette in the ashtray on her bedside table with unexpected viciousness.

'He doesn't give a fig where I go, as long as I'm out of his hair.'

'I'm sure that's not true,' said Wilhelm, although they both knew it was. Ever since Ines's elopement, Charles Père had withdrawn into an increasingly sullen, embittered world of his own. Charles Fils, desperate to get away from the stultifying atmosphere at Place Dauphine, was already threatening to join up. Genevieve had no intention of being the sole sibling left in Paris with only her father for company.

Her own personal safety wasn't a consideration. Like most French families, the Challants considered it impossible that Hitler would succeed in invading French territory, believing themselves comprehensively protected by the well-fortified Maginot Line. Wilhelm had said nothing to Genevieve directly, but privately he was by no means so sure that Paris would remain safe and was pleased that Genevieve would be leaving the city for the quieter backwater of Beaulieu.

'At least you'll be able to work on your play in peace,' he told her, lovingly pushing a stray wisp of hair away from her eyes.

'That's true.' She smiled gratefully. Not since Aurelian had anyone encouraged her with her writing, or taken her remotely seriously as an artist. Dear God, when she thought about Aurelian now! About how in love with him she'd been! It was embarrassing, really. He'd never been half the man that Wilhelm was. No sooner had he got married than he'd completely abandoned his own literary ambitions, accepting a job with his father-in-law's company and enthusiastically embracing the meaningless, comfortable, bourgeois life he had once claimed to abhor. A hypocrite, that's what Aurelian was. A hypocrite and a coward.

Wilhelm, meanwhile, radiated integrity and honesty and *truth*. He might not be creative himself, but he admired creativity in others, and encouraged it in Genevieve out of love and respect for her. That was something she had never experienced before, and hadn't even realized she needed until she met him.

Tracing a finger slowly down his cheek and along the line of his jaw, like a blind person trying to imprint the image of his face through touch, she steeled herself not to cry. But inside, her heart was breaking. What would she do without him?

'I don't want to let you go,' she whispered.

'You're not letting me go,' he replied gruffly, kissing her with painful urgency. 'We're not letting each other go.'

'But . . .'

'It won't be forever, Genevieve.'

Won't it?

'I'll hold on to you. You'll hold on to me.'

She nodded bravely, closing her eyes, willing herself to believe it.

'And when it's all over, we'll both come back here to Paris and pick up where we left off.'

She clung on to his words like a mantra. The war would not be forever. They would find their way back to each other.

They had to.

CHAPTER SEVENTEEN

Paris, France, December 1939

Charles Challant dutifully sang out the last verse of the ancient Christmas carol, his resonant bass voice merging with those of the rest of the congregation.

> *Il est né le divin enfant*
> *Chantons tous son avenement.*

There was a defiant joy to both the singing and the thundering pipes of the organ in the modest church of Sainte Marguerite, just a short stroll from Place Dauphine, this Christmas morning. People were determined to continue as normal, with their carols and *sapins de Noel*, their *Reveillon* feasts of duck and prunes wrapped in bacon, and their gaudily wrapped *cadeaux*. And yet there was no escaping the fact that this was a Christmas like no other. Europe was at war, and although France herself remained peaceful, Paris in December 1939 was a completely different city to the one that had celebrated these same traditions last year. British Tommies wandered the streets in uniformed packs, Christmas shopping and admiring the sights alongside their French comrades. The Allied troops were welcome, and yet their presence was in itself a reminder of the danger that lurked just beyond France's borders.

Closing his eyes, Charles inhaled the sweet, heady smell of the incense swinging from the priest's chasuble and tried to shake the deep melancholy that seemed to have settled over his heart in recent weeks like poured concrete. It wasn't only the outside world that had changed. The very fabric of the Challant family, once such a tight flock, seemed to be disintegrating. Perhaps, in truth, that had been the case ever since Clotilde's death. But for Charles to be spending Christmas in Paris at all was jarring, and to be spending it alone, without any of his children, felt desolate.

Ines, he still couldn't bring himself to think about, after her devastating betrayal. He had loved her so desperately, so profoundly. Of course he'd known that she must marry one day, and leave him. But he'd expected to orchestrate that wedding, when it came. To select the groom, decide on the timing, and direct the path his daughter's life would take. After everything he'd done for her, for all his family – was that too much to ask?

But instead, ungratefully and deceitfully, Ines had abandoned him, just like the others. Renée remained in London, apparently engaged in important war work, but increasingly distant from the rest of her family. Genevieve had written to say she was settled and happy at Beaulieu and had no plans to return to the city. And Charles Fils, who had joined up in October, was spending his ten days of leave in Megève skiing with old friends.

To give the boy his due, he had asked if his father might join him there. But Charles hadn't the energy. If Paris felt changed, he knew that Megève was unrecognizable. That something deep in the marrow of the mountain town he so loved was already infected and turning rotten. His friends the Rothschilds had recently decamped to Switzerland, fleeing a growing tide of antisemitism within France that worried Charles deeply. The idea that a Frenchman might feel compelled to take Swiss citizenship out of fear of his own fellow countrymen appalled and shocked the patriotic Charles. It seemed yet another sign of the pernicious influence of Nazi ideology, which seemed to be sweeping through Europe even faster and more effectively than Hitler's jackbooted army.

'The mass is ended.' The priest's familiar words rang out, jolting Charles temporarily out of his depressing reflections. 'Go in peace to love and serve the Lord. And a very Happy Christmas to you all.'

Buttoning his heavy overcoat, Charles hurried out of the church, eager to avoid the exchanging of festive pleasantries with anyone he knew. While the Christmas bells pealed out from Sainte Marguerite's plain wooden belfry, he made his way on foot through the frosty streets of Charonne, back to the lonely comfort of Place Dauphine.

'Some lunch, sir?'

Lisette, one of the newer housemaids and part of the skeleton staff still working on Christmas Day, took his coat and hat. As a younger man, Charles would have noticed the girl's high cheekbones, her slender waist and the pretty turn of her calves as she walked. But these things were all invisible to him now. Or at best they existed as shadows, of pleasures once felt but no longer savoured, even in memory.

'*Non, merci.*' Charles waved her away. After last night's traditional Christmas feast, and this morning's brooding, his stomach felt as sour as his spirits. 'I'll be in my study for the rest of the day. Unless I ring I am not to be disturbed.'

Christmas cards already lined every shelf and mantelpiece, but a new, unopened stack had appeared on Charles's desk. With a sigh, he began to open them. As a pillar of three communities, in Paris, Megève and Beaulieu, he was inundated every year with *Joyeux Noel* wishes from countless local tradesmen, civil servants and dignitaries whose names meant nothing. Clotilde had been a marvel at handling all that when she was alive. She'd remembered everybody.

After about twenty minutes, almost at the bottom of the pile, Charles slit open an innocuous-looking brown envelope and gave a cursory glance to the card, a cheap, gaudy representation of an angel blowing a trumpet.

Without interest he opened it.

Spidery, looped handwriting filled one side of the card, a script he recognized immediately. The other side was blank, unsigned. With a heavy heart, Charles read the single-line inscription:

Je sais ce que tu as fait.

172

I know what you did.

He'd received several of these 'notes' over the years since that fateful summer of 1928. None were signed, and none overtly threatening. But the malicious intent of the author was clear. This was psychological warfare, the gradual, insidious tightening of a screw. And it worked. Charles felt his blood run cold and the small hairs on the back of his neck shiver upright, like ears of corn blowing in a suddenly chill wind.

Would he never be free of it?

Picking up the discarded envelope, he once again scanned it for clues, a name or an address. But of course there were none. Only, this time, a smudged, barely legible postmark indicating that it may have been sent from Villefranche.

A short drive from Beaulieu.

Getting unsteadily to his feet, Charles reached for the brandy decanter in the drinks cabinet behind him and poured three fingers of Rémy Martin into a cut crystal tumbler. Swirling the amber liquid around, he watched it for a few moments before draining it in one, long gulp, tears stinging his eyes as the burning sensation swept over his tongue and down his throat, before settling like a fireball in his chest.

Refilling the glass, and slipping the hated card back into its jagged envelope, he took both upstairs. Clotilde's rooms – the private bedroom and dressing area that she'd kept, separate to their marital suite – had remained largely untouched in the decade since her death. Charles had seen Ines go in from time to time, to sit among her mother's things. Once in a blue moon, Genevieve or Renée might do the same. Perhaps the printed silk screens of exotic birds or the kidney-shaped dressing table beneath the window, still covered with perfume bottles and trinket boxes, brought Clotilde back to her daughters in some way? But Charles Père never entered the shrine. It was too painful, even now.

Like his children, Charles missed and grieved for his wife. But his was a grief interlaced with other, torturous emotions. Guilt. Anger. Frustration. Together they had combined over the years to form a thick, bitter stew. Yes, he had done wrong.

He had made mistakes. Sinned. But hadn't he tried to make amends?

And then there was the secret that haunted him, all these years later. The truth of what really happened that stormy night, when Bernard died in the grounds of the bastide. A secret that Clotilde had taken to her grave – and which he'd vowed to, too.

Staring down at the hateful card in his hand, the anonymous writer's message squatting over his conscience like a fat, poisonous toad, he began to cry.

Yes, he had survived. He had defeated his enemies. He had escaped prison. He had kept hold of his reputation, and his fortune, multiplying the latter several times in the years that followed. But there were those who hated him for that.

And Charles had also suffered. Why did nobody understand that? He had lost Clotilde, for God's sake! And now Ines. He was alone, quite alone. But still some vengeful, cowardly son-of-a-whore had sent him this card, this latest reminder that he would never truly be free. At Christmas.

May you rot in hell, whoever you are.

Pressing his hand down into the softness of the bed where his wife had drawn her last breaths, Charles tried to pray. But neither the words, nor the feelings would come. It was too late for absolution. What was done could never be undone. *That* was his punishment.

So instead he rested a hand on Clotilde's pillow, sipped his cognac, and from time to time whispered her name as the soft, wet snowflakes began to fall outside the window.

At Gunn and Ines's rambling cottage in Cornwall, an infinitely happier Christmas afternoon was unfolding.

'It's a book. Four words. Third word : "the".'

Gunn shouted out guesses as their neighbour and friend, Edward Turnbull, took his turn at charades in front of the fire. The same age as Gunn, Edward was a sweet, shy man who'd inherited the large farm further up the lane. This he managed

174

almost single-handedly despite a partially paralysed leg, the result of childhood polio.

'First word: amorous?'

Edward shook his head, walking over to Ines and miming gently stroking her hair.

'Randy?' offered Gunn.

'Oh, do get your mind out of the gutter, man!' Edward reproached him grinning. 'It's "tender".'

'Oo, oo, *Tender Is the Night*!' shouted Laura, Gunn's sister, from the threadbare sofa next to the Christmas tree where she sat with their mother Edie.

'Yes!' Edward pointed at her, grinning, and flopped back into his own armchair, relieved to be no longer the centre of attention. 'That means you're up.'

After several secretive entreaties from Ines, Laura Gunn had agreed to drive over with Edie for Christmas lunch, the first thawing in Gunn family relations for several years.

'It's not about forgiving him, or sacrificing your principles,' Ines wrote, despite not fully understanding exactly what it was that Gunn and his sister had fallen out about in the first place. 'It's about being together one last time before he has to leave. It would mean so much to him, and to me.'

After much cajoling and negotiation, Ines had succeeded in keeping Gunn at home for the last few months. But on the 29th December he was finally to join his father's old regiment, the Devonshire, at a training camp in Taunton before receiving his orders sometime in the new year. Neither of them had spoken much about it since the letter came, other than to agree that they must make the most of their first married Christmas and have as jolly a time as possible. Ines had promised him a 'special' Christmas present, and Gunn had been impossibly touched when Laura telephoned a few days ago to confirm she would be joining them.

'She's a good sort, your new wife,' Laura told her brother brusquely. 'Too good for you, I daresay.'

'I agree,' said Gunn.

'But she's right about families pulling together, especially in times like these.'

After a long and boozy lunch, the centrepiece of which had been one of Ines's unfortunate geese, followed by the opening of a few modest presents around the tree, Edie's proposal of a game of charades had been eagerly seized on by everyone. But a few rounds and several sloe gins in, things had already descended into a raucous but good-natured free-for-all. Even Edie, who at intervals was clearly bewildered by proceedings, gamely shouted out guesses in between bites of Ines's home-baked macarons, which everyone pronounced infinitely tastier than boring old mince pies.

Later, while Gunn drove his mother and sister home, Ines began the washing-up in the tiny cottage kitchen, listening to the wireless news while Edward carried the dirty plates and glasses in from the sitting room.

'Can you believe they cancelled the Christmas service in Westminster Abbey?' she said, carefully drying a wine glass with a cotton tea towel.

'No.' Edward frowned. 'Why?'

'No choirboys, apparently,' said Ines. 'They've all been evacuated to the countryside.'

Edward watched his neighbour's young French wife. He hadn't known the Gunns very long, but he liked both of them. Gunn was marvellous company, full of fun and curiosity and with the sort of exciting, bohemian background that made Edward's quiet, country life seem depressingly humdrum by comparison. But it was Ines who really fascinated him. The way that she'd embraced not just marriage, but an entirely new way of life at such a young age, was impressive. Less flamboyant than her husband, she nevertheless more than matched him in intelligence, and her creative side was evidenced everywhere throughout the cottage in her artfully de-signed rooms.

'Here.' Setting down the last pile of dirty plates, Edward nudged Ines to one side. 'You wash, I'll dry. It's the least I can do after all your hospitality,' he insisted, seeing her open her mouth to protest.

'You know, I wouldn't mind having an evacuee or two here,' Ines said idly, as the news finished and the haunting opening lines

176

of 'Once in Royal David's City' filled the airwaves. 'Once Gunn's gone, the house is going to feel awfully quiet. And I love children.'

Edward caught the wistfulness of this last comment.

'Do you and Gunn plan to start a family?'

'Eventually.' She looked away shyly. 'I mean, of course, one day. We've talked about it. I think he'd like to make a bit more money first.'

'Fair enough,' said Edward.

'His secret dream . . . don't tell him I told you . . . is to earn enough eventually to be able to buy back the house that he and Laura grew up in. It's not far from here. He says it would be the most magical place to raise a family.'

'I'm sure it would,' said Edward, watching the way that Ines's eyes lit up at this fantasy. He suspected it was the children part that excited her, whereas Gunn was more focused on the grand old house part. But he kept the thought to himself.

'Anyway,' said Ines, plunging another dinner plate into the sudsy water. 'It's hardly the time to be thinking about a family now. Not with so much . . . uncertainty.'

'He'll be all right, you know,' Edward said kindly.

Ines smiled tightly, rubbing a stubborn smear of icing from a silver fork.

'Lovely cards,' Edward changed the subject, admiring the long string of brightly coloured Christmas cards that Ines had hung across the top of the kitchen window. 'I can't believe you've got so many. I suppose your family and friends in France must miss you.'

'Actually, almost all of the cards are for Gunn,' Ines replied. She said it matter-of-factly, without self-pity, but Edward nonetheless sensed an underlying sadness.

'Do *you* miss home?' he asked her.

'Sometimes,' Ines admitted. 'The thing I'm saddest about is my father. We're very close. I mean, we *were* very close,' she winced. 'But he didn't want me to marry Gunn and he hasn't spoken to me since. I'd hoped, at Christmas, you know . . .' She let the sentence tail off. 'But he didn't get in touch. Not even a card.'

'Well. These things can take time,' said Edward. 'Just look at Gunn and Laura. That was a brilliant thing you did, you know, getting everyone together today.'

Ines blushed. 'I hope Gunn was happy.'

'You're joking, aren't you?' said Edward. 'The man was beside himself with joy. Anyone could see it. You made his Christmas. And both of you made mine. Thank you so much for inviting me.'

'Don't be silly.' Ines tapped him playfully on the arm. 'We could hardly leave you up at the farm all on your own. Besides, Gunn never helps me clean up.'

'Ah. So it was all a ruse in aid of free maid services?'

'Exactly,' Ines grinned.

She loved having Edward around. Gunn was utterly perfect, but there was an intensity to being so helplessly in love, especially with the war and looming separation hanging over them, that made her grateful for the lightness and ease of another man's company. Selfishly, she was glad that the army had refused to let Edward join up, because of his leg. She knew he wanted to fight, every bit as badly as Gunn did. But the thought of having nobody to talk to when Gunn was at the front was really too awful to contemplate.

Perhaps she *would* take in an evacuee child from London?

'Would you mind?' she asked Gunn later, in bed.

With everyone gone and the cottage clean, they'd sat by the fire together, roasting chestnuts and drinking sweet tea like an old married couple. Then Gunn had led Ines upstairs, and they'd made love for hours like a young married couple, the heat from their bodies banishing the winter chill of their tiny gabled bedroom, where the cold night air seemed to seep through the walls no matter how many fires they lit.

'Hmmm? Mind what?' Gunn asked distractedly.

'Mind me taking in a city child in the new year,' Ines chided him gently. 'Haven't you heard a word I've said in the last five minutes?'

'Sorry.' Gunn reached over and pulled her closer. 'I'm afraid I was miles away.'

'No, I'm sorry.' Ines nuzzled into him. Here she was, worrying about herself and how she was going to cope at home once he'd gone. While he must be lying there, contemplating the horrors of the battlefield. 'Are you frightened?'

'Frightened?' he looked surprised. 'Of what?'

'Of going to war.'

'Nooooo.' He chuckled, kissing the top of her head as if the very idea were ridiculous. 'I wasn't even thinking about that. I drove past Maltings today,' he added after a pause. 'Once I'd taken back Laura and Ma.'

'Ah,' said Ines. 'I wondered what took you so long. That's forty minutes out of your way, isn't it?'

He nodded. 'I hadn't planned to go. But I suddenly wanted to see it again.'

'I understand,' said Ines.

The pull of a childhood home, with all its precious memories, was something she could appreciate. Par-ticularly when those memories were intimately entwined with a parent who had died. Gunn might not be afraid of going to fight consciously, but clearly his subconscious mind was anxious, leading him back to a place of safety and innocence.

He had shown Ines Maltings before right after their wedding, walking her past the house and around the walled gardens at the back, pointing out which window gave on to his childhood room. But when Ines had suggested they knock on the door and introduce them-selves to the owner, he'd been adamant in his refusal.

'I won't set foot inside,' he insisted. 'Not till the day I can buy it back. And when I do, I want Ma to be the first to walk in. It was her home more than any of ours.'

'How was it?' Ines asked him now. 'It must have been pitch black when you got there.'

'Actually, the lights were on inside,' said Gunn, 'which I wasn't expecting. It's been empty since early November, but the owner must have found a new tenant.'

'Could you see anything?'

'No,' Gunn lied. 'Not really. Not from the road.'

In fact he'd seen a Christmas tree, brightly lit, right in the bay windows of the drawing room, where his parents always used to have theirs. He'd seen children flitting back and forth, a boy and a girl, and the shadowy figures of their parents, the man tall and animated, the woman seated close to the fire.

He had stood and watched from the road, freezing, his breath escaping his lips in little smoky clouds. And for the first time in more years than he could remember, he'd cried.

'I love you,' he told Ines now, kissing her.

'I love you more.'

She knew that inside his emotions were scattered. That the trip to Maltings had awakened feelings that consumed and troubled him. But she also knew that he didn't want to talk about it. Not yet. Not tonight.

Gunn held her until she fell asleep. Then he lay, staring at the ceiling, a kaleidoscope of loves and wants and wishes, past and present, rolling through his mind like a broken reel of film. Christmas, Maltings, seeing Laura again, and his mother. Here, in this house with Ines, his old life merging miraculously with his new one. It had been joyous. No question. But it had also been bittersweet.

I've been happy in this cottage, he admitted to himself. But happiness had made him complacent. There was still so much he needed to do.

Leaving to fight was an important first step. But Gunn had more than one war he needed to win.

There would be many battles ahead.

CHAPTER EIGHTEEN

Beaulieu-sur-Mer, France, November 1942

On 10 November 1942, the charade of freedom in Vichy France abruptly came to an end. Within days, German troops had fully occupied the entire south-eastern region controlled by Petain's puppet government, in retaliation for the French navy's scuttling of its own fleet off Toulon. From that winter on, nowhere in France was free of an Axis military presence.

For Genevieve, in Beaulieu, the occupation brought mixed feelings. On the one hand, like most Frenchwomen, she bitterly resented being forced to live among enemy soldiers, and to submit to the hated Nazi yoke. Hearing German spoken in the town square and cafés, lining up at the *boulangerie* behind men who, for all she knew, might have shot at her own brother or the brothers of countless friends, felt surreal and awful. But on the other hand, every one of the grey, jackbooted *boche* reminded her of Wilhelm, whose face and voice she now had difficulty calling to mind clearly, even though she thought of him every day.

At the start of the war, they'd exchanged letters. Gen had attended his grandmother's funeral in Paris as she'd promised, and had sent him long passages of her play when she first got to Beaulieu. But by early 1941, their communication had dwindled to a trickle. And by the summer of that year, it had stopped completely. Gen had learned through mutual friends from Megève that Wilhelm's battalion had been one of the scores of regiments sent to Russia. But beyond that she knew nothing. What his feelings were. Whether he still loved her. Whether he was even still alive. It was an agony of uncertainty, anxiety and loneliness. And although for a while Gen did her best to fill it with writing, and creative, positive things, by that Christmas the temptation to drink had become overwhelming.

Most of 1942 had been 'lost', Genevieve weaving in and out of a drunken state that numbed her feelings, but that also distorted time and memory. She had made a New Year's resolution to stay sober – keeping it for almost two weeks – and told herself she had to get a job. But for all her outer bravado, she lacked the confidence to go out and ask for one. Frankly, she found it hard to imagine on what basis anyone would want to hire her, with no experience, no practical skills and an education that had prepared her for nothing beyond flower arranging and throwing parties. Without that routine to hold on to, it wasn't long before, inevitably, she began to slip back into her old ways.

One particularly grey and dreary afternoon, she found herself in a café on the Place de Liberté, sipping café au lait and reading *Le Monde*, the new government-approved newspaper that occasionally reported real, unfiltered news. Beaulieu was still beautiful, even blighted by the stamp of occupation as it now was. Grey-uniformed Germans might be swarming the streets like ants, but the sea was still blue and the shuttered houses still charming as they leaned into one another like drunks, weaving up the steep hill from the harbour, their window boxes overflowing with flowers.

Glancing up, she noticed one of the German soldiers sitting a few tables away was staring at her. Not in a threatening way. Admiringly, if anything, although he looked away as soon as he realized he'd been seen and left soon after with his companions. Draining her coffee, Gen allowed herself to feel a little cheered by the attention. It was nice to be found attractive. Nice to be seen at all, in fact. She rarely left the bastide these days, and had only one or two acquaintances in town whom she saw with any regularity, and no real 'friends' in Beaulieu. She'd considered returning to Paris, if only to mitigate the loneliness. But the idea of living day to day with Papa again, having him meddle in her life – and her drinking – was not appealing. And once back at Place Dauphine, she knew it wouldn't be easy to make a second escape.

Signalling to the waitress for the bill, she reached down into her handbag and took a surreptitious swig of cognac from the small silver hip flask she carried with her everywhere. It was more out of habit than any deep need, or so she told herself. But the familiar, spreading warmth of the alcohol added to the sense of contentment she'd felt from the young soldier's fleeting interest, and she found herself smiling as the waitress returned.

'Here.' She held out a five-franc note as a tip, her unexpected happiness making her generous. 'For you.'

The girl shook her head and batted away Genevieve's hand. 'No, thank you.'

For the first time, Genevieve noticed the hostile look on her face.

'But . . . it's a tip,' she explained, confused.

'I know what it is,' the girl replied curtly. 'I don't want it. Not from a Challant.'

There was so much vitriol in the last word, Genevieve recoiled. Over the years she'd witnessed intermittent bad feeling towards her father in Beaulieu, both over the lenient treatment Charles received back when Bernard Angier died, and regarding his reputedly 'shady' finances. But the loathing had never been directed at *her*. It was like being spat at by a snake.

'What's that supposed to mean?' she demanded pugnaciously, shock and alcohol combining to turn her dismay into anger. 'If you've something to say about my family, you'd better come out and say it.'

'I've nothing to say,' the waitress snapped back, un-bowed. 'I just won't be taking your money. Good day, mademoiselle.'

The conversation was over. Genevieve had been dismissed. The smattering of other customers who'd witnessed the exchange returned to their own coffees and cakes. But although nobody said anything, Gen got the distinct impression that they had sided with the girl. That it was she, Genevieve, who'd brought awkwardness and shame into the room. She who was the problem, guilty by association. By simply being a Challant.

Pulling on her coat, she ran into the street, the brief glow of happiness she'd felt just minutes ago now thoroughly extinguished.

It astonished her to think that the townspeople's anger really ran that deep, for an event that had happened almost fifteen years ago now. An accident, for heaven's sake! And the idea that anyone would blame *her*? Well that was just awful.

On the other hand . . . perhaps she did bear some responsibility? Not directly. But her long, troubled relationship with her father had required the conscious forgetting of many things. Repressing dark memories about both her parents, and about that night. Perhaps the act of forgetting was in itself a form of collusion?

Back at the house, Gen hurried inside. It was already almost dark, and cold outside, and she had no wish to linger in the gardens where her mother's aviary used to be, the source of so much tragedy.

Heading straight to the drinks cabinet in her father's study, without even taking off her coat, Genevieve poured herself a second large brandy, followed by a third. It was years, well over a decade, since she'd thought actively about the events of 1928. About that awful summer when, piece by piece, her world had collapsed. How dare that stupid waitress, that nobody, dredge it all up again? And when Genevieve had been trying to be kind, trying to do something nice? *Putain.*

She was about to flop down onto the leather Chesterfield sofa to set about finishing the rest of the decanter, when she suddenly caught sight of her reflection in the antique gilt mirror behind her father's desk. Her hair was messy from the wind, and her cheeks still flushed from the cold walk back from town. But it wasn't that that struck her, so much as the dreadful sadness etched on her face.

I look so desolate. So old and ruined.

Was that what the soldier in the café had been staring at? Was that what Wilhelm would see when he finally came back to her? *If* he ever came back?

Genevieve knew that Renée was right. She had to find *something* to do, some meaning to her life. Charles Fils was off fighting in North Africa with the Free French. Renée had her war work in London. Even Ines was running her little smallholding somewhere in the English countryside, taking in evacuee children. All the birds of Beaulieu had flown the nest and were making their own way in the world.

All except me.

Why am I the only one with nothing?

Turning away from her reflection, Gen gazed down instead at the brandy glass in her hand. Almost imperceptibly, she noticed, it had begun to shake. A tiny tremor, starting at the wrist, spreading up through her long, bony fingers as they coiled themselves around the crystal tumbler, gripping it tightly, like the talons of an eagle wrapped around a mouse.

This was her answer. This, drink, was what made her different to her siblings. She knew it, knew it in her bones. But the knowing didn't help. Because she couldn't let it go.

It's my alpha and omega.

The root of my fear, and the cure for my fears.

The source of my weakness, and my only strength.

With tears in her eyes, Gen realized that the glass in her hand and the precious liquid it held was all that stood between her and the floodgates opening; to all the terrible memories of the past. To all the things she had forced herself to forget. To Wilhelm and her desperate, fading hope that one day, some miracle would bring him back to her.

Sinking slowly down onto the sofa, her eyes closed to hold the tears in, she raised the glass to her lips.

'To your health, old man.'

Gunn's friend Captain Arthur 'Norms' Norman took a slug from his hip flask before passing it across to the other side of the wildly bumping jeep.

'To home!' grinned Gunn, swigging gratefully. The Devonshire's 2nd Battalion had been in Malta for what felt like an eternity. Having successfully depleted the Axis's supply chain, scuppering Hitler's long-planned advance into Egypt and helping the Royal Navy's destruction of two-thirds of the Italian merchant fleet, the prospect of imminent leave felt well deserved.

Norms, who had four small sons he talked about every single day, was beside himself with delight at the thought of three whole weeks back home in Hampshire with his family. Gunn was also excited to see Ines, although a part of him always found the transition from 'soldier' to 'husband' anxiety-provoking, for reasons he could never quite define.

With the arrival of two evacuees in their Cornish cottage, Ines had also started to mention children. Gunn wanted a family, at least in theory. It went without saying that children would be a part of their future, once the war was finally over. But the more time he spent away, the harder Gunn found it to visualize himself slotting back into a quiet, domestic routine. Although he felt guilty to admit it, he loved army life and the adrenaline and excitement that came with it.

Handing back the hip flask, he reached into his pocket and pulled out the small, enamel cockatoo brooch he carried with him everywhere in a roughly sewn felt pouch. It was a replica of the one he'd pressed into Ines's hand when he left her back in Mürren, after winning the Lauberhorn. Back when he knew he loved her, but saw no path forward towards marriage or any kind of future together.

How long ago that felt now! But then, how long ago so many things felt for everyone since this nightmarish war had started. Rattling along Maltese lanes so rutted they were barely passable in summer, he realized that it now felt as much like home as anywhere.

'Thinking about your young wife, are you?' Norms asked with a wink. 'Back in your own soft bed? Don't worry, I don't need the details.'

'Good,' said Gunn. 'Because you won't be getting any.'

'As the actress *didn't* say to the bishop!' laughed Norms.

Nothing could dampen Gunn's good humour today. *And nor*

should it, he reflected. He wished he didn't always overthink things quite so much.

He was looking forward to seeing Ines. His wonderful cockatoo. Wild and un-trappable. *Beauty and brains.*

Closing his eyes, he rubbed the brooch between his fingers like a talisman as the jeep rattled on.

CHAPTER NINETEEN

Cornwall, England, November 1942

'Put that glass down. Jimmy, I mean it!' Ines shouted helplessly, as a nine-year-old boy with filthy hands and a face more freckles than skin ran towards the stairs. In his hand was a water glass containing a wolf spider – a fat, hairy monster of a thing – with which Jimmy intended to surprise his older sister, Agnes.

As thirteen-year-old Agnes had a phobia of spiders bordering on the hysterical, Ines was keen to put an end to this practical joke before it brought the house to a shrieking, deafening standstill. Especially as Renée and Charlotte were staying with them for the weekend, and poor Charlotte had already taken to her bed with a migraine.

'Jimmy! I mean it. You take that creature upstairs and you won't get a bite of rice pudding. Not one bite.'

The little boy hesitated. This was a major threat. Ines had used the very last of the delicious condensed milk on tonight's pudding, in honour of their guests. Jimmy had been salivating over the thought of it for days.

'All right,' he said grudgingly, scuffing over to Ines in his heavy lace-up boots and thrusting the unwanted glass into her hands. 'Would have been fun, though. That's the biggest one I ever caught.'

Jimmy and Ag had been living with Ines for over a year now, and she'd grown tremendously close to both of them. The first few months had been awful. Both children resented having been sent away, and Jimmy in particular decided early on that Ines was the enemy, greeting her every question or attempt at kindness with crossed arms and sullen silences. Cornwall was 'ugly', the countryside 'boring' and Ines 'a Frog' who 'shun't even 'ave been in England in the first place'.

In the end, it was this last complaint that helped Ines to build bridges with both Jimmy and his sister. She, too, was finding her way in a strange place, far away from the home she'd grown up in and everyone she loved. She knew how lonely and frightening that could be. The fact that she was so young, only ten years older than Ag, probably also helped, enabling her to step into the role of an adult sister, rather than trying to usurp their mother's place.

One weekend, to welcome Gunn home on leave, Ines had decided to stencil the entire staircase at the cottage with colourful, exotic birds as a surprise for him. She still longed for adventure, and hoped one day to explore the Andean cloud forests that her mother had told her about and that had so enchanted her as a child. But for the time being, all her hopes and dreams were confined within the four walls of this tiny cottage. Painting the birds would be some sort of release.

With nothing else to do, the children had agreed to help, and the day had proved a real turning point in their relationship. Jimmy loved that Ines didn't seem to care at all when he spilled paint on the floor, or got it on his hands and face. And Ag was simply in awe of the riot of colour and life being unleashed onto the cottage's plain, whitewashed walls.

'It's like livin' in a painting, ain't it?' she'd laughed to Ines.

'I suppose it is, in a way,' Ines smiled.

'Or a jungle,' added Jimmy. 'Or a zoo. Do you reckon Gunn will like it?'

'Course 'e will,' said Ag. 'How could anyone not like it? It's bloody marvellous.'

'How about a walk before supper? While it's still light?' Renée drifted into the kitchen, instinctively grabbing and tickling Jimmy just because he was there. In heavy, baggy slacks and a thick Aran sweater that covered every inch of her shape, Renée radiated the same calm, self-contained happiness that Ines remembered so well from her childhood. She loved having her sister here, and Renée clearly loved it too. Not just seeing

Ines, but having a chance to be in the countryside, among animals and nature and all the things she missed so keenly in her life in London.

'Ugh. I hate walks,' grumbled Jimmy, wriggling free. 'So does Ag.'

'No I don't.' Agnes appeared at the bottom of the stairs, all skinny limbs and tangled hair, a vision of unkempt beauty. 'I'd like to get outside actually. I feel like I've been cooped up all day. Oh my God. What's *that*?'

Her face blanched when she noticed the glass in Ines's hand.

'Nothing,' Ines said hurriedly, slipping on her boots and opening the door to release the spider into the garden. 'Coats on, everyone.'

Jimmy groaned. 'Do we *have* to go on a walk? It's so boring.'

'Yes!' Renée grabbed him again, making him giggle despite himself. 'We do, Mr Misery Guts. Poor Charlotte needs some peace and quiet in this house. And you can show me your camp by the river. Ines told me it's really good.'

'It is.' Jimmy's little chest swelled as his sister handed him his duffel coat. 'Oh, all right then. I s'pose I could show you,' he told Renée graciously.

They walked together across the lane and up the steep hill on the other side, frost-stiffened grass crunching beneath their feet. It was a cold day but a bright one, and as Jimmy and Agnes both raced ahead, chasing one another in circles like overexcited puppies, Renée hung back with Ines, taking it all in. Below them, the Tamar valley stretched out, grey-green and endless. And above, the fields and hills gradually began to flatten out, with clumps of bare woodland popping up at intervals, along with various old stone buildings, most in various stages of disrepair.

'It's beautiful,' Renée sighed, slipping her gloved hand into her little sister's. 'So peaceful. You must love living here.'

'I do,' Ines replied thoughtfully. 'For a while, after Gunn was called up, it was a bit *too* peaceful. But the children changed all of that.'

As if on cue, Jimmy began hurtling down the steep sides of an old Saxon burial mound, shouting like a banshee as his sister watched from below, her red hair blowing wildly in the wind.

'I'll miss them when they go,' Ines added wistfully.

'Look at you, all maternal!' Renée teased. 'I wouldn't fret too much if I were you. You and Gunn will have your own children running around soon enough.'

'Do you think so?'

The note of anxiety in Ines's voice was unexpected.

'Of course,' said Renée. 'Why? Don't you?'

Ines shrugged. 'I'm not sure. I mean, I hope so . . .'

'Are things all right between the two of you?' Renée asked, suddenly worried.

'Yes! Oh, yes, absolutely,' Ines insisted. 'We adore each other, and I miss him so much. It's not that.'

Renée waited for the 'but'.

'It's just that sometimes I feel there's a sort of *restlessness* that he has. I'm not sure if it's ambition or what it is exactly. He wants to make a lot more money, I know that.'

'Well, that's not a bad thing,' said Renée. 'Is it?'

'No.' Ines sounded hesitant. 'Not by itself. But every time he comes home on leave he's talking to me about connections he's making through friends in the regiment. Wealthy, powerful people. People that he's excited about. And I feel . . .'

'What?' Renée asked, when she didn't finish the sentence. 'What do you feel, love?'

'Ugh,' Ines groaned. 'I don't know. I suppose I feel left out. And a bit threatened, maybe? Like he's rushing headlong into a world I know nothing about. A world I might not like at all.'

'I understand,' Renée said kindly. 'But I'd try not to think too far ahead if I were you. None of us know when, or how, this bloody war is going to end. Any plans Gunn, or you, make now are bound to change. He's probably just focusing on the future to help him survive the present.'

'I'm sure you're right.' Ines smiled gratefully, but it was clear from her tone she wasn't convinced.

They walked on, Renée stopping every now and then to pick

up an interesting stone or part of a blue speckled bird's egg, fallen from the nest. 'They're for Charlotte,' Renée explained. 'She loves these sorts of treasures. They remind her of home, I think.'

'You're very close, aren't you?'

Ines let the question drop casually, without slowing her pace or even making eye contact. But Renée understood its significance, and was conscious of the alertness with which her younger sister awaited her answer.

'We are,' she replied simply. 'I don't think I could do . . . the work I do . . . without her.'

Ines nodded. She'd grown used to these sorts of coded conversations with Renée, whose work at the Foreign Office was clearly not just secret, but important and, Ines suspected, dangerous. But it was her sister's personal life she was more interested in.

'You're happy, though?' she asked. 'You and Charlotte?'

A slow, shy smile suffused Renée's features, and there could be no doubting the sincerity of her answer.

'Very. We're very happy.'

For the briefest of moments, a flicker, the girls' eyes met. But then Jimmy came running back, grabbing Renée's hand with ruddy-cheeked excitement.

'This is where my camp is,' he announced breathlessly, as they reached the edge of a small copse. 'Come on. I'll show you.'

The tour of the camp took a good twenty minutes, Agnes waiting patiently in the cold while her little brother explained the purpose of every sharpened stick or piece of dangling rope. No one was happier than Ag when Edward Turnbull's distinctive, cut-glass English voice came ringing through the trees, followed by the man himself with his distinctive limp and ever-present smile.

'Hello, you lot. I saw you coming into the woods from my kitchen window. I wondered if I could interest anyone in hot tea and crumpets?'

'*Actual* crumpets?' Jimmy's eyes widened. This was a treat indeed with rationing in full swing.

'Well I'm hardly likely to invite you over for imaginary crumpets, now am I?' Edward teased him. 'You must be Renée,' he said, turning to Ines's sister.

But before Renée could answer, Agnes had grabbed his hand impatiently. 'Can we save the introductions for later please? I'm *freezing* and *starving*.'

Edward exchanged an amused glance with Ines. 'Yes, I can see you've been treated terribly, you poor children. Come along then. Follow me.'

The crumpets were indeed real, warm and delicious, toasted over an old-fashioned range fire in the kitchen of Edward's farmhouse.

Renée was struck at once by what a charming place it was, handsome and yet entirely unpretentious, not unlike its owner. Beneath the baronial, vaulted ceilings, the floor was laid with ancient flagstones, dipped and worn smooth from centuries of use and covered in parts with faded antique Persian rugs. The furniture, although dark and heavy, was quite in keeping with the room. A large oak dresser dominated one side of the kitchen, decorated with pretty, mismatched china, and on the opposite side stretched a truly vast Jacobean dining table. A vase of rather hastily arranged berries and holly had been plonked in the middle of the table, next to a bowl of some sort of potpourri that made the room smell of cloves and oranges. The walls were hung with a mishmash of paintings and tapestries, some obviously valuable, others looking more like junk shop finds. And in a basket next to the range, a shaggy, scruffy-looking Irish wolfhound slept contentedly.

'What a lovely home you have, Mr Turnbull,' Renée observed, sipping a second cup of tea quietly with Ines while the children disappeared off to play Tommy Dorsey records on Edward's fancy new turntable.

'Thank you,' said Edward. 'I do love it, but it's far too big for me most of the time, rattling around on my own up here.

It only really comes to life when your sister drops by. And the children,' he added hastily.

'Edward's been so kind to us, with Gunn being away,' Ines told Renée. 'He lets Jimmy and Ag run wild around the house and the farm, which they really don't have space to do back at the cottage.'

'No,' Renée agreed. 'Your house is idyllic but it is rather small.'

'Yes, and Edward's forever coming over to fix things and do all the sort of man-jobs that I'd ask Gunn to help me with if he were home,' Ines gushed. 'Although, come to think of it, even when he *is* home he does precious little in terms of helping with the house.'

'I daresay he wants to spend every second with you and the children,' said Edward, diplomatically. 'I'm sure I'd be the same if I were away at the front.'

Yes, thought Renée. *I'm sure you would. And I'm sure you'd do the same now, if you had the chance.*

She liked Edward, very much. The kindness shone out of him, and it was clear from the way he carried himself that he was a decent, honourable man. But it was also clear that he carried a serious torch for Ines.

'It must be wonderful for the two of you to spend time together like this,' said Edward, wisely changing the subject while offering Renée the last buttered crumpet. 'With the rest of your family so far away.'

'It is,' confirmed Ines, smiling.

'Have you had any news of your brother or sister?'

'Charles is still in North Africa, as far as we know,' said Renée, biting into the warm dough with real relish, and trying to remember the last time she'd tasted butter. The food situation was even worse in London than it was in the country, where people could supplement their rations with homegrown food, so Edward's 'tea' was a real treat.

'You must worry about him.'

Renée shrugged. 'Everybody's fighting somewhere. One can't think about it too much. To be frank with you, it's our sister Genevieve I worry about more.'

Ines had shared dribs and drabs of information with Edward over the years about Gen and Wilhelm, and her leaving Paris for Beaulieu at the start of the war. But Renée filled in many of the blanks, specifically about Genevieve's drinking and loneliness.

'Our mother's death hit her harder than the rest of us, I think,' said Renée. 'Not that it's a competition,' she added swiftly, clocking Ines's look of surprise and distress. 'It was awful for everybody. But Ines, Charles and I were all able to find our paths forward as adults. Whereas Gen became almost stuck. It's a terrible shame, really, because she's quite brilliant. Funny and clever and creative.'

'She's fearful,' Edward summarized, having listened intently to Renée's description.

'Exactly,' said Renée. 'And Papa . . . the way our father is . . . hasn't helped.'

'Perhaps, after the war, bridges will be built?' said Edward. 'You never know. You might all come back together yet. One "flock", like you used to be.'

'Ines told you about the birds thing?' asked Renée, surprised but delighted that Ines would share this particular piece of Challant family lore.

'You can't really miss that wonderful bird staircase she painted down at the cottage,' said Edward.

'Ah,' Renée nodded. 'No. You certainly can't!'

'I asked her what had inspired her to do it, and she told me all about the "birds of Beaulieu". I think it's a wonderful idea. All of you migrating here and there, but then finding your way back home.'

The loveliness of the metaphor had been tainted over the years, since the fateful night back in Beaulieu when someone had opened the door to their mother's aviary and all Clotilde's precious birds had flown. But perhaps here, in England, with her new friends and new life, Ines felt able to revive its magic? Renée hoped that was the case.

*

'What made you say all that to Edward earlier?' Ines asked later that night, after dinner. 'About Genevieve, and Maman and Papa?'

The two sisters were alone. Charlotte, who'd rallied enough to come down for eggs and rice pudding, had since retreated back to her sick bed. And Jimmy and Ag were both sleeping peacefully in their shared attic bedroom, exhausted after such a long and eventful day, leaving Ines and Renée to clear away the supper things and play cards by the fire.

'He seemed curious,' replied Renée, frowning. 'Why? Shouldn't I have said anything? I got the impression that the two of you were close, but I didn't mean to speak out of turn.'

'We are close,' said Ines, who felt irritated, although she didn't know why. 'Edward's a dear friend. I just haven't told him all there is to know about Challant family history, that's all.'

'You told him about the birds,' Renée pointed out reasonably.

'Yes, but . . . that's different,' Ines muttered.

Renée dealt the next hand, unsure what it was she had done wrong, or what Ines was upset about, but deciding that the best thing was to stay silent.

'I'm sorry if I was cross,' Ines said awkwardly a few minutes later. 'It's just that Gunn feels . . . sometimes feels . . . that Edward behaves too much like a member of the family. He got upset with me last time he was home, said I talked to Edward too openly about our private affairs.'

Ah. This made more sense.

'Gunn's not keen on Edward?'

'No, no, no, he is,' Ines insisted. 'They're friends. But there are certain things Gunn gets touchy about.'

'You mean he's jealous?' Renée cocked her head to one side.

Ines opened her mouth to reply but then closed it again.

'Does he have reason to be?'

'To be jealous of me and Edward?' Ines looked affronted. 'Of course not. Why on earth would he?'

'Perhaps because you and Edward spend a lot of time together?' suggested Renée, innocently. 'Maybe Gunn feels a bit usurped, with Edward coming over and helping out as much as he does.'

'Well if he does, what am I supposed to do about it?' demanded Ines, exasperated. 'You see how hard I work, Renée. But there are some jobs I need a man for. Physically. Edward's here, and he offers to help. Gunn's not. He was supposed to have leave this month, right now in fact. But of course it all got changed at the last minute, again.'

'I'm not blaming you, my darling.' Reaching forward, Renée squeezed Ines's hand. 'I know it must be hard. I'm just saying that I can imagine how Gunn might feel uncomfortable around Edward. Especially as the man's quite plainly in love with you. Your turn,' she added, uncovering the six of clubs from the stack of cards in the middle.

'What do you mean?' Ines flushed scarlet. 'Edward's not in love with me. We're friends.'

Renée raised an eyebrow but said nothing.

'He's not in love with me!' Ines insisted. 'He's more interested in the children than he is in me, I assure you.'

'If you say so. Your turn,' Renée said again.

'They both adore him,' Ines persisted, playing her card. 'And Edward feels the same way. But he and Ag are especially close. Between you and me, I expect she may have a little bit of a crush on him.'

And I expect she may not be the only one, thought Renée. But she kept her musings to herself. Unwittingly or not, she'd rocked the boat violently enough for one day.

'Well,' she said eventually, after winning yet another hand, her third in a row, 'I'm sorry if I said too much about Genevieve's problems. I do worry about her, though.'

'Me too,' said Ines, yawning.

'Bedtime, I think.' Picking up Ines's empty mug Renée took it back into the kitchen, along with her own.

'Wouldn't it be wonderful if Edward were right?' Ines called from the other room, slipping the cards back into the beautifully inlaid jet case that Gunn's late father had once brought back from China. 'If after the war, Papa changed his mind about things, and we all came back together again? Me, you, Genevieve and Charles?'

'It would be nice, dearest,' Renée called back, cheerfully. But inside she felt sad.

A lot of things would be 'nice'. But that didn't mean they were going to happen.

Renée liked Edward Turnbull, very much. But for all sorts of reasons, she went to bed worrying about his relationship with her younger sister, and what it might mean for Ines's happiness.

CHAPTER TWENTY

North York Moors, England, December 1942

'Who *is* that man?'

Anna Grierly, an attractive, wealthy and famously predatory American divorcee, leaned conspiratorially to the man on her left at dinner.

'He's married,' the man replied wryly. 'Hands off.'

'I didn't ask if he were married,' chided Anna. 'I asked who he is.'

'Gunn. Hector Gunn, I believe, although no one uses his first name. He's a friend of Harry's from the Devonshire. A skier.'

'He's divine,' Anna pronounced, idly twisting the enormous diamond ring on the fourth finger of her right hand. Originally an engagement ring from her first husband, who'd tragically died from a stroke just a few months after their wedding, leaving Anna temporarily heartbroken and permanently rich, she had once worn the ring on the opposite hand. Since her divorce from husband number two, however, *that* finger remained conspicuously bare. Although there was no shortage of expensive gems on display at Anna's throat, ears and wrists, adorning her naturally slim figure and further enhancing the appeal of her pretty, elfin features.

'He's a chancer,' her neighbour replied. 'Not to be trusted. And as I said, married. To some ridiculously young French girl, apparently. Very much *not* for you, Anna my love.'

'Don't tempt me, Sebastian,' Anna purred coquettishly. 'You know I love a challenge.'

They were all guests at an unusually grand dinner party at

Brocklehurst Hall, an ugly but enormous Victorian pile in the North York Moors. Brocklehurst was the family seat of Lord and Lady Hemming, whose son the Hon. Harry Hemming had become a great friend of Gunn's in the regiment.

Gunn had felt guilty lying to Ines about his leave, slinking off to Yorkshire instead of coming home. But the shooting party at Harry's family estate was too good an opportunity to pass up. At tonight's dinner alone was the head of a venerable British investment bank, a chap who'd just acquired two gold mines in Peru, and an American oilman in his late sixties named Grayson, who spoke loudly and pretty much without a break about all the money there was to be made in Texas 'after this darned war'.

Gunn justified his deception by telling himself that he was developing these connections for their future as a family. He knew that Ines would despise the Texan, and would certainly consider the mine-owner to be a profiteer. (With some justification, to give her her due.) But she seemed to have no understanding of how important it was for Gunn to cultivate social ties that might lead to an income. A job. A chance. The last time he was at home, it almost felt as if she resented him for trying, comparing him yet again to Edward. As if their circumstances were the same!

'Edward farms for a living, and he seems to be doing all right.'

'Edward inherited four hundred acres!' Gunn had snapped back, exasperated. 'We have a few geese and a paddock. Besides, I'm not sure Edward *is* doing all right. He lives like a hermit up at that house, and dresses like one too. I don't think he's bought a stick of new furniture since his father left him the farm. If that's the sort of life you want, darling, you married the wrong man.'

He'd regretted that last barb as soon as he said it. But it was irksome sometimes, coming home from the utter hell of Malta, where his regiment had been relentlessly bombed by the Axis during a brutal eight-month siege, to find Ines waxing lyrical about another chap, just because he'd boarded up one of the chicken coops or helped to comb the nits out of Jimmy's hair.

They'd patched things up, and made love afterwards, as quietly as possible so as not to wake Jimmy and Agnes. But Gunn couldn't face the inevitable arguments about spending his next five days' leave in Yorkshire, which would have meant Ines leaving the children behind. A white lie had seemed easier, and what she didn't know wouldn't hurt her.

'I'm told you're taken?' Anna Grierly made a beeline for Gunn after dinner, introducing herself over port in the Hemmings' magnificent drawing room. 'How *crushingly* disappointing.'

Gunn laughed. 'It's my wife who feels crushingly disappointed most of the time, I can assure you.' His quick eye roved over Anna, assessing her in a blink. Her Christian Dior evening gown and impressive array of diamond and emerald jewellery gave immediate proof of her wealth; but her forthright manner and relatively youthful confidence made it equally plain that she had come into money later in life, rather than been born to it. She was sexy, and charming, but altogether over-the-top for a country shooting weekend with her glamorous clothes and her bright red lipstick. Before the war, he'd have taken her to bed before she could finish her first glass of port. But things were different now.

'So you're not married?' he asked her, clocking the bare ring finger. 'I find that hard to believe.'

'Oh, I've had a husband or two,' replied Anna, mischievously. 'I just have a terrible habit of misplacing them. I understand you're a skier?'

Gunn raised an eyebrow. 'Who told you that?'

'It's not true, then? And here was I all impressed. Harry said you won the men's downhill in Mürren before the war?'

'That is true.' Gunn gave what he hoped was a humble smile. 'It all feels like a very long time ago now, though. God knows if or when I'll ski again.'

'Oh, don't be so defeatist,' said Anna, laying a red lacquered hand briefly on his upper arm. 'I'm sure you will if you want to.'

Later that night, in the rather cold, draughty bedroom

201

to which he'd been assigned, Gunn's thoughts drifted back to skiing and Mürren and the winter he'd met Ines. To competing with her brother Charles Fils, who he hadn't seen in person since those days. To Julia Valaperti, who'd brought him out to Megève in the first place, and been so generous and kind to him throughout their affair. He'd lost touch completely with Julia since the war began, and found himself wondering now where she was and how she was faring in these strange, turbulent times.

It all felt so long ago. And yet, at the same time, immediate, as if he could stretch out his arm and stroke the memories with the tips of his fingers. So much had changed since that winter. Everything had changed, in fact. But nothing more so than Gunn himself. He had fallen in love, and found a joy in marriage that he never knew existed. And yet he was aware there was also a restlessness in him, an innate longing for adventure and novelty that the war, for all of its horrors, had provided. With an unpleasant jolt, Gunn realized that he was afraid of the war ending.

He thought about Anna Grierly, the American. About how sexy she was, but in an aggressive, confident way, the absolute opposite of his sweet, romantic Ines. And about what she'd said to him after dinner, about resuming his skiing career.

'You *will* if you *want* to.'

The problem was that Gunn didn't know what he wanted. Only what he didn't want.

He didn't want to be poor.

He didn't want to be bored.

He didn't want to go home and find Edward bloody Turnbull sniffing around his wife. Or two very sweet but unrelated children taking over his entire house, monopolizing Ines's time and affection. His own children would be different, of course. Their children. But he found it impossible even to imagine future offspring without Maltings in the picture.

Closing his eyes, he pushed all other thoughts aside and brought to mind the familiar image of his beloved childhood home. Maltings was the one thing that always encouraged a sense of calm, and called him back to himself, to his essence, his purpose. If he focused only on that, he told himself, on reclaiming the happy house that had forever been his North Star, eventually he would find peace.

CHAPTER TWENTY-ONE

Cornwall, England, September 1944

By September 1944, there was a palpable feeling throughout England that Germany was certain to lose the war, and what had once been a question of 'if' had now become 'when'. Since D-Day back in June, the success of the Normandy landings, and most recently the fall of Orléans to the Americans, had transformed the situation in France, which was naturally the primary focus of Ines's attention. Combined with the Soviet victory in Operation Bagration and the punitive airstrikes on Japanese forces in the Palau islands, the sense that the tide had turned inexorably in the Allies' favour was pervasive.

In Cornwall, day-to-day life for Ines and the children was largely unchanged. But the shift in everybody's mood was profound. While Ines dreamed of peace and of returning to France with Gunn to reunite with her siblings and, she hoped, eventually make peace with her father, Jimmy and Agnes were also growing restless to move back to London.

'It's not fair,' Agnes grumbled to Edward one warm Sunday afternoon, which felt more like summer than the onset of autumn. 'All the children from Manchester and Birmingham have been allowed back home. I don't see why they're picking on us Londoners.'

They were in the dilapidated barn up at the farm, Ag dangling her long legs from the top of a pile of stacked hay bales while Jimmy 'helped' Edward to fix the engine of an ancient, broken-down tractor. It was plainly beyond repair, but had proved a useful diversion for eleven-year-old Jimmy, who bored easily and lacked his sister's ability to simply sit around and chat. Edward had promised Ines to take both children off her hands for the entire day, so that she could deep clean the house and get everything ready for Gunn's upcoming leave which, once again, seemed to have been delayed for several days.

'I wouldn't call it "picking on you",' Edward pointed out to Agnes reasonably. 'London's not safe yet, that's all.'

'Course it is,' interjected Jimmy scathingly. 'Ol' Hit-ler's finished.'

'Is that right?' replied Edward, amused. 'And who are your sources for that, Jimbo?'

'Eh?' Jimmy cocked his oil-smeared face to one side, confused.

'He means who told you,' said Agnes.

'Nobody told me,' replied Jimmy. 'I just know. Everybody knows. We've practically won the war already.'

'Ed?'

Ines's voice was so quiet that none of them heard her at first.

'Edward,' she tried more loudly. Turning around, Edward saw her standing in the barn doorway, the skirt of her rose-printed muslin dress blowing in the wind.

'Hullo,' he said cheerfully. 'What are you doing here?'

Only as he drew closer did he realize something was wrong. Ines's face was ashen and she was trembling, shivering like a child turned out naked into the snow. A paper fluttered in her hand.

'What is it?' he asked. 'What's happened?'

She raised the paper wordlessly. Edward saw it was a telegram.

'Oh God,' he said quietly. Nine times out of ten, a telegram meant only one thing.

The children were less restrained. 'Is it Gunn?' Agnes gasped, her hand flying to her mouth in horror. 'Has he been killed? Is that why he didn't come home, when the other men did?'

Jimmy, who worshipped Gunn and, despite seeing him only rarely, had come to view him as a surrogate father, dropped the spanner he was holding into the dust and let out an awful, animal howl. 'Nooooooo!'

Marching over, Ines took the boy firmly by the shoulders and crouched down so that their eyes were level.

'It's not Gunn, Jimmy,' she told him. 'Gunn's fine. Try to breathe.'

Jimmy gulped for air, wiping his eyes and nose frantically with a dirty sleeve.

'It's not Gunn?' he stammered.

'No,' Ines reassured him. 'Gunn will be home any day now, I'm sure. This telegram is from my sister Renée.' Holding out the paper, she handed it to Edward, who read it in silence. 'It's . . . it's our brother who's been killed. Charles,' her voice cracked.

Jumping down from the hay bales, Agnes ran over to Ines and instinctively wrapped her arms around her.

'I'm so sorry, Ines.'

'Me too,' sniffed Jimmy, guiltily.

Ines caught Edward's eye, and read all the sympathy and love in his expression. Like the children's warm, tight bodies pressed against hers, it was comforting. But it was Gunn's comfort she needed. Gunn whose love she had come to depend on so utterly. He had known Charles Fils, and loved him – not in the same way that Ines did, of course. But still. She wanted to talk about Charles with someone who shared at least some of her memories of him. She wanted to talk and scream and sob and be made love to until all the pain went away.

Ines longed for her husband in that moment more than she had since the first, breathless days of their marriage. But as usual, Gunn wasn't here. The rest of the men from his battalion were all home on leave. But some mysterious business was keeping Gunn away, at the one moment Ines needed him the most.

'I'm so very sorry,' murmured Edward helplessly. 'If there's anything I can do for you. Anything at all . . .'

'Stay with us tonight,' Ines blurted. 'I'll make you up a bed on the sofa. I just . . . I don't want to be alone.'

'Of course.' Edward nodded gravely. 'Whatever you need.'

Genevieve was at home in Beaulieu when she heard the news. It was Marie, the family's old cook, now in her eighties, who'd received the telegram from the post boy and brought it to her.

'Mademoiselle?' Nervously, the old woman tapped Gen's shoulder as she lay slumped on the chaise longue, drunk and only half awake. 'This came for you. From London. Mademoiselle Genevieve, can you hear me?'

Since her husband, Géraud, had died, Marie had been all alone at her little cottage down by the harbour, and had gladly accepted Genevieve's invitation to move into the bastide and 'help out' while Gen remained living there. Although she didn't regret her decision, it had been hard for the elderly widow to watch the girl she'd known since childhood – so vivacious and full of promise – sink into such a defeated, drink-addled state.

Blearily, Gen took Renée's telegram and opened it. It took a few moments for the import of the words to sink in. When they did, Gen just sat there staring at them, unreacting.

She'd shed so many tears over Wilhelm. Self-pitying tears, she berated herself now. Tears because they were apart and she was lonely. *Dear God.* And now Charles was dead. Dead! Killed in a mortar attack in Alsace, by Wilhelm's comrades. And she seemed to have no tears left. When genuine tragedy struck, she was empty, as cracked and barren as a dried-up river bed.

'You've lost someone, mademoiselle?' Marie asked gently.

Gen looked up at her with blank desolation.

'It's Charles,' she told her. '*Notre Niverolle. Il est mort, Marie.*'

Handing the cook the telegram, she slumped back down onto the chaise longue and pressed her face into a silk pillow. *Strange*, she thought, *how much you miss feelings, even the bad ones, once you've drunk them away.*

In London, Renée had cried, loudly and messily, in Charlotte's arms before she sent the telegrams to her family. To be forced to break the news in such a cold, formal way felt profoundly wrong. But there was really no other option, other than waiting for the regiment's official telegram to arrive at Place Dauphine, and that might take weeks.

Renée had begun fearing the worst three days ago, when intelligence first reached the Foreign Office about the extent of the Free French casualties in Haguenau, once a sleepy market town close to Strasbourg, but latterly the scene of intense and bitter fighting. But she'd only been able to confirm that Lieutenant Charles Challant was among the dead late last night and had very little opportunity to process the news herself before passing it on.

The worst part was that she found herself struggling to retrieve any particularly warm or personal memories of Charles. Within their once tight family flock, her brother had felt the most distant to Renée, always off with his own friends, or sometimes with Ines, or being whisked away into mysterious and apparently important 'male' activities with Papa.

Or perhaps it was she, Renée, who'd been the distant one? More than once during her childhood, she remembered feeling like the cuckoo in the nest, bigger and uglier than her glamorous, shimmering siblings. It seemed impossible that Charles Fils, the only son and most golden of them all, was gone.

'Should I say it was a mortar attack?' she asked Charlotte, agonizing over the content of the telegram. 'Does that make it worse or better?'

'Neither,' said Charlotte. 'He's dead, my love. Nothing can be worse than that, and nothing can make that better. But for what it's worth, yes. I do think you should tell them how he was killed. They have a right to know everything you do.'

'All right,' said Renée. 'Thank you.'

She was so deeply grateful for Charlotte. For her innate ability to combine compassion with practical, sensible advice. For her love, but also her complete lack of histrionics, which made a welcome change from Renée's own upbringing. In the midst of tragedy, it helped to know that she had a steadying, reliable first mate standing beside her on this stormiest of ships. As long as she had Charlotte, she wouldn't sink.

'I did love him, you know,' Renée told her quietly, once the telegram was sent.

'I know you did.' Wrapping an arm around Renée's shoulder, Charlotte pulled her close, kissing the crown of her head as they walked back to their flat. 'And I'm sure he knew it too.'

For Charles Père, in Paris, the shock was debilitating.

Paris had been liberated only two weeks before, and the mingled sense of euphoria and disbelief still hung in the air like an intoxicating cloud. Everywhere one went, people were smiling or laughing, strangers greeting one another on the streets with a strange, dazed delight.

Like everybody else, Charles Challant had gathered on the Champs-Elysées for the liberation parade on the 26th of August, cheering on the French 2nd Armoured Division amid the 'Vive De Gaulle' banners and riotously waved French flags. But in his heart, he'd struggled to feel the same sense of joy and relief as his fellow Parisians. Not only was his personal war not over – the anonymous, threatening cards and letters continued to arrive, locking Charles Père into an apparently endless battle with the faceless enemies of his past – but the real war wasn't over either, not for the Challant family. Charles Fils was still fighting down in Alsace, at the foot of the Vosges mountains. Closer to home, physically, than he'd been at any time since the war started. But still not safe.

When Renée's telegram arrived, Chares had had to read it several times before the dreadful truth sank in. When it did, the effect on his body was immediate. All the strength in his legs left him and he fell hard and painfully onto his knees on Place Dauphine's marble-floored hallway. The noise of his collapse immediately brought the household staff running. But Charles was barely aware of their panicked questions and ineffectual attempts to help. As they fluttered around him like ghosts, all he experienced was a sharp, stabbing sensation down the entire left side of his body, like a million shards of glass being pushed up through his skin from underneath.

Doctors were called, and powerful drugs administered. It was determined that Charles had likely suffered a 'mild' stroke, exacerbated by extreme shock, and that above all he needed complete rest. But while his broken body recuperated, his mind raced frantically, fuelled by an almost manic bitterness.

Charles Fils was dead. His son, dead.

And with him, all of Charles Père's remaining hopes for the future. The empire that he had spent his life building had all been intended for Charles Fils. Without him, there would be no legacy. No point to any of it. The injustice of it was unbearable. He needed someone to blame. Someone to *hurt*, now that his own life had been brought to ruin, and all that was left was ashes and dust.

The Germans were too amorphous a target for his hatred; vague and unsatisfying. So he searched for another.

If Charles Fils's death were some sort of cosmic vengeance, punishment for the sins of his father, then God himself was the enemy. But the deep roots of Charles's Catholicism made this impossible for him to contemplate. Just as the even deeper roots of his sense of privilege and victimhood made it impossible for him to blame himself.

Casting around for a more palatable culprit, his mind began to turn to the women in his life.

To Clotilde, the long-dead wife who still haunted him. But she'd been no saint, whatever their children might believe. She, too, had done terrible things, Charles knew. One terrible thing, in particular. Perhaps it was *her* sins that Charles Fils had had to die for? Was that it?

Eventually, his fevered imaginings rested upon his three daughters.

With his rational mind, Charles understood that Genevieve, Renée and Ines had had nothing to do with their brother's death. That they, too, had lost someone whom they dearly loved, and were no doubt devastated with grief. But in the roiling sea of emotion that raged beneath his rational mind, it was easy to imagine all three girls as guilty.

Renée, for her absence, and for being the bearer of the appalling news.

Genevieve, for her violent jealousy of Charles Fils, the family's son and heir.

And then there was Ines. Ines, whom Charles had loved most of all his children, but who had proved herself so grossly unworthy of that love, abandoning him for that hateful, immoral Englishman, Hector Gunn. As he saw things now, through his wildly distorted lens of loss, Ines had tricked him out of a love that he had rightfully owed her brother all along. A wrong that he could never now put right.

Alone and tortured, Charles Challant's hatred grew like a tumour.

In Cornwall, Ines moved through the hours and days mindlessly, like a clockwork doll. The cottage that she had always loved and considered a place of sanctuary suddenly felt small and claustrophobic, its uneven, whitewashed walls trapping her and its beamed ceilings bearing down gloomily from above.

Jimmy and Ag were sweet and did their best, Jimmy in particular displaying a previously unknown talent for tidiness and washing his own clothes. And Edward was a godsend, his constant, quiet presence filling an unspoken need in Ines for comfort and protection. But the cloak of sadness that had settled on Ines since she first heard the news refused to shift.

For much of her childhood, especially during the early, happy years when Maman was still alive, Charles had been Ines's closest playmate. Not until she met Gunn had she adored anyone quite so deeply. She associated the two of them, somehow, husband and brother. Their shared love of the mountains, and of her. Their energy and masculinity and confidence. Ines had always hero-worshipped her father, but that was different. Papa had been on a pedestal, whereas Charles Fils, and later Gunn, had been confidants. Equals.

Now Charles had been killed and Gunn spared. As nonsensical as it was, a part of Ines felt guilty about that. But then with each day Gunn failed to come home for his leave, her anxiety grew. What if he *hadn't* been spared after all? What if he, too, were lying dead on a battlefield somewhere? What if she'd lost both of them?

She was in the kitchen, mindlessly reorganizing the pantry cupboards, when it happened. The creak of the door made her look over her shoulder, expecting Edward or Agnes, who'd been out all day blackberry picking. But instead Gunn, handsome and tanned in civilian clothes, stood shimmering in front of her like a mirage.

'Where have you *been*?' Ines heard herself saying, unable in that moment to fling herself into his arms, even though his embrace was what she longed for more than anything.

'I'm sorry.' He set his kitbag down on the floor and moved towards her. 'I heard about Charles.'

Ines took a step back. This wasn't what she'd expected at all. Now that he was actually here, Gunn felt almost like a stranger.

'I needed you!' Her eyes flashed with fury.

'I know.'

Outside, in the tiny front garden, a murder of crows swooped down suddenly from one of the sycamore trees, cawing loudly as they strutted around, stabbing the grass in search of worms. Ines watched them, mesmerized. It felt like an omen.

'I'm so sorry, my love.' Gunn's voice reclaimed her attention.

'Yes, but where *were* you?' Ines demanded.

In lieu of an answer, he reached out and pulled her forcibly into his arms. 'I'm here now,' he said gruffly. Ines struggled and cried at first, lashing out at him with her thin, exhausted arms. But Gunn kept tight hold of her like a human straitjacket. And before long his smell and warmth and all the love between them reasserted itself and when he pressed his lips to hers she kissed him back with raw, ravenous hunger.

'It will be all right, Ines,' he whispered, his face pressed close to her ear. 'I promise.'

Looking past him through the open door at the flock of sinister blue-black birds, Ines shuddered. *Would* it be all right? Some deeply buried, superstitious part of her strongly doubted that it would.

CHAPTER TWENTY-TWO

Cornwall, England, April 1945

Jimmy and Ag returned home to their parents in London in the early spring of 1945, a joyous day for them, but an emotional and difficult one for Ines.

For once, Gunn was at home for this important moment, and his love and understanding meant everything. 'I know how much you loved them,' he told Ines the evening after the children left. They'd spent the entire afternoon in bed, lovemaking being the one activity certain to distract them both, and by the time they staggered downstairs for supper, a lot of Ines's more intense emotions had already been released.

She had hoped that Jimmy and Ag's departure, and the imminent end of the war, might naturally prompt a conversation about her and Gunn starting a family of their own. But by the time he left to rejoin his unit, Gunn still hadn't broached the subject. Ines decided it would be easier to wait until he was home for good than to bring it up now, which perhaps he might see as tempting fate? Charles Fils being killed so close to the end of the war, and just weeks before France's full liberation, had brought home to all of them just how fragile life still was.

But at last, the war *was* over, and in Cornwall as everywhere else, the mood was euphoric. While soldiers drifted back to England in dribs and drabs, on overcrowded boats and trains, women, children and those already back home threw themselves into frenzied preparations for the grand VE Day celebration on 8 May.

Gunn's sister Laura had invited Ines to join her and her friends making Union Jack bunting, which was hung in endless, looped yards along Saltash High Street. It was the first time the two women had spent any real time together since the Christmas at the start of the war, and Ines was both pleased and surprised to have received the invitation. On the grand day itself, they attended the parade together, along with Gunn's mother Edie, who Ines was shocked to see looking so frail.

'The dementia ages her,' Laura explained, matter-of-factly. 'I don't think my brother realizes quite how bad things are. He thinks I'm exaggerating.'

'Gunn tries not to dwell too much on difficult things,' Ines replied diplomatically. The truth was that Laura was right. Gunn stubbornly refused to accept that Edie was anything more than 'occasionally confused' and maintained an almost mythical belief that returning 'home' to Maltings would cure her of any ailments and restore her to her youthful, vital self. This delusion had once again strained his relationship with his sister, who was responsible for all their mother's day-to-day care and felt belittled and dismissed by Gunn's attitude, shattering the fragile truce that had been built between them back in 1939.

As Gunn's wife, Ines felt honour-bound to defend him. But holding Edie's bony, liver-spotted hand today as they waved their flags and sipped from bottles of homemade cider, it was clear that Laura was right and her brother wrong.

'Here.' Ines handed her barely touched bottle to her sister-in-law. 'You have mine. I'm not feeling too great. I actually think I might head home.'

'Already?' Laura frowned. 'Oh come on, you can't! Things are just getting started.'

'That's what I'm worried about,' said Ines, as another group of young drunk revellers careered into them, almost knocking Laura flying. The crowd was good-natured, but it was also huge and growing. Combined with the heat, the alcohol, and the fact that she'd been too busy hanging bunting to remember to eat breakfast, or lunch, Ines was beginning to feel distinctly dizzy.

The bike ride back to the cottage was eight miles, but miraculously Ines was able to hitch a lift for most of the way on a rickety farm truck, whose elderly driver had also had enough flag waving for one day. 'I'll raise a glass from me own front room,' he told Ines. 'Leave all the hoo-haa to you youngsters.'

By the time Ines finally wheeled her bicycle through the front garden gate and staggered into the cottage, she didn't feel remotely like a youngster. Hot, clammy and dizzy, she rushed straight to the loo at the back of the house and was violently sick. Afterwards, although the nausea had subsided, her head still throbbed painfully, and heavy dark spots swam before her eyes. She'd had heat stroke once, as a child in Beaulieu. This felt similar, except for the fact that it was warm outside rather than roasting. Maman used to suffer from migraines, Genevieve too from time to time. Ines had never had one before, but if this was what they felt like, she felt guilty for not being more sympathetic at the time. Thank God she hadn't stayed at the parade!

Eventually she made her way back into the kitchen, and brewed herself some tea, which she sipped at weakly while nibbling on a digestive biscuit. It was several minutes before she noticed the envelope, lying on the mat by the kitchen door.

White, small and nondescript, it was addressed to *Mrs H. Gunn Esq.* and had the words 'BY HAND' written in capitals on the bottom right-hand corner. Too ill to feel curious, Ines nevertheless shuffled over and picked it up, placing it on the table beside her until she had the energy to open it.

It had already been the longest of long days.

Two weeks later, an elated Gunn jumped down from the front seat of the lorry that had given him a lift all the way from London. He was at a small country crossroads, less than three miles from the cottage, and was more than happy at the prospect of walking the final stretch, back to his darling Ines and the new life they were about to start together.

It was a glorious day, sunny and bright, as if nature had conspired to pull out all the stops to welcome him home.

Despite his heavy pack, Gunn felt ridiculously light as he strolled along the lane, delighting in the astonishing beauty of the Cornish countryside. The views towards the valley and broad, winding river were grandly spectacular. But it was the smaller, more intimate things than entranced him the most. The high hedgerows were overgrown with honeysuckle and buzzing with insects and bees, attracting swooping starlings which flitted across Gunn's path like bats. The verges, reeking of wild garlic and festooned with buttercups, dandelions and tall Queen Anne's lace, the delicate white flowers swaying shyly in the spring breeze. There were butterflies and birdsong, and every now and then a crumbling stone wall, presaging the appearance of a farm or cottage, with washing hung cheerily out to dry on lines casually strung between apple trees.

It seemed impossible to think that the fighting was over. That there would be no more leaving, no more terror, no more death. And yet at the same time, this new peace felt as natural and right as the sun rising in the east, or the soft, familiar bleating of goats in the distance. Like waking from an exciting but frightening dream into a reality so vivid and lovely, it was hard to believe it *was* real.

How foolish he'd been, to worry about the war ending. To think that peacetime might mean boredom and dull domesticity, an end to ambition and adventure. It was so clear to him now that the opposite was true. That victory meant freedom, to pursue whatever adventures he wanted, with his beautiful wife by his side. The *true* adventure of his life was just beginning. It would be up to him to make a success of it. To put his mistakes behind him and move forward, a new and better man. On this perfect late May afternoon, Gunn felt optimistic bordering on the invincible.

Quickening his pace, he broke into a jog as the roof of their cottage came into view. Soon they would leave this place behind. He already had big plans for making their fortune and buying Ines the home and life she deserved. But at the same time, a part of him would miss this place. Their first marital home, it held many happy, cherished memories, even if at times he and Ines had argued here. *Only because I stayed away too long,* Gunn told himself now, unlatching the front gate, his heart pounding. *Or because we let other people come between us.*

Setting down his pack in the garden, he pushed down on the latch and opened the door triumphantly. 'I'm home!'

The words began as a joyous shout, but they quickly faded and died on his lips.

The kitchen was empty. Not just empty of people. Completely empty. Stripped bare. Upstairs it was the same story. Beds without sheets, floors scrubbed clean. In his and Ines's bedroom, Gunn's few items of civilian clothing hung lonely in the wardrobe. His box of cufflinks remained on the bedside table, but the rest of his meagre possessions had all been packed into crates, leaning against the far wall. Nothing of Ines's remained, except for a single white envelope addressed to her, propped open against the pillow on her side of the bed.

Confused, and more than a little panicked, Gunn picked up the envelope.

Inside were several photographs of himself in the company of Anna Grierly, the American divorcee he'd first met up in Yorkshire in '43. Some were groups shots, innocent enough – apart from the locations and dates, all of which coincided with his 'missed' leaves, and which the letter-writer had helpfully spelled out in black ink on the back of each photograph. Others were unmistakably intimate.

Accompanying the pictures was a typed note, reading simply: *'Your husband is not the man you think he is.'*

In corroboration of this claim, copies of two hotel receipts had been enclosed, one from London in January of '44 and the other from the Palace Hotel in Brighton, just a few months ago.

Gunn sank down on the bed, momentarily stunned. But while his body was still, his mind raced. Who had taken the damning pictures of him and Anna, pictures that made everything seem far worse than it was? And who hated him enough to send a letter like that to Ines?

*

Edward Turnbull was upstairs shaving and listening to the wireless when he heard the thunderous banging on the front door.

'Turnbull? I know you're in there. Open this damn door!'

His face still half covered in a white beard of shaving foam, Ed ran down to find a murderous-looking Gunn looming menacingly on his doorstep.

'Where is she?' Gunn demanded, pushing past him into the hallway, then striding purposefully on into the empty kitchen. 'Where's my wife?'

'I have no idea,' Ed replied truthfully. But there was a disdain in his tone he made no effort to hide.

'You know she's left me though, don't you?' Gunn snarled, opening drawers and looking behind furniture, as if he expected to find Ines shut inside a cupboard or hiding under a pile of coats. His fear was making him angry, but also ridiculous.

'Yes,' said Edward. 'I know she's left you.'

'And you expect me to believe she didn't confide in you? About where she was going?' Gunn squared up to him aggressively.

'Frankly, I don't give a rat's backside what you believe,' Ed replied coolly. He didn't bully easily. 'But I found out in the same way that I expect you just did. I walked into the cottage and Ines was gone.'

Gunn hopped from foot to foot in impotent misery. For a moment Ed thought he might be about to hit him. It took every ounce of his self-control not to flinch. But in the end Gunn uncoiled his fists and sank, defeated, onto one of Ed's wicker chairs.

'You saw the letter?' he asked.

'Yes. I saw it.'

'Did you send it?'

'Me?' Ed sounded genuinely taken aback. 'Of course not. Why would *I* send something like that to Ines?'

'Because you love her?' Gunn looked up, holding Ed's gaze unflinchingly.

Ed cleared his throat, choosing his words carefully. 'No one who loved Ines would have sent that letter. Those pictures were intended to wound. To destroy.'

'I need to find her. To talk to her,' wailed Gunn, pulling at his hair desperately. 'Do you think she might have gone to her sister in London?'

Ed shrugged. 'Perhaps.'

'Those photographs . . . it's not what it looks like,' mumbled Gunn.

Ed raised a deeply sceptical eyebrow.

'I mean, it was like that, once,' Gunn clarified. 'For a very short time. Ages ago. But I'd broken it off. I love Ines.'

'What about the hotel in Brighton?' asked Ed, reasonably. The receipt in the envelope had been for February of this year.

'I agreed to meet her in Brighton,' Gunn admitted. 'One last time, before she went back to America. But only to talk. Like I say, I'd broken it off, but Anna was insistent. She wouldn't take no for an answer.'

Ed frowned. This all sounded somewhat implausible in his opinion. But it was Ines who Gunn needed to convince, not him.

'Do you really not know where she is?' Gunn pleaded.

All the aggression and swagger was gone now. Gunn's misery was entirely of his own making, but Ed couldn't help but feel at least a little bit sorry for him. On the other hand, because of Gunn's selfishness, he, Edward, had lost Ines as well. Heaven knew when, or if, he would ever see her again. And Gunn had been right about one thing – Ed did love her. Hopelessly, perhaps, but it was no less deep a love for that.

'I really don't know where she is,' he reiterated. 'To be honest with you, I also thought she would have confided in me. But the fact that she didn't . . .'

He left the sentence hanging, but both men knew what came next.

The fact that she hadn't meant only one thing.

Wherever she'd run to, Ines didn't want to be found.

PART THREE

SPRING

CHAPTER TWENTY-THREE

Beaulieu-sur-Mer, France, April 1951

'Eternal rest grant unto him, oh Lord, and let perpetual light shine upon him. *Puisse-t-il reposer en paix.*'

The three Challant sisters, Genevieve, Renée and Ines, watched silently as their father's heavy, brass-handled coffin was lowered into the grave. Even in death there was a certain weight to Charles Challant, a gravitas and sense of importance that not even the gaping pit could swallow entirely.

The spring air of the Côte d'Azur felt clean and clear compared to the grey skies of Paris. Riotously blossom-ing fruit trees surrounded the churchyard, peaches and apricots with their delicate-smelling, pale pink flowers. Had it not been for the sombre circumstances, just being here would have made Ines feel hopeful, mindful of nature's beauty and of the summer to come. As it was, none of it touched her. Closing her eyes, she listened to the sound of soil falling onto the coffin as the grave was filled, each thud reminding her what she already knew: Papa was dead.

Her beloved father, her childhood idol, the man she had adored, disappointed and ultimately lost, was now more than lost.

He was gone. Gone forever.

Remember, man, that you are dust, and to the dust you shall return.

It had surprised many people, his daughters among them, that Charles Challant had chosen to be buried in Beaulieu, and not in the family plot in Paris alongside Clotilde and Charles Fils.

In his later years Charles Père had rarely visited the bastide, and while he had never sold the property it was clear that he no longer felt happy there. The tragic events of 1928 had cast a permanent cloud over the family's one-time idyll.

The choosing of Beaulieu over Paris was by no means the only surprise at Charles Père's funeral, however. Local mourners were shocked to see the changes in the Challant family pew. Not only was Charles Fils's absence keenly felt; but of course all three of the girls had aged, although none more dramatically than the eldest, Genevieve. Rake-thin, with sunken cheeks and long, grey hair, she looked decades older than her forty-something years. A toxic combination of loneliness, disappointment and alcoholism had evidently taken a terrible toll on both her physical and emotional state.

By contrast Renée looked healthy and well as they filed out to the graveyard, if a little fuller figured since the onset of middle age. In a simple black shirtwaister dress and matching cardigan, she had come without Charlotte, her inseparable companion of the last fifteen years, in solidarity with her sisters, who were both alone. Or almost alone, in Ines's case.

Still a beauty, the youngest of the Challant daughters looked magnificent in her mourning outfit, an im-maculately tailored Christian Dior dress in jet-black crepe, teamed with a floor-length coat and chic pillbox hat, with mantilla-like lace netting at the front, covering eyes red-raw from crying. Unlike her older sisters, Ines wore her grief on her sleeve, sobbing with obvious devastation at various points during the service and clinging to Renée for support when their father's coffin was first carried into the church.

Afterwards, at the graveside, she approached Renée again.

'Who's that?' she asked, gesturing towards an elegant older woman in a black lace dress, standing apart from the other mourners. Dabbing her eyes repeatedly with a white cotton handkerchief, she was clearly moved by the service. But Ines had never seen her before in her life.

'That's Madame Faubourg,' Renée replied, as if this cleared the matter up. 'Alissa.'

'Who?' Ines frowned.

'I'll explain later,' said Renée quietly. 'I think you're needed now.'

Looking down, Ines felt a tugging at the hem of her coat.

A small blond boy, no more than five years old but dressed like an adult in a formal dark suit and tie, looked up at her plaintively.

'Can we go back to the house now, Maman?' he begged, hopping from foot to foot and screwing up his sweet, freckled face in discomfort. 'I'm reeeeally hungry. Also, I need to do a wee.'

'*Bien sûr, Matthieu.*' Ines smiled at her son, grateful as always for his presence and the miracle of his love. 'We'll go right now.'

Taking his small, clammy hand in hers, Ines followed the throng in the direction of the bastide, leaving the gravediggers to finish their sombre work.

Matthieu's birth had been the single, dazzling bright spot in one of the darkest periods of Ines's life.

Gunn's betrayal had shattered her into a million pieces. Just as the war was ending, in what ought to have been a moment of joy, the fateful letter had arrived, bringing with it a crushing darkness. Ines knew at once that she had to leave him. That a clean and final break was her only hope of ever mending her heart, or regaining some semblance of sanity. She would return to France, make amends with her father, and restart her life as if Gunn and Cornwall and all her hopes and dreams of the last six years had never been in it.

That was the plan anyway. For several reasons, how-ever, things didn't quite work out that way.

Returning to Paris proved relatively easy. Ines knew she could rely on Renée to help her, and to keep her whereabouts secret from Gunn, should he try to come after her. (Which he did, repeatedly, until Renée informed him bluntly that her sister categorically never wanted to see him again, and that if he wished to make amends, the best thing he could do would be to admit his adultery to allow a speedy divorce, and let her go.)

Unfortunately for Ines, persuading her father to forgive her, or even to see her at all, proved far more difficult. In her mind, reconciliation ought to have been easy. The wedge between herself and Papa had always been Gunn. Now that the marriage was over, Ines couldn't see a reason not to piece together the relationship.

Charles Challant saw things differently. The years since Ines's elopement had been profoundly painful ones for him. From the pressure of the anonymous, sinister letters arriving at Place Dauphine, to the loss of Charles Fils, followed by his own emotional and physical decline. In order to survive, Charles had clung ever more tightly to his growing sense of victimhood. Forgiving Ines, and allowing himself the joy that their restored relationship might bring, would mean abandoning his identity as a wronged, innocent man. For Charles, this was unthinkable. Resentment had become his oxygen, self-righteousness his artificial lung. To let go of either meant death.

The birth of Matty, an illegitimate son, gave Charles the perfect excuse to turn his back permanently on his youngest daughter, without inviting the world's censure. And so father and daughter remained lost to each other.

The pain of their estrangement might well have destroyed Ines, had it *not* been for Matty. Haunted by the spectre of her mother's multiple miscarriages, and terrified throughout her pregnancy of losing her baby, Ines had felt only unadulterated joy at Matthieu's safe arrival into the world. Refusing from the start to name the boy's father, all Ines would say was that he had been a 'good' man who had comforted her in the wake of Gunn's affair, when she first got back to France, but who would not be involved in the child's upbringing.

'Are you sure you don't want to name him, dearest?' Renée had asked her, concerned. 'Even on the birth certificate? What if you and the child need his support later?'

'We won't,' Ines insisted. 'I intend to get a job and support myself.'

To everybody's surprise, including Ines's own, she achieved this goal quickly and with quite marked success; a feat that her poor mother Clotilde had never been able to pull off, as Ines was acutely aware. Bringing to bear all her experience of decorating the cottage and Edward Turnbull's farm, she set herself up as an interior designer, starting work just a few months after baby Matthieu's birth. Approaching old friends and connections first, her business rapidly began to spread by word of mouth. Although her early commissions were small, involving a lot of sewing of curtains and reupholstering of tired furniture in the latest, vibrant post-war fabrics, more ambitious projects swiftly followed. For those with means, the end of the war meant a fresh start, rebuilding homes and spaces that had been tired and neglected for six long, painful years of conflict. Ines's natural flair for colour and pattern, combined with her technical skill and burning passion to succeed, not just for herself but for her new baby son, made her a popular choice among Paris's fashionable elite.

But no matter how successful Ines became, Charles Père stubbornly refused to see her, or to acknowledge his only grandchild. Walking past the closed gates of Place Dauphine, her childhood home, pushing 'Matty', as the baby quickly came to be known, in his English Silver Cross pram, Ines felt her heart breaking all over again.

'The bottom line is, I betrayed Papa and he can't forgive me,' she told Renée, the Christmas after Matty was born. 'If anyone should be able to understand that, it's me. After Gunn, after – well – everything . . .'

It didn't matter how many times Renée or Genevieve insisted that the situations were quite different. That Gunn was Ines's husband, not her child. That Gunn had cheated and lied to her, whereas Ines's only 'crime' towards their father had been to marry the man she loved. Ines would have none of it. Just as Charles Challant clung to his victimhood, Ines needed to keep her father on a pedestal. After everything else she'd lost, letting her idol fall would have been more than her wounded heart could bear.

Back at the bastide, guests mingled over chilled Chablis and hors d'oeuvres, while Matthieu and the few other children present ran around in the grounds. Genevieve, already the worse for wear, retreated upstairs to bed early, leaving Renée and Ines to play host.

'I can't believe how shabby the house looks,' Ines whispered to her sister, peeling a loose shard of dried paint the size of a bottle top from one of the walls. 'Doesn't Genevieve *see* this?'

'If she does, she doesn't care.' Renée shrugged sadly. She was worried about the house, and even more worried about Genevieve, but now wasn't the time to dwell on such things. At least they'd been able to tidy up sufficiently to invite people home after the funeral, and provide some simple food and drink. It was a far cry from the old entertaining days of their childhoods. But then the whole world had changed since then.

'Look. There she is again.' Ines grabbed Renée's arm and pointed. Alissa Faubourg, the elegant stranger from the graveside, was putting on her coat near the door, and appeared to be saying her goodbyes. 'Lots of people seem to know her,' observed Ines. 'Who *is* she again?'

'A friend from Paris,' said Renée, vaguely. 'No one important.'

'Well I'm going to introduce myself,' Ines announced, draining her wine glass and setting it down purposefully on the side table. 'Before she leaves.'

'Don't.' Renée put a restraining hand on her shoulder.

Ines looked at her curiously. 'Why not?'

Glancing around for a suitable escape, Renée's eyes lighted on their father's old study. 'Come with me,' she said, taking Ines's hand.

Closing the door behind them, Renée locked it before gesturing to Ines to sit.

'My goodness, what is it?' Ines asked, anxiously. It wasn't like Renée to go in for this sort of drama. Unless something really serious was going on.

'There's no easy way to say this,' Renée began, inauspiciously.

'So I'm just going to jump right in. Alissa Faubourg was Papa's companion. Of the last eight years, at least.'

Ines blinked. Opened her mouth to say something, then closed it again. It took several seconds for a cogent question to form.

'"Companion" . . . as in friend?'

Renée shook her head.

Ines sat down, sinking shakily onto the sofa.

'Papa had a *mistress*?'

There was no mistaking the naked astonishment in Ines's voice. This was going to be even harder than Renée had feared.

'He had several mistresses, darling, over the years.'

Ines shook her head, unable to make sense of such information.

'But Alissa was an important one. She's a nice woman.'

'Is she married?' Ines interrupted. 'Or widowed? You said Madame Faubourg.'

'She's married,' said Renée.

'Then, with all due respect, she is *not* a nice woman,' Ines thundered, outraged. 'She's an adulteress and a . . . a whore!'

Renée's eyes widened. 'Now *you* sound like Papa,' she chided. 'Were you a "whore" for having Matty?'

Ines blushed scarlet, recognizing the irony of her position. 'I just don't understand,' she muttered. 'Papa *abhorred* sex outside of marriage. He was sickened by the very idea. How many times did we hear him say it? "Adultery's a mortal sin."'

Renée nodded in silent sympathy. They had all heard Charles Père repeat this mantra, countless times. 'I understand it's a shock, dearest. But I can assure you Alissa is a kind woman, kinder than Papa deserved. Unlike some of the others.'

The others . . .

Ines felt dizzy.

'So if you want to blame anyone, I'm afraid you'll have to blame him,' Renée continued. 'He's the one who betrayed his own values, after all. His own beliefs. Although I don't want to speak ill of him, today of all days. These things are complicated.'

Ines started to shake. It didn't seem 'complicated' to her.

Just awful. *Wrong.* She felt as if she'd stumbled into some horrid, dystopian dream and was unable to wake herself up.

After what felt like an interminable silence, she asked Renée a question that would have been unimaginable half an hour ago.

'Do you think he was unfaithful to Maman, when she was alive?'

Renée sat down beside her on the couch, and took Ines's hand in hers.

'I don't know, my love,' she answered truthfully. 'It wouldn't surprise me. But I don't know, and I don't want to know. They're both dead now. I prefer to let them rest in peace.'

'Did Genevieve know?' Ines fought back tears. 'About Alissa and . . . the others?'

Renée nodded.

'What about Charles? Before he was killed . . .'

'We all knew,' Renée admitted.

'Why didn't you tell me?!' The question was so laden with anguish it was almost a wail.

'Oh, Ines.' Now it was Renée's turn to well up. 'We tried, my love. Over the years. We all tried to tell you that Papa was never the saint you imagined him. That he was human and fallible, like everybody else. But you wouldn't listen. You decided he was perfect, and that was that. I did think about telling you about Alissa specifically. But in the end I decided that Papa had hurt you enough. And it would only hurt you more if you knew.'

'It's not your fault,' Ines rasped, choking on the words. This was all too shocking, too terrible, too much for her to process. Just hours ago, she'd been sobbing in church, destroyed by grief for a man that, she now realized, she may never have known at all. And if Papa was capable of this, what other secrets might he have carried to his grave? 'I just need to be by myself, that's all.'

Renée watched, wretched, as her sister left the room.

Poor, poor Ines. She felt dreadful telling her, but it was an inevitability. Ines was no longer a child. And no one could live in the dark forever.

CHAPTER TWENTY-FOUR

The morning after the funeral, Charles Challant's longtime lawyer, Yves Dubonnet, arrived at the bastide to read the will.

'Where would you like to do this?'

The elderly *avocat* looked at Renée, who seemed to be taking charge of proceedings. The older daughter, the one who lived here, appeared confused and dishevelled, with smudged eye make-up and mismatched clothes that hung pathetically from her scrawny frame. Grief, Yves presumed.

He hadn't been inside the house for years, and tried to hide how appalled he was by its current state. Paper peeled from the walls in the hall and entryway, and there were visible stains on the carpet. Several light bulbs had burned out without being replaced, and a general air of dirt and neglect pervaded what had once been a dazzlingly impressive home, full of colour, laughter and life.

'Your father's old study, perhaps?'

Ines shot a glance at Renée. The last place she wanted to hear their father's will being read was in the study, on the same sofa where just hours ago her world had been blown apart by the revelation about Alissa. But needs must, and it was undoubtedly less of a wreck than some of the other, larger rooms.

'Good idea,' said Renée. 'After you.'

As soon as all three daughters had taken their seats, Yves moved behind Charles's desk and got straight down to business.

'I've prepared full copies of your father's will and letter of wishes for each of you.' He laid the documents down on the desk with a thud. 'With your permission, however, I'd like to walk you through the main points first, as there's a fair bit of detail to wade through in the documents.'

'That sounds sensible to me,' said Genevieve.

'And me,' said Renée, praying that Gen wasn't drunk already. She'd seemed all right at breakfast, but that was two hours ago. 'Ines?'

Ines nodded her agreement. She looked tense, and had been uncharacteristically short with Matty when he ran in in search of a toy, shooing him away quite crossly.

'I'll start with you, Ines, if I may,' the lawyer began. 'Although it distresses me to say it, I believe you have been aware for some time of your father's decision to rescind your inheritance?'

'Yes,' said Ines, her voice barely more than a whisper. 'I knew he'd cut me out of the will.'

'Bastard,' Genevieve muttered under her breath.

A few days ago, Ines would have corrected her. Told her that the rift with Papa was her own fault entirely. But now that she knew about Alissa, she wasn't certain what to think, or how to feel. It was all so unsettling.

Turning hopefully towards Yves, she asked, 'I wondered if perhaps I might have been left some small personal items? Nothing of value, but maybe some sort of memento? Perhaps some of his or my mother's things?'

'I'm afraid not,' the lawyer cleared his throat awkwardly. 'In his last letter of wishes, your father made it clear that he wanted neither you, nor your son, to receive any items from his estate whatsoever. Of course, your sisters will be free to use their own judgement with regard to their share,' he added, trying to find a silver lining to Charles Père's shameful instructions.

'Of course you shall have some of Maman's things,' Genevieve assured Ines. 'We'll sort it all out dearest, don't you worry.'

Ines nodded gratefully, but the tight knot in her stomach refused to dissipate. Even in death, it seemed, Papa was determined to punish her. So much for 'Let he who is without sin cast the first stone.'

It was a relief for all of them when Yves moved on. Charles had left the chalet in Megève to Renée, and the bastide to Genevieve, 'Since she has chosen to make it her home.' Further, modest trusts had been left to both the older girls 'for the purpose of maintaining the properties' as well as some smaller, personal gifts.

'The last important point I need to raise with you relates to the remainder of your father's estate,' the old man told them. 'I'm not sure to what degree he discussed this with any of you. But excluding the properties and assets left to Genevieve and Renée individually, everything else has been bequeathed to the Archdiocese de Paris.'

All three girls exchanged astonished glances.

'He left everything to the church?' Renée asked, neatly articulating all three sisters' shock.

'He did,' Yves confirmed.

'Even Place Dauphine?' Ines looked close to tears. It was bad enough that she'd been left nothing, not even a brooch or a painting to remember her parents by. But at least the other homes were remaining within the family. Ines might not own the bastide or the chalet, but she could still visit, and spend time there with her sisters. She could still keep alive that precious thread to her childhood, her past. But to lose Place Dauphine completely, and to the *church*? That was just terrible. What had Papa been thinking? If there was one institution in France with absolutely *no* need of more money, it was the bloody church.

'Ah, well. No, Ines.' Yves Dubonnet blushed, visibly embarrassed. 'The remainder of your father's estate takes the form of cash and securities. To a total sum of . . .' Glancing down at his papers, he read out the relevant figure.

'Then who gets Place Dauphine?' Ines asked the obvious question.

'The bank, darling.' It was Genevieve who answered. Poor Renée had been the bearer of bad news yesterday. Even in her inebriated state, Gen knew it wasn't fair to leave *all* the heart-breaking to her sister.

'I don't understand,' said Ines. 'Why the bank?'

'Papa was in hock to them, since the . . . shtart of the war,' Genevieve slurred. 'Handing over the house was the only way.'

Ines looked from Gen to Renée to her father's lawyer, willing one of them to contradict this lunatic statement. Or at the very least to explain it. When nobody did, she clutched her head in her hands.

'Am I *actually* going mad?' she asked. 'Are you telling me Papa was in debt?'

'Substantial debt, I'm afraid,' replied Yves, matter-of-factly. 'Over the last decade, it seems your father borrowed very heavily against the Paris house. It reached the point where he had no obvious means of repayment on those loans. So, the bank now own the asset.'

'All right,' Ines said hoarsely, allowing this new in-formation to settle into her addled brain. 'But why?'

'Why?' the lawyer repeated. 'Why what?'

'Why did Papa need to borrow so much money?'

'Ah, well. On that point, I'm afraid I have no idea,' Yves replied truthfully, getting to his feet. 'I'll leave you now, to review the paperwork. Please don't hesitate to contact me if you've any questions.'

Any questions . . . Ines turned the words over in her mind as Renée showed the old man to the door. She had countless questions! Nothing but questions.

'You knew.' She rounded on Genevieve accusingly as soon as Renée left the room.

Genevieve looked at her blankly.

'You and Renée *knew* we'd lost Place Dauphine, before Monsieur Dubonnet came here today.'

'We suspected,' Genevieve corrected her.

'Call it what you like,' snapped Ines. 'The point is, you didn't tell me. That was *our house*! I know I always had mixed feelings about it, but Maman died there.'

Genevieve winced at this cold truth but said nothing.

'Why didn't either of you tell me?'

'You di'n' ask.' Genevieve hiccupped the words, drink once again getting the better of her. In other circumstances, Ines would have felt sorry for her. But in this moment, anger blocked out all finer feelings.

'How do you think it feels, knowing you and Renée have been hiding things from me?' she shouted. 'Deliberately keeping secrets?'

'I don't know, Ines.' Gen jabbed a bony finger un-steadily back at her. 'How do *you* think it feels when you and R'nee never come to see me from one year to the next? I'm s'posed to ring *you* up, am I? To *chat* about Papa's finances?'

'I never said that,' Ines said awkwardly. But Genevieve was on a roll.

'And why would I talk to you about Papa?' she rambled on. 'So you can tell me what an amaaaaazing father he was? Well guess what? He wasn't. You d'in even know him, Ines. Not the real him.'

And with that she weaved her way out of the room, leaving a shell-shocked Ines alone.

She wasn't sure why exactly, what impetus had driven her. But ten minutes later Ines found herself standing down at the bottom of the bastide gardens, in the place where Clotilde's aviary had once stood. Just like at the churchyard earlier, the springlike cheerfulness of the surrounding flowers and cherry blossoms, with their bright colours and sweet scents, jarred painfully with the tragic ghosts that haunted this spot. And no one was more haunted than Ines.

Part of her, a deep, important part, remained forever trapped in the summer of 1928. Standing here, now, where the terrible accident took place, Ines was once again the terrified little girl in the rain and the darkness, afraid of the storm and what it meant, afraid of the barking dogs and the screeching birds and the loud bang of thunder that had snatched her from sleep. If she closed her eyes, she could still see the shadows of her parents, frozen with their backs to her. And other shadows too, shapes half remembered, that Ines didn't understand. Didn't *want* to understand.

There's something I need to remember, she thought to herself. *Something here, right here, that hasn't clicked into place.*

At times, she could almost feel it getting closer, rising to the surface from the depths of her psyche. But at other times it was lost to the mists of time, gone completely.

Sinking to her knees, Ines finally gave way to tears.

Much later that night, having finally cried herself out, an exhausted Ines heard a knock at her bedroom door.

'Can I come in?' Renée asked softly.

'Of course.'

Ines sat up, turning on the bedside lamp and patting the covers for her sister to sit.

In an old-fashioned muslin nightgown and with her thick hair brushed out, Renée looked touchingly young, almost like she used to as a teenager. Seeing her like that dragged Ines straight back to childhood summers at Beaulieu again, begging Renée to let her tag along at the farm because Charles Fils was too busy with his friends to make time for her. It struck her then forcefully, that whatever else happened, she must *not* lose Renée. No matter what, the two of them must find a way to stick together.

'Can't you sleep?' Ines asked her.

'I haven't tried yet,' Renée admitted. 'I feel terrible about earlier, Ines.'

'It's all right,' Ines sighed.

'No, it isn't,' insisted Renée. 'We . . . *I* . . . should have told you about Place Dauphine, and Papa's debts. But you know, I wasn't aware myself for a long time. And once I did know, it just never seemed the right time to break it to you. And then Papa died, and there was no more time. I'm sorry.'

'Really, it's all right. I was never going to inherit anyway, so it doesn't affect me directly. I suppose it's just . . . after yesterday, finding out about Alissa and that whole side of his life? Genevieve's right. Here I am mourning Papa, *trying* to mourn him. But I never really knew him at all. I only knew a ghost.'

'Gen isn't right,' Renée said firmly, squeezing her little sister's hand. 'You knew him. You knew the best parts of him, which were as much "him" as the worst parts. That's what you're mourning, and what you have to try to remember. We all do.'

Ines shook her head. It was nice sentiment. But it wouldn't do. She didn't want to grieve for half a father, even if it was the 'good' half. She wanted to know all of him, and knew she would have no peace until she did.

'What do you think happened?' she asked Renée. 'With him getting into debt and mortgaging the house. How did that happen?'

Renée flopped back on the bed, propping her head up on one of Ines's spare pillows.

'I honestly don't know. Gen's convinced it harks back in some way to 1928, and what happened that summer.'

Ines turned to face her, resting on an elbow. 'Really?'

It seemed unlikely, if only because it was all so long ago.

'Do you agree?'

Renée thought about it. 'I don't think so, no. Although I don't have any answers myself. And I do know that Gen's been harassed on more than one occasion since she moved down here, by locals who still feel angry about the boy's death. But even so, it's a stretch. You know as well as I do that Gen's always been partial to a good conspiracy theory, especially where Papa's concerned.'

Ines smiled. 'True. Perhaps it's the frustrated playwright in her, always seeking out drama.'

'Or the drinking,' Renée said bluntly. 'She's much worse.'

A familiar cloud descended over both of them, as it always did when they discussed Genevieve's addiction.

'Do you suppose it's because of Wilhelm?' Ines asked.

Renée shrugged. After the war, Wilhelm had written to Genevieve; a kind letter, full of compassion and fond memories, letting her know that he had survived the fighting, but also that he was engaged to be married to a German girl from his home town. Too much had happened, too much time had passed and blood spilled, for them to pick up their old romantic connection where they'd left off. There was no rancour, no ill-will. And in her more honest moments, Genevieve could admit that no part of the letter had been a surprise. But it nevertheless marked a formal, tangible end to all her hopes, all her fantasies of a happy, married future.

'I think she drinks because she's an alcoholic,' Renée said at last. 'I'm not sure one needs another reason. But I imagine losing Wilhelm didn't help.'

'She's lovely with Matty,' Ines observed, clutching as usual for chinks of light in the darkness. 'So playful and patient and funny. He adores her.'

'Matty's good for her,' Renée agreed. 'I do worry though. About how things will be once you and I go home. How she'll cope. Beaulieu belongs to her now, but she hasn't the faintest idea how to take care of it.'

The same thought had occurred to Ines. She didn't begrudge her older sister her inheritance. But it made her sad to think of this wonderful bastide, so full of memories, sinking ever deeper into disrepair and decay. Especially now that Place Dauphine was to be lost completely.

The latter thought brought her back to Papa, and the mystery surrounding his finances.

'Gunn said something to me once, years ago, about Papa's business affairs. I think it was before we married. But he asked me whether I knew of any dangerous or shady people who Papa had invested with. It was all rather vague, and of course I didn't know of any such people, so I forgot all about it. But do you think it might be connected in some way to these debts?'

'Again, I doubt it,' said Renée. 'I heard those rumours too. We all did. But the fact that it *was* decades ago makes me think it can't be connected to whatever was happening recently.

'All I remember is that, back in 1928, Papa seemed very tense and on edge, even before the summer. He bought those awful doberman dogs for protection, if you remember? So he was scared of something, or someone, and I think Maman was scared too, although she tried not to show it.'

Ines listened, on tenterhooks. Her own memories of that summer were so worn and re-worn that she no longer trusted them; no longer knew what was a genuine memory and what

238

was a dream. Every word from Renée was precious.

'Anyway. Whatever they were afraid of, whatever the trouble was, it was clearly resolved after Maman died. As sad as Papa was, the decade that followed was probably his most successful, business-wise. He certainly wasn't in debt to man or beast the year that you ran off with Gunn. I reckon he could have bought ten Place Dauphines that summer, if he'd wanted to.'

'So what changed?' Ines asked. 'Did he make some catastrophic investment? Was he . . . gambling? Or something criminal? I mean, I know that sounds unlikely,' she added, clocking Renée's amused face. 'But this time last week I would have eaten my hat if anyone had told me he'd had a mistress, never mind more than one. Whatever happened between us, I always believed Papa to be a moral man.'

'I think he was a moral man,' said Renée kindly, seeing her sister on the verge of tears again. 'Just not a perfect one. He made mistakes, and he struggled with that. But you *did* know him, love. And as for the debts, like I say, I don't know what changed,' she went on. 'But truthfully, I'm not sure it matters that much any more. That's also why I came to see you tonight.'

'Oh?' Ines cocked her head to one side, curious.

'I know today must have been hard for you,' Renée went on. 'Not being left anything at all in the will. We won't argue about Papa's motives or the rights and wrongs of it,' she added hastily, seeing Ines open her mouth, preparing to do just that. 'And I know Gen already said you could choose some personal things from her share, as you can from mine. But I also wanted to let you know that I've decided to give you half my share in the chalet. It's only right, Ines, and I can have the paperwork drawn up easily as soon as I get back to London.'

Deeply moved, Ines squeezed Renée's hand tighter. But she shook her head.

'I love you so much for the thought, Ren. Truly, I do. But I can't accept.'

'Of course you can,' said Renée.

'All right, technically I can,' Ines clarified. 'But I don't *want* to. Please don't misunderstand me. I couldn't be more grateful

239

for the offer. But Megève holds too many painful memories for me. Of the Christmas after Maman died. Of Charles Fils. It's also where I met Gunn,' she added, an unmistakable trace of bitterness creeping into her voice.

'But that's silly,' Renée countered robustly. 'You had lots of happy memories there too. But quite apart from all that, it's a valuable house. I'm not sure you realize quite how much it's worth these days.'

'I'm sure you're right,' said Ines. 'But I don't care a fig about the money. Perhaps I would if Matty and I were struggling, but we aren't. We have a lovely flat in Paris and we're doing just fine on our own. It was Papa's wish for you to have that house, Renée. And it's my wish, too.'

Renée looked down at her younger sister's earnest, impassioned face. It was clear that she meant what she said.

'All right,' she said. 'I don't understand you. But all right. Just as long as you know that if ever you change your mind . . .'

'I won't,' she said, squeezing her sister's hand again.

After Renée had gone, Ines lay awake, thinking. It had been such a painful day on so many levels. An awful, painful few days. And yet as she pulled up the blankets on what had once been her childhood bed, she found herself feeling both happy and hopeful.

Renée's kindness was certainly a part of it. Knowing that she had her sister's love in her life was more precious than any inheritance, any piece of jewellery or even any house. But there was a deeper, more profound source to the warm spring of contentment welling within her as she lay in the darkness.

I'm free, she realized. *Free from Gunn. Free from Papa. Free from the past, if I choose to be.*

She would dwell no more on why her father had had to give up Place Dauphine. Or what the real truth was behind his affairs. Or the events of that terrible night in the summer of 1928. Renée was right. At the end of the day, what did any of it matter now?

In the darkness Ines could just make out the faded silk screen of exotic birds that she and her mother had made together all those years ago.

All Maman wanted for me, for any of us, was freedom.

Ines had that now. She would build a new life for herself and Matty, far away from the howling ghosts of the Challant past.

She couldn't speak for her sisters. But this bird of Beaulieu fully intended to soar.

CHAPTER TWENTY-FIVE

Aspen, USA, December 1951

'Another glass of Sancerre over here,' Anna Grierly-Gunn instructed the waiter imperiously. 'And what the hell happened to our apple fritters?'

'I'm sorry, ma'am,' the flustered young man apologized. 'Our kitchen's been really backed up today.'

'Not my problem,' Anna snapped, waving her hand in curt dismissal. 'If I order something I expect it to arrive promptly.'

'Give the guy a break,' mumbled Gunn, embarrassed by Anna's rudeness. 'He's only doing his job.'

The Gunns were spending the Christmas holidays in Aspen, without question America's chicest and most monied ski resort, with a group of friends from New York. They were with Anna's friends, although Gunn had been warmly embraced as her handsome third husband and was now a part of the Grierly 'set', for good or ill. The mountain hut where the party had chosen to stop for lunch was newly open and busy – fully booked, in fact. Although Anna had insisted on a table for eight, and in Aspen, what Anna Grierly wanted, Anna Grierly got.

'That's the whole point, darling.' She smiled at Gunn but there was a steely glint in her eye that left him in no doubt she was displeased at being corrected in public. 'He's *not* doing his job. Or at least not doing it well. And as I'm the one paying, I'll complain if I darn well please.'

A sycophantic chorus of 'hear hear's and 'good for you's rang out around the table and Gunn did what he always did when Anna played the money card: retreated into resentful silence.

How on earth had he got himself into this predicament? What was he *doing* here, in a foreign country, eating lunch with people he barely knew and a wife he was growing actively to loathe, and who he suspected felt the same about him?

Unfortunately, Gunn already knew the answer to those questions. He also knew he had only himself to blame.

After Ines left him over six years ago, making it clear she never wanted to lay eyes on him again, Gunn had been temporarily at a loss. He did not contest the divorce. As Ines's sister Renée had impressed on him forcefully, the very least he owed his wife was her freedom, after all the pain he'd caused. But despite his heartbreak and devastation, he was also aware that it wasn't *only* Ines herself that he had lost. All of the schemes and business opportunities he'd been cultivating during the war years had relied to some degree on his marriage and connection to Ines's family. Estranged or not, the Challant name still opened doors, and while there was a possibility of a rapprochement with his uber wealthy father-in-law – particularly if Gunn and Ines were to provide the old man with grandchildren – other rich investors remained interested. Once that hope was removed, Gunn had little to offer, and no discernible skills beyond his wit, charm and ability to ski to the bottom of a mountain faster than almost any other man alive.

So when Anna Grierly swept back into his life, making it clear that she wanted not just to rekindle their affair, but to make him her third husband, he was torn.

On the one hand, he bitterly regretted ever meeting Anna. He never did find out who spilled the beans about their liaison to Ines. Although he grudgingly accepted that it hadn't been Edward Turnbull who sent the fateful letter, he struggled to think of who else might want to see his marriage wrecked for the sake of what, for Gunn, had been a mere passing attraction; a stupid slip that he'd regretted almost at once.

For Anna though, their relationship had been much more significant from the start. It wasn't that she loved him. To be frank, Gunn wasn't sure whether Anna was even capable of love, other than a narcissistic regard for herself. Instead it was

243

a matter of control. Of power. Of winning a game that had swiftly become a battle from the moment Gunn ended things between them and went back to his wife. For Anna, 'losing' a lover to a younger, more beautiful woman felt like a death. The fact that the woman in question was Gunn's wife mattered not a jot.

On the other hand, not to put too fine a point on it: Anna was rich. She was rich, smitten, and she was all Gunn had. In fairness, she was also intelligent and attractive and could be terrific company when she chose to be. And Ines was gone after all, lost to him forever.

So they married, and after a vulgarly decadent society wedding in New York, Gunn moved into Anna's palatial townhouse on East 71st Street. For a few months, he was happy, allowing himself to enjoy the novel feeling of having large amounts of money at his disposal, and being courted and fawned on by Manhattan's movers and shakers. He ignored the nagging voice inside, reminding him these things were due solely to his connection to Anna and the Grierly fortune. But the voice would not be quieted, and it wasn't long before Gunn's new life began to turn sour.

Anna was generous with her fortune. But her largesse came at a price. *She* was the breadwinner. *She* was the boss. Allowing Gunn to dominate her in bed was one thing. But socially, and in all other spheres of their life, she expected him to defer to her wishes. If he failed to do so, she was quick to belittle him, mocking his slow reading and lack of education and patronizing him in front of their 'friends' to the point where he often felt like little more than the gigolo his sister accused him of being.

'You make Anna out to be the devil,' an exasperated Laura told him, during their final, spectacular fight last year. Laura Gunn had married immediately after the war and had recently given birth to twin girls, an unexpected later-life blessing that had softened her generally, and prompted a renewed effort to improve her relationship with Gunn. Brother and sister had been having lunch in an expensive restaurant off Piccadilly, paid for by Anna of course, when the argument erupted. Partly because Gunn appeared to see no irony in slurping down oysters and champagne at his new wife's expense while eviscerating her character as shallow and mercenary.

'For all I know, she is the devil,' said Laura. 'But *you* sold your soul to her, Hector. Willingly and with your eyes wide open. So don't come whining to me if you're unhappy. Fix things. Leave.'

Her words stung because Gunn knew they were true. But leaving was a lot easier said than done. Leaving meant poverty. It also meant two failed marriages. Back to square one.

So he'd returned to New York. Last year he'd tried to heal the rift with his sister by finally buying back Maltings, fulfilling the promise he'd made long ago to return it to Edie. He'd had to wheedle and cajole, abasing himself to Anna in order to get the funds. But he'd done it at last, extracting at least one good thing from the disaster of his marriage. And it was a big thing, too. His goal and his dream ever since the day his father died. But even that spectacular triumph had been destined to turn to dust in his hands.

Deciding to travel back to England unannounced and surprise his mother by driving her to the old house and handing her the keys, Gunn arrived at Edie's cottage to find her frightened and confused. It had been over two years since he'd last seen her in person, and her mental decline had been far more precipitous than Gunn had realized. Standing on her doorstep, he realized with an awful lurch that, for the first few moments at least, his mother didn't know who he was. 'It's me, Ma,' he tried to reassure her. 'It's Hector.'

Eventually, even if momentarily, Edie's memory re-turned. But when he drove her to Maltings, with its distinctive, bay-windowed Victorian wing glued like an eccentric carbuncle to the original Elizabethan manor, Edie stared at it vacantly. The idea that she might be forced to leave the familiar surroundings of her cottage to live in this strange, enormous, building filled her with abject panic.

'Why didn't you warn me?'

Gunn confronted Laura afterwards. He'd been convinced that if he physically took Edie back to Maltings, seeing the house would jog her memory. But there'd been nothing, not even a flicker.

'I tried to,' Laura defended herself, listening to her brother rant while she pushed her daughters around the park in their pram. 'For years I've been trying to get you to see what's been happening with Ma. But you didn't want to hear it, Hector. You just ploughed on with your own plans, like you always do.'

This was true, too. It was all true.

Ines had understood his yearning for Maltings, his need to buy it back at all costs, both to honour his father's legacy and to repair his mother's grief. She'd supported his dream, even when they'd been living in a tiny Cornish cottage with barely enough funds to feed themselves, or room to swing a cat. Even when it had seemed impossible. A childish, whimsical part of him wished he could call Ines up now and cry on her shoulder. Share the grief of his mother's lost memory, of it all being too late, with the one person who was certain to empathize. But of course, he'd lost that right long ago.

Feeling lower and more trapped than ever, Gunn once again returned to New York and Anna, who wasn't remotely interested in Maltings or Gunn's family issues.

'Do cheer up, darling,' she chastised him. 'I'm having the Aspen house completely done up in time for Christmas, and we're going to throw *the* most fabulous party. Look at the pictures the designer sent me.'

The platter of apple fritters finally arrived, piping hot and smelling of cinnamon and burned sugar. Anna and the others dived in, but Gunn had no appetite.

'I think I'll head back up the mountain,' he announced, pushing back his chair with an awkward, creaking sound.

'By yourself?' Casey Webber, a Wall Street guy and one of the least objectionable of Anna's friends, looked at him askance. 'Don't do that, old man. Give me a few minutes and I'll come with you. We'll leave this lot to finish the vino.'

'Thanks,' said Gunn. 'But I'd prefer to ski alone for a bit. Clear my head.'

'Oh, just leave him, Casey,' snapped Anna, viciously gulping down her third Sancerre. 'He's sulking. Did I tell you Gunn used to be a ski teacher, back in Europe? Helping snotty-nosed rich kids clip up their boots so he could afford to stay for the season. Can you imagine? I believe that was how you met your first wife, wasn't it darling?'

But Gunn had already fled, out into the snow and as far away from Anna as he could.

By the time he got back to the chalet that night, Anna was home alone. Sitting in a Frank Lloyd Wright armchair, an artfully dressed Christmas tree looming behind her, she looked as coldly beautiful as a statue. Wearing black, wide-leg pants and a matching cashmere turtle neck, with an enormous emerald ring glinting on her left hand and a full tumbler of Jack Daniel's clasped in her right, she radiated the angry, dangerous energy of a rattlesnake, discreetly coiled yet poised to strike.

'You missed dinner.'

Gunn walked silently to the bar and fixed a drink for himself.

'We had a table at the Red Onion,' Anna went on, her voice so slow and deliberate that it made him wonder whether she'd been drinking solidly since lunch. 'Everyone else went on to the Jerome. But I thought I'd come home and wait for you. Like a dutiful wife.'

She smiled, but there was no joy in the expression.

'We can't carry on like this, Anna.' Gunn looked at her, taking a long, fortifying slug of his own drink.

'Can't we? I don't see why not.'

'Yes you do. We don't love each other. I'm not sure we even like each other.'

'Are those things prerequisites for marriage?' Anna swirled the whiskey around in her glass contemplatively. 'I'm not convinced. I don't like being alone. You don't like being poor.'

Gunn raised an eyebrow. Not because it wasn't true, but because he was surprised by her honesty.

'And we're attracted to each other,' Anna continued. 'That counts for something, doesn't it?'

Gunn looked away. His silence spoke volumes. The longer it went on, the darker and more belligerent Anna's expression became until in the end she could contain herself no longer.

'You're not still holding a torch for the French girl, are you?' she spat contemptuously. 'Your *child bride*?'

'Don't speak about Ines,' Gunn muttered through clenched teeth.

'I'll speak about whomever I choose,' Anna retorted. 'It's my house. I can do what I like.'

Gunn's jaw clenched and a muscle in his cheek began to twitch, but he said nothing.

'It's just a pity that your devotion to dearest Ines didn't come to the surface earlier,' said Anna, her sing-song tone laden with spite. 'Before you decided to take me to bed, all those times. In Yorkshire. In London. In Brighton.' She counted them off on her fingers.

'It is a pity,' snapped Gunn.

'And just *imagine* our being photographed together, in *all those places*?' Anna fluttered her eyelashes and adopted a look of faux surprise. 'And *someone* sending the pictures to poor Ines? It's just too much.'

Gunn set down his drink. He almost laughed.

'My God. It was you. *You* sent the letter.'

Anna smirked.

'It's so obvious. But somehow I didn't think of it. It just never occurred to me that you'd be so . . .'

'Resourceful?' Anna offered, sweetly.

'Vicious,' Gunn corrected. 'I know better now though.'

Marching into the bedroom, he began pulling his clothes out of the wardrobe. As awful as it was, Anna's admission made things easier somehow. He'd been torn about leaving her this afternoon. As she rightly said, he did not relish being poor. Or alone. Although truth be told, he didn't think he'd ever felt quite as lonely as he had this past year, stuck in New York and his miserable marriage.

'If you leave, you'll get nothing,' Anna roared, staggering in after him. 'Not one cent. And I'll make sure your name is mud with anyone who knows us. You can forget going cap in hand to your "chums" in the regiment. No one will want to know you. Are you listening to me?'

But Gunn wasn't. Tossing the last of his things into the smart, monogrammed valise Anna had bought him for their honeymoon, he closed the brass fastenings with a satisfying *click* and walked towards the door.

'Think hard,' Anna glared at him, stretching her thin arms across the doorway to block his path. 'If you go tonight, there's no coming back.'

Gunn pushed past her.

'You'll regret it.'

'No, I won't,' he said quietly.

His future had never been more uncertain. But he was one hundred per cent sure about that.

CHAPTER TWENTY-SIX

Paris, France, February 1952

'*Pardonnez-moi*. I'm so sorry I'm late. Oh my goodness. Excuse me.'

A flustered Ines weaved her way through the tables at Chez Maurice, fanning her flushed face.

'I got stuck at the hotel,' she panted, arriving at last at her friend Sylvie's table. 'The design meeting went on *forever*. Lucien Toulon is just so specific and detail-orientated, I couldn't get away. Do you hate me? Are you starving?'

Sylvie smiled, amused by the chaos that Ines seemed to bring with her, like the asteroid tail of a particularly glamorous and enchanting comet. In a fuchsia-pink dress and cinched Chanel boucle jacket, teamed with a tur-quoise silk headscarf that she untied now with a flourish and tossed carelessly onto the table, Ines was certainly the most strikingly dressed woman in the restaurant, and almost certainly the most beautiful – although at Chez Maurice, there was always competition in that category, especially on a Friday lunchtime. Reservations here were like gold dust.

'I don't hate you, but I am starving,' said Sylvie, turning around to look again for a waiter. For the last ten minutes she'd been invisible, but the moment Ines sat down, two servers raced to their table at once, like genies from a newly rubbed lamp.

'*Qu'el-que chose à boire, mademoiselles?*'

'We're madames,' Sylvie said crossly. 'And yes, we would both like a drink. And to order some food as soon as possible. I'll have a salade niçoise to start with, and my friend . . . ?'

'I'll have the same,' said Ines absently. Reaching across the table, she clasped her friend's hand. 'It's so good to see you.'

'You look well,' observed Sylvie. 'Happy.'

The two women had met in the park several years ago when both had babies the same age and had become firm friends, despite their wildly different lives. Sylvie was a conservative, happily married mother to three children whose life revolved around her family and who rarely left Paris. Ines, by contrast, was fast becoming one of France's most highly sought after interior designers, who lived equally for her son and her work, but who always seemed to be jetting off to one glamorous location after another on exciting-sounding 'business'. Her latest commission, completely redesigning the iconic Lafayette hotel for its new millionaire playboy owner, Lucien Toulon, had been in all the society gossip pages and was the talk of the town.

'I am happy,' gushed Ines. 'Exhausted but happy. I actually think this hotel's going to be incredible when it's finished. But it's a far bigger job than I realized. I've no idea how I'm going to juggle my other projects at the same time.'

'What's he like?' asked Sylvie. 'Toulon?'

'I told you,' said Ines, helping herself to water and bread with all the enthusiasm of a starving prisoner. 'He's demanding. Knows exactly what he wants, or thinks he does. I really have to push to get him to see my vision, my ideas.'

'Is he as handsome as they say?' Sylvie pressed her.

'Handsome?' Ines frowned. 'I don't really know. I suppose so.'

It was baffling to Sylvie, and to everyone else who knew her, how a woman as young and vibrant as Ines could remain so resolutely uninterested in romance. It wasn't just that she didn't want to marry again. That part Sylvie could have understood. Ines never spoke about her first marriage – never, ever – but it was clear that the end of that relationship had hurt her badly, and was an experience she had no wish to repeat. But this was Paris, in the 1950s! A new era, and a new world for single, financially independent women. She could have taken a lover; several lovers, if she chose to. She could have allowed herself to be wined and dined, or flirted with any one of the myriad, eligible men who tried, unsuccessfully, to woo her. But she simply refused to engage. 'I have Matty,' was her mantra, whenever anybody asked. 'What more do I need? And besides, I simply haven't the time.'

Recently, this latter excuse may have become true. Even Sylvie had had to make an appointment to meet Ines weeks in advance. But she was pleased to see her smiling. The last time they'd met, for a drink at the Georges V, Ines had looked sleep-deprived and frazzled, and had been complaining of recurrent nightmares.

'How are the dreams?' Sylvie asked, once their salads arrived. 'Have they stopped?'

A cloud descended over Ines's pretty features. 'No. I'm waking less at night, but no. The dreams are still there.'

'Still with your mother's birds?'

Ines nodded grimly. 'For so many years now. Birds screeching. Dogs barking. But now increasingly, right before I wake up, this BANG!' She gave a little shudder. 'I honestly sit up clutching my chest, like I've been shot. It's horrendous.'

'It sounds it,' said Sylvie. 'Did you go to see the man I suggested? Clemenceau?'

'Several times.' Ines stabbed frustratedly at her bitter *frisée* salad leaf with a fork.

'And?'

'Money for nothing.' She sipped the cold Chablis that had just been placed in front of her, cheering slightly as the crisp, gooseberry deliciousness invaded her senses. 'God, that's good wine.'

'Really?' Sylvie was disappointed. 'He didn't help you at all?'

'I mean, we talked, and he was very nice. He had a lot of theories about my father.'

'Oh?' Sylvie tilted her head, interested. Ever since reading a book on Freudian analysis, she'd become fascinated with the whole field of examining the subconscious. Disappointingly, her own dreams tended to be mundane affairs. But she felt sure that her friend Ines was a rich mine of angst and repression, just waiting to be tapped.

'He basically said the dreams were caused by my anxiety, and my anxiety was caused by my "unresolved attachment" to my father,' said Ines. 'But I mean, it doesn't take Freud to work that out. And now it turns out that everything I thought I knew about my father was basically a lie, I honestly don't know how I'm supposed to "resolve" anything.'

'Hmmm,' breathed Sylvie, sympathetically. Ines had told her about all the revelations from her father's funeral, with the mistress turning up and the various surprises in the will. 'Well what about this tremendous bang at the end of your dreams? That's new, isn't it? Does Clemenceau think that's significant? Because I think it *must* be.'

'Ugh. I really don't know,' groaned Ines. 'Can we please talk about something else?'

Their conversation moved on to their respective children. Sylvie's eldest, Martin, had just been accepted into a prestigious lycée for senior school, and her younger daughter Anaïs was giving a piano recital at the Conservatoire de Paris.

'Does Matty still play?' Sylvie asked.

'Very badly,' said Ines. But the mere mention of her son had lit her up from within, like someone flicking a light switch. 'He's slightly into drawing at the moment. And Gothic ghost stories. Although since he became an altar boy he's started spending a huge amount of time down at the church.'

Sylvie laughed. 'You say that like it's a bad thing. It's church, Ines, not the Folies Bergère.'

'True,' Ines smiled. 'I don't know, though. Matthieu does have a tendency to become a bit obsessive. You know, when he's really into something.'

Her friend gave her a knowing look. 'You don't say? I wonder where he gets that from?'

After lunch, the two women parted, heading in opposite directions to pick up their children from their respective schools.

253

Ines's walk was longer, close to two miles, across the river and through her old neighbourhood at the western end of the Île de la Cité. Ordinarily she would have hailed a cab. But for once she had a little time on her hands, and it was such a beautiful afternoon, she relished the prospect of a stroll.

It had been nice to see Sylvie. Ines's busy life left little time for socializing, but the few close friendships she had, she cherished. With Sylvie in particular, it gave her comfort that their lives were *so* different. Sylvie didn't care that Ines was from a famous family, or that she designed homes for film actresses and socialites and their high-rolling financier husbands. Nor was she interested in Ines's past before they met. With Sylvie, Ines existed solely in the present – which was just how she liked it. She already spent far too much of her life in the company of ghosts.

Paris was full of them. Especially the streets she walked now, the avenues close to the river where she used to stroll with her mother in the springtime as a child, in between the Challant flock's winter and summer migrations. Back then Paris had always felt like a stopgap, a humdrum waiting room of a city that had to be endured before the excitement of Beaulieu or the thrill of Megève. Perhaps Genevieve had felt a deeper attachment to Place Dauphine. But Ines and Renée were both summer birds. For them, Beaulieu had always been the big draw, just as Charles Fils, the snow finch, had lived for Megève and the mountains.

And yet it was Paris where they'd all spent by far the most time. Paris where they went to school, and where Papa worked. Paris where Charles Père and Clotilde had met and married. Where all the Challant children had been born, and where both of their parents had died. It was Paris Ines had returned to after the war and after Gunn, with her shattered heart and, not long afterwards, her precious new baby. So perhaps, deep down, the city had always meant more to her than she'd chosen to admit?

Turning the corner past L'Église Sainte-Marguerite, where the Challants had sat in the front pew at mass for generations, the echoes of the past felt deafening. Ines remembered standing beside her father, bored and cold and stiff in her uncomfortable woollen coat and muffler, reciting the Latin prayers that they'd all learned in infancy. She remembered how her eyes would wander to the bright colours of the stained-glass windows, which seemed as exotic and cheerfully out of place in this cold stone church as Maman's tropical birds had in their aviary at Beaulieu. In her childish mind, Ines had associated her mother with both the birds and the windows, and her father, much as she loved him, with the stone and the cold and the bars of the cages. That latter association made her feel guilty and ashamed, although she wouldn't have been able to name either of those emotions at the time. Rather, she would have said she felt sick. Ines was often 'sick' at church.

It was one of the reasons she found it so hard to understand her son's natural and growing affinity for religion. The building that, for her, had always felt like a place of conflict, a place where the two sides of her nature were torn, was becoming Matty's sanctuary and his playground. He loved the pageantry and magic of the mass, the robes and the incense and the swell of the organ music. Serving as an altar boy seemed to make him more joyful than almost any of his other activities, even riding his bike which was a close second now that he'd fully got the hang of it.

Sylvie's right, Ines told herself. *Matty liking church is a good thing, not a problem.* But she couldn't fully shake her unease.

'Maman!'

Running down the steps of the school, his satchel flapping behind him like a tailfeather, Matty launched himself with unselfconscious abandon into Ines's arms.

'I *have* to tell you about today. You won't *believe* what happened!'

At seven years old, tall and slim with an unruly mop of blond hair and moss-green eyes that crinkled into little slits when he smiled, Matthieu was known affectionately to his teachers and classmates as *un bavard*: a chatterbox. Curious about everything, and with the sort of inexhaustible energy unique to a certain type of child, he rarely drew breath on their walks to and from school, regaling Ines with tale after tale of his friends' antics, or the latest *amazing* fact he'd learned in science.

'The moon, right? You know the moon? It's more than three-hundred and eighty thousand kilometres away! Did you know that? Madame Dupont asked us all to guess, and I was the second closest because I said two hundred thousand, but do you know what Amelie said? *Twenty kilometres!* I mean, how can you think the moon is twenty kilometres away?'

Ines mumbled a few words in Amelie's defence as they started home, but Matty was having none of it.

'Orsay is twenty kilometres away. That's like thinking Orsay is the moon!'

As he nattered on, skipping contentedly beside her, Ines found herself turning left into Place Dauphine. It wasn't their usual route home, and in general she made a point of avoiding the grand garden square where she'd grown up. Her Paris was now a triangle, its three points formed by her and Matty's Marais apartment, her office in the Quartier Saint-Louis, and Matty's school. Somewhere in the middle of that triangle was the small church where Matty served on the altar. But today, for some reason, Ines felt an urge to see her old home again.

The square was now fully restored after its wartime damage and more radiantly beautiful than ever. But the house itself was in a shockingly dilapidated state. The once gleaming wrought-iron gates hung part-rusted from broken hinges. Behind them a scraggly, weed-infested front garden led up to a house that clearly hadn't been lived in for several years. Crumbling walls, destroyed in places by aggressively invasive ivy, framed filthy windows with rotting frames. Missing tiles above the gabled windows gave the façade the look of a decrepit old man with a mouthful of broken teeth.

Without realizing it, Ines stopped and stared, her hand clamped over her mouth and her eyes welling with tears.

'Oh, Maman!' Matty hugged her, confused and clearly worried. 'Don't cry, Maman. What's the matter? Is it that sad old house making you upset?'

Ines nodded, hugging him back and hurriedly pulling herself back together. *That sad old house.* Of course Place Dauphine meant nothing in particular to her son. Why would it? To Matty it was just a building, like any other. Charles Père had made sure of that in his will.

'Yes darling,' she sniffed. 'I think it is, a little.'

'But why?' He looked up at her, perplexed. 'I mean, it does look sad. But it's not our house.'

'No.' Ines forced a smile. 'You're quite right, Matty. It's not our house. I'm being silly.'

Perhaps it was for the best that he didn't know. About the house, or his grandfather's will, or any of it. Despite his curious nature, Matty was too happily immersed in his own present to worry about his mother's past.

Very occasionally he would press Ines for more details about his own father: who he was, where he was, and why they couldn't see him. But for the most part he was happy to accept her explanations. That she had made a solemn promise never to name the man, for reasons that she couldn't divulge but that she promised Matty were honourable. That he had been a good man and they had parted as friends.

The little boy's world had always consisted of himself and his mother, no one else. It never occurred to him that there was anything missing.

'I know. Let's get a tarte tatin from Café Flo,' he suggested now, tugging Ines's hand to draw her away from the horrid, spooky old house. 'That'll cheer us both up. And then we can go into St Bernadette's and say a prayer that whoever lives in the house comes back and tidies it up.'

Bending down, Ines kissed the top of his head.

Cake and prayer. Those were Matty's answers to everything.

*

In bed later that night, as she lay sketching out design ideas for her new commission at the Lafayette Hotel, Ines's mind kept boomeranging back to Place Dauphine.

The house belonged to the bank. At first it had baffled her, why a rich, financial institution would take so little care of such a valuable asset? To let a grand old mansion like that fall derelict seemed foolish in the extreme. But eventually she realized that that was her heart talking, not her head. And that banks had no heart. If the bank had declined to invest in the house, it could only be because they stood to make greater profits by abandoning it. After all, the costs of upkeeping those grand old *hôtels de villes* were eye-watering while the value of the land they stood on rose exponentially year after year, at no cost at all. Especially in a prime Paris address like Place Dauphine.

Leaving the place to rot must make good business sense, or they wouldn't be doing it. But as both a Challant and a lover of beautiful homes, it broke Ines's heart to see it in such a sad, depleted state. *It would have broken Papa's heart, too.*

No. She mustn't think about Papa. She must focus on the present. On the work in front of her.

Turning back to her sketches, Ines's mind gradually began to wander again, but this time in a different direction. Sylvie had asked her at lunch today whether her new client, Lucien Toulon, was handsome. The truthful answer to that question was yes. Stockily built with strong, Roman features and thick dark hair only slightly greying at the temples, it was easy to see how Lucien had become such a sought-after lover among Paris's bored, wealthy wives. And although she did a good job of hiding it, Ines too had registered his charms, filing them away under 'Caution' alongside his subtly flirtatious manner. It wasn't that she didn't *notice* men any more, despite what her friends might think. She wasn't dead. And the wistful, romantic part of her that still believed in love and romance and happily-ever-after was still somewhere within, albeit battered and bruised. But whatever passing desire or yearning she might feel to experience love again was held very firmly in check by her newly developed instinct for self-preservation.

Loving, like remembering, was dangerous.

Ines had learned this the hard way. But still, this afternoon, some force outside of herself had led her back to the ghosts, back to both love and memory. Standing in front of the wreck of her childhood home, gazing up at all that had been lost, something had shifted inside her. She felt as if she were being called back, called to *do* something. But what?

All of a sudden, the random thought came to her: perhaps the *BANG* that ended her recurring nightmares was not a clap of thunder. What if, instead, it represented the firing of a starter pistol, telling her to move, to run, to begin the race?

But a race to where? And for what purpose?

Exhausted, she set down her sketch book and turned off the bedside lamp. She really mustn't let Sylvie's Freudian mumbo jumbo get to her like this. Dreams were just dreams. They didn't have to mean anything.

Even so, Ines hoped that tonight she might be spared the birds and the dogs and the bang. She'd had more than enough ghosts for one day.

CHAPTER TWENTY-SEVEN

Cornwall, England, April 1953

Gunn stood in what had once been his father's study at Maltings, now an empty, pathetic-looking room with scuffed floorboards and peeling cornicing, watching the light spring rain scatter across the lawn, dusting the apple blossoms with water.

He'd come down to Cornwall to make a decision. With Maltings now his only asset after the divorce from Anna, he must either move in himself and attempt to find enough work locally to support himself, furnish the place and pay for its upkeep; or sell it; or, conceivably, rent it out to a family in more fortunate circumstances than his own, until he got fully back on his feet. Whenever that might be.

The agent Gunn met with yesterday had been unequivocal in his advice.

'Sell. It's really the only answer. Rambling old houses like this burn money like you wouldn't believe. Heating the place alone will be a small fortune, and because prospective tenants know it, the rental yields are dreadfully low. Whereas buyers, if they're wealthy enough, are still happy to cough up for the dream. For their name on the letterhead.'

Gunn didn't doubt that it was sound advice. But the trouble was, Maltings was still *his* dream, albeit a broken one. And one he couldn't bear to part with.

Leaving the study, he creaked his way through the empty rooms and corridors. The house itself was still stately and beautiful, its mullioned windows and fine stone fireplaces crying out for people and colour and *life*. For furniture and bright tasselled cushions and children's laughter and toys and books. Gunn could envision it, even if he wasn't a designer like Ines.

Ines. Her beautiful face drifted into his mind with increasing frequency these days. No doubt she could have transformed the place with a click of her fingers. Even Anna, for all that he loathed her, knew how to 'pull together' a room, just as long as she had limitless cash at her disposal with which to do it. Gunn had neither Anna's cash nor Ines's artistic vision. But he loved Maltings like a person, like a beloved child. And he remembered it as a vibrant, happy house. Come what may, he couldn't leave it like this.

Gliding upstairs like a ghost, the dust on the bannisters sticking to the palm of his left hand in a filthy, grey film as he climbed, Gunn moved from his childhood bedroom, to his parents', weighing up his options.

Sell, stay, rent. Sell stay rent. The words echoed through his depressed brain like a mantra. Finally he mounted the rickety ship's-ladder stairs up to the attic. The floors here had been dangerous for years, and Gunn instinctively trod cautiously, stepping from beam to beam without resting any weight on the flimsy planks between. A bare light bulb flickered overhead when he hit the switch, revealing a lot of cobwebs and not much else. Like the rest of the house, the attic was largely empty, save for a few fossilized-looking packing crates stacked together at the far end, beneath the skylight.

How long have those been there? wondered Gunn. Even from a distance the boxes looked ancient. A closer inspection revealed that they were indeed pre-war, and perhaps even nineteenth century, back when crates of that type were made from hardwood and nailed together. *They might even be ours*, he thought, with building excitement. After all, it wasn't impossible that a crate or two had been left behind in the chaos after William Gunn's death. And none of the owners since had taken them.

Hurrying back downstairs, he darted out to his car in the rain and retrieved the tool box from the boot. Armed with a screwdriver and hammer, and with his hair and jacket still dripping, he returned to the attic and knelt gingerly beside the crates. Prying open the nearest one, he pulled out the splintered planks and reached into the wood-shavings within. The sensation was wildly nostalgic, like sticking one's hand into a lucky dip at a children's birthday party. But he quickly found his fingers closing around something soft and familiar, big enough that it needed two hands to grip it properly.

Extracting the treasure at last, Gunn found himself staring at a pristine, white-feathered, stuffed bird on a stand. And not just any bird. He would have known that crested white head and proud, almost regal tilt of the neck anywhere. Even without the brass plate reading '*Cacatua alba Muller, Indonesia 1918*'.

A cockatoo.

Ines's favourite bird.

Beauty and brains.

Gunn used to believe in signs. But the older he got, the more cynical he'd become. So he was surprised to find himself unable to stop his hands shaking, or his pulse racing, as he stared into the bird's glassy eyes. It was one of William's specimens, that much was for sure. A solid, tangible link between all three of the great losses of Gunn's life: his father; his adored childhood home; and the only woman he had ever truly loved.

Gently placing the stuffed bird back into its crate, Gunn walked back downstairs. He'd felt sad and reflective before, but now his sorrow was so heavy it threatened to overwhelm him.

'I can't stay here,' he said aloud, to the empty hall. 'If I stay here, I'll drown.'

And in that moment, the decision was made.

The rain outside had stopped. Resting his hand lovingly on the oak-panelled front door, Gunn pulled it open and walked out into the pale spring sunshine.

Three days later, in the British Museum in Bloomsbury, Professor Horatio Chapman stood back and watched from a distance as a young man approached one of the exhibits. Perhaps 'young' was the wrong term. Although fit and handsome in a well-cut pair of Oxford slacks and a V-necked sweater, the fellow might have been forty. But then youth was a relative term, and to Professor Chapman's rheumy old eyes, the man staring intently at the Ecuadorian *Tsantsas*, or shrunken heads, appeared very much in his prime.

Chapman had worked at the museum for forty years, the better part of his adult life, and was familiar with all its treasures. But the small side room that housed the Gunn collection had always been one of his favourites. Smaller now than it had been when William Gunn first bequeathed it to the museum, and with fewer objects on display, it remained a miniature Aladdin's cave of the absurd with its tribal artefacts, extinct birds' eggs, rare fossils and more. The professor stopped in regularly, and although he occasionally encountered a tourist or two idly glancing at William Gunn's exhibits, these days they tended to drift swiftly in and out, on their way to the more famous Egyptian mummies or Saxon burial displays.

This fellow, however, had stood in the same spot for more than ten minutes now, transfixed by the tiny, sightless eyes looking back at him.

'Marvellous, aren't they?' Professor Chapman slowly approached him.

'I'm not sure that's the word I'd use,' the man replied, without taking his eyes off the heads. 'They're certainly compelling. But it's terribly sad.'

'Sad that they're dead?' the professor probed.

'Sad that they ended up like *that*,' said the man. 'With their heads hanging from a string in a glass case, thousands of miles away from where they lived and died.'

'Horatio Chapman.' The old man extended his hand, eager to meet this empathetic and curious person. But when the man turned around he was taken aback. 'Good grief!'

'Is something the matter?'

'No, no, it's just that . . . you look so like him.'

'Like who?'

'Like William. Like your father,' said Chapman. 'I assume I *am* talking to William Gunn's son?'

Now it was Gunn's turn to be taken aback. 'You knew my father?'

'Certainly,' Chapman smiled. 'I knew your father very well. Very well indeed.'

Gunn had stopped into the museum on a whim, on his way to meet his sister Laura for lunch. After leaving Maltings he'd jumped straight on a train to town, in need of busy streets and life and action to combat his depression, but also because he wanted to let Laura know his decision about the house.

Seeing the rest of their father's collection again felt strange and emotional enough, especially after his discovery of the cockatoo in the attic. He hadn't set foot in the British Museum since his youth, back when he was squiring Tig Hanborough around town. But to run into somebody who'd actually known William? That was surely a coincidence too far . . . that the house should lead him to the bird, which led him to London, and the museum, and now this?

'We worked together on several expeditions,' Chapman explained, sensing Gunn's bewilderment. 'I was the one who persuaded William to leave his collection to us in his will.'

Gunn looked at him curiously. 'Did he need persuading? I'd have thought he'd have been only too delighted to have all this on display.'

'He *did* need persuading,' Horatio Chapman chuckled. 'Your father had what might nowadays be described as a "love–hate" relationship with the British Museum. He admired the place, of course. But the trustees weren't always as forthcoming as he might have wished with funding for his expeditions.'

'Ah,' said Gunn, smiling ruefully. It felt strange, but oddly comforting, to be talking about his father again after so many years. Remembering both his strengths and his foibles.

'There were some here who felt that the breadth of William's interests diminished the value of his work,' Chapman went on. 'He was something of a magpie, you see. Anything shiny that interested him, he took.'

Gunn nodded.

'Most scientists are specialists. Archaeologists are too,' the professor explained.

'Yes, but Pa wasn't a scientist or an archaeologist,' said Gunn. 'He was an adventurer.'

'Exactly!' Chapman's eyes lit up. 'And therein lay the rub.'

Silence fell for a moment. For the first time, it struck Horatio Chapman that there was an air of sadness about William Gunn's son. An almost tangible loneliness, in fact.

'And you, young man?' he asked kindly. 'Are you an adventurer?'

Gunn laughed, but it was a brittle sound, without much merriment.

The term 'adventurer' had certainly been used to describe him in the past, but not in the way that Professor Chapman meant.

'I'm afraid not.'

'So what do you do?'

'That's a very good question,' said Gunn. 'To be honest, I'm rather between jobs just now.'

To his own surprise, he found himself telling this complete stranger about his divorce from Anna, the mixed emotions of returning to Maltings, and feeling at a loss as to what he should do next.

'I never was much good at school or exams, you see. I have trouble with reading,' he heard himself admitting, matter-of-factly. 'Apart from ski racing and fighting in the war, I don't really have much experience of anything. So to be perfectly frank with you, I'm not sure how employable I am.'

Horatio Chapman listened. William Gunn's son might look like him. But William would never have spoken about his weaknesses with such humility and honesty. This man's self-awareness and courage both spoke well of his character, in Chapman's opinion. And he was clearly intelligent, and interested in many of the things that had interested his father. Curiosity was what had made William Gunn such a brilliant collector, albeit in his own, maverick way. Chapman found himself wondering whether his boy had inherited the trait, along with his father's charm.

'Would you care to have lunch?' he asked, once Gunn had finished his story. 'There's a tolerable café over the road, if you've the time.'

Gunn's face fell. 'I'd love to, professor, I really would. But I'm afraid I can't today. I'm meeting my sis . . . Oh Lord.' He glanced anxiously at his watch. He hadn't realized how much time had passed since he'd wandered in. 'I'm frightfully late as it is. It was a pleasure to meet you, though.' Pulling a pen from his inside jacket pocket, Gunn hastily scribbled his temporary London address on the back of the paper map of the museum he'd been given at the door. 'Perhaps another time?'

'Don't even say it.' Laura held up her hand in a firm 'stop' motion as Gunn approached the table, excuses and apologies tumbling from his lips like rapid-fire bullets. 'You'll be late to your own funeral, and we both know it.'

'Sorry, sorry . . .'

'It's an illness at this point,' said Laura. But she was smiling, much to Gunn's relief. 'So I suppose that means it would be unfair for me to blame you. Or something.'

Laura smiled much more these days, Gunn had noticed. Since he'd walked out on Anna she'd been very kind, and made a sincere effort to support him and put their prior differences behind them. The simple fact was that his sister was happy, living in a big house in Battersea with her loving husband Michael and their two adorable girls, Julia and Mary. Their mother Edie was now finally settled in an old people's home in Polzeath, well cared for and as content as she could be under the circumstances, which had lifted an immense burden from Laura's shoulders. She'd been a devoted daughter and sole carer for decades, but now that Edie no longer recognized either of her children at all, the time had come to let go. It was awful in one way of course. But Laura had waited so very long to be able to enjoy her own family life, and her renewed smiles spoke volumes.

'Not an excuse.' Gunn held up his hands like a footballer

admitting a foul. 'But I actually got stuck at the British Museum.'

'How unexpectedly cultured of you,' Laura observed, handing him a menu. 'Please choose something immediately, I'm starved.'

Gunn ordered a large plate of spaghetti and a green salad, while Laura plumped for some sort of fancy-sounding fish pie.

'What were you doing at the museum?'

'I stopped in to see Pa's collection,' said Gunn.

Laura gave him an astonished look, but said nothing.

'I wasn't sure anything would still be out on display, after so many years. But there it all was. They had the Ecuador heads hanging in a big glass case in the middle.'

Laura shuddered. 'I always hated those. What on earth made you decide to go?'

'I'll get to that in a minute,' said Gunn. 'It's why I wanted to see you, actually. But first I have to tell you about this morning. The most unlikely thing happened, you won't believe it.'

He told her about his run-in with Professor Horatio Chapman and how he and their father had been close friends.

'Chapman would have been older than Pa, but they were thick as thieves apparently. Did you ever hear that name?'

'No,' Laura shook her head. 'And I think I would have remembered it if I had. There aren't too many "Horatios" to the pound.'

'What are the chances though?' Gunn went on, enthusiastically. 'Of me running into someone who actually knew Dad, on the one day I happen to go to the museum?'

'You think it's fate?' Laura looked at him archly. She was teasing, but to her surprise Gunn took the bait.

'I don't know,' he shrugged. 'Maybe.'

Well, this was a turn-up for the books. Throughout his adult life, Gunn's selfish, mercenary streak had led him down one destructive path after another. But as a child, Laura's brother had been different. Romantic and imaginative, he'd believed fervently in things like fate and magic, in adventure and passion and wishing on stars. Laura used to think that that side of his nature was one of the few things that he and

Ines Challant had had in common, back in the tumultuous days of their marriage. They'd both been dreamers, back then. But it was years since she'd even glimpsed any of those qualities in her brother.

As their food arrived, Gunn began to tell her about his trip to Maltings, and stumbling upon the stuffed cockatoo in the attic.

'It reminded me of Pa, obviously. And of Ines. She adored those birds.'

'I remember,' said Laura.

'She and I used to talk about Maltings all the time you know, during the war.'

'Did you?'

Gunn nodded. 'About moving back there one day, having children of our own. It's a house for children, don't you think?'

'I suppose so,' said Laura, not at all sure where all this was going.

'Anyway,' said Gunn, after a few contemplative sips of Pinot Grigio. 'The whole cockatoo thing helped me come to a decision.'

He paused and stared warmly at his sister. 'I want you to have the house.'

'Me?' Laura spluttered, reaching for her napkin.

'Yes,' Gunn smiled. 'You and Michael and the girls. You can make it a home again. That's something I can't possibly do. Not now.'

'Oh, Hector,' said Laura, choking up with emotion. 'That's . . . my goodness, that is such a kind and generous offer. But I can't possibly accept.'

'Of course you can!' Gunn insisted. 'Why not?'

'Well,' she cleared her throat. 'For one thing it's a valuable property and it's the only asset you have left since the divorce. I hate to point out the obvious, but you can't afford to simply give it away. As of today you don't even have a job.'

'Yes, but . . .'

'No "buts", Gunn,' Laura cut him off, kindly but firmly. 'I know the agent said it wouldn't rent for much, but not much is

268

a lot better than nothing, and you need that income. And then one day, when you're ready, you can either sell it . . .'

He shook his head, but she ignored him again.

'. . . or, if you choose to, live in it yourself. Who knows, you may yet marry again and have children of your own.'

'I'm touched that you think so,' he smiled sadly. 'But I'm afraid I'm far too long in the tooth for all that now. I wonder if things would have been different if Anna and I had had children . . .' he mused aloud.

'She never wanted them?' asked Laura.

'Never. Ines did. But with the war and everything, I put it off. And of course by the time I got home it was too late.'

'I don't suppose you ever hear from her, do you?'

Gunn sat back, recoiling as if stung.

'No. Look, are you really sure you don't want Maltings? For Julia and Mary's sake, if not your own? Shouldn't you at least discuss it with Michael?'

Reaching across the table, Laura squeezed her brother's hand.

'No, darling. Buying back Maltings was your dream, not mine. I already have my dream,' she added, smiling. 'Michael, the girls, our home.'

'I'm happy for you,' said Gunn, sincerely.

'I know you are. And if Maltings isn't your dream either any more, then that's OK. Things change,' Laura told him. 'There's no shame in selling it, Gunn, and rebuilding your life with that money.'

Except that there *was* shame in it. Not only the shame of failure and betraying his long-held ambition. But the shame of knowing that he'd bought Maltings back with Anna's money. If Laura would only take the house, he'd be off the hook. He could tell himself that he'd done something honourable, something unselfish and good with the ill-gotten gains from his miserable second marriage. But if she didn't want it, and he couldn't live in it alone, then what? If it was really just an 'asset', did he have any moral right to it at all?

But of course, it would never be 'just an asset' to Gunn.

Maltings was all that was left of his father, his happy childhood, and the decent, morally certain person he used to be.

What on earth was he to do?

After lunch Gunn took a long, circuitous walk around Kensington and Chelsea, trying and failing to shake his restlessness. By the time he got back to the rundown mews house he was staying in close to the river, a loan from an old friend, it was already getting dark. He passed the Cross Keys pub, warmth and light emanating invitingly from its windows, and contemplated going in. But he thought better of it. Drinking when you were happy was one thing. But drinking when you were sad was a slippery slope, and one that Gunn had no intention of falling down. He'd fallen far enough as it was.

Instead, shaking off his self-pity like a wet dog drying itself after a swim, he went straight inside, took a hot bath, and set about making himself some supper. During his time living in Rome with Julia he'd learned to cook a couple of pasta dishes, and though his repertoire wasn't extensive he was quietly proud of his spaghetti amatriciana. Chopping the red onion and finely slicing the streaky bacon that he used instead of pancetta felt therapeutic. It helped him think things through more calmly.

He would put Maltings up for rent in the morning, unfurnished as it was, and see what happened. All other decisions about the house he would postpone.

In the meantime, he needed a job. The alpine ski season began in about six months. If he hadn't secured himself some other permanent employment by then, he would bite the bullet and offer his services as a private ski guide. His medal-winning days were far behind him now, but they still added a cachet that he could use to raise his prices, teaching the spoiled children of rich families how to perfect their parallel turns.

It was a deeply depressing thought. But the time had come for him to grow up. Beggars could not be choosers.

The knock was so soft and tentative that at first Gunn didn't even register it. But eventually the rapping became louder and more insistent. Turning down the heat beneath his pasta sauce, and wiping his hands on a tea towel, he opened the front door.

'Mr Gunn. Good evening to you. May I come in?'

Professor Horatio Chapman looked smaller than he had done today at the museum, not much more than a child's height as he stood smiling in the doorway. He had a bottle of cheap French wine in one hand and a briefcase in the other, and he held both up with an equally childlike excitement.

'I have a proposition I'd like to discuss.'

An hour later, warm and sated after the pasta and wine, Gunn sat in a tatty armchair opposite his father's old friend, wondering if the conversation they'd just had was actually real, or whether he'd dreamed the whole thing.

South America. Huayhuash, Peru. The Elqui Valley in Chile. Kaa Iya, Bolivia. Chapada Diamantina, Brazil. The exotic names stirred long-buried memories of his father, returning home to Maltings after extended absences, tanned and elated, bearing gifts and treasures and regaling Gunn and Laura with endless tales of danger and adventure. It had all seemed so very far away from Cornwall, from school and home and reality. That sense of otherness, of unreality, was just as strong now, listening to Horatio Chapman talk. Only this time, Gunn was being asked to come to these places, not to imagine them or experience them vicariously through his father's eyes. A two-year expedition, funded by the British Museum and other private benefactors, sailed for Brazil in ten days' time. Chapman was offering Gunn a seat on the boat.

'The pay will be dreadful,' the professor reiterated cheerfully. 'You'd be starting at the bottom, helping prepare equipment, taking notes. Possibly cooking,' he added, patting his stomach appreciatively after two helpings of Gunn's amatriciana. 'But I could tell when I met you this morning that you're an intelligent fellow with a genuine passion for other cultures. And I sense you've also inherited William's restless, adventurous streak. In spades, I suspect,' he added knowingly.

'I don't know what to say,' said Gunn.

He was surprised to find himself flattered by these comparisons to his father. After so many years trying *not* to be like him, *not* to repeat his mistakes, it was bizarre that Chapman's comments about their similarities should trigger feelings of such happiness and pride. 'What makes you think I'm qualified?'

The old man shrugged. 'Instinct? You've been in the army and enjoyed it, so I don't doubt you're up to the rigours of exploration, physically or mentally. And as I say, you'd be starting at the bottom.'

'Yes but I'm not academic. I'm not an intellectual.'

Chapman laughed loudly. 'Heaven protect us from *intellectuals*, dear boy! What we're looking for is the raw materials. We don't need diplomas. We need intelligence and passion. I suspect you have both. Plenty of highly intelligent people struggle with reading, you know,' he observed casually. 'There's more to life than the written word.'

Gunn swallowed, momentarily panicked that he might be about to cry. Here he was, a grown man in his forties. But no one had ever said this to him before.

'Thank you.' He cleared his throat, pulling himself together.

'Does that mean you'll go?' asked Chapman.

Gunn paused for a moment, then smiled. 'Yes. I think it does.'

South America. A new world. A new life, far away from the mess he'd made of this one. *Why not?*

Reaching for the bottle of Bell's on the drinks trolley beside him, he slowly poured two fingers of whisky into two tumblers. Passing one to Chapman, he resumed his seat and raised his own glass in a toast.

'To new beginnings.'

The professor lifted his glass and nodded approvingly. What a miraculous, unexpected day today had been, meeting William Gunn's son of all people.

'To new beginnings. And adventure,' he added, with a wink.

272

CHAPTER TWENTY-EIGHT

Paris, France, March 1956

Lucien Toulon watched his new interior designer step out of her cherry-red Renault 4CV onto his gravelled forecourt. It was the first time he'd met with Ines Challant at La Poulette, his country house just outside Paris. Most of their meetings took place at the hotel, but this weekend he'd been trapped at Lourmarin on other business, and he'd decided that what he had to say simply couldn't wait until Monday.

The Lafayette was Lucien's baby. He'd renovated and redeveloped hotels before of course. But nothing with such an iconic heritage and, not to put too fine a point on it, nothing this expensive. Every franc Lucien had, and several more that he didn't have, were at risk in this latest venture. So entrusting something as fundamental as the Lafayette's interiors to another human being was always going to be stressful.

Reaching down to pet his beloved doberman, Lefou, he steeled himself for the conversation ahead. Ines wasn't going to like it, but it couldn't be helped.

'Mademoiselle Challant has arrived,' the butler announced, unnecessarily. 'Will you meet in here, or should I show her into the study?'

'In here.' Lucien stood up, stretching his stocky legs and bending his broad back with an audible crack. 'Offer her a drink and then bring her through.'

Moments later, Ines appeared in the doorway. Unusually muted in a slate-grey pencil skirt and matching tailored jacket, the one flash of colour in her outfit was a bright enamel parrot brooch on her lapel.

'You didn't want anything to drink?' Lucien asked, seeing she was empty-handed.

'No, thank you. It's a lovely house.' Ines smiled politely.

'Thank you.' Lucien returned the smile. 'It's an indulgence for a single man. Far too big. But I like the space.'

Just then Lefou emerged from behind his master's chair and barked loudly, before making a friendly advance towards Ines.

'Agh!' She froze, not quite screaming but clearly profoundly unnerved.

'He won't hurt you,' Lucien assured her. 'He's a big softie really.'

'I . . . I'm afraid I can't be around . . . that sort of dog,' Ines stammered.

It was the first time Lucien had ever seen her ruffled. Up until that moment, he'd wondered whether fear was even an emotion in her repertoire. But clearly he'd been mistaken.

'Would you take him out, please?'

'Of course.' Grabbing Lefou by the collar, he led him out of the room, handing him off to one of the staff. 'You don't like dogs?' he asked Ines when he returned, gesturing for her to sit on the antique Louis XVI banquette by the window.

'Just dobermans.' Ines gave an involuntary shudder. 'I had a bad experience as a child.'

'I see,' said Lucien, who didn't, but got the clear sense she did not wish to be pressed further. This was one of the traits he found both most compelling and most frustrating about Ines. She was a profoundly private person. Any attempt, however subtle, to break through her professional boundaries and engage the real woman beneath, was instantly and skilfully rebuffed.

'Listen,' he began, changing the subject and cutting to the chase before his own nerve failed him. 'I asked you here today because I've made a decision about the chinoiserie in the foyer and bar areas.'

Ines cocked her head to one side, listening.

'It's not that the silk printing isn't beautiful,' Lucien

continued, more awkwardly than he'd intended. 'It's exquisite in its own way. But all the flowers and the birds . . . it's just too much for such an important part of the hotel. I'm sorry. I just think it's too busy. Too feminine. I want something calmer.'

'Then you should have it,' said Ines, smoothing down the front of her skirt.

'Thank you.' Lucien smiled, relieved. He hadn't expected her to acquiesce so easily on an artistic matter, but perhaps things were finally turning a corner.

'I have a couple of colleagues I'd be happy to recommend,' said Ines, getting to her feet. 'Well-respected designers who can take over from here. Jules Martin is an angel, and much more conservative than I am in his aesthetic. And Pascal Receneau . . .'

'No, no, no, you misunderstand,' Lucien clarified hastily. 'I'm not *firing* you.'

'Oh, I know you're not,' said Ines. 'I'm quitting. Enjoy the rest of your weekend, Monsieur Toulon.'

'What . . . wait!' Lucien shouted after her as she turned on her heel and reached for the door. 'Slow down. *Sit* down. Please.'

Without thinking, he'd put a hand on her waist and was pulling her gently, guiding her back into the room. Ines stiffened, registering the intimacy. She could feel the warmth of his palm through the fabric of her skirt, a sensation both unfamiliar and yet embedded somewhere deep in her memory. For a moment it threw her off her stride. She found herself sitting, as he'd asked.

'Are you always so *hasty*?' Lucien asked her. 'So emotional in your decisions?'

'I wasn't aware I was being emotional,' Ines bristled.

'Well you are.' Lucien frowned.

It sounded so petulant and childish that, catching each other's eye, they both laughed.

'I don't understand you, Ines,' he observed, more relaxed now that the tension had been broken. 'May I call you Ines?'

'Of course,' said Ines. She would have preferred to keep hiding behind the formality of using full names, but she could hardly say 'no' under the circumstances. 'I'm not sure there's much to understand. You hired me for my artistic vision.'

'True,' said Lucien. 'But I must be able to make business decisions about my hotel without you taking umbrage.'

'I fully agree,' said Ines, regaining her composure now that the physical distance between them had been restored. 'And I'm not taking umbrage.'

He raised an eyebrow, staring at her with an intensity that was both flattering and unnerving.

'I'm merely recognizing the fact that our "visions" for the Lafayette are not aligned.'

'Because I don't want so many birds?' he laughed.

Despite herself, Ines blushed. 'You need a designer who sees things the way you do, Monsieur Toulon.'

'Lucien,' he corrected her, not crossly but firmly. 'What I need is a designer who's willing to collaborate. Who's at least open to the *idea* of taking direction. I mean, really, what is it with you and these birds?' He gestured towards the brooch on her jacket. 'Do we have to have birds on absolutely everything?'

'Of course not,' Ines stammered. Did she put birds on everything? It was true that she often incorporated vivid, natural themes in her work, with lots of colour and floral accents. And perhaps that was her mother's influence. But she hadn't realized that Clotilde's birds were featuring so prominently in her work. That they were becoming overwhelming.

It was true, too, that her dreams still continued. Her mother's flapping, desperate birds were still her nightly companions, along with the barking dogs and the frightened, screaming boy: Bernard.

'*Pardon?*' Lucien Toulon looked at her curiously and Ines realized to her horror that she'd said the word out loud. '*C'est qui, Bernard?* Is that the name of your son?'

'No.' She shook her head, mortified. 'It's . . . he's no one.'

'Very well then,' said Lucien, not taking his eyes from hers. He felt he had made some progress this morning. But breaking down Ines Challant's barriers was going to take time. If Bernard was an old lover, whose name was still on her lips, he would discover it eventually. Just as he was determined to discover why his difficult designer was so terrified of his dog.

'To business. Let's see if we can compromise on this lobby wallpaper, shall we?'

You're being ridiculous, Ines told herself, walking briskly away from her apartment in the vague direction of the river, but with no plan, no fixed destination.

She'd spent the entire drive back to the city from Lucien Toulon's mansion berating herself. How could she have been so unprofessional? Blurting out things, private, personal things, that she had no wish for anyone to know, least of all her most important client. More significantly, why had she done it?

Lucien had criticized her artistic judgement, which she didn't like one bit. That may have had something to do with it. But what if he was right? What if all the memories and symbols haunting Ines's subconscious *were* starting to spill out into her real life? Or worse, into her work, the one precious thing that she had built for herself?

Then there was Toulon's dog, the doberman, and how frightened it had made her. She hadn't expected that. And afterwards, that touch. Lucien's hand on her waist, warm and shockingly intimate. The intensity of his gaze as he looked at her, as if he were unravelling secrets about her psyche that even Ines herself didn't know.

That was all bad. Very bad.

May I call you Ines?

Quickening her pace, Ines forced herself to stop catastrophizing. After all, if she looked at it another way, the only thing that had *really* happened today was a silly squabble over some hotel wallpaper. But if that was the case, why did she still feel so anxious?

Looking up, she found herself at an unfamiliar corner. A row of shops ran east to west, and on the other side of the road was a small church, really little more than a chapel, that she'd never noticed before. She must have passed it a hundred times.

The Marais was too small for her to have 'missed' any streets completely. But for whatever reason, she'd never stopped and looked, as she did now.

A flock of pigeons swooped down, some perching on the railings at the front of the church and others along the kerb. In their midst Ines saw a sign indicating the name of the church and the times for Sunday masses. At the bottom, someone had written in bold script:

'Confession today, 5.15 p.m.'

Ines looked at her watch. *5.10 p.m.*

Matty went to confession regularly. Ines worried about him. What sins could her sweet, lovely boy possibly feel he needed to be forgiven, week after week? But her son assured her he found the experience both joyful and calming, and he certainly didn't seem upset afterwards.

Oh, what the hell.

Before she could talk herself out of it, Ines crossed the road and entered the church.

Two penitents, both older women, were already in line before her, kneeling in the pew nearest to the confessional, waiting for the priest to call them. Removing a cushion from its brass hook, Ines knelt beside them, a few feet away. Closing her eyes, she pretended to pray, trying to remember the words of the sacrament. She knew it began with 'Forgive me Father for I have sinned,' but after that it was all a blur. Her mind began to wander, but it was senses, not thoughts, that distracted her. The rough texture of the embroidered cushion, pressing into her bare knees, contrasting with the smooth, polished wood of the pew beneath her palms. The cool, still air of the stone church filling her lungs, while the lingering scent of incense, wood polish and candle wax wafted into her nostrils, transporting her back to the uncomfortable Sundays of her childhood. After a minute or so, the *clack, clack* of the first woman's heeled shoes as she walked across the nave to the confessional. Ines couldn't claim to feel joyful. But there was a certain peace that she hadn't expected. Moment by moment, breath by breath, the agitation that had been dogging her all day began to subside, like the lapping waves of a slowly retreating tide.

And then, all at once, it was her turn. Stepping into one side of the tiny box of a room, she could hear the priest's breathing through the small metal grille that separated them.

'Forgive me Father for I have sinned,' Ines heard herself saying. 'It's been . . . many years . . . since my last confession.'

'I see, what is it you want to confess?'

The voice on the other side sounded kind and much younger than she'd expected. The priests of Ines's childhood had all been old men, mostly of the austere and clipped variety. But despite the young priest's com-passionate manner, a lump still formed in her throat.

'I . . . I don't know. Lying, I suppose, or . . . being selfish?' she stammered.

'I see. Can you try to think of a specific example when you have committed those particular sins?'

'Er . . .' Ines hesitated. This was ridiculous. There must be a hundred instances of where she'd been selfish or told a lie. Everybody did those things, all the time. And yet asked to come up with just one, she drew a blank.

'Take your time.'

And then, like a lightning strike, it came to her. Why she was here. The words forming on her lips before she even knew she'd thought them.

'God's been trying to tell me something.' She swallowed hard. 'In my dreams at night. Sometimes in the day, too. In my thoughts. But mostly at night.'

'What has he been trying to tell you?'

'I don't know,' Ines blurted, the violent *BANG* of her nightmares ringing in her ears. 'I haven't listened. I haven't let him in. That's what I need to confess.'

The priest digested this in silence for a moment. Eventually he asked, 'Why do you think you haven't listened?'

'Because I'm afraid.'

'Afraid of God?' the priest asked, after another short pause. 'Or of what you think he's trying to tell you?'

Ines opened her mouth to answer, but no sound came out. She felt dizzy, suddenly. Overwhelmingly nauseous, like she remembered being in the early stages of her pregnancy with Matty. Clutching the sides of the confessional, she let out a sob.

'My father.' The two words came out of her spontaneously, like vomit. 'I'm afraid my father may have done something terrible, a long time ago. Something . . . unforgivable. God's trying to tell me what it is. But I don't want to know.'

'Because you love your father?' the priest ventured.

'Loved him,' Ines broke off, struggling for breath. 'He's dead. But yes, I loved him. I'm the only one who really loved him. Although I'm not sure he felt the same.'

Sensing a crisis building, the priest chose his words carefully.

'Love is never wrong, my child,' he said gently. 'Nor is any sin "unforgivable". Not in the eyes of God. You don't have to tell me about these dreams if you don't want to. But you should trust in whatever it is the Lord has to tell you.'

Ines relapsed into silence, hot tears streaming down her cheeks. If only she believed that! That no sin was unforgivable. That absolution was possible for all things, all crimes, all betrayals, no matter how heinous. What a beautiful place the world would be if that were true. But of course, it wasn't.

'Would you like me to offer you a penance, my child?' the priest asked. But his question drifted through the grille in the confessional and hung unanswered in the air. Ines wasn't there to hear her penance, nor the absolution that might have followed.

She had already thrown open the door and fled.

The next morning, at nine a.m. sharp, Ines made a phone call to the coroner's office in Villefranche.

'I'd like to see a copy of a report, please. It relates to an accidental death,' she began.

'I'm sorry, madame. Coroner's reports are not available to the general public until ten years after the fact. Before that, they remain the property of the court. You can apply to have a specific document unsealed, but . . .'

'Oh that's all right,' Ines interrupted. 'The report I need was issued more than twenty years ago. It relates to the case of a child, in Beaulieu.'

'I see.' The voice on the other end of the line brightened. 'And what was the name?'

'Angier,' said Ines, her hand trembling. 'Bernard Angier.'

PART FOUR

AUTUMN

Ten years later . . .

CHAPTER TWENTY-NINE

Beaulieu-sur-Mer, France, 1966

Genevieve Challant sat at the dressing table in the room that had once been her parents' bedroom, dissecting her reflection in the mirror. In her mid-fifties, she knew she looked older, her sunken cheeks accentuated by the long, grey hair that she wore scraped back into a tight bun. The overall impression might have come across as stern or severe, were it not for the general air of frailty and vulnerability that clung to Genevieve everywhere, like a misting of morning dew. Her skin was so paper thin, it was almost translucent where it stretched over her cheekbones, and her fragile arms hung from her body like wintry, leafless twigs that might snap at any moment. There was still a certain elegance about her, a poise and flair for accessories and fashion that kept her from outright ugliness. Truth be told, even as a young woman she had never been classically pretty in the way that her sisters were, especially Ines. But in her youth, Genevieve's elegance had gone hand in hand with her wit and humour, with a certain joie de vivre that was missing from the older woman. Somewhere along the way, an inner light extinguished. Partially at first, but now completely.

Still, she thought stoically, tying a silk Dior scarf around her crepey neck and pinning it with a pretty gold brooch set with garnets. *Today was not a day for melancholy. Or regrets.* Her nephew, Matthieu, was coming to stay with her at Beaulieu for a few days, the first time he'd visited in over a year. He was expected in time for lunch, and the prospect of his company after so long an absence brought Genevieve more joy and excitement than she liked to admit, even to herself.

She rarely went out any more, spending most of her days reading, sleeping and drinking alone up at the bastide. The Duponts, the couple who took care of her, loved her enough to be honest about her limitations. 'You're in no fit state to be out and about today, madame,' Hélène Dupont would tell her, on the rare occasions when Genevieve expressed a desire to be driven into town. Overweight and jowly, with fat-fingered hands, and a strange face full of exaggerated, rubbery features that almost made her look as if she were wearing a mask, Hélène was no beauty. But she was capable and confident, and her older husband, Georges, clearly doted on her. 'Think how embarrassed and upset you'd be if anything were to happen? If you need something, Georges or I will be happy to run in and get it for you.'

It was the drink that was the problem of course. Genevieve now needed a brandy the moment she opened her eyes in the morning, and at no less than two hourly intervals after that. Without it she simply couldn't function. Although she wasn't *so* far gone that she didn't realize she had a problem. And within the very limited confines of her world up at the bastide, she managed things reasonably effectively, at least while the sun was still up; dressing herself, bathing, taking small meals or modest 'turns' around the garden without incident. It was only when there were changes in her routine that things had a tendency to go wrong. Anxious, and unused to being around other people, Gen would drink more and more on the days she planned to venture out, with predictable results. Once, in church in Beaulieu, she had passed out cold during the bidding prayers. Another time, at a little café on the harbour where she'd spent many happy evenings in her youth, she'd forgotten her purse and drunkenly accused the waiter of stealing it. Having viciously berated the poor man, she then realized she had made a mistake and proceeded to burst explosively into tears, causing a scene that the Duponts informed her had been the talk of the town for weeks afterwards.

Genevieve told herself she was happy to stay home at the bastide day after day, week after week. But the loneliness grew oppressive. There were only so many games of whist one could play with one's housekeeper and her husband before one went mad. And as kind as they were, Hélène and Georges Dupont were hardly scintillating company. It didn't help that her contact with her two sisters had dwindled to little more than occasional letters and phone calls. This distance and growing sense of tension was largely Genevieve's own doing – she was the one who had withdrawn from the family – but that didn't stop her feeling hurt by it.

The only exception was her nephew Matty. She couldn't say why, but from the moment Genevieve first laid eyes on Ines's baby son, she'd always adored him. Even as a very small boy, there had been a maturity about Matthieu, a wisdom and a kindness that set him apart from other children and made him easier for Genevieve to relate to. Ironically, this curiously grown-up little boy had managed to bring out the child in his much older aunt. Matty alone had the power to revive the spark that had once burned so brightly within her, even if only temporarily. Perhaps because he genuinely enjoyed her company, drunk or sober, jolly or sad, engaged or withdrawn. Unlike her sisters, he never judged her. Genevieve loved him for that most of all.

A knock on the bedroom door jolted her from her reverie.

'Your morning medicine, madame. And a little top-up for before lunch, just to see you through.'

Hélène Dupont bustled in, a wobbling triumph of efficiency, with two small glasses of brandy on a silver tray. Setting the tray down briskly on the dressing table, she smiled brightly at her mistress.

'You must be excited to see Monsieur Matthieu.'

She spoke slowly and with the exaggerated intonation one might use with a small child, or someone very elderly.

'I am excited,' Gen nodded meekly, downing the first brandy with a single flick of the wrist. 'It will be lovely to have him here. Even if it is only for a few days.'

'I wonder what it is he wants to talk to you about?' said Hélène, fussing about the room straightening cushions and refolding the scarves Genevieve had discarded earlier. 'Must be something important for him to have driven all this way just for the weekend.'

'Hmmm,' Genevieve shrugged. 'We'll see, I suppose.' She was in no mood for gossip – although she was also curious about the 'news' Matty had alluded to on the telephone. More pressingly, however, she wanted to drink the second brandy that her housekeeper had brought her, and without being watched.

'That'll be all for now, Hélène. Thank you.'

After she'd gone, Genevieve waited a few seconds before walking over to her bedroom door and locking it. Then she turned and, extending her hand as if towards a lover, reached towards the glass of amber liquid, glinting seductively in the autumn sunlight. She'd feel better after the second drink. Stronger.

Today was going to be a good day.

'*Merde!*'

Matty Challant cursed under his breath as his ancient Renault spluttered to a halt for the third time in as many minutes. Thankfully he was only a couple of miles from the bastide. He could walk it at this point if he needed to. But he had to be back in Paris in a few days' time, and he really couldn't afford to have his car give up the ghost on him now.

Stepping outside he opened the bonnet, scuffing aside the brown leaves piled on the verge and pushing his thick blond hair back out of his eyes as he tinkered with the engine, his expert fingers coaxing it back to life. In blue jeans and a white linen shirt, his face and forearms still lightly tanned from the Paris summer, he looked at ease in his surroundings.

At twenty years old, Matty was fit, handsome and generally capable, as good with his hands as he was his academic work. Ines had written proudly to both her sisters when he'd been awarded a scholarship to the prestigious Sciences Po in Paris, but Matty himself never really broadcast his achievements. He was equally modest when it came to his effect on women, who regularly tripped over themselves, and each other, in their eagerness to flirt with this tall, athletic and naturally charming boy.

'Are you lost?' Right on cue, a stunning brunette in a pink minidress that barely skimmed the tops of her thighs appeared next to him on the roadside. 'I'm local.' She fluttered her eyelashes seductively. 'Maybe I could help?'

'Thanks, but I'm not lost,' Matty replied, wiping his oil-stained hands on his jeans and closing the hood of his car before hopping back behind the wheel. 'I'm only headed a couple of miles up the hill.'

Trying the ignition, he grinned triumphantly as the engine once again roared back to life. 'Bingo.'

'Where are you staying?' the girl asked, brazenly thrusting her entire upper body through his driver's side window before he sped off and she lost him forever. 'I'm Antoinette by the way.'

'Matty.' They shook hands. 'Lovely to meet you, Antoinette, but I'm staying at my aunt's house and I'm late as it is. I really must get going.'

'That's my house over there.' Stubbornly refusing to extricate herself from the car, Antoinette pointed to a modest *gîte*, set back from the road. 'If you ever get bored at your aunt's house, you know where to find me.'

'Thank you,' Matty's eyes met hers, lingering just a beat longer than they needed to. 'I'll bear it in mind.'

The girl kissed him on the cheek, reluctantly stepping back from the window as he slid the Renault into gear. Moments later he was gone, dust flying up from beneath his rear wheels as he sped away, waving cheerfully behind him.

Georges Dupont was the first to see Matty arrive, his decrepit old Renault belching fumes from its ancient exhaust pipe in a most unhealthy manner before shuddering to a halt on the bastide's gravel forecourt.

A short, hefty fellow with a tonsure of white hair around his bald pate and a bushy white beard to match, Georges's jovial, Father Christmas-like appearance belied the cynical, occasionally bitter man beneath.

'I wonder if it's money he's after?' he observed waspishly to his wife. 'Hard to imagine he's broke, what with his mother's earnings. But his car's clearly on its last legs.'

'Wouldn't surprise me,' Hélène Dupont muttered, joining Georges at the salon window. Her sharp eyes narrowed as she watched Matty step out of the vehicle, stretching his long, jeans-clad legs and extracting a small overnight case from the boot. 'Best keep a close eye,' she warned her husband. 'You know how Madame dotes on that boy. We don't want her doing anything stupid.'

'Bit late for that,' scoffed Georges. 'Come on. I'll help the young prince with his bags. You see if you can steer the old girl into the dining room.'

Matty enjoyed his lunch, a simple but delicious feast of crayfish, endive salad, brie and fresh baguettes, still warm from the bastide ovens. He was tired and hungry, despite having broken his journey down from Paris last night at a guesthouse in Lyon.

'I don't suppose you know a good local mechanic, Aunt Genevieve?' he asked, tearing himself off another large hunk of bread, his third, and trying not to focus too much on the dilapidated state of their surroundings. The bastide looked even worse than he remembered, with big ugly damp patches spreading untreated across the walls, and carpets that looked as though they hadn't been cleaned or beaten in years. Whatever it was the Duponts were 'taking care' of, it sure as hell wasn't the house. 'My car's not been sounding too clever.'

'I don't drive any more, my darling,' Genevieve told him, smiling indulgently at his youthful appetite. She herself ate like a bird, but it was nice to see good food being appreciated. Nice to see Matty too, looking so handsome and vibrant and full of life. 'But I daresay the Duponts might know a man.'

'Don't worry about it.' Matty waved away the sug-gestion. 'I'll work something out.'

Although he couldn't entirely put his finger on why, he was not a fan of the Duponts. Perhaps their obvious laziness around the house was a part of it. But worse than that, last time Matty had come to visit he'd had the distinct impression he was being watched around his aunt, an intrusion he didn't appreciate one bit. No one had his Aunt Genevieve's best interests at heart more than he did, and he'd tried very hard over the years to heal the rift between her and her sisters, although with no marked success.

'Now listen, Matty.' Clearing her throat, Genevieve decided to take the bull by the horns. 'You told me on the telephone you had something important to talk to me about. I've no idea if it's a good something or a bad something, but whatever it is I don't want it hanging over us all weekend. So come on. Out with it.'

Matty laughed. 'I do love that about you, Aunt G. You're so direct.' Picking up his napkin, he twisted it awkwardly, wondering how to begin. In the end, he too opted for the direct approach. 'I hope you won't be too upset. But I've decided,' he cleared his throat. 'I've decided to take holy orders. I'm going to become a priest.'

Gen's eyes widened. Not in dismay, but certainly in surprise. This wasn't what she'd expected at all. Although perhaps, thinking about how keen on church and altar-boying he'd been as a young child, it shouldn't have come as a total shock.

'Don't be sad.' Watching her reaction, his face fell. 'I've given it a huge amount of thought and I'm certain it's the right path for me.'

'I'm not sad, darling,' Genevieve assured him. 'If it's truly what you want then I'm pleased for you. I'm just surprised. To be frank, I thought you were going to tell me you were getting married.'

'Yes,' he frowned, setting down his knife and fork unhappily. 'Maman thought the same thing.'

'Ah.' Genevieve nodded understandingly. Poor Ines. There

291

were times, many times if she were honest, when Genevieve envied her youngest sister. For her beauty, her independence, her glittering career. But mostly for having lived through heartbreak and survived. More than survived. *Thrived*. That was something that Genevieve herself had never been able to do and for that, as unfair as it was, she envied and resented her sister. But she did feel compassion for Ines about this. To lose Matty, her only son, to the church? No daughter-in-law. No grandchildren. That must be terribly hard.

'Have you and your mother argued?'

Matty shook his head. 'Not argued. But she cried. A lot. She doesn't understand. She kept saying, "But you *love* women." As if that were a reason for me not to heed my vocation!'

'And do you?' asked Genevieve.

'Do I what?'

'Love women? Because, you know, it's all right if you don't. Not everybody . . .'

Matty laughed again, holding up a hand. 'I'm not homosexual, Aunt G. I would say if I were. And yes, I do like girls and giving up that side of things will be a challenge, I'm sure. I just wish she could see that the priesthood isn't a denial of love. It's choosing a different kind of love, that's all.'

'Well,' said Genevieve, setting down her own knife and fork and ringing a bell for Madame Dupont, who arrived so promptly it was clear to Matty that she must have been listening at the door. 'Give her time. I'm sure she'll come around.'

'Anything I can help with?' Hélène Dupont asked eagerly, bestowing beady smiles equally on her mistress and Matty as she cleared away the plates.

Genevieve opened her mouth to reply, but Matty was too quick for her.

'No thank you, madame.' He had no intention of discussing his personal life or family business with this officious busybody of a woman. On the other hand, he tried never to be rude, and he knew that his aunt was fond of her. 'Lunch was quite delicious, by the way,' he told her. 'Thank you.'

'Of course,' Hélène nodded, still smiling, but with a tighter, more strained edge to her expression. 'Your aunt will need a rest now for at least a couple of hours, so you'll have time to settle in to your room and freshen up.'

'Right,' said Matty.

He was tired, and could use a nap himself, but something about the way the housekeeper spoke bothered him. Almost as if she were ordering his aunt to take a siesta. The Aunt Genevieve he remembered would never have stood for that. But looking at her properly now, she did seem older and more passive, somehow. Depleted.

I must stop worrying about my own problems while I'm here and focus on her, Matty told himself. As the only family member with whom she had regular contact, he felt the responsibility of caring for Genevieve quite deeply. Her drinking had always been a problem. That hadn't changed, and it wasn't in his power to change it. But something else *had* changed, something that troubled him.

'Perhaps we'll take a walk together into town later, Aunt G? Once you've had a rest,' he suggested kindly.

'I'd like that,' Genevieve looked at him lovingly. She supposed, once he went off to the seminary, he wouldn't be able to visit her any more, or at least not for a while. The thought made her sad. She must be sure to make the most of their time together now.

They never did go into town. Instead their 'walk' was reduced to a slow circuit of the bastide grounds, never venturing beyond the high walls at the rear of the property, or through the grand gates at the front. Despite these limitations, Matty had enjoyed his aunt's company, grateful for the occasional flashes of sarcasm and sharp wit that he remembered from his boyhood. And Aunt Genevieve seemed to have genuine compassion for his own situation.

Joining the seminary was the right thing. He had no doubts about that. But as he lay in bed that night, staring up at the dusty, cobwebbed ceiling of his guest bedroom, he still felt guilty. Mainly for hurting his mother, who'd been unable to hide her devastation at the news.

'I'm sure our father's attitude to religion has tainted Ines's view,' Genevieve told him earlier, when he'd described his mother's shocked and tearful reaction. 'Your grandfather made a great show of piety, you see, Matty. But he was a shameless hypocrite. Righteous and upstanding at church, but quite the monster when he got back home.'

Matty didn't correct her, although he knew that his mother did not share Genevieve's view of their late father. Despite the fact that he'd cut her and Matty out of his will completely, Ines persisted in remembering Charles Challant Père as a fundamentally good and decent man. No, Ines's issues about his vocation were all about *him*, or rather the two of them. Because it had always *been* just the two of them, mother and son, with an unbreakable bond. And nothing Matty said could convince Ines that his becoming a priest wouldn't break that bond. In his mother's mind, he was abandoning her. It was as simple as that.

She'll get over it in the end, he told himself. *Once she sees that she hasn't lost me. That I'm still her son.* But it wasn't only his mother making him feel guilty. Ines had her work, after all, and her friends, a full, happy, purposeful life in Paris. Aunt Genevieve had nothing and no one, apart from this sad mausoleum of a house and the ubiquitous Duponts, whom Matty was starting to view with increasing dislike and suspicion.

He must make a point of raising his fears with his mother as soon as he got back to Paris, and before he entered the seminary. This ridiculous distance between Aunt Genevieve and both of her sisters had gone on for too long. He must redouble his efforts as peacemaker. Closing his eyes, and turning off the bedside lamp, he offered up a prayer.

'Dear Lord,' he began. 'Give me the grace and wisdom to help heal the rifts in my family. Bless my mother and my aunts. Bless this house. Forgive all of us our sins, and let love and trust once again flow freely at Beaulieu. Amen.'

There was more to say. More to be thankful for, and more divine guidance to be humbly requested. But Matty was bone-tired. It would have to wait till morning.

As sleep slowly began to creep over him, images from the day tumbled one by one through his fading consciousness. His Aunt Genevieve's sunken cheeks and thin, frail body. Hélène Dupont's resentful glances. And finally Antoinette, the beautiful girl at the roadside with the shiny, chestnut hair and oh-so-deliciously suggestive eyes . . .

Some parts of the priesthood *would* be hard. But then Matty had always known that the Lord worked in mysterious ways.

CHAPTER THIRTY

Megève, France, December 1966

'What is it with you and hoteliers?' Renée teased Ines, refilling both of their glasses. It was Christmas Day, and Ines had accepted Renée and Charlotte's invitation to spend the holiday with the two of them at the family chalet – now Renée's chalet – in Megève. It was a kind offer, designed to help distract Ines from Matty's taking orders back in the autumn. But Ines was starting to have second thoughts about her decision to accept.

'She's always had a thing for them, you know,' Renée informed Charlotte, chuckling at her little sister's discomfort. 'Lucien Toulon's simply the last in a loooong line.'

The joke related to an article that had come out in December's *Vogue*, profiling Ines's refurbishment of the latest Toulon hotel, a chic boutique affair in Venice. The journalist had made much of the 'decades-long partnership' between the millionaire hotelier and his 'adored' interior designer, strongly implying that Ines and Lucien either were or had been lovers.

'Remember David Walton?' Renée teased, turning back to Ines.

'Oh God!' Ines groaned, clutching her head with a shudder. 'Don't.'

'Who's David Walton?' Charlotte asked, happy to play along with the sisterly banter. Without anything ever overtly being said, it was understood by everyone who knew them that Charlotte Mortimer and Renée Challant were in love, and that after the better part of thirty years were to all intents and purposes a married couple. Making harmless fun of Renée's singleton younger sister was just something older married couples did. It amused Charlotte to see Ines getting so flustered.

'David was a rich American business partner of Papa's,' Renée explained. 'He stayed with us here, in fact, the Christmas before the war. Ate lunch *at this very table*. No wonder Ines is feeling nostalgic.'

'Oh, do shut up,' said Ines, scrunching up her napkin and tossing it playfully in Renée's general direction. 'I am not feeling nostalgic. Papa was terribly keen to have at least one of his daughters marry well,' Ines explained to Charlotte. 'He rightly identified Renée as a lost cause.'

Charlotte smiled, silently placing her hand over Renée's. 'Fair enough.'

'And Genevieve was always falling in love with wildly unsuitable, bohemian types,' Ines went on. 'So I was the great white hope. Unfortunately, my father's idea of a suitable match tended to be rich men twice my age. David Walton's probably dead by now.'

'Oh, he is *not*,' Renée gasped, then giggled because it wasn't impossible. How old would David Walton be today . . . late sixties? 'I thought he was a nice man.'

'He was a nice man,' Ines agreed. 'I just didn't want to marry him. I was a teenager, for heaven's sake.'

'Not that that stopped her from running off into the sunset with Gunn,' Renée winked at Charlotte. 'Love's young dream, the two of you, back then,' she said to Ines. She hadn't meant it remotely unkindly, but as soon as the words left her lips she regretted them. The change in Ines was immediate. All the light-hearted playfulness was gone and her expression shifted from amused embarrassment to genuine pain.

'Oh lovey, I'm sorry,' said Renée. 'I didn't mean to upset you. It was all so long ago, I didn't think . . .'

'No, no. It's fine.' Ines shook her head firmly. 'You're quite right. It *was* so long ago. And it *was* a part of my history. Of all of our histories. You're allowed to say the man's name.'

'Personally, *I'd* rather hear more about Lucien Toulon,' said Charlotte, breaking the tension as she stood up to clear away the plates and bring in the traditional, steamed English Christmas pudding she'd insisted on making for today's meal. 'Exactly how close *is* your partnership? That's what I want to know.'

Later, as the light began to fade, Ines and Renée set out for a snowy walk through the deserted streets of town. Last night the square had been full, with hundreds or perhaps even a thousand people gathered around the enormous Christmas tree, singing carols by candlelight. Church bells had rung out in the still alpine air, and a sky full of stars had bathed the traditional yuletide vigil in magic and wonder of the kind Ines hadn't felt since her early childhood, back when her mother was still alive.

Today, things were very different. All was quiet. Lights glowed warmly from the chalets and hotels, where families gathered around their fires to drink and laugh and admire their presents. But the shops and restaurants were all shut, and even the churches had finished with their Christmas services, so there was no reason to ven-ture outside.

'It's nice, isn't it?' Renée asked Ines, linking arms. 'Having the place to ourselves?'

They were both dressed in thick fur coats, Renée's rabbit, Ines's mink, with gloves and hats and fur-lined snow boots to shield them from the cold. In the last few minutes, snow had started to fall again, heavy, wet flakes that stuck only briefly to clothes or skin before melting, but which somehow enhanced the lovely, muffled feeling of peace.

'It is nice,' Ines agreed. 'I'd honestly forgotten how beautiful Megève was. It's been such a long time.'

'It hasn't changed much, though, has it?' said Renée. 'Papa was probably the last developer to make a significant impact on the town. Only one new hotel's been built since he died, can you believe it?'

Ines shook her head. She hadn't really thought about it, but now that Renée pointed it out, it was bizarre the degree to which Megève had remained frozen in time.

'There was the new ski lift of course, in 1960. A few more fancy homes went up after that. But since then, nothing. It's essentially the same village we grew up in.'

On the surface, perhaps, thought Ines. But underneath, nowhere was the same as it had been before the war. Nowhere in Europe, anyway. An innocence had been lost, a simpler, happier, more rooted way of life that could not be recreated now, not even here in the timeless beauty of Megève.

'Are you thinking about Matty?' Renée asked, noticing her sister's sad, pensive expression.

'Actually, I wasn't – for once.' Ines smiled ruefully. 'I was just remembering Charles Fils. In my mind's eye I can see him, running across the square in those baggy ski trousers he was so proud of. Do you remember those?'

'Of course!' Renée laughed. 'He looked ridiculous, like a cartoon aviator. Remember the goggles that went with them?'

Ines nodded, feeling happy and sad at the same time. 'I don't think about him very often,' she admitted, guiltily. 'I did in the first few years, but not now. Here though, it's like he's everywhere. This really was his place.'

'It was,' Renée agreed, squeezing her sister's arm more tightly. '*Niverolle.*'

'When I think back to those days now, that last winter before the war, it doesn't feel real,' said Ines. 'Charles Fils. David Walton. Gunn and me.' She swallowed hard. 'I'm sorry I made such a fuss about that at lunch, by the way.'

'You didn't.' Renée waved away the apology. 'Honestly, it's fine.'

'Genevieve and Wilhelm,' Ines went on.

'Heavens.' Renée sighed. 'I haven't thought about Wilhelm in forever. I wonder whatever happened to him?'

'He married and settled down in Germany, I believe, after the war,' said Ines. 'Matty says that Gen still talks about him sometimes. Usually when she's drunk.'

'And is that still "usually"?' Renée asked archly.

This led them into a longer conversation about Genevieve, and their doomed efforts to reestablish contact.

'I think, after a certain point, I took the hint that she didn't want to see me and rather let it go,' confessed Ines. 'Partly because I've been so busy with work, and because I always had Matty as a go-between, I let myself off the hook. But if I'm honest it's also because I just find her so difficult to be around.'

'We all do,' said Renée.

'I sometimes think, if only I'd been able to get clarity from the coroner over Bernard's death, I might have spared Gen some of the worst of her paranoia. But if anything all those missing sections only made it worse.'

Over the last ten years, Ines had made titanic efforts to find out what exactly happened on the night that poor Bernard Angier died at the bastide. After her confession with the priest in Paris, not to mention multiple heart-to-hearts with her friend Sylvie, she'd decided that the only way she was ever going to find peace from her dreams was to cut through all the rumour and blurred memories and establish some cold hard facts. But facts had proved frustratingly hard to come by. The official coroner's re-port, when Ines finally read it, suggested that the child had died from a broken neck, probably the result of a fall from the high garden wall, and that the injuries sustained from Charles Père's dobermans had occurred post-mortem. Mysteriously, however, the document had been redacted in several key areas. The man who had written it had died from lung cancer several years ago, and nobody else in the Villefranche coroner's office seemed able, or willing, to explain the omissions, or to fill in any of the blanks.

Frustrated, Ines had spent years visiting everyone she could think of who knew Papa, to try to unearth some answers. She'd had three separate dinners with the quite charming Alissa Faubourg, and tracked down several other of her father's former mistresses, in hopes Charles might have confided in one of them about that fateful night. But it seemed he'd never spoken of it.

At first those meetings were hard for Ines. But over time, as she reluctantly let go of the last vestiges of her childhood image of her 'perfect' father, she came to find them quite comforting. In a strange way, she was finally getting to know the man she had loved so blindly, for so long.

In the end, the closest Ines ever came to finding answers to the questions surrounding Bernard's death came through a chance meeting she had with an old hunting friend of her father's at a cocktail party in Paris.

Arnaud Champalimaud was a doddery old fellow, but his mind remained sharp as a tack. He remembered that Charles Père had spoken repeatedly of being 'tormented' by loan sharks and unscrupulous former business partners in the months leading up to that terrible summer. That both he and Clotilde had been living under a cloud of fear. But that while he was in Beaulieu, just days before the tragedy happened, he'd written to Arnaud to say that it was 'all over, thank God'.

'He seemed very relieved,' Arnaud told Ines. 'Happy with your mother. Happy altogether. That's what made all the terrible things that happened afterwards so sad, so ironic. Your father had genuinely believed that the worst was over.'

In short, Ines hadn't found out anything that explained why the coroner's report into Bernard Angier's death had been tampered with, and nothing that would shift Genevieve's view of Charles Père as an irredeemable monster.

'Papa killed that boy,' she would insist, drunkenly and vociferously, whenever the subject arose. 'Then he bribed the coroner to cover it up, and bullied poor Maman into silence. The guilt of it killed her too!'

The fact that Charles Père had no motive for killing an innocent young boy carried no weight with Genevieve. 'Papa didn't need *reasons* to be cruel,' she insisted. 'It was who he was.'

Turning sharp left out of the town square and up the steep, snowy cobblestone hill that led towards the church, Renée put a comforting arm around her sister.

'I don't think it would have mattered what you found out, from the coroner or anyone else,' she told Ines. 'Genevieve needs someone to blame for her own unhappiness. For all the failures and disappointments of her life. Papa was always going to be that person. Especially now he's not here to defend himself.'

'Maybe,' Ines replied hesitantly. 'I'm still worried about her though.'

Renée nodded. 'Me too.'

'Matty stayed with her just before he entered the seminary. He told me she seemed weak and frail and that the house was in an appalling state. She has some couple living there, the Duponts, but Matty's not at all sure about them.'

'Really?' Renée frowned. She didn't see Matty terribly often in person, but she knew him to be a kind and sensible boy, and she was inclined to trust his judgement. 'Maybe you should go down there? See for yourself?'

'She won't have me!' said Ines. 'All this business about Bernard and Papa has really come between us. You know how impossible she is.'

'Don't tell her you're coming then,' said Renée. 'Just show up.'

'Why me?' Ines retorted, crossly. 'Why don't *you* just show up?'

'It's easier for you from Paris than it is for me from London,' Renée replied reasonably. 'Plus I'm working. You did say you were between jobs at the moment.'

'For a heartbeat!' protested Ines. 'I was planning to rest. Take a break.'

Renée rolled her eyes. 'Please. You're rubbish at resting.'

This was true.

'You know if you stay in Paris all you'll do is sit around and brood about Matty. Why not go?'

'I'll think about it,' Ines mumbled grudgingly.

They'd reached the top of the hill. Behind them, vast but barely visible in the darkness, was the awesome, looming presence of Mont Blanc. Below them, all the lights of the town twinkled invitingly, a vision of Christmas card perfection and wonder.

Would Genevieve be spending Christmas alone? Ines wondered. Or with this couple that Matty felt so uncomfortable about?

She tried to picture Matty himself, in the seminary with the other trainee priests. *Postulants*, they called them. Ines couldn't imagine Christmas there. Was there a tree and presents, or was it all mass and bible readings and feeding the poor?

Either way, she told herself, her son was probably happy. It was what he'd chosen, after all. But being without him, today of all days, felt desolate. It was the first Christmas they had spent apart since he was born.

The more Ines thought about it, the more Renée's suggestion began to make sense. She wouldn't look forward to seeing Genevieve, exactly. Nor to returning to Beaulieu, a place that brought back even more mixed memories than Megève. But it would be a distraction, something she badly needed. And someone needed to check on Gen.

Family was family at the end of the day, and there was more to Ines's family than just her son. The Challant flock might be depleted, and scattered. But those who survived still belonged to one another. The old patterns of migration, from Beaulieu to Paris to Megève, remained hardwired into each of them, an instinctive pull drawing them back into a rhythm that nothing, it seemed, could completely erase.

'I'm so glad you came to us for Christmas.' Renée smiled at Ines as they stood together, admiring the view. 'I hope it will be the first of many.'

'It will be,' Ines promised, allowing her head to rest on Renée's shoulder, as she had when she was a little girl. 'I'm glad I came too.'

It was memories of Gunn, she realized now, that had kept her away from Megève for so long. But like Beaulieu, this place was part of her history. Part of who she was. Perhaps now, the time had come to move on from the pain of the past, and make this magical village a part of her future too? A future that stretched ahead of her as pure and white and endless as the Christmas snow. If only she would let it.

CHAPTER THIRTY-ONE

En route to New York, USA, January 1967

'Excuse me, sir? Can I interest you in another drink?'

The stewardess smiled suggestively at the handsome passenger in row 5. The Pan Am flight from São Paolo to New York was full, but there were precious few 'interesting'-looking men on board. Plenty of the female passengers were attractive, a mixture of curvaceous Brazilian brunettes and slim, blonde Manhattan types. But the guys were mostly businessmen, middle aged, bald and paunchy: not much of a distraction.

This one was different, though. He was older, with greying hair and a beard to match, as well as a clearly etched fan of lines at the corner of each eye. But he carried the years well, with his tanned skin, great bone structure and immaculately cut clothes that somehow made him look both chic and effortless.

Glancing languidly up from his in-flight magazine, he returned her smile.

'Do you know what? I believe you *can*,' he drawled, in the most divine British accent the stewardess had ever heard.

'I'm sorry?' she blushed, flustered at having forgotten her own question.

'Interest me.' He grinned wolfishly. 'A drink?'

'Oh, yes. Of course! Sorry,' the stewardess stammered. 'Gin and tonic, wasn't it?'

A few minutes later, sipping his second G and T while admiring the stewardess's bottom as she made her way further up the cabin, Gunn reflected on what a good start to the year he was having.

1967! Christ. How had that happened? Was it really possible that so many years had passed since he first came to South America? On the other hand, he'd packed a lot into those years. Changed his life completely, in fact. And he had his father's old friend, Professor Horatio Chapman, to thank for it.

That one chance meeting at the British Museum, shortly after his divorce from the awful Anna Grierly, had set Gunn on the path to the life he led now, as a Professor of Archaeology at the University of São Paolo. *Professor Gunn.* No matter how long he lived, he didn't think he would ever get used to hearing those words side by side. Him, Hector Gunn, the boy who struggled so much with reading that he'd failed his Common Entrance papers as a boy and dropped completely out of mainstream education and working life. A university professor! More than that, a damned good one, whose class in Tribal Cultures was one of the most popular and oversubscribed in the entire school.

With Horatio's help, after accepting a dogsbody role on that first British Museum expedition to South America, Gunn had worked to overcome his childhood dyslexia and gone back to college, paying his fees with the modest rental income he now earned from his tenants at Maltings. Ironically, given his struggles with the written word, he'd always had a natural gift with languages, and had picked up spoken Portuguese astonishingly quickly, along with a growing, encyclopaedic knowledge of some of the cultures and regions that had so fascinated his father. Now that Gunn was experiencing these places for himself for the first time, he felt stirrings of the same passion, the same intellectual curiosity that had so consumed William Gunn, taking him away from his family and responsibilities for years at a stretch.

But Gunn had no family. No responsibilities, other than to himself. And to Horatio – to repay his kindness by making the most of the unexpected chances he'd been given. This he did, diligently working to earn his equivalent of the Brazilian high school diploma, followed by an undergraduate degree in archaeology, and finally his master's, with an acclaimed thesis on the Yanomami tribe's use of plant-based poisons in their hunting tech-niques. Academics from all over the world sought Gunn's opinion on his specialist subject, and his pupils at São Paolo universally adored him.

Especially the girls.

Stretching out his long legs and taking another sip of his drink, he idly picked up the in-flight magazine and began flipping through it, his thoughts returning again to what a great year this was shaping up to be, and how excited he was about this trip to New York. Incredibly, he hadn't been back to the States since his short-lived and unhappy second marriage. But that was long enough ago now for any painful memories to have faded. The archaeology conference he was headed to at NYU looked set to be a fantastic event, full of speakers that Gunn was excited to hear from. Plus the organizers had paid to put him up at the Knickerbocker Hotel on Broadway and 42nd, in a beautiful suite with views over Times Square. A full week of excellent dinners, scintillating conversation and hopefully at least a few glamorous parties filled with glamorous American women beckoned. Gunn couldn't wait.

'Have you stayed there?'

The man in the seat next to him nudged Gunn, pointing at the picture in his magazine. It had fallen open at a feature on another Manhattan hotel, The Regent, a sumptuous boutique in the West Village being showcased for its flamboyant interiors.

'It's supposed to be incredible. My buddy had one of the best suites when it opened last fall. Said it was like waking up in the rainforest.'

'Is that a compliment?' Gunn raised an eyebrow. As someone who *had* woken up in a rainforest, several times, he didn't particularly recommend it.

'The designer's French, and she has this really trippy vibe,' his neighbour went on. 'She does all Lucien Toulon's hotels. The Lafayette in Paris, Villa St Victoire in the South of France and that new one in Venice, I forget the name.'

Gunn looked more closely at the article in front of him. The photograph showed a bedroom that was really more of a *boudoir*. It had wildly over-the-top wallpaper, full of jungle flowers and humming birds in every conceivable colour, an ornate four-poster bed and fitted closets sprayed white and gold. But it was the text below that really made his heart stop.

'*Reclusive interior designer Ines Challant talks exclusively to* Clipper *about Lucien Toulon's Stateside sensation, New York's Regent West Village.*'

'Well, I'll be damned . . .' Gunn muttered under his breath.

He'd heard vague rumours from friends back in England, years ago, that Ines had moved back to Paris after she left him and become an interior designer. But he'd never probed any further – memories of Ines were always potentially painful, even after all these years, and Gunn had learned to stop choosing pain on purpose. So he had no idea she'd ended up becoming a household name, one of the best in the business. Fancy European hotels were not the sort of thing one read or talked about down in São Paolo. As wonderful as Gunn's life at the university was, it was pretty insular.

Flipping the page, he hoped to see a picture of Ines as she was now, but there were none. Only more images of riotously decorated bathrooms, the clawfoot tubs covered with yet more painted birds and butterflies. The room was beautiful in its own way, Gunn conceded, although one wouldn't want to walk in there with a hangover. For the first time in years, he remembered the little cottage he and Ines had shared in Cornwall during the war years, and the pretty, rainbow birds she'd painted up the stairway to welcome him home from leave. Something in his chest tightened, a sharp unexpected pain making him wince. He read on.

'"*The Régent was the first time I was given completely free rein, creatively,*"' Ines was quoted as saying. '"*There was an appetite for something much more vibrant and explosive in New York than would have been appropriate, or even commercially viable, back in Europe. That felt celebratory to me. I hope that people will feel that joy when they stay there.*"'

Gunn tried to link the words and the voice behind them to the girl he remembered. The girl he'd loved more than anything, once. But he couldn't. Ines Challant, Designer, sounded like a mature, confident woman, a professional and an artist at the top of her game. The Ines he'd betrayed and so foolishly lost had been totally different: young, naïve, diffident. She'd always had talent. Always been creative. But back then she'd subordinated that talent to her love for him. The entire sum of her ambition had been to be a good wife, the best wife. And she had been.

Most of the rest of the article focused on the hotel, its famous guests, and its French owner, Lucien Toulon. At the very end of the piece, the journalist asked Ines about her hopes for the future, and what ambitions she still had left to fulfil.

'"*I try not to think in those terms,*"' she answered. '"*Designing beautiful spaces and watching them come to life is its own reward. As long as I can do that, and as long as my son is proud of me, that's really all I need.*"'

Gunn closed the magazine and put it away quickly, as if holding it any longer might burn his fingers.

So, Ines had a son.

Really, there was no reason why this information should have surprised him. She'd always wanted children, after all, and she'd been so young when they split. He'd always assumed that she would have remarried – although there was no mention of a husband in the article, which pleased him, as ridiculous as he knew that was. But somehow, he'd never actually thought about Ines having children. For some inexplicable reason it made him deeply sad. It was as if someone had lifted off the lid of a huge, hor-rible, unexpected well of regret. It was rising up now like a flood, threatening to burst out of him.

How old was this son? What was his name? Who was his father? After years of suppressing the memories, Gunn now found himself consumed with a need to know more about Ines Challant, and this boy whose pride and approval was 'all she needed' – just as his had been, once.

'Another drink, sir?'

The stewardess was back, as pretty and solicitous as ever.

'Yes. Please.' He handed her his empty glass. 'Same again.'

But Gunn no longer registered her smiles, or the way her hips swayed suggestively when she moved down the aisle. Instead he gazed sullenly out of the window, anxious and perturbed for reasons he couldn't fully explain, even to himself.

CHAPTER THIRTY-TWO

Beaulieu-sur-Mer, France, July 1967

On a muggy, humid Thursday morning in July, Ines Challant found herself sweating uncomfortably in the upstairs waiting room of a private investigator's office in downtown Beaulieu, picking nervously at a loose thread on her blouse.

'Madame?' The overweight, harassed-looking recep-tionist waved in her direction, just as Ines was con-templating calling the whole thing off and scuttling back to the bastide. But she couldn't back out now. Not after she'd come this far.

'Monsieur Tremont will see you now.'

It had taken Ines until the summer, just before Bastille Day, to finally visit Genevieve. So many forces had been pulling her back to the bastide. Worry about her sister. The state of the house. And most of all, Matty's misgivings about the couple his aunt had hired to 'take care of her': the Duponts.

But equally strong forces had held Ines back, fear being the main one. Of leaving Paris, where Matty still was, even if she couldn't see him regularly at the seminary. And where work still was, even if she was taking a long-overdue and well-earned 'hiatus'.

'Ines my dear, I'm hardly going to start working with someone else, just because you go to Beaulieu for a few months,' Lucien Toulon assured her, amused by her insecurity after their decades-long partnership. 'So if you want an excuse not to see your sister, I'm afraid you're going to have to find someone other than me.'

'I don't want an excuse not to see Genevieve,' Ines replied, defensively. She was spending the weekend with Lucien out at La Poulette, finalizing the snag lists on their most recently finished project, and neurotically obsessing about handing over the reins to her temporary stand-in.

'Good,' Lucien said firmly. 'So go.'

He was still attracted to Ines Challant. She remained a beautiful woman, youthful, chic and, most importantly, aloof, the nut he'd never been able to crack. But he'd also developed a genuine affection for her over the years, one based on friendship, admiration and the mutual pleasure they took in the huge success of their partnership. Ines's vision, married to Lucien's investing and marketing genius, had helped elevate them to the very tops of their respective trees. The idea that Lucien would move on without Ines, or switch loyalties to another designer, was unthinkable. At this point, *Toulon et Challant* went together like *pain et beurre*.

While she was resigned about the need to go to Beaulieu, Ines was also apprehensive about turning up on Gen's doorstep unannounced. She and Renée had long since agreed that this was the only way. That any 'advance warning' would lead to a litany of delays and excuses from Genevieve and the Beaulieu trip being postponed for so long it was effectively cancelled. But at the same time, Gen's temper could be formidable, especially when she was drunk. Which, in the absence of any other information, Ines assumed would be most of the time.

As it turned out, Genevieve had seemed pleased to see Ines, and touched that she had made the effort to come to Beaulieu. But while her reception from Gen was better than she'd expected, Ines found other things had been worse. Most notably Monsieur and Madame Dupont, whom she found every bit as insincere and troubling as Matty had almost a year earlier; fawning over Genevieve, taking her money while doing little or no housekeeping or maintenance, and radiating resentment towards Ines, or anyone Gen appeared close to.

It was concern about the Duponts that had led Ines to today's private investigator, Alain Tremont, a short, unprepossessing-looking fellow with a tonsure of greasy brown hair and huge, spreading sweat marks beneath the arms of his brown rayon shirt.

'A pleasure to meet you, Mademoiselle Challant.' He greeted Ines warmly, clearing a messy pile of papers from a chair so that she could sit down. 'How can I be of assistance?'

Ines cleared her throat, embarrassed. Now that she was actually sitting here, it seemed ridiculous to start accusing a couple she barely knew of . . . what? Whatever she was accusing the Duponts of, it was simply based on a 'feeling'. Even if it was a feeling that she and Matty shared.

'My family have owned a small, er, a small estate here for several years,' she began awkwardly.

Tremont nodded encouragingly. 'The Challants are a household name in Beaulieu, mademoiselle. I know the house well.'

'Yes, well, it passed to my sister Genevieve on my father's death,' Ines blundered on, not totally sure why she seemed to be finding the conversation so torturous. 'She had been living there alone. But her health has been declining for some time, and a year or two ago she hired a couple by the name of Dupont to move in and help to take care of her. And the property.'

Tremont pulled a notepad and mechanical pencil out of his desk drawer and wrote the single word 'Dupont' in large, elaborately curled script. Looking up, he smiled expectantly at Ines.

'You see, my sister has been estranged from the rest of the family,' Ines coughed again. 'But my son Matthieu had come to visit his aunt and he expressed concern about this couple.'

'The Duponts . . .'

'Yes.'

'What sort of concern?'

Ines blushed. 'That's the thing, Monsieur Tremont. He wasn't able to specify. So a few days ago I arrived to see for myself. And I also felt . . . uncomfortable around them. My sister's rather vulnerable, you see, and I suppose I'm worried they might be manipulating her or . . . mistreating her in some way,' she finished lamely.

312

'Has your sister complained of any mistreatment?' Tremont asked, a frown briefly corrugating his shiny forehead.

'No,' Ines admitted. 'Quite the opposite, in fact. She speaks well of this couple.'

'I see,' Tremont mused, cocking his head to one side. 'But you, and your son, believe there may be nefarious motives at play?'

'I honestly don't know,' admitted Ines. 'It's a gut feeling.'

'I try never to ignore those.' The investigator smiled, and for the first time Ines began to relax just a little. 'So you'd like me to look into them? See what I can find out?'

'Exactly.'

Exhaling, Ines began to take in her surroundings for the first time. She turned first towards the window, but it was obscured by so many filing cabinets and stacked boxes that it was impossible to see anything through it. Chaos and mess were everywhere, from the desk to the floor to the little side tables covered with overflowing ashtrays and endless piles of coffee-stained documents.

'How can you work like this, Monsieur Tremont?' she heard herself saying, her inner designer breaking spontaneously forth.

'I beg your pardon?'

'I'm sure I couldn't think straight surrounded by so much clutter.'

'Oh.' Tremont blushed, looking at the detritus all around him as if seeing it for the first time. 'I suppose I hadn't really thought about it.'

'I'd be happy to suggest some improvements,' Ines offered brightly. 'If you decide you'd like to change things. But in the meantime, I hope this will be enough for you to get started?'

Pulling a neat stack of fifty-franc notes from her wallet, she placed them on a rare mess-free spot on his desk and stood up.

'We'll meet again once you have some information,' she announced, all business suddenly now that her nerves were gone. 'I'm staying at the bastide, but don't contact me there. I've a mailbox at the post office. I'll leave the details with your assistant so we can stay in touch.'

A week later, Ines and Genevieve were eating breakfast together on the terrace at the bastide. Or rather, Ines was eating. Genevieve just sat there, staring straight ahead.

'Are you sure you don't want an egg, darling?' Ines asked, worried. 'You've barely touched your toast.'

'For heaven's sake. Of course I'm sure,' Genevieve snapped. 'I'm perfectly capable of ordering my own breakfast.'

In the seven long, oppressively hot days since her meeting with Tremont, Ines had tried to focus on the tentative process of reacquainting herself with her older sister up at the bastide. It wasn't easy. Genevieve was prickly at the best of times, quick to take offence and on a permanent state of alert. To make matters worse, she often defaulted to patronizing Ines, whom she still instinctively viewed as the baby of the family.

For her part, Ines felt exhausted from the effort of biting her tongue, and depressed by everything from Genevieve's drinking to her bird-like appetite and the genuinely shocking state of the house. Either Matty had understated how dire things were, or the situation had worsened since his visit. Electrical wires hung loose and dangerous from countless fixtures, where the ceilings or walls around them had rotted away with damp. There was mould in several of the carpets, dry rot in the woodwork, and it appeared that nothing had been repaired or repainted since before the war. But however gently or politely Ines broached the subject, Genevieve instantly bridled and shut her down.

'I don't know why you've come here if all you're going to do is complain.'

'I'm perfectly happy with things the way they are.'

'I daresay you're used to all sorts of luxury in Paris. But here in Beaulieu we live a more simple life.'

This last barb had been particularly hard for Ines to swallow, from an older sister famous for spending money like water, and who for most of her younger life had been obsessed with both Paris and luxury. What modest creature comforts Ines enjoyed now she had worked hard for and earned entirely on her own merit. Unlike Genevieve who'd inherited Beaulieu *and* a fund to pay for its upkeep, presumably long since drunk away.

When Hélène Dupont emerged from the house to clear away the breakfast things, Ines made a point of thanking her and smiling. Until she heard more from Monsieur Tremont, her policy was to keep her friends close and enemies closer. If, indeed, the housekeeper and her smarmy husband really *were* enemies.

'Will you come down into town with me later?' Ines asked Genevieve, once Mrs Dupont had gone. 'It's market day. I thought we could potter around the stalls together like we used to in the old days. Maybe pick up some good cheese and bread for lunch?'

'Well, I . . . I'm not sure.' Genevieve sounded hesitant. But at the same time there was a yearning there, Ines was sure of it. As if she wanted to get out of the house but was afraid to do so.

'Come on,' Ines encouraged, gently. 'It'll be fun. We can buy some cheeses to make ourselves a lovely, fattening lunch later.'

'Hélène will make us lunch,' Genevieve announced imperiously. 'Anyway, I do wish you'd stop banging on about meals all the time. I eat when I want to.'

'You're very skinny,' Ines pushed back bravely. 'I know you get cross with me, but you must see it yourself. I'm worried about you.'

Genevieve opened her mouth to deliver some pithy retort, but then closed it again. She resented Ines's 'concern' – meddling by another name – and the fact that she had turned up at the bastide out of the blue with a suitcase and simply announced that she was staying for the summer. But at the same time, despite her bad temper, Genevieve was pleased to see her sister again after all these years. Pleased that, as hard as she had pushed Ines and Renée away, for her own self-protection, the love that they shared as siblings was still there. The flock, though depleted, was still intact.

'I'll see how I feel,' she mumbled grudgingly.

*

To Ines's surprise, Genevieve did come with her to the market. Wandering together around the bustling square, meandering between the different stalls with their bright red and white striped awnings, selling everything from fresh fish and local farm cheeses, to flowers, honey and embroidered linens, Ines was delighted to watch her sister come alive for the first time since she'd got to Beaulieu. Smiling and engaging with stallholders, wrinkling her nose at the smells, even agreeing to taste little samples of this and that, Genevieve seemed, if not her old self, then at least a much better, brighter version of the frail recluse she had become.

'It is nice to be out in the world again,' she admitted to Ines, almost guiltily, as they packed a selection of muslin-wrapped cheeses into the wicker basket they'd brought with them for the purpose. 'One forgets, you know. The energy of it all.'

'I'm pleased.' Ines squeezed her arm. 'I hope you'll start to get out more. There's really no reason why you shouldn't, is there?'

A shadow of uncertainty flickered across Genevieve's face. 'I worry sometimes,' she told Ines, her voice dropped close to a whisper. 'What people think of me. What they're saying.'

Ines stopped and turned to face her. 'What are you afraid that they might be saying?'

'I don't know exactly,' said Genevieve, suddenly sounding distressed and confused. 'Hélène and Georges hear all sorts of things. They try to protect me. From the gossip, you know.'

'What gossip?' Ines asked. She herself had made several expeditions to town since she arrived, and had generally been received with openness and kindness by the locals. So she assumed that whatever rancour might once have been felt towards their father, it was now water under the bridge. 'I don't believe you need protecting, Gen. You saw how friendly everybody was today.'

'This time, perhaps,' said Genevieve. 'But not always. We should get back anyway. I'm tired.'

'OK,' said Ines, deciding that now was not the time to push it. But these latest revelations about the Duponts' influence over her sister were telling. And the question remained: what *was* their mysterious agenda up at the bastide?

Renée was in bed with Charlotte and just drifting off into a contented sleep when the telephone rang.

'Do you know what time it is?' she said, yawning loudly as she drew her dressing gown more tightly around her in the hallway of her London flat, receiver in hand.

'I'm sorry,' Ines said, 'but this is important. I didn't know who else to call.'

'Are you in Beaulieu?' Renée rubbed her eyes sleepily, bracing for bad news.

'I'm still in Beaulieu, but not at the bastide,' Ines replied breathlessly.

'Well, where are you?'

'I checked myself into a little pension in town. Gen threw me out this evening.'

'*What?*' Pulling up a chair, Renée sat down, listening carefully as Ines explained what had happened. How she and Gen had had a lovely afternoon together at the market. But that when they got home, Gen had gone upstairs for a rest, 'helped' by Hélène Dupont, and then a few hours later announced that having 'guests to take care of' was too exhausting on her nerves, and that she must insist Ines found somewhere else to stay.

'She wasn't angry or drunk or anything,' Ines went on. 'I almost would have preferred it if she were. She was just *passive*. Numb. It's as if she's being brainwashed by the Duponts into believing that she's ill or weak or incapable of making her own decisions.'

'Did you go and see that investigator you were thinking about?' asked Renée. 'To do some digging on them?'

'A week ago,' Ines confirmed.

'And what did he say?'

'He still hasn't come back to me with a report. I might chase him in the morning.'

'Do,' urged Renée. In her experience, all service providers in the South of France needed regular chasing. She assumed this applied to private detectives as surely as it did to plumbers.

'I thought about driving back to Paris, now that Gen's kicked me out,' said Ines. 'But then I changed my mind. It's clear that's what the Duponts want: to get rid of me. So I've decided to stay down here, at least for a while. See what Monsieur Tremont comes up with, and keep an eye on poor Genevieve, even if it's from afar. I'm worried, Ren. Matty was right about these people.'

'Matty's right about a lot of things,' Renée replied, gently.

They both knew she was alluding to his decision to join the priesthood. But Ines was grateful that she didn't spell it out in so many words. She had enough to worry about this evening, without letting her mind wander back to *that*.

'You'll never guess who I bumped into by the way, just as I was checking in here,' she said, deftly changing the subject.

'Who?'

'Old Marianne Blanchet.'

Marianne. It took Renée a second to place the name. 'You don't mean Marie's friend? From church?'

Ines laughed. 'Can you believe it?'

'But, she was as old as the hills when we were children!' said Renée, remembering the garrulous, gossipy friend of the Challants' beloved old cook. 'She had warts and a stick! She can't possibly still be alive. Are you sure it was her?'

'Quite sure,' said Ines. 'She introduced herself, said how nice it was to see me. She was a bit stooped but still walking, and seemed to have all her marbles. Anyway, she's invited me to her cottage for tea and macarons tomorrow afternoon.'

'How lovely. See if you can get her to tell you how she's still hobbling about Beaulieu and hosting tea parties at a hundred and ten!' joked Renée. 'That's what I'd like to know.'

They talked for a few more minutes and then Renée rang off.

Back in their London bedroom, Charlotte was now wide awake.

'How are your sisters?' she asked Renée.

'Oh, you know. Insane, as usual,' Renée rolled her eyes.

'Is everything all right?' Charlotte asked.

Now that's a question, thought Renée. The truth was that so much was not as she would want it to be. Genevieve's frail state of health. Ines's apparently insatiable need to pick away at the past.

But as she slipped under the covers, Renée leaned over and kissed Charlotte, a long lingering kiss of gratitude and contentment for the lovely, peaceful life the two women had built together. And she heard herself answer, quite sincerely.

'Yes. Yes, everything's all right.'

Because as long as she and Charlotte were together, it always would be.

CHAPTER THIRTY-THREE

Paris, France, July 1967

Matthieu Challant sat shirtless on the end of his bed in the seminary, his black cassock, belt and shirt discarded at his side. It had been a punishingly hot summer in Paris. And while Matty had no complaints about his accommodation at the seminary, the stifling air and paucity of windows that could actually be opened often left him feeling more like a chicken in a broiler than a postulant, nearing the end of a profound spiritual journey.

His faith hadn't wavered since he began his priest's training. If anything it had strengthened, as he became ever more deeply immersed in the intricacies of the liturgy and the divine mystery of the sacraments that he would one day, soon, be administering. And yet some things about his new life were not as he'd expected. As the weeks passed, he realized to his disappointment that he was, in fact, exactly the same person he'd been before he chose to follow his vocation. No profound rebirth had occurred, or at least not yet. Matty was still his mother's son, still a part of the messy, extended Challant family. He found himself eagerly awaiting Ines's regular letters from Beaulieu, updating him on all the dramas unfolding with Aunt Genevieve and the dreadful Duponts. Matty's mother was a naturally witty, gossipy writer, and he wondered whether the intense delight he got from immersing himself in her descriptions of Tremont the investigator and Beaulieu life in general might be, if not sinful exactly, then at least a bad sign in terms of his personal piety.

And then there was the other letter he'd received, several weeks ago now. The letter he was re-reading at this very moment, having once again extracted it from his 'personal items' drawer like an addict returning to his fix. Matty had told nobody about this letter. Not Pierre, his closest friend at the seminary. Not Father Gerard, his spiritual mentor. Definitely not his mother. And yet at some point, he knew, he would have to share its contents with Ines. Because the letter posed questions – one question in particular – that ultimately only she could answer.

A knock startled him. Slipping the letter back into its envelope, he was reaching for his shirt and about to call out '*Un moment, s'il vous plaît*' when the door suddenly swung open. A young woman carrying a mop and bucket in one hand and an unwieldy array of dusters in the other swept into the room, too weighed down and preoccupied at first to even notice he was there.

Matty noticed her, though, with her slim figure and flushed cheeks, and her stray auburn curls that stuck stubbornly to her sweating forehead, no matter how many times she tried to blow them back into place because she had no hands free.

Instinctively, he stood up to help her, reaching for the mop and bucket first as those looked to be the heaviest. 'Please, here. Let me.'

It was only when she let out a gasp, followed by an audible whimper of embarrassment, that he realized he was still shirtless.

'Father! Oh my, I am so sorry. I didn't realize . . . I thought the room was empty. I'll come back another time.'

'No no, please. Don't go. It's fine,' stammered Matty, setting her cleaning things down to one side before hurriedly slipping his shirt back on over his head. 'I was just . . . I popped back to my room to . . . check. On something. And then, well, er, it was hot. So I took my cassock off for a minute and then I thought, you know, I might as well . . . anyway. You don't have to go.'

The girl paused for a moment, looking at him curiously.

Then she smiled, a wonderful, all-encompassing smile that lit up not just her face but the whole room. Or at least, so it seemed to Matty.

'OK then,' she said, starting to dust the desk beneath the window. 'I'll be as quick as I can.'

Matty sat dumbly, watching her work, berating himself for his awkwardness. What a fool he must have appeared to her. Or was it worse than foolish, for a priest – soon to be priest – to feel such obvious desire? Did it count as a 'sin of the flesh' if one didn't act on it? Or only an 'impure thought'? Either way, it wasn't good.

I must pray for strength, he told himself. *And for God's grace. That all these sinful longings will one day leave me, so I can devote myself body and soul to Him.*

'There we are now, Father. All done.' The girl smiled at him again. 'I'll get out of your way.'

She seemed half amused, half pitying. Neither half made Matty feel any better.

'I'm not actually a "Father". Not yet,' he heard himself telling her. 'My name is Matthieu. What's yours?'

She looked surprised by the question.

'Sophie,' she replied. 'My name is Sophie. *Au revoir*, Matthieu.'

'Go easy!' Gunn protested, as his teenage niece Julia sloshed more neat Pimm's into the depleted jug on the garden table and poured him a glass. 'Who taught you to make drinks that strong? Your father?'

'I resent that,' Michael Hartley called back, emerging from the house carrying a tray laden with fruitcake and berries. Gunn's brother-in-law was around his own age but looked considerably older, having gone completely grey in his forties. He also looked stereotypically British in his summer shorts and shirt, lard-white arms and legs beginning to turn pink from their sudden, unexpected exposure to the sun. But he was a lovely man, funny and engaging, and Gunn enjoyed his company immensely. 'Everyone knows it's the Gunn side of this family with the alcohol problem.'

'Not a problem,' Gunn's sister Laura piped up, raising her own glass in her husband's general direction from her deckchair on the lawn, without glancing up from her E.M. Forster novel. 'Just a fact.'

They were all in the back garden at Laura and Michael's Battersea house, a sprawling, perennially messy Victorian villa that they'd bought when the girls were babies and grown into rather than out of over the years. Gunn – Uncle G to Julia and Mary – was staying for a few weeks while attending a conference in London. Weeks that had serendipitously coincided with a prolonged heatwave, and a lot of long, lazy afternoons in the garden like this one.

'I can make you a cup of tea if you prefer?' Julia asked her uncle guilelessly, prompting snorts of derision from Laura.

'Ha! The day your uncle chooses tea over Pimm's will be the day you know he's *not* really your uncle at all, but some fiendish alien imposter.'

'I'll take some cake though, sweetheart,' Gunn grinned at his niece, taking a deep, thirsty gulp of his newly refilled drink. 'Two slices, if they're going.'

Once everyone had eaten and drunk as much as they wanted, and the girls had gone back inside, conversation among the adults turned to Gunn's love life. Or lack thereof.

'Do you really not want children of your own one day?' Michael asked him bluntly. It was easier, as both an in-law and a man, for Michael to say things to Gunn that Laura wanted to but couldn't, or at least not without a row. 'You're so good with our girls.'

'I adore Julia and Mary,' Gunn admitted. 'I do. And I wish I saw them more. But being a good uncle is not the same as being a good father. Besides, I'm far too old to start all that now.'

'A younger wife might disagree,' observed Michael.

Gunn smiled wryly. 'One of the many reasons I haven't remarried.'

'His last girlfriend looked about twelve,' Laura commented, more waspishly than she'd intended.

'Paola was twenty-six,' Gunn shot back defensively. 'And very mature for her age.'

Both Michael and Laura snorted with laughter at this, although not unkindly. 'She can't have been that mature, if she was going out with you!' Laura teased. Then, seeing his crestfallen face, 'Oh come on, Hector. I love you dearly, but even you have to admit that you're turning into a bit of a cliché. The hot, middle-aged professor who seduces his students.'

'For your information, I didn't *seduce* anyone,' Gunn said crossly. Then, turning to Michael, he added, 'The truth is, I did want children when I was younger. Very much, actually. But after I messed things up with my first wife . . .' he shrugged sadly. 'I suppose I missed the boat.'

It was a rare admission of vulnerability, and both Michael and Laura took it as such, taking in what Gunn had said in silence.

'Funnily enough, I've been thinking about Ines recently. I read an article about her on a plane. She was being interviewed about a fancy new hotel she'd just designed in New York.'

'Did that make you feel nostalgic?' Michael asked.

'A bit,' he admitted. 'She has a son.'

Laura sat up, interested. 'Really? I never knew she'd remarried. Not that I *would* know.'

'I'm not sure if she did remarry,' said Gunn. 'Perhaps she did, but there was no mention of a husband in this piece. Just the son.'

He looked away, troubled all of a sudden, his jolly mood quite banished.

'Listen old man, I'm sorry I brought all this up,' said Michael sheepishly. 'I didn't mean to upset you. Laura and I want to see you happy and settled, that's all.'

Gunn stood up, shaking off his melancholy as quickly as it had appeared. 'Nothing to be sorry about,' he smiled, clearing plates from the table. 'Ines and I were aeons ago. And I am happy and settled in Brazil. Very. Just because I'm not married . . . I love my work, my life, my colleagues. Being Julia and Mary's favourite uncle is more than enough, believe me.'

'*Do* you believe him?' Laura asked her husband whilst Gunn carried the plates into the house. 'Do you think he's happy?'

Michael thought about it. 'Yes,' he said eventually. 'I think I do. We all have regrets. But on balance, I'd say your brother has a good life. Although he clearly still carries a torch for the first wife.'

Later that evening, walking by himself through Battersea Park and across the river into Old Chelsea, Gunn thought about the conversation in the garden.

He was too old for marriage and fatherhood now. That much he felt certain about. And he *was* happy and settled in São Paolo. Happier and more settled than many of his married friends. And yet . . . there was no doubt that the things he'd read about Ines, hearing about her life again, her son, had stirred up emotions in him that he'd believed were long buried.

It wasn't that I wanted children, he realized in a moment of clarity. *It was that I wanted children with her.*

A couple of days later, Renée Challant emerged from her office in Whitehall onto the street just as the heavens opened. The thick, humid London weather had been threatening to break for days. And now, with a spectacular, single clap of thunder, it did so, bruise-grey clouds cracking open to unleash a monsoon-like deluge onto the street.

Opening her umbrella, Renée was about to make a run for it towards Westminster tube when a figure on the opposite side of the street caught her eye. The man was tall and well dressed in a summer suit and Panama hat, both of which would have been ruined had it not been for his own, oversized umbrella, big enough to shield a small family from the downpour. But what really drew her attention was the fact that the man was looking at *her*. And now he was crossing the street, walking towards her purposefully.

He knows me, thought Renée. And as he walked, she realized that she knew him too – she recognized that loping, almost arrogant gait – although she couldn't place it until he reached her side of the road and was standing at the foot of the steps to her building, waving at her as if no time had passed.

'Hello Renée.'

'My God,' she waved back, shaking her head in astonishment. 'Hector Gunn.'

'I'm sorry to ambush you at work. But I have something important I need to ask you. Can you talk?'

CHAPTER THIRTY-FOUR

Beaulieu-sur-Mer, France, July 1967

Stepping into Marianne Blanchet's cottage in Beaulieu's old town was like stepping back in time. The entire ground floor was really one room, a modest salon-cum-*salle-à-manger* comprised of two armchairs and a scrubbed pine table and chairs, wedged against a stone wall. A large, soot-blackened fireplace provided all the heat for the house, and Marianne also used it to boil water for cooking and her morning café au lait. There was a tiny 'kitchen' set off to one side, but this was barely more than a cupboard with a porcelain sink at one end and a single shelf for food at the other. Ines counted three cats as soon as she walked in, two tabbies and a fat ginger that lay in front of the hearth purring like a pampered king. But she suspected, rightly, that more of the animals lurked upstairs, in Marianne's single, cell-like bedroom.

It's like coming to tea with a witch, Ines thought, half looking around for the old woman's broomstick. Except that there was nothing sinister about dear old Madame Blanchet. Everything about her hunched, wizened figure and wrinkled, sunken face suggested kindness, and she fussed over Ines with obvious delight.

'I don't get many visitors nowadays, mademoiselle,' Marianne informed Ines, pressing a plate of hand-baked macaron cookies into her hand. 'So this is really quite a treat. All my friends are dead, you see,' she added matter-of-factly.

'I'm so sorry . . .' began Ines, but the old woman waved her away.

'Nothing to be sorry about,' she said cheerfully. 'That's just what happens once you get to my age. I'm lucky to be here. And I've still got my kitties, of course.' Pursing her lips, she made a soft, mewing sound that immediately brought the two tabbies running over to her chair and hopping up into her tweed-skirted lap. Renée was right, Ines reflected, watching Marianne's skeletal, liver-spotted hand stroking her beloved pets. She must be at least a hundred years old.

'I was talking to my sister Renée about you on the telephone yesterday,' said Ines, making conversation as she bit into the macaron. 'We were remembering what great friends you used to be with our old cook, Marie Lancon?'

'Oh, Marie! Dear Marie!' The old woman's eyes misted over. 'She adored you children, you know.'

Ines smiled fondly. 'And we her.'

'She loved your mother too,' Marianne mused, her gaze off somewhere in the distance. 'Once she knew the truth about your father, I think she did all she could to protect Madame. Although of course, in her position, it wasn't easy.'

Ines felt her heart rate quicken and a tingling sensation in her palms.

'What "truth" about my father are you referring to?' she asked the old woman, doing her best to keep her voice neutral. 'Specifically?'

'Oh, well, you know.' Marianne lifted her own tea cup unsteadily to her lips. 'The awful business with Bernadette.'

It took the old woman a few moments to notice Ines's blank, questioning expression. When she did, she set her cup back down with a clatter, clamping a hand over her mouth.

'Oh heavens! I'm so sorry, my dear. I assumed, after all these years, that you knew. Please, forget I said anything.'

'I can't do that, Marianne,' Ines said kindly. She felt bad for the poor woman who was obviously in distress. 'I'm sure you can imagine, my sisters and I have heard whispers and rumours about our father for most of our lives. But to be candid with you, we've been desperately short of facts. Now that both my parents are dead, it would mean a lot to me . . . it would be a kindness, truly . . . if you would tell me whatever it is you know.'

Marianne Blanchet winced. She looked thoroughly miserable.

'I doubt it will feel like a kindness when you hear the story,' she sighed, shaking her head and muttering. How she wished she'd kept her foolish mouth shut! 'But I suppose you do have a right to know. If you're sure?'

'I'm sure.' Leaning forward, Ines gave the old woman's hand a reassuring squeeze. 'Please.'

Marianne cleared her throat.

'All right then. The events I'm going to describe happened before you were born. I learned them myself from Marie, who only shared them with me because she desperately needed a friend to lean on. And though I've no proof of my own that any of what she told me is true, I knew Marie to be unfailingly honest.'

'She was,' Ines agreed.

'So to the best of my knowledge, my dear, these are facts. Just not very pleasant ones.' Frowning, she went on.

'Shortly after your brother Charles was born, your parents entered a difficult period in their marriage. As you may know, your mother suffered a number of miscarriages during her childbearing years.'

'I was aware, yes.'

'One of these losses, not long after your brother's birth, was especially devastating to Clotilde as it happened late in her pregnancy. She became severely depressed. Your father brought her to Beaulieu to recover.'

'All right,' said Ines. So far the picture Marianne was painting tallied with what she already knew.

'During their stay here, I'm afraid to say that your father developed an obsession with a young woman from the village. A very young woman. Her name was Bernadette Debray.'

Ines turned the name over in her mind, but nothing came up. No one she had spoken to had ever mentioned a Bernadette, until today.

329

'At your father's bidding, the girl was hired to work as a maid up at the bastide. And at some point during her employment there, it appears he made his feelings known to her. However, Bernadette did not in any way return his affections. She rejected all his approaches as forcefully as their respective situations in life allowed.' Marianne's ancient eyes met Ines's young ones. 'Your father did not take kindly to this at all.'

'Did he fire her?' Ines asked, after a moment of silence.

'The official version of events,' said Marianne, 'is that she left voluntarily.'

'I see.'

'As a result of her pregnancy.'

Ines's stomach lurched as the full import of the old woman's words sank in.

'My father got Bernadette pregnant?' she mused aloud. 'But you said . . . she rejected him.'

'She did.'

A painful silence fell, the awful implication of this last statement hanging in the air, too shameful to be spoken aloud. When Ines looked down into her lap, she noticed that her hands were beginning to shake.

'He was never formally accused of anything,' Marianne said, choosing her words carefully.

Of course not, thought Ines. *Men never were, especially not in those days*.

Closing her eyes for a moment, she tried to picture the father she remembered in her mind's eye. The devout giant of a man with the big beard, like a prophet's, radiating authority, but yet also indulgent and loving when he wanted to be. Where *was* that man? Had he ever really existed? Or had Ines created him, conjured him up from her own daughterly adoration?

Genevieve had certainly long thought so. She'd been convinced for years that Papa was fundamentally rotten. Not a good man who might have done some bad things, but a bad man. A wicked man. To be unfaithful to one's wife might conceivably fall into the former category, at least in Ines's view. Taking a mistress might have made Charles

330

Père weak, and it certainly made him a hypocrite. And perhaps these things could be perceived in shades of grey.

But forcing yourself on a servant girl, getting her pregnant and then casting her out without a penny? There wasn't much nuance there.

'Did Bernadette have the baby?' Ines heard herself asking.

'She did,' Marianne replied in her reedy, old woman's voice. 'A son. Unfortunately, the boy was born with certain mental disabilities. Bernadette attributed his slowness to the violent nature of his conception. But there were those who chose to see the child's challenges as divine punishment, presumably for his mother's sin. People can be terribly cruel in this world. Especially to women.'

Ines couldn't have agreed more. But in that moment, her mind was engaged beyond the feminist struggle, racing as she tried to put the pieces of the puzzle together: the dates; the illegitimate child, born and never acknowledged by his father.

When she looked up at Marianne, there were tears in her eyes.

'It was Bernard, wasn't it? The boy who died on our estate. He was Bernadette's son.'

The old woman nodded solemnly. 'That's right. That was what Marie confided in me. That Bernard was, in fact, your father's son.'

'My brother,' murmured Ines, her voice barely audible.

'Poor Bernadette never recovered from the trauma of what happened to her,' Marianne went on. 'I'm afraid to have to tell you that she drowned herself off the Plage des Fourmis when Bernard was just a toddler.'

'No!' Ines gasped, her face contorted in real anguish.

'After her death, Bernard was raised by his aunt, Bernadette's elder sister Eloise, and her husband Louis Angier. Nobody spoke about the scandalous rumours surrounding his birth, or the tragedy of his mother's death, and your father's reputation remained largely intact at that time. But a few people knew.'

'Like Marie,' said Ines. 'No wonder she was so awkward around him. I'm surprised she kept working for us.'

'As I say, Marie loved your mother, and all of you. She was fiercely loyal,' Marianne explained. 'But, naturally, resentment towards your father lingered. And when that poor child met his death, in your bastide, of all places? Well, it aroused a lot of suspicion, especially among those who knew the truth about his parentage.'

'I'm sure.'

It had been more than suspicion, though, Ines remembered. It had been a heavy black cloud of loathing and anger, of unspeakable (wholly justified, it now appeared) rage, that had descended over the Challant family that summer, choking the happiness out of all their lives. And breaking poor Maman's heart.

Ines didn't remember leaving Marianne's cottage. But at some point she found herself walking aimlessly through the old fish market, while thoughts, memories and emotions tumbled chaotically through her head like a troupe of drunken acrobats.

She had no doubts about the truth of what Marianne had told her. Poor, darling Marie, their cook and friend at the bastide for so many years, had clearly confided in her friend in a moment of moral crisis over what she knew. And Marie would never have peddled in gossip or rumour, especially not about something as serious as this.

No, these were facts, or as close to fact as Ines was ever likely to get.

Papa was a liar and a bully, certainly, who had abused his power and position and ruined an innocent young woman's life. There was every chance he might also have been a killer. It was too much to take in all at once.

Had Maman known? Ines wondered. About Bernard? She was sure she remembered Clotilde being kind to the boy when they ran into him in town that day, at the cinema. But she no longer trusted her childhood memories, not without corroboration. She'd been wrong about so much, after all.

I must talk to Renée, she thought, turning left into the alley leading towards the harbour. But as the clock tower struck three, she suddenly stopped and retraced her steps. There was somebody else she had to talk to first, and she was already late for their appointment.

CHAPTER THIRTY-FIVE

'I'd almost given up on you,' Tremont wheezed when Ines walked into his office, flushed from her fast walk up the hill.

Clearly the PI had failed to take her advice about decluttering. If anything, his desk looked even more overloaded than it had the last time she was here. But Ines hoped that meant he'd made some progress regarding the Duponts, as he'd hinted when they spoke on the phone.

'I'm sorry I'm late,' she said, setting her handbag down on the floor and clearing a place for herself to sit. 'I was visiting an old friend and, as it turns out, she had important things she needed to tell me. About my father.'

'Oh?' The PI raised a curious eyebrow as he shuffled around among his stacks of papers like a confused mole searching for worms.

'And if they're true,' Ines exhaled heavily, 'which sadly I suspect they are, then they're really quite terrible.'

Tremont listened intently as she recounted everything Marianne had told her. About the young maid Bernadette, Bernard's birth and his mother's suicide. The diminutive PI looked fascinated, but not as surprised as Ines had expected.

'Did you already know?' Ines asked him. 'That Papa was Bernard's father?'

'Er . . . well, yes,' he admitted, his beady eyes lighting up as a second, mole-like dive into his papers yielded unexpected success. Grasping a sheaf of printed spreadsheets, he put them to one side. 'But I only found out in the last few days. Whilst I was delving into the background of our friends the Duponts.'

Ines frowned. 'I don't understand. What could Genevieve's

housekeeper and her handyman husband possibly have to do with things my father may or may not have done with a maid more than thirty years ago?'

'A lot, believe it or not,' Tremont replied excitedly. 'Bernard Angier, you see. He's the key to all this. After his mother's suicide, you said that Bernard was raised by his aunt Eloise, and her husband.'

'That's right,' said Ines. 'Angier was his uncle's name. His mother had been . . .'

'Debray,' the PI interrupted. 'Bernadette Debray. Well, it turns out that Bernadette had two sisters. Eloise, the older one, who took in little Bernard. And Chantal, the youngest. Chantal married a fellow named Luc Aubert from Nice, and moved down there. They had one child, a daughter named Hélène.'

'OK,' said Ines, not sure where this was going.

'When Hélène was a teenager, her dad died suddenly. Heart attack. Her mother, Chantal, decided to move *back* to Beaulieu, where she grew up. And then a year or two later, *she* died as well.'

'So Hélène was all alone?'

'Yes, but not for long. At nineteen she married a local painter and decorator by the name of *Georges Dupont*.' Tremont smiled at Ines triumphantly. 'They've been to-gether ever since.'

'Georges and Hélène Dupont!' Ines gasped. 'Well, well. So Hélène Dupont would be . . .'

'Bernard Angier's first cousin,' Tremont confirmed. 'Now, that may not seem like much of a link at first glance. Especially as the two of them grew up in different towns and never knew one another as children. But after Hélène and her mother returned to Beaulieu, she would have heard all the stories about her cousin Bernard and how he'd died up at the bastide in somewhat mysterious circumstances. It's my belief that she became obsessed with your family from quite a young age.'

Picking up the spreadsheets he'd retrieved earlier, he handed them to Ines.

'Here. Take a look at these.'

'What am I looking at?' she asked, scanning the rows of figures.

'Bank transfers,' Tremont announced, running a grubby finger down the list. 'Each of these transactions shows a separate transfer of funds between offshore accounts traceable to your late father, and Georges and Hélène Dupont's current account in Villefranche.'

'My father?' Ines studied the statements more closely. It was all there in black and white. Regular payments, totalling a very significant sum, made out to the Duponts. And starting several years before Charles Père's death.

'I don't understand,' she said at last. 'Did the Duponts used to work for my father? Because they never mentioned any prior connection to Genevieve when she hired them. I'm sure of that.'

'I'm sure of it too,' the PI replied archly. 'People don't usually shout it from the rooftops when they've been engaged in extortion, to the tune of nearly a hundred million francs. The Duponts were blackmailing your father, Mademoiselle Challant. Very successfully. It's all here in the financial records if you look. It was their increasing demands leading up to his death that lost him the house at Place Dauphine.'

Ines sat for a moment, digesting this information.

'Blackmailing him with what?' she asked, eventually, setting the papers Tremont had given her down on the desk. 'What hold did they have over Papa?'

The little man leaned back, interlacing his fingers with an audible crack.

'That's what I've been spending most of the past week trying to ascertain,' he told Ines. 'Hélène Aubert – now Dupont – almost certainly knew about your father's paternity of the dead boy, Bernard. But so did several other people. Those rumours had been swirling around locally for decades. But they'd never been proved. I think it's safe to assume that whatever threat they may once have posed to your father had passed, long before the date of these transfers.'

'So, what then?' Ines frowned. 'It must be connected to Bernard. If Hélène was involved.'

'Yes,' Tremont nodded. 'It must be. And it must be something serious, something for which your father would have been sent to prison, or would have caused him to lose everything. From what I've learned about the man, I don't believe he would have given up Place Dauphine for anything less.'

Ines held her breath, waiting for him to go on.

'What I'm about to tell you is my theory. My opinion,' he began, ominously. 'Unlike the transferred funds, I have no piece of paper to give you that proves it to be true. But based on all of my research and interviews, and on the circumstantial evidence, it is what I believe.'

'Go on,' said Ines.

Tremont took a deep breath and held Ines's gaze. 'I believe that your father murdered Bernard Angier. And that Hélène Dupont and her husband claimed to have evidence that would prove it.'

Ines swallowed hard but said nothing.

'I think that once Bernard began showing an interest in your mother and her birds that summer, and repeatedly showing up at the family home, your father became in-creasingly paranoid that your mother was going to find out the truth. Perhaps he worried that Bernard himself knew about his paternity, and planned to tell Clotilde, or otherwise blurt it out, I don't know. But your father was already under significant emotional strain during that summer. The boy sneaking into the property the night of the storm was the last straw. So in a fit of anger, or panic, or both, your father shot him, and bribed the coroner to cover it up, making it look as if the dogs had attacked and killed him.'

'You think Bernard was shot?' Ines closed her eyes and rubbed her temples.

'Several groundsmen and staff recalled hearing a gun go off that night.'

The *BANG* from her nightmares! Of course!

Ines had always told herself the dreadful noise was a clap of thunder. But it could just as easily have been a gunshot. A *real* gunshot. The fatal shot that executed poor Bernard.

My God.

'As I say, this is only my theory, mademoiselle,' the PI

reiterated, taken aback by Ines's glazed eyes and suddenly bloodless face.

'You believe it to be true, though,' she whispered.

'I do. It makes the most sense, based on the evidence still in our possession. Although to prove it we would need the original, unredacted coroner's report.'

'Could that be what the Duponts used to threaten my father? Do you think they somehow got hold of that report?'

'The thought crossed my mind,' said Tremont. 'Although if they do have it, they can't use it any more. Not now that they've taken so much money from your family. It would implicate them as blackmailers.'

'They *are* blackmailers!' seethed Ines. 'And they're living under Genevieve's roof.'

'Yes,' Tremont looked concerned.

'What do you think their game is?' Ines asked him. 'With my sister, I mean. Is it money they're after?'

'A very good question,' he replied. 'To which the answer is almost certainly yes. But if so, they're playing a long game. I looked into your sister's finances as soon as you hired me, but she doesn't appear to have paid them any more than they might legitimately expect to earn for their jobs up at the bastide. No big gifts of money, or paintings or jewellery. And the three of them seem to be on good terms.'

'Better than good,' Ines rolled her eyes. 'My sister's been completely brainwashed by these two. She relies on them for everything. Of course, if she knew about Papa and the blackmail things might be different. But I'm not sure she'd believe me, even if I told her.'

'Well,' Tremont smiled at Ines kindly. 'I'll leave that up to you, mademoiselle. But my guess is that the Duponts' ultimate intention is to get their hands on the bastide. If your sister were to name them as beneficiaries in her will, for example . . . I understand her health is not good?'

'Good Lord!' Ines gasped. 'You don't think they mean to harm her, do you? Physically, I mean?'

The PI fixed her with a steady stare. 'All I know is that if it

338

were my sister, I'd find a way to get rid of them. Sooner rather than later.'

A gentle breeze blew through Beaulieu as Ines left Tremont's office and walked alone through the town. Wandering through the steep cobbled alleys and hidden squares that had been her childhood playground, she wondered whether she would ever feel peace again. Her thoughts flew in endless different directions, like a frantically trapped flock of birds, trying to escape through closed windows. No matter which way she turned, she ended up bruised and battered.

Thinking about her father, and what he had done, was almost unbearably painful. The misery of that poor girl, Bernadette. The way Papa had abused her. How much he had *owed* her and her son. Their son. And how shockingly he'd behaved, even before Bernard's death.

As for that . . . had he really shot the boy in cold blood, as the PI believed? Ines still struggled to accept that. With her rational brain it made sense. Papa had a motive. There *had* been a shot, she was sure of it now. And the coroner had clearly concealed something about the boy's death, something significant and material. But with her heart? *No.* It just didn't feel right. Ines had come to terms with the fact that her father had been a hypocrite and a womanizer. But she also remembered the other side to Charles Père, the loving, protective, decent, paternal side to him. She needed to believe that that was still true. *No. He couldn't have deliberately shot a child to death. Any child, never mind his own.*

As for her mother's role in all this, that was even harder to fathom. She may not have known about Bernard, specifically. But she must have at least suspected some of her husband's other betrayals. And yet she had stayed with him. *Was that for us?* Ines wondered. Or had there been real love between her parents, despite everything?

Turning left at the harbour, Ines continued walking past her pension in the direction of the bastide. She still wasn't sure what she was going to say to Genevieve about today's revelations. But Tremont was right about one thing. She couldn't simply leave Gen alone, at the mercy of the Duponts. Not knowing what she now knew.

As she walked, her thoughts turned to marriage, and forgiveness. First to her parents' marriage. And then to her own. To Gunn.

For twenty years now she had successfully kept the door to that chapter of her life closed, locked and bolted at the back of her mind. But today, on so many levels, the floodgates were opening.

Ines had loved Gunn. Totally. Uncontrollably. With a love bigger and more all-consuming than any she had ever felt for another human being, before or since – apart from her love for her son of course. And Gunn had betrayed her. That was a simple statement of fact.

Yet in comparison to her father's betrayals – of her mother, of Bernard and *his* mother, of Ines and her siblings, even of himself – Gunn's infidelity was surely less grave an offence. Even today, after everything she'd learned, she was still tying herself in knots, trying to find new ways to forgive Charles Père's behaviour. To mitigate, to explain.

Why?

And why had she been unable to do the same for Gunn?

How different would her life have been if she'd taken him back? she wondered. Part of the reason she'd left him, running back to France and never looking back, was because she'd hoped to reconcile with her father. But Charles Père had never shown Ines the forgiveness that she showed him, even now.

Memories of her time with Gunn swooped down out of nowhere, like a flock of hungry starlings pecking at her happiness, pulling it apart. She pictured again their little cottage in Cornwall. Edward and the geese. Jimmy and Ag, the children Ines had taken care of during the war. Lovemaking in the rain, and painting birds on the staircase. Watching and waiting at the window for Gunn to return from the war. She remembered the love and pain, hope and disappointment, joy and despair, as if it were yesterday.

As she approached the bastide, its thick stone walls looming above her in the darkness, the question haunted her: had she walked away from the one true love of her life, for the sake of a man who had never truly loved anyone but himself? For a fraud?

Bracing herself for Hélène Dupont to answer the door, Ines knocked loudly, rapping the brass lion's head knocker three times against the thick oak. But it was Genevieve who appeared in the hallway, alone and dishevelled-looking in a thin black dress that hung from her bony frame like a shroud.

'Ines!'

Ines couldn't tell if she was pleased or irritated to see her. Either way, she took advantage of her sister's surprise to step inside, closing the door behind her.

'Are the Duponts not home?' she asked. Glancing around, it was clear that the house was in an even worse state than usual. Dirty mugs and plates littered the side table in the hallway, and at least four days' worth of newspapers lay piled, unopened on the floor.

To Ines's astonishment, Genevieve's face crumpled, then dissolved quite suddenly into tears. 'They've gone!' she sobbed. 'I sent them away. Oh, Ines. It's been awful. Just *awful*.'

Ines made them two strong black coffees and dug out some pâté and cheese from the kitchen, to go with this morning's untouched bread.

'Try to eat something,' she urged Gen, as they sat together at one end of the dining table, swapping stories.

Genevieve explained how her lawyer had written to her, informing her that he'd been approached by Georges Dupont. 'He was trying to have me certified as mentally unfit so that he and Hélène could apply for power of attorney over my affairs. My *avocat* felt it was a blatant attempt to force me to change my will. At first I refused to believe it. But then I remembered a story Wilhelm had told me years ago . . . you remember Wilhelm?'

'Of course,' Ines said kindly, moved by the nostalgic look of love in Genevieve's eyes.

'His grandmother, or perhaps it was a great-aunt, was cheated out of a vast estate in Bavaria by a nurse who took care of her in her latter years. The family spent a decade in court trying to get the thing reversed, but they never did. The ghastly woman walked off into the sunset with everything. Anyway, I never forgot it. So I showed my lawyer's letter to Hélène Dupont. She denied it of course, but from the look on her face I knew at once it was true.'

'Just a bite of brie, dearest,' Ines tried again, nudging the cheeseboard in her sister's direction. But Genevieve shook her head, sipping at her coffee like a nervous bird. Ines noticed her cup rattling against the saucer each time she set it down thanks to her permanently shaking hands. Years of drinking had broken her physically, although emotionally, Ines suspected, other things had hurt her more.

She was surprised and relieved to hear that the Duponts had packed up and left without too much of a fight. Evidently the lawyer's letter had panicked them.

'Oh, Georges cursed and screamed a bit,' Genevieve told her. 'How dare I accuse him, and this and that. He was quite bullying in his demeanour. But of course, I'm used to that, having grown up with Papa. I just let him vent, get it all out of his system. And then off they went. But I . . . I cried afterwards,' she admitted, welling up again.

'Why?' Ines asked. 'I don't understand. Once you knew what their intentions were?'

'It didn't matter,' Gen replied. 'They'd been all I had, my only friends, for years. I was frightened, Ines. Frightened to be without them. Even after I knew. Isn't that pathetic?'

'No,' said Ines. 'I don't think so, love.'

Although it was pathetic, deeply so, in the true sense of the word.

'They were cunning, manipulative people. They took more from Papa than they ever succeeded in taking from you. And you know how tough *he* was.'

She told Genevieve then about the blackmail. Not about Tremont's theory regarding Bernard's death. That was only a theory, after all, and poor Genevieve had been through enough trauma. But about Bernadette, and Bernard Angier having been their half-brother.

'Hélène and Georges extorted a fortune out of Papa, from the war years on. It was because of them that he lost Place Dauphine. They targeted you from the beginning, Gen. But there was no way you could have known. No way any of us could.'

'I'm sorry I sent you away,' Genevieve said after a long pause, looking down at the swirling, dark liquid in her cup. 'The Duponts wanted you gone, but I shouldn't have listened.'

'It's OK,' said Ines. 'I understand.'

'It's not OK,' Genevieve replied firmly. 'And not just because you were right about the Duponts. But because the bastide is your home, too.'

Ines's face clouded over. 'Not any more,' she said sadly. 'Papa made it very clear in his will that he wanted you to have it.'

'*Baise Papa!*' Genevieve's eyes blazed angrily. 'After everything you've just told me, Ines, why do you care what he thought? This house may have been his to give legally. But morally, emotionally, Beaulieu has always belonged to us all. It was Maman's place more than anybody's, and she would have wanted us to share it.'

Ines looked away. It was still so hard to think about their mother.

'I should never have shut you and Renée out the way I did, after Papa died,' Gen went on. 'But at the time I just felt as if I'd lost so much. Ever since Wilhelm . . .'

Her voice cracked. Reaching across the table, Ines squeezed her hand.

'You had Matty and your career,' Genevieve continued, collecting herself. 'And Renée had Charlotte and *her* career. I had nothing. Except the brandy, of course.' She laughed bitterly. 'I think deep down I always knew that the Duponts were taking advantage of me. Trying to widen the gulf between us. But they were there, and they made me feel less desperate. Less alone. Oh God.' Setting down her coffee cup, she sank her head into her hands. 'How could I have been so stupid?'

'You're not stupid,' Ines told her loyally. 'You're unwell. And yes, the Duponts did take advantage of that, but that reflects on them, my love, not you. They're criminals. Blackmailers and thieves.'

'Yes, but Papa was a criminal too,' said Genevieve, looking up. She wasn't crying. It was too late for tears. But her face was ashen, as bloodless as a ghost's. 'If Hélène was Bernard Angier's family, you could argue she had reason to do what she did.'

'You most certainly could not,' Ines said passionately. 'I don't believe Hélène gave two hoots about Bernard, or his mother. Their tragedy merely served as an excuse. A cover story for her and Georges's avarice.'

Genevieve shrugged. For a few minutes the two sisters sat in silence, each lost in their own thoughts. Then Genevieve said, matter-of-factly, 'I need help, Ines. Real help. To stop drinking. I've tried before, but I'm not sure I ever wanted it badly enough those times.'

'Do you think you want it badly enough now?' Ines asked.

'I know I do. I'm not a young woman.' Genevieve smiled sadly. 'But what life I have left I want to *live*. Really live. Do you know, I'm not sure I've really lived at all since the war. Since Wilhelm. All I've done is existed. If it hadn't been for your lovely son, I doubt I would even have done that,' she added, wistfully. 'Does Matty know? About your private investigator, and Marianne, and everything you've discovered?'

'Not yet,' said Ines. 'I'm not allowed to telephone or see him now until he's ordained. But I'll write and tell him of course. He was the one who persuaded me to come down here in the first place, and look into the Duponts. Well, him and Renée.'

'I'm grateful to all of you,' Genevieve said humbly. 'And I know you've already done so much. But I have one more favour to ask you.'

'Of course,' said Ines.

'There's a place in the Alps, a clinic, not far from Megève

344

actually.' Genevieve smiled weakly. 'They've an excellent track record, but you need to commit to stay there for at least three months. I was wondering if, perhaps, you might consider moving into the bastide while I'm gone? I thought, you know, with you being such a brilliant designer and everything, perhaps you could restore the house? There's a bit of money left in Papa's trust that you could use . . .'

Ines opened her mouth, then closed it again, not sure for a moment how to respond. On the one hand, she'd already stayed in Beaulieu far longer than she intended. The idea of leaving Paris and her business for another three months, or perhaps longer, was terrifying. But on the other, she was delighted Genevieve was seeking help and that she trusted her enough to ask her for something as important as this. Did she really want to refuse? This opportunity to restore the bastide to its former glory, *and* put her own creative stamp on it? To reclaim it as a Challant family home? As *her* home.

'I'd love to.' The words were out of her mouth before Ines had a chance to second-guess herself.

'Truly?' Genevieve gasped, tears welling in her eyes. With relief, with overwhelming gratitude, with love. 'I mean, I know you're terribly busy. And I hate to impose. But I'm not sure I could trust anybody else.'

'I'm not busy,' Ines insisted. 'And I need something to take my mind off Matty and . . . everything. We'll be helping each other.'

Standing up, Ines walked around the table and hugged her sister's skinny frame before heading out of the dining room and back into the hallway. Looking around her, it was clear this would be a big job. Big, expensive and all-consuming. But despite its threadbare, dilapidated state, the bones of the house were still intact, and still as magnificent as ever. The high ceilings and elaborate cornicing, the sweeping, graceful curve of the staircase, the magnificent views from the bedrooms over the rooftops of the town to the azure jewel of the sea beyond.

Closing her eyes amid the dust and the darkness, Ines could already picture it all. What had been and what would be.

Matty had found his vocation. Perhaps here, in this house that had been such a huge part of her life for better and worse, Ines had finally found hers.

The birds of Beaulieu would fly again.

CHAPTER THIRTY-SIX

'It's stunning, Ines. Really. Properly breathtaking.'

Charlotte Mortimer slowly turned the pages of the leather-bound photo album that Ines had given her and Renée, showing the completed renovations at Beaulieu. After four intense, backbreaking months, Ines had finally handed Genevieve back the keys a week ago, letting her into a house so utterly transformed it was unrecognizable. Watching her sister's stunned delight had been one of the high points of Ines's year. Although spending Christmas Day here in Megève with Renée and Charlotte had certainly been another.

'I'm so glad you both like it,' she smiled, watching as Charlotte and Renée pored over the images together. 'I decided to go all-in with the colour and prints, so it's very vibrant. Which isn't to everyone's taste.'

'It's like something from one of Maman's dreams. All the exotic birds and flowers,' sighed Renée. 'She would have loved it.'

'Thank you,' Ines said, tearing up. 'I hope so. Although it was really Gen who I was thinking of. She's worked so hard to get sober and change her life. I wanted to breathe life back into the bastide. So she could come home to somewhere hopeful, somewhere new.'

'Well it seems to have worked,' Charlotte laughed. 'Ren and I couldn't believe it when you told us she had a new beau.'

'And that she'd invited him to spend Christmas with her!' Renée added, still glued to Ines's photo album. 'I mean, how long can she have known him? A few weeks?'

'I think she's seizing the day,' Ines replied happily. 'And not before time. Poor Gen's been sleepwalking through life since long before Papa died. Did I mention she's writing again?'

'No.' Renée smiled broadly. 'Is that this chap's influence?'

Ines shrugged. 'Could be. I'm just so pleased to see her living again. Finding her purpose. She deserves that.'

A loud crack from one of the fire-logs startled Ines for a moment, but she quickly recovered, drawing her legs underneath her on Renée's overstuffed couch and reaching for one of the myriad cashmere throws that lay strewn around the chalet. Over the past few years, Renée and Charlotte had put their own stamp on the place. And though their style was much more muted than Ines's – lots of taupes and creams and various shades of caramel – it was no less warm and welcoming.

The original idea had been for all three sisters to spend Christmas in Megève together, for what would have been the first time in decades. But when Genevieve announced she had met someone in rehab – 'a friend', she insisted, although her mischievous expression said otherwise – and that she'd invited him to spend Christmas with her at Beaulieu, Ines had been happy enough to leave her behind.

'It's not only because of Pierre,' Genevieve had told her. 'You can't go and create something this beautiful and then expect me to up sticks and leave the minute I get home. We'll do something all together next summer, down here. Who knows, maybe by then Father Matthieu will be able to join us?'

'What's this?' Renée asked, opening the album at a photograph of the gardens. 'This wooden sort of mini-tower thing?'

'It's a dovecote,' said Ines. 'I built it on the site of Maman's old aviary.'

'It's pretty.'

'I wanted there to be birds again at Beaulieu,' Ines explained. 'But no more cages. The doves can fly free whenever they want to.'

'And they're symbols of peace of course,' said Charlotte.

'Peace and freedom,' Renée mused. 'I like the fountain too, with the stone bench beside it. It all looks very serene.'

'The bench is dedicated to Bernard Angier,' said Ines. 'And the fountain's at the spot where he was found. I wasn't sure about either of them to be honest with you. After the things Monsieur Tremont told me. But I felt we needed to do something to commemorate Bernard. He was our brother, after all. Even if Papa . . .'

She left the sentence hanging. Renée and Charlotte were exchanging glances.

'What?' Ines asked. 'What is it?'

Although she'd held back certain things from Genevieve, Ines had disclosed the whole sorry tale to Renée. Not only about Charles Père's paternity of Bernard, but the possibility that he'd murdered the boy on that terrible night in 1928. Although shocking, Renée had found the latter theory easier to believe than Ines did.

'People are capable of all sorts of things when they're frightened,' she observed. 'And in the heat of the moment. I'm not saying he did do it. But can I imagine it? Absolutely.'

Yet despite Renée's more sanguine reaction to the possibility that their father was a murderer, something was clearly troubling her now.

'There's something I need to show you,' she told Ines seriously, closing the photo album and getting to her feet. 'It's up in the attic.'

'Should I come too?' Charlotte asked anxiously, placing a hand on Renée's back. But Renée shook her head.

'It's all right, love. This is between Ines and I.'

Worried, Ines followed her sister up the winding pine stairs into the attic where as children they'd played hide and seek, and rummaged around among the boxes and chaos, searching for 'treasure'. There was no chaos now, though, or cobwebs, or rusting mousetraps left scattered around. Like the rest of the chalet, the attic had been completely made over by Renée and Charlotte, everything tidied and organized into neat, labelled boxes.

'Here.' Renée gestured to two small chairs that had been placed under one of the skylights. There was a low wicker table between them, on which a brown manilla folder had been carefully placed.

'What's this?' Ines asked, turning the folder over nervously in her hands. There was no label, nothing to suggest what lay inside. The outer cover was clearly old, the card stained and damaged in places and there were even signs of mould on one of the corners. But the papers inside, though yellowing, looked intact.

'I found it two weeks ago. Or rather, Charlotte did. She was looking for Christmas decorations up here, and one of the boards in the wainscotting suddenly came loose. This was behind it, taped to the inside in a waterproof bag.

'I thought about calling you right away,' Renée went on, wringing her hands anxiously as Ines began to leaf through the papers. 'But in the end I thought it would be better to talk about it face to face. And better for you to see for yourself. We've waited thirty years, after all. I reckoned another few days wouldn't matter.'

Ines was vaguely aware that her sister was speaking, but she heard nothing. Her eyes were glued to the document in her hand. A document she'd read scores of times over the last decade, but only in its redacted form. Never in its entirety, as it was first written.

Tracing her finger along the embossed title – 'RAPPORT DE CORONER' – she proceeded to read in silence, finally filling in the blanks that had haunted her for so long.

When she finally finished, she looked up at Renée, distraught.

'So Bernard *was* shot.'

'Yes.' Renée bit her lip.

'That was the cause of death. One shot to the heart.'

Renée nodded.

'And everything else, the dogs, the mauling . . . was all a cover?' Ines's voice was fraught with emotion, getting faster and more high-pitched as her distress worsened. 'All to save Papa's skin?' She shook her head furiously. 'So Tremont was right.'

350

'No,' said Renée, putting a hand on Ines's knee. 'He wasn't right. The report's just the start of it, Ines. There are letters, confessions of sorts.'

Taking the coroner's report from Ines's trembling fingers, Renée pointed to the stash of loose papers and envelopes still in the folder.

'Some are between Papa and his mistress at the time, and with an old schoolfriend. One is to my godfather, Marcel Devereux. Do you remember him? He locked Charles Fils in the cellar once at his chateau as a practical joke. Poor Charles was terrified.'

'Vaguely,' murmured Ines, who had already begun to read the first letter.

Renée waited patiently as Ines made her way through them all, her facial expression shifting from sadness, to surprise, to confusion and occasional flashes of disbelief as her eyes scanned the pages. She wondered if she had looked the same two weeks earlier, when she and Charlotte had sat in these same attic chairs together, and read the contents of the file for the first time. It felt like a lifetime had passed by the time Ines finally spoke.

'It was Maman.' She sighed, sounding as tired as she did sad. 'I can't believe it. *Maman* shot Bernard. All the paying off of the coroner, all the lies Papa told? That was to protect *her*. Not himself?'

Memories of that night came rushing back to Ines now, more vividly than they had in forty years. Maman, frozen with shock, staring at the dark shape on the ground. A shape that Ines could see clearly now as a body. Bernard's body.

Papa, beside her, holding the gun, screaming at Ines to go back to the house. But the gun was cocked, Ines remembered now. Open. Papa must have grabbed it from Clotilde, rushing to make it safe. But it was too late! The deed was done.

'He loved her,' she murmured aloud.

'Oh, I'm sure he loved her,' said Renée. 'But there was more to it than that. Maman didn't intend to kill Bernard. She would never have done that. It's all there in the letters. She was terrified. She and Papa had been receiving threats all summer, from someone whom Papa had double-crossed in business. Serious, physical threats. He basically admitted as much to Marcel. It was why he bought those dogs in the first place – to protect us at Beaulieu.'

Yes, thought Ines. *Yes*.

At long last it was all coming back to her, the pieces slowly starting to fit.

'It was dark,' Renée went on. 'Raining heavily. Maman's nerves were in shreds. She thought she heard an intruder – or perhaps one of the servants said they'd seen a figure, jumping over the wall. Maman took the gun to protect herself – to protect us – and when Bernard came running towards her in the darkness, she panicked and fired. When Papa found her she was just standing there.'

'That's right,' whispered Ines. 'She was in shock.'

Slumping back in her chair, she rubbed her eyes.

'Those letters Papa wrote to the woman in Paris . . . Louise?' She looked across at Renée. 'They read like a confession, don't they? They're so detailed. Every image, every sound. When I ran out there that night and saw Maman and Papa it must have literally just happened. Seconds earlier.' She shuddered.

'It was the moment his life changed,' said Renée, choking up herself now. 'He acted on instinct, taking the gun from Maman, commanding her to say nothing.'

He sent me inside, thought Ines.

'And then setting the dogs onto the body. The body of his *son*, as we now know.'

'While Maman stood there and watched!' gasped Ines. She had been back inside, frightened but safe. But poor Maman had actually seen it happen. Seen the blood, the carnage. 'Can you imagine the horror?'

'Papa blamed himself,' said Renée. 'Because it was his greed, his dishonesty, that had put them under threat in the first place. He put Maman and all of us in danger, and if she hadn't been afraid for her life, she would never have gone out there with a gun, never have made the horrific mistake that ruined so many lives.

Including her own, in the end. The fact that it was Papa's illegitimate son she killed was a tragic irony. But Maman never knew it. Only he did. You can see how he must have thought it was all some sort of divine punishment.'

Perhaps it was, thought Ines. After all, her father *had* been guilty of so much. So very, very much. Just not the one thing that Tremont, and presumably others, believed he had done: taking the life of an innocent child.

'One of the saddest parts for me was when Marcel wrote to him after Maman's funeral, asking about her birds,' said Renée. 'And Papa admitted he was the one who'd released them.'

'I've got it here.' Ines fumbled around for the letter in question, reading the passage aloud.

'*I came to see those birds as a curse,*' Charles Père had written. '*A curse on me, on my house, on my children. It was those damned birds that lured the boy in in the first place. Clotilde couldn't see the harm they were doing, to her and all of us. She was obsessed with them. Anyway, she'd become so ill, from the shock. And the birds would cry and shriek all night, this dreadful noise that so upset her and the children, shattered everybody's sleep. So one night I walked down to the aviary, opened the cage and let them go. I believed, sincerely believed, that Clotilde would improve once those birds had flown. I did it for her, Marcel, you must believe me. But instead it was the thing that broke her; the beginning of the end.*'

'Good God, what a mess.' Ines placed the letter carefully back into the folder. 'Why do you think he kept all this?' she asked Renée after a while. 'I mean, why not burn it? Especially the coroner's report. But even the letters are incriminating.'

'I wondered that too,' said Renée, pensively. 'Especially as he obviously wrote, but never sent them. Maybe he kept them out of guilt? As a tangible reminder of that time, like some sort of penance? He did try to save Maman. But in the end he clearly still held himself responsible, not only for her death but for her unhappiness in life.'

'He doesn't reflect much on Bernard's death though, does he?' Ines observed. 'And he doesn't mention poor Bernadette once. Maman seems to be the only person he feels badly about.'

'Perhaps there were other letters?' Renée suggested lamely. But they both knew that there weren't. Facing up to a small portion of the pain he'd caused had been agony enough for Charles Challant. To admit it all would have killed him.

'I wish we had some of Maman's letters,' Ines sighed wistfully. 'I'd love to know how *she* really felt, about the accident and Papa and all of it . . .'

'Would you?' Renée shuddered. 'I wouldn't. I'm glad we finally have some answers, about what really happened that summer. But if I could un-know Papa's mental torture, I would. At least Maman's feelings died with her and remain her own. One of our poor parents gets to rest in peace.'

CHAPTER THIRTY-SEVEN

Later that night, up in her bedroom in the chalet's eaves, Ines reflected on Renée's words as she sat at the dressing table, removing the day's make-up with a cotton wool ball and Pond's cold cream.

Was Maman resting in peace? She hoped so. She really did.

Heaven knew she'd known little enough peace on this earth, in her marriage. But then, nor had Papa. Perhaps, after all her exhausting seeking out of the truth, the only thing Ines had really learned was that life was rarely black and white, and marriage never was. It was all just shades of grey. Loving. Failing. Regretting. Trying again. Of course, not every marriage engendered as much tragedy as Charles and Clotilde Challant's. Nor left so many innocent victims in its wake. *Poor Bernard.* But that was all in the past now. With the last piece of the puzzle in place, Ines could finally let go.

As for her own life, 'peace' still felt tantalizingly elusive. Examining the face looking back at her in the mirror, Ines judged herself to be holding up well for a woman of almost fifty. Her skin was still firm and bright, notwithstanding the latticework of fine lines around her eyes and beginning to etch themselves into her forehead. There was no grey yet in her hair, and she still had the high cheekbones and soft, bow lips that had defined her as a beauty in her youth. And yet sometimes – now, for example – she found herself feeling old, wearily fighting off the sense that her best days, all the important milestones of her life, were behind her.

Why is that? she wondered, brushing out her hair with the gilt brush that had once been her mother's. After all, she was still working and earning, a successful and respected designer with friends and interests and a full life that many people would envy.

Part of it was Matty. Losing him, not just to the priesthood but to adulthood in general. As he'd matured and become independent, it had been painful to a degree Ines hadn't anticipated. Whatever sense of failure she'd felt as a daughter, and a wife, it had ceased to matter the day she became a mother. Motherhood was something she was good at. As Matthieu's mother she had come to life and shone, just as she had in her career as a designer. It was agonizing to have to let that go. But she knew that she must, for her own sake as well as her son's. All baby birds must one day fly the nest, just as she had when she married Gunn. Charles Challant's inability to let her go had ended up blighting both their lives. Holding children back was a path that led only to bitterness and despair. Ines was not about to make the same mistake.

Besides, losing her identity as a mother was only part of her current sadness. Loath as she was to admit it, a part of her missed being married. The love, the companionship, the coming home to someone and sharing life's triumphs and disappointments. After all, what was the point of looking youthful and attractive if there was no one in one's life to notice or appreciate it?

She'd left Gunn for good reasons, and it had certainly felt right at the time. But all these years later, she couldn't help but wonder how different things might have been had she stayed. There were men she'd been attracted to over the years. Lucien Toulon, at one point, and a couple of others. But no one that she'd come close to loving in the same wild, all-or-nothing way she'd loved Gunn.

Spending Christmas here in Megève, with Renée and Charlotte, had brought it home to her even more forcefully. Work was wonderful and Ines was grateful for it. But she needed more, something for herself, a purpose and identity beyond her career.

Cracking open the window, Ines stuck her head outside into the freezing alpine air. The sharp tang of woodsmoke filled her nostrils, and above her a dazzling blanket of stars spread across the night sky, clear and cloudless on this holiest of nights, banishing all the painful thoughts about her parents' lives and her own. Yesterday, snow had fallen relentlessly from dawn till dusk, leaving behind a thick layer of frosting that lay on the ground now, muffling every sound. In the warmth of her chalet bedroom, Ines felt cocooned and, for that one moment at least, content.

That's the trick, she thought. *Stringing those moments together, one by one, like threads into cloth.*

Patiently.

Diligently.

Happiness was something one had to create, like a beautiful room. It didn't just happen. It took work.

Tomorrow, Ines and Renée would ski on that snow, working off the excesses of today's feast. It would be the first time in many years that Ines had strapped on a pair of skis, and she was childishly excited about it, and the prospect of recapturing the thrill of her youth. Tomorrow, a bright blue day would vanquish the darkness of night.

A new chapter would begin.

CHAPTER THIRTY-EIGHT

As it turned out, Ines slept deeply and late. By the time she came down for breakfast, Renée and Charlotte were both already out. They'd left a note for her on the table, along with a warm pot of coffee, some berries, fresh bread and butter and two boiled eggs in a bowl, covered with a chequered tea towel to keep them hot.

Groggily, Ines drank the coffee and ate one of the eggs, dipping the crusts of her bread into the soft yolk as she came to. Then she had a bath scented with violet oil, before getting into her new Fusalp ski jacket and Ellesse stretch pants. The latter were in neon yellow, with bright white racing stripes down the sides, and, if Ines did say so herself, she looked pretty good in them. Whether her skiing would do them justice after such a long break from the piste remained to be seen. But at least she would look chic when she joined Renée and Charlotte for lunch at Maxim's, the fondue hut at the top of the mountain that was this season's go-to meeting spot for fashionable Megève.

She was deciding which hat to wear when a loud rap on the front door interrupted her thoughts. A package to be signed for, probably. Tossing both options onto the bed, Ines raced downstairs, running a hand through her tousled hair as she pulled open the door.

'Hello, Ines.'

Ines went white. Grabbing the door frame, she steadied herself against it.

'Good God.'

A man, older and greyer but otherwise exactly the same as she remembered him, was standing on the chalet doorstep. He wore a long, black cashmere overcoat, maroon scarf and soft leather gloves. And he was carrying a suitcase. Louis Vuitton, if Ines wasn't very much mistaken.

'Can I come in?'

Hector Gunn.

Half an hour later, after another coffee, this one liberally laced with fortifying brandy, Ines sat with Gunn out on the chalet's rear terrace. The initial shock of seeing him again was quickly replaced by indignation when he explained that Renée had in fact invited him.

'I've lived in Brazil for many years now,' he explained. 'But I looked your sister up in London when I was there earlier in the year, and she was kind enough to ask me out to Megève.'

'What do you mean, you "looked her up"?' asked Ines, indignantly. 'Since when do you and Renée *look each other up*? And why were you in London in the first place, if you live in Brazil?'

'A conference,' said Gunn, as if it were obvious. 'Plus I needed to check up on Maltings as I'm between tenants and there was quite a lot of work needed on the . . .'

'Hold *on*,' Ines raised a hand, frustrated. 'Please slow down. Did you say Maltings? You bought it back?'

He looked up at her, unable to stop the smile from spreading across his face as their eyes met.

'I bought it back. Finally.'

'Well,' said Ines, determined not to smile back. 'That's . . . good news. I'm happy for you.'

'Thank you.'

'But I still can't imagine what possessed Renée to invite you here. In secret.'

'She knew I wanted to see you again,' Gunn said simply. 'To talk to you. She was being kind.'

'Kind? To whom?' Ines demanded crossly. 'Kind to you, perhaps. But what if *I* didn't want to talk to *you*? Did nobody think of that? I mean, shouldn't I have had a say in this?'

'Don't you want to talk to me?' Gunn asked guilelessly.

Ines's eyes narrowed.

'Oh no. No, no, no. Don't you do that.'

'Do what?'

'You know very well what,' she chided. 'Play the victim. As if I'm the one being unreasonable here. When you've basically co-opted my own sister to ambush me.'

But eventually she calmed down. The truth was, having successfully *not* thought about Gunn, almost since the day she left England, recent events had brought him and their marriage back to the front of her consciousness. So much so that it was hard not to believe that she hadn't manifested his appearance at the chalet in some way. Wished him here, like a genie. And she could hardly blame Renée for that.

'I like your trousers.' Gunn sipped his coffee, trying hard not to betray his own nerves.

'Really?' said Ines, a smile playing on the corners of her lips despite her best efforts. 'Well, thank you. But I'm guessing you didn't wangle an invite from Renée and come all this way just to compliment me on my fashion sense.'

'No,' he admitted. 'I didn't.'

'So why are you here, Gunn?'

Gunn ran a hand through his hair. It was hard to know where to begin. So much had happened, so many years passed, he felt as if he were standing at the foot of a mountain so tall, he had no way to see the summit, let alone reach it. But he knew that if he didn't grasp the nettle now, he never would. The chance would be lost to him, perhaps forever.

'I wanted to say sorry, in person. For what I did to you,' he said, forcing himself to look Ines in the eye. 'Meeting Anna. My affair. It's the single biggest regret of my life.'

Ines shifted uncomfortably in her seat.

'I see,' she said eventually. 'Well, I think perhaps we both owe one another an apology.'

Gunn looked at her with frank astonishment. 'I don't see how. Unless . . .' his face fell. 'Oh God. You didn't have an affair with Edward Turnbull, did you? I always wondered . . .'

'No!' For a moment Ines was indignant. But looking at Gunn's stricken face, she relented. 'For heaven's sake. You're not really still jealous of Edward, are you? After all these years?'

'Of course not,' Gunn muttered, unconvincingly. 'It's just when you said we should both apologize . . .'

'Good,' Ines cut him off. 'Because I didn't have an affair with anyone. I was madly in love with you.'

'Then what do you have to be sorry for?' Gunn asked.

'For running, I suppose?' Ines replied. 'Disappearing and never looking back. For never giving you a chance to explain or, I don't know, make amends? I told myself I hated you, that you deserved to come home to an empty house, an empty life. But looking back now I can see that there was more to it than that. My father . . .' she broke off awkwardly. 'I think perhaps, with hindsight, he played a part in my decision. More than he should have.'

'You thought that if you left me for good, he'd take you back? Is that it?' Gunn hit the nail on the head.

Ines nodded. 'Something like that. But of course, he never did.'

A thoughtful silence fell.

'I never stopped loving you, you know,' Gunn blurted, breaking the spell. 'Never.'

Ines swallowed hard. Had she ever stopped loving him? Perhaps not, she realized now. Although heaven knew she'd tried.

But this was a dangerous path to go down, more than twenty years after the fact. Too much had happened. Too much had changed. One couldn't just apologize, declare one's love, and pick up where one had left off. That was the stuff of fairytales or Hollywood romances. Not real life.

'I hardly know you any more,' she told him. She hadn't intended for it to come out as harshly as it did. But Gunn pulled a face as if she'd just squirted lemon juice into his eyes.

'That's not true,' he insisted vehemently. 'You know me better than anyone.'

'In one sense, perhaps. But I don't know your life,' Ines

361

clarified. 'I don't know anything about you *now* at all, Gunn. What you do, in . . . did you say Brazil? What you've been doing, for the past however long it's been.'

It was the perfect opening. For the next hour, Gunn gave her a potted history of everything that had happened since the two of them had parted ways. Some parts he skimmed over lightly, such as his brief but disastrous marriage to Anna, and his mother's long decline into dementia and eventual death. Other parts – buying back Maltings, meeting Horatio Chapman, becoming an academic, building a new life for himself in Brazil – he lingered over, painting a vivid, genuinely fascinating picture of the life he'd led and the man he'd become.

Afterwards, he probed Ines about her own life. Her business, initially, and the tremendous success she'd achieved professionally as a designer.

'I read an article about you in the Pan Am magazine last summer,' he told her. 'A feature on some hotel you'd worked on in New York.'

'The Regent?'

'That was it. The pictures were a knockout.'

'Did you think so?' Ridiculously, Ines found herself blushing.

'Absolutely,' said Gunn. 'Some of those rooms, with the stencilled birds and flowers, reminded me of our little cottage down in Cornwall. Do you remember?'

'Do I remember?' Ines looked at him curiously. 'What a question! How could I forget? Those were some very happy days.'

'They were,' Gunn nodded, choking back emotion.

'For a while,' murmured Ines.

Their eyes locked, for an interminable moment. Then at last Gunn found the courage to ask the question that he'd really travelled all this way to put to her.

'You spoke about a son,' he said, clearing his throat. 'In the magazine article.'

Ines's face lit up. 'Matthieu. Matty. He's in Paris at the moment. Believe it or not he's training to become a . . .'

362

'Is he mine?'

The question took Ines aback. Perhaps it shouldn't have. But it did.

She looked down at her hands in her lap. Then to her left, out of the window framing the snowy loveliness of Megève. Then back to Gunn.

'Let's go for a walk,' she said.

'Do you think she's all right?' Renée asked Charlotte, roaming the chalet kitchen like a trapped bird. 'She wouldn't have done anything silly, would she?'

Several hours had passed since they'd returned from the slopes. Ines never had made it up the mountain to join them. The presence of an overnight bag in the hall, presumably Gunn's, explained her absence, but not how long she'd been gone.

'Like what?' said Charlotte. 'She's hardly going to throw herself under a train because you invited her ex to stay.'

'I suppose not,' Renée fretted.

'She might throw *you* under a train,' Charlotte added. 'But wherever they are, they're obviously together so it can't have gone that badly. He probably took her out for supper or something.'

Letting out a little gasp, Renée grabbed her arm. 'There they are.'

She nodded towards the kitchen window. Two figures were making their way up the hill in the snowy twilight, arm in arm. 'Oh Charlotte, look! She's leaning into him.'

'It's cold, Ren,' said Charlotte, with an affectionate roll of the eyes. 'For heaven's sake don't go leaping to any conclusions.'

Outside, walking with Ines, Gunn stopped to gaze up at the night sky. On a cloudless night, the stars above Megève were some of the most beautiful anywhere, adding another layer of magic to this fairytale town.

'I've missed this,' he told Ines. 'Megève. The Alps. I mean, I adore Brazil and the life I have now. But you can't replace this, can you?'

'No,' she agreed. 'You can't. But you can't go back-wards either.'

He turned to look at her. 'What do you mean?'

'Only that this place was a huge part of your youth. Of both of our youths. We can come back to the place, but not the time. And I suspect the time is part of what you miss.'

'Hmmm.' Gunn thought about it. 'Perhaps. I don't know, though. Tonight, at least, I feel more excited about the future than I have in a long time. And more at peace with the past.'

'Me too,' said Ines. Only yesterday, she'd been wondering if she would ever feel truly at peace again. But walking with Gunn here, like this, she did.

Until he'd shown up out of the blue and asked her to her face about Matty, Ines hadn't realized how heavily the lie about her son's paternity had been weighing on her. She'd repeated her cover story so often, about a one-night stand with a married man, that in the early years of Matty's life it had begun to feel true. But as the boy grew older, and she'd seen more and more of Gunn in him – his smile; his walk – the magnitude of her deception had begun to hit home.

It wasn't keeping the truth from Gunn that she felt bad about. After all, she'd never expected to see him again. When she finally told him, he'd been understanding about her decision to keep her pregnancy a secret, and to raise their son alone.

'It was my behaviour that drove you into that corner,' he acknowledged, graciously, once his initial, profound shock had worn off. *A son. He had a son!* 'I wish things had been different, that's all.'

But Ines had also lied to Matty. That was wrong. He deserved to know the truth about his father, and who he really was. And though the thought of telling him was nerve-wracking in one way, it was also a relief. Ines's own parents' secrets had wreaked unimaginable havoc in their children's lives. Ines had taken the first step in breaking the cycle of lies down in Beaulieu, and Renée's discovery of the coroner's report and letters had brought them even further. But Gunn coming to Megève and asking about Matty had forced Ines to realize that the job was not yet complete.

As for the two of them? Well, there the future remained to be seen. Tonight, they were friends, and for Ines at least, that was enough. Forgiveness. Honesty. Affection. These were all huge things, unhoped-for gifts to be cherished and nurtured.

She must thank Renée. Just as soon as she'd finished strangling her.

'Let's go inside,' said Gunn, looking up at the warm, orange glow of lights through the chalet windows, and the welcoming spiral of smoke snaking up from the chimney. 'Your sister's probably wondering where on earth we've got to.'

'Yes, let's,' said Ines, reaching for his hand and en-twining her fingers in his, surprised by how natural and right it felt.

She wasn't worried about Renée. She wasn't worried about anything, in fact. For the first time in a long, long time she looked forward to going to bed tonight. Because she knew now for sure that her nightmares were finally over.

EPILOGUE

Beaulieu-sur-Mer, summer 1968

'For heavens' sake you two, stop *pawing* each other!'

Renée did her best to sound disapproving. But it was hard to keep the smile off her face. Not for a very long time, perhaps ever, had she seen her sister so happy.

'We're newlyweds,' Genevieve beamed, resting her head sweetly on Pierre's shoulder. 'We're allowed.'

'Too right,' her new husband concurred, removing his glasses and carefully polishing them with an old-fashioned spotted handkerchief before putting them back on. 'We may not be spring chickens. But one's never too old for romance, right darling?'

They were all out on the lawn at Beaulieu in the midst of a friendly, but amusingly competitive, game of boules. Everyone had descended on the bastide for Genevieve and Pierre's wedding last Saturday, an intimate but joyous affair, toasted by both the bride and groom with sparkling water. 'They all' being Renée, Charlotte, Ines and Hector Gunn, who Genevieve hadn't laid eyes on since before the war, but who appeared to be firmly back in Ines's life, albeit on a part-time basis.

The revelation that Gunn was Matty's father had not particularly shocked either of Ines's sisters. But the rekindling of their romance had certainly surprised Genevieve, who'd spent the last twenty years under the impression that her youngest sister loathed her ex-husband with a passion bordering on the murderous.

'Things change,' Ines had explained breezily. 'Look at you.'

Genevieve laughed. That much was certainly true. Her life had changed beyond all recognition in the last year, and she had her sisters to thank for it. Not only had she met and married Pierre, but she had finished the first draft of a new play and had already had a couple of bites of interest from agents in Paris.

'I'm not expecting to become the new Gaston Baty,' she told Ines and Renée. 'But to see something of mine performed on a stage, anywhere? That would really be a dream.'

She was thrilled to see Ines's dreams coming to fruition too, although her younger sister played down the latest developments with Gunn.

'It's not as if we're getting married or anything,' Ines insisted. 'We both have our own careers and lives. But now I get to spend some time in São Paolo, which is just stunning by the way. And at Maltings, which is honestly the most divine house, I have *so* many plans for it . . .'

'Plans, eh?' Gen teased her. 'So let me get this straight. You're back in Cornwall, nesting in his house, but you're *not* getting married?'

'I am not *nesting*!' Ines protested, rolling the word off her tongue with profound distaste. 'Any more than Gunn is *nesting* in Paris. Which he loves by the way. We're splitting our time. I suppose you could call it a new form of migration.'

'I suppose you could,' Gen smiled.

'The point is, we're happy.'

They did seem to be. Although Genevieve couldn't help but worry for Ines, at least a little bit. 'Losing' Matty to the church had been so very hard for her, a truly crushing blow. And Gunn had already broken her heart once. Still, so far at least, he'd been on his best behaviour and had certainly charmed everyone at Beaulieu. Especially Pierre. But then Pierre liked everyone, God bless him.

'Bugger romance,' announced Renée, bending down on one knee as she prepared to roll her last boule, laser-focused on the *cochonnet* at the far end of the lawn. Gunn and Ines were currently in the lead, but not by much, and Renée and Charlotte were determined to overtake them. 'You're putting me off my game.'

Moments later they were all distracted by the sudden, dramatic arrival of a bright red MG sports car, being driven at a quite phenomenal speed. So fast, in fact, that it was impossible to see who was inside it, thanks to the arcing spray of gravel that shot up into the air like water from a hose pipe before raining back down with a clatter as the convertible skidded to a halt in the driveway.

'Friend of yours?' Ines looked at Gunn archly.

'You could say that.'

Was it Ines's imagination, or was Gunn behaving nervously all of a sudden? He seemed to have developed a weird tapping motion with his feet, and kept wiping his hands on the front of his linen trousers, as if his palms were sweating.

The passenger door of the car opened. Out stepped a very young, *very* pretty girl, blinking in the sunshine, her auburn curls blowing softly about her face in the breeze. She wore a floaty, white peasant blouse over a pair of perhaps the shortest shorts Ines had ever seen. And she was pregnant. Heavily pregnant.

'Hello there, mademoiselle. Can we help you?' Pierre stepped forward, edging gently but kindly past an open-mouthed Ines.

But before the girl could answer, the driver's side door opened. A familiar, much loved pair of legs – long, male legs, wearing trendy wide-flared jeans – unfurled themselves.

'Hello everyone.' Matty, looking nervous but happy and distinctly un-priestly in a paisley shirt and with a mop of shaggy hair flopping constantly into his eyes, scuttled round to the girl's side, wrapping a protective arm around her. 'This is Sophie. Sophie, *voici toute ma famille*.'

After what felt like an eternity of stunned silence, Genevieve stepped forward, arms thrown wide, and hugged her nephew.

'Lovely to see you, my darling.'

'You too, Aunt Gen. And you must be Pierre?' Matty thrust out his hand, smiling broadly. 'Congratulations.'

It was Renée who asked the obvious question.

'So, er, Matty. What happened to the priesthood?'

Matty shrugged. 'Change of plan?' Looking sheepishly at his mother, he added, 'They do say God works in mysterious ways.'

Awakening from her stupor at last, Ines ran forward and kissed him. 'They do indeed,' she said, grinning from ear to ear at Sophie as she took in the truly vast size of her pregnant belly for the first time.

'Did you know about this?' Ines turned accusingly to Gunn, who'd gone uncharacteristically quiet behind her.

'Don't be angry with him, Maman,' pleaded Matty. 'He drove up to the seminary to visit me, unannounced, the same week that I left. Father Girond gave him my temporary address. Sophie answered the door when he turned up, didn't you, my love?'

The beautiful girl nodded at Matty, the two of them exchanging such besotted glances, there could be no doubt they were hopelessly in love.

'So then the cat was out of the bag. But I swore him to secrecy.'

'He did,' Gunn confirmed, to a sceptical-looking Ines.

'I needed to tell you myself, Maman,' said Matty. 'About Sophie and the baby. I know I've put you through a lot, but . . . oh, Maman, don't cry!' His face fell. 'Are you upset? Please don't be. We're so very happy. And we . . .'

Ines cut him off, raising a finger and pressing it to his lips. Tears still streamed down her cheeks. But when she looked up at him, there could be no mistaking the joy in her expression.

'I'm not upset, Matty,' she assured him. 'Just shocked. But in a good way. The best way. I'm so very, very happy for both of you.'

Gunn wrapped an arm around her shoulder and pulled her close.

A grandchild. Their grandchild.

Gunn's thoughts drifted to Maltings, and how magical it would be to welcome a child there again at last. But Ines could think only of Beaulieu.

Here, in this beautiful garden, so full of memories and now so full of hope for the future, she finally felt at peace.

The birds of Beaulieu had completed their long migration. She was home at last.

ACKNOWLEDGEMENTS

Thanks once again to my agents: the tireless Hellie Ogden, and everybody at Janklow & Nesbit in London and New York. Especially the lovely Luke Janklow who has guided and helped me with all my books from the beginning. Also to the whole team at HarperCollins, in particular my patient and insightful editor Charlotte Brabbin, but also Holly MacDonald in Design, Sarah Shea in Marketing, Harriet Williams and Tom Dunstan in Sales, Sophie Waeland in Production, and the eagle-eyed Rhian McKay and Simon Fox for copy-edits and proofreading. I am hugely indebted to all of you for such a gorgeous finished product.

Home and family are two big themes in the story of *The Secret Keepers*. This year has been an emotional one for my family, uprooting from Santa Monica where we spent many happy years to move back to our home in London. For me, the joy of finally waking up in England again every morning is indescribable. I have missed my country and my family and friends here more than words can possibly express. But for my husband Robin, and our younger children Zac, Theo and Summer, the move has been challenging at times. I want to thank all of you for the sacrifices, big and small, that I know you have each made in order for us to embark on this new chapter together. And to my oldest daughter Sefi, who has waited so long for our return – thank you too my darling.

Last, but definitely not least, I would like to thank all my readers, past and present. I hope you enjoy reading *The Secret Keepers* as much as I have enjoyed writing it.

TB 2024

Escape to a beautiful Burgundy château in another historical epic by Tilly Bagshawe

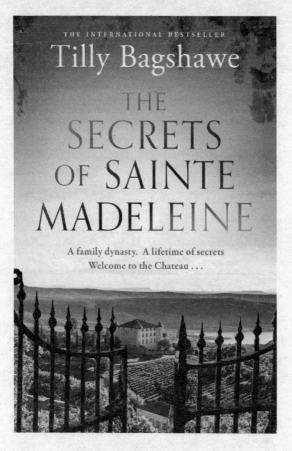